JOIN THE COVEN

The story doesn't have to end when the page does! Join the Coven and get exclusive content just for subscribing.

THE LINE OF TEPES

E A WILLIAMS

CHAPTER 1

Of course, it was raining. In every movie Emma had ever watched the funeral scene was always raining and the graveyard was populated by stoic mourners with classy black umbrellas. Gram's friends didn't have black umbrella money. They had a rainbow of cheap threadbare raincoats and poncho's covering their church-best kind of money.

It made Emma feel better that not a single one of Gram's neighbors had missed the funeral and not a single one was anything close to stoic. Losing the woman who had raised her was paralyzing. She had spent two days staring through the doorway into Gram's bedroom before she had even been able to cry, and since then she had barely been able to stop. Only when Miss Lily from next door had shown up with her half-blind pug, Mr. Bug, was Emma able to calm down. Miss Lily had handed her Mr. Bug's leash and made two phone calls. The first was to Mrs. Abernathy and her son, Simon. They blew in on a gust of white-knightly bravado and the empathy of the only approximation of family she had ever enjoyed. Emma and Simon had known each other since diapers racing the big wheels down the street. Simon had hugged her tight, letting her sob it out.

The second call had been to Miss Lily's nephew who owned a pizza place and from whom she ordered enough pizza to feed an army. Miss Lily's unspoken motto had always been "when you're feeling blue food stays true." Not much of a surprise from the retired baker.

Mrs. Abernathy had helped Emma get the funeral plans together. Having buried four husbands and being currently married to the director of the funeral home, she had finagled the best of everything for Iliza King.

At the end of the service, every one of her grandmother's neighbors smiled weepily at Emma as they left the grave site. They offered shaky hugs and made her promise to call if she needed anything before they wandered to their cars, tracking streaks through the mud.

She watched the hodge-podge of vehicles pull away except for one, a sleek dark sedan. One of those expensive cars she had seen in action movies but never in real life. Emma knew there wasn't a soul Grams knew who could afford one of those things. It took her a second to spot the car's owner, a man paying his respects to the tallest stone standing in the small family plot. Grams had told her that it was the oldest one standing and belonged to the woman who had brought her whole family over from Romania.

The man had one of those classy black umbrellas and two bouquets of the most beautiful roses Emma had ever seen. He pulled out one flower and left it at the base of the stone before turning to find Emma's gaze and stalking over. She was struck by how truly sad he looked and how certain she was that she had never seen him before. It was his eyes. She doubted anyone who had seen those fathomless pits could forget them. Even at this distance she felt transfixed by them. She shivered despite the heat of the day and looked up into the sky as the rain continued pelting down to sizzle and puddle on the ground. He moved towards her slowly, the way large dogs approach small children. It was as if he were making deliberate steps not to frighten her away. If she were being honest, it didn't help.

The man was tall and lean with a stern face and a hooked nose. At best the man could be described as not ugly, but by even the most generous accounts he could never be considered handsome. The suit he wore looked expensive and the rain that touched it didn't seem to soak the material, choosing rather to bead up and roll down the lapels. When he finally stood in front of her, Emma was surprised to find that he was only a few inches taller than her. He carried himself in a manner of a much larger man.

"You are Emma, no?" His voice was rough with tampered grief and an Eastern European accent she couldn't place. Emma nodded, trying not to stare at him. "Iliza sent photographs, but I have not seen you in person since you were very small."

"I'm sorry, I don't know you." Emma took a small step back looking for a quick escape route in case things got sketchy. Just because this guy knew Grams' name did not mean he wasn't a creep. She had had enough experience with those to stay alert.

"Nor would I expect you to." The man smiled without teeth, tilting his chin down slightly, in a way that gave Emma the impression he was trying to reclaim composure. "It was many years ago. I am Vlad. Forgive me, I did not wish to cause you alarm."

"No, no alarm." Definitely alarm. Dude looked like a bad guy from any action movie made after 1996. "I don't want to be rude, but I have, like zero idea who you are."

Despite her inner sirens going crazy Emma forced her eyes to stay soft, schooling her mouth into as close to a smile as she could achieve standing next to Gram's grave.

"There is no rudeness in this." He stepped away from her, kneeling to put his beautiful roses amongst the daisies and carnations that crowded Gram's grave. "I am a stranger to you. I would not wish for my presence to cause you more strain at such a terrible time."

Standing, mud caking his fine shoes and one knee of his dark slacks, he offered her the second bouquet. Not knowing what else to do, Emma took them, the scent of roses filling her nose and sending a hot wave of sadness through her. She bit the inside of her lip hard, hoping she could stem the flood of tears before she broke down in front of a total stranger.

"I know that they are not enough." He looked into the clouds and whether he was blinking back his own emotions or giving Emma time to collect her own was unclear, still she appreciated the moment to wipe her eyes. "I know that any words of condolence will not be sufficient, however, I would like you to know that Iliza will be truly missed. Her passing has left a hole in my world."

"You were close?" Emma's curiosity reared its head. "She never mentioned any acquaintances like you."

"Like me?" He smiled again in his sad way that didn't stretch across his entire face, or bring any humor to his eyes. "Foreign?"

"Rich." Emma shrugged embarrassed. "Grams never had money or a reason to associate with anyone who did."

"Well, Iliza is more family than acquaintance."

"So, you're what? Her great-nephew twice removed?" Emma hid her curiosity in the sweet, musky scent of the roses. She tried to imagine what her soft, kitschy grandmother would have looked like standing beside this bespoke tycoon. "She never mentioned you."

"I would not expect her to." He looked down at his watch. "We only saw one another in person twice. Once when she was visiting the old country and once here, when you were an infant. Might I walk you to your car? I believe the other mourners will be waiting for you at the wake."

He turned with her towards the trail of grassy broken

asphalt laying a large hand delicately on Emma's elbow. When she didn't pull away he tucked her closer to him, guiding her with practiced gentility towards the shabby rectangle of asphalt that her car occupied.

"Will you come?" Emma couldn't explain the instant connection she felt when he took her elbow. He tilted his umbrella so that it sheltered her as they walked arm in arm to her shabby second-hand Toyota. "Grams would have wanted to have family there."

"Unfortunately, I cannot." He opened the door, shifting the umbrella over her so that she could slide cleanly into the vehicle. "You would not want me there. I have maudlin tendencies and this is a time for the comforts of the familiar, not for strangers."

"You have been to a lot of wakes?" She stood at her door, one foot in her car, and one foot still planted in the mud.

"Too many I am afraid." His black eyes watched her as she slid gracelessly into the car, careful not to crush the flowers he had just given her.

"I don't know your last name." She felt stupid. They had an entire conversation. How could she have not learned his name?

"Rudeness on my part, it is Tepes." He pulled a thick vellum card from his breast pocket and handed it to Emma. "You must call if you need anything. I know it means little, but if I can ease your suffering in any way, I would dearly like to help."

"Thank you." Emma relaxed into the car as much as she could manage with her plastic poncho.

"I mean it Emma. Even if it is just to talk. I am available day or night."

"You might live to regret that statement." Emma smiled at him in what she hoped was a kind way.

"That I very much doubt, but I invite you to do your worst." He waited for Emma to click her seat belt into place before shutting the door.

The roses filled the entire passenger seat of her little sedan. They probably cost more than her car payment. She immediately and inexplicably missed him. His business card was heavy in her pocket. The black vellum read

V. Tepes

with a phone number in curving golden script. Running her thumb over it, she felt embossing and watched as Vlad's car slid gracefully out of the cemetery. It was a pity she would probably never see him again.

CHAPTER 2

It was finally quiet. There had been people buzzing around, shoving plates of food into her hands, taking away the plates she had pushed food around just to distract herself from their well-meaning sympathy. Now they were gone, their casseroles and pies stored neatly in the fridge. All the dishes sat drying on the counter, the displaced chairs had been moved back to their places beside Gram's long dining room table.

Emma wished that they had left it, wished that they had been even the slightest bit inconsiderate. Not that she was ungrateful, it was simply that her neighbors had poured through the house with love, filling its small rooms with kindness. They had filled up those places left silent by Grams' passing and in their wake each room was silent again.

Picking up an ugly clay mug that was still drying by the sink, Emma set about making tea. Miss Lily left a bundle of her homemade blends. Each flavor picked out just for Emma. She felt love and grief bulge in her throat. Tears trickled unkempt down her cheeks. Flecks of dissolving mascara streaked along the corners of her eyes quickly destroying the careful façade of calm she had spent the whole day affecting.

The stove clicked insistently as it tried to ignite. She wiped the black streaks from her under eye with the sleeve of her sweater. Standing in Grams' tidy white kitchen, waiting for the kettle to boil, the hard press of silence burst. A sob shuttered out of her chest, too loud in the small space. She folded over the counter, the ugly clay mug slapping onto the linoleum floor and by some miracle not shattering into a thousand pieces. Any strength she had been carrying left her and she let her body crumple next to the ugly brown thing. Sobs rolled through her like summer storms stacking up on the horizon. There was something about weeping that felt good. As if somehow if she cried hard enough she could wipe out the sorrow sticking to her ribs.

Above her the kettle whistled, adding its high clear scream to the symphony of cries filling the air. She ignored it. A daze was overtaking her and she was happy to let it.

A scrape replaced the whistling as someone took the kettle off of the burner and Emma could make out the thin frame of a woman in black picking the mug off of the floor. One of the neighbors come to check on her no doubt. Mrs. Abernathy or Miss Lily both had keys, she wouldn't be surprised if it was either. Emma struggled to sit up, to calm herself against the onslaught of emotion she had been so dutifully shoring up. It was useless. The harder she tried the worse it got. She was hiccupping, her belly seizing with every breath. Snot and mascara laced tears blotching her face, running unhindered into her open mouth. Her vision blurred and burned.

The warmth of the woman who Emma was certain must be Ms. Lilly or Mrs. Abernathy lapped at Emma's back and she let herself be dragged backwards into her lap. Boney knees poked Emma's sides and the heat drained out of her body, certain that none of her neighbors was bony enough of or nimble enough to be the woman holding her.

"Shh," The woman murmured into Emma's hair, petting it with sharp fingertips. "It'll be alright, Emmy. Shhh."

Every nerve in Emma's body exploded with rebellion. That saccharine voice belonged to the one person who hadn't bothered to show up to Grams' service, or her grave. The only person who could make all of this worse.

"It's okay baby girl, Momma's here." Melissa Caldwell-King squeezed Emma's head too tightly against her breasts, knocking her daughter's nose into her protruding collar bone. "I've got you baby. I've got you."

Emma pushed out from her mother's arms, scrambling across the narrow kitchen floor to sit on her knees. She watched Melissa as if she were a coyote who had let itself inside.

"What are you doing here?" Emma's voice was hoarse and she felt a tingling weakness in her arms. She allowed herself one last snuffle and wiped the last of her black tears on her sleeve.

"She was my mother, Emma." Melissa folded her feet underneath her, calm as a monk. Her face was a placid slate of familiar features, slightly withered by long periods in the sun but almost the same ones Emma saw in the mirror. "I'm allowed to come and say goodbye, aren't I?"

Immediately Emma felt guilty. She tilted back off her knees and let herself back fall into the wall behind her, disarmed.

"Of course." Emma took a long slow breath, looking around for her mug. "You weren't at the service. I didn't think you would come."

"Mom's friends don't like me." Melissa reached up to pluck the mug off the counter, and hand it to Emma. "I thought it would be harder for you if I was there."

She wanted to believe her mom wanted to be the first thought Melissa had had when she had decided not to come. If Emma didn't look too closely she could pretend, so she didn't look. Nodding, Emma took the mug, tea already steeping in its fat belly, and stared into it for a long while before taking a sip. When she finally took a sip it was lukewarm and bitter. She waited until her mother looked away to spit it back.

"I would never leave you alone." Melissa fiddled with the sleeve of her black smock. It was the same shabby linen as usual, but Emma could appreciate the effort she had taken to dye it for the occasion. There was a dangerous flicker of hope deep in Emma's gut, some place that still called Melissa "Mommy."

They sat there for a while, neither speaking. Emma pretending to sip the tea Melissa had made for her. Melissa was calm tonight, it was odd. Not that Emma would have preferred for her to be her usual manic self. A flash of her mother being escorted by security from her high school graduation blipped in her memory. She wouldn't let it bloom into the anger that would inevitably follow that train of thought. There wasn't room for that ugliness tonight, not with the grief filling up the room between them.

"How's the tea?" Melissa broke the silence first, both of them knowing she was always the one who broke first.

"A little cold." Emma shrugged noncommittally.

Melissa stood up, putting out her hand to take the mug. Shaking her head Emma followed her up, handing over the brown ceramic. Her mother took it and popped it in the microwave.

"Careful." Emma smiled cautiously at her. "Not sure that thing is gonna make it."

Melissa watched it turn in the microwave wistfully. Her features seemed different from the glazed look of fanaticism that so often graced that profile in almost all of Emma's memories.

"I made that for her." Her voice was lower than usual. Lost

in a happy memory. "I didn't know that she kept it. Here you go baby girl."

She blew against the steaming surface of the tea before handing it to her daughter. Emma took it, wincing as the scalding hot ceramic burned her fingertips. The desire for Miss Lily's calming tea blend had lessened since her mother arrived, but this was nice. It felt as though she were not the only one floating in grief and like countless times before she thought perhaps there might be a bridge between she and Melissa. She was hopeful that in this at least they could come together. She sipped the tea tentatively, its bitter flavor filling up her mouth until her lips and tongue tingled with the heat of it. Then they were numb. Too much anise maybe, funny that she hadn't tasted it. Emma would have to ask Miss Lily.

"Grams kept everything." She stared at her mother. "I wouldn't be surprised if she still had your report cards."

"Mortal only knows what we will find when we go through it all." Melissa sighed leaning against the counter.

"Yeah, who knows." Emma purposely avoided her mother's mention of her icon, glazing over it with veiled annoyance. Why her mother thought she was going to help go through Grams' things Emma had no idea. The day had been long and she didn't feel the need to make the night even longer by starting that fight. She had seen Melissa's cult run roughshod over the woman's better judgment her whole life, it was better to ignore it and keep her calm. There was no way Emma would let her mother touch Grams' stuff. She had lost that right the moment she had chosen the Order over her family, over taking care of her daughter.

Emma took a sip of the bitter tea one more time, giving herself a reason not to say anything else. At least she felt calmer now, even with Melissa watching her so intently. Everything was going a little fuzzy where before it had been so sharp and cruel with sorrow. There was a chance it was better that way and Emma hated it. She put the mug on the counter, the walls of the galley kitchen felt like they were pressing in, trapping her in the narrow room.

As she fled, Melissa reached out, brushing her fingers over Emma's arm. She didn't flinch away from it but it was a very near thing. There was still a scar along her elbow where Melissa had thrown her onto the asphalt outside after an argument with Grams when Emma was eight. It wasn't the only scar her mother had given her and it was hardly the worst.

The air in the dining room felt cooler and even though it wasn't a large room it felt less oppressive.

"Why didn't you come to the grave?" Emma didn't need to look back to know that her mother had followed. Absent-mindedly she rubbed the jagged cluster of skin on her elbow, grounding her thoughts.

"I thought it would be too dramatic." Melissa herded Emma around, trying to hand her the still steaming mug. "I know that mother had many friends and they deserved to say goodbye as much as I do."

"Maybe more." The words were out of her mouth before she could stop them and whipped around the room with loud, pointless veracity.

Melissa flinched away from them, her lips pursed tightly.

"I'm sorry." Guilt, like a lead weight, dropped in Emma's stomach and she sank into one of the dining room chairs. "That was rude."

"Yes, it was." Melissa's face was now a hard mask and her voice had that treacle sweetness once more. "I should apologize too, I suppose."

Emma was speechless. Her mother never apologized for anything. She was a woman who had in her own mind, never done anything wrong in her life. Emma continued on in silence waiting to hear her mother's contrition.

"I never should have left you alone when you needed me."

Melissa sat down carefully, finally setting the mug on the table. The sound of its hard body hitting the wood of the table sounded like a shot, some of its bitter contents sloshing onto the lacquer tabletop. She watched Emma without blinking regularly.

"That's it?" The anger that Emma had thought she no longer carried with her clawed up her throat, cold and bitter.

"I'm sure that you're angry." Melissa cocked her head to the side the way dogs do when they expect a treat. "Losing Mother must have been hard for you, but it is the natural order. It is our human right, a gift protected by God and the Divine Mortal."

Melissa blinked slowly at Emma, waiting for some kind of reaction. Whatever it was that she wanted from Emma she never got.

Emma heard the proverbial other shoe drop, of course her mother wasn't here to share the burden of mourning with her only daughter. She had come on another mission from those freaks. Emma knew name-calling would get her nowhere, knew from experience that screaming would do nothing, and she was well and truly tried. Her bones felt ancient tonight and more than anything she didn't want her memories of Grams to be colored by yet another fight with her mother.

"The Divine Mortal teaches us not to grieve, but to celebrate our deaths." Melissa gave another slow blink. "And when you're ready to apologize I will forgive you."

Her ears buzzed with white noise as Emma watched Melissa through a haze. Time felt like it was crawling and her lips still tingled from the tea. How she had ever even hoped for something else from her mother she couldn't remember.

"Forgive me?" Emma's lips barely curled around the words, let alone the idea that she had anything for which she needed forgiveness from Melissa Caldwell-King. No amount of breathing exercises would quell the burning hot rage filling her lungs.

"Yes." The look of confusion on Melissa's face was infuriating. "You were incredibly hurtful last time we spoke and I am ready to forgive you."

When last, they spoke? Emma wracked her memories trying to think of when the last time she had actually had a conversation with her mother was. There were two dozen or so hateful voicemails, and a request sent from Melissa's new husband, Cult Master Extraordinaire, to attend an Order function, but she had never responded. She watched Melissa blink and nod dumbly, clearly thinking Emma's silence was penitence for her past misdeeds.

"What are you talking about?" Emma watched as Melissa's calm façade cracked just a little.

"When I visited you at school, Honey." The corner of Melissa's eye twitched, her voice getting more childlike by the syllable. "I stopped by your dorm room and you were very rude. You let that whore of a roommate speak to me like a criminal. It's okay though, I forgive you."

"When you stopped by my dorm?" Realization skittered over her in an unwelcomed caress. The vigorous way her mother was nodding was making Emma dizzy.

"I'm so glad you don't speak with her anymore." Melissa pushed the tea a little closer, a peace offering. Emma's stomach rolled with suspicion. "She was such a untenable person."

Melissa babbled on, but Emma was trapped years in the past by the memories of her sophomore year breaking over her.

Finals week had been kicking her ass. Both Emma and her roommate had thrown in the towel before eight o'clock. She had been out cold when someone had started screaming. She smacked her elbow on her desk as her roommate dragged her out of bed desperate to get her away from a nearly feral Melissa. The image of her mother being dragged screaming from her dorm by three security guards, screaming slurs at anyone unfortunate enough to enter her peripherals, played on a loop in Emma's head.

Unbelievable, Emma starred at her mother, or rather the woman who had given birth to her, mouth agape. For a moment she had thought, really wanted to believe, that Grams' death had unlocked a morsel of human compassion behind the Order's rhetoric. Still her mother babbled on, pausing only to do her head tilt routine expectantly.

"What?" Emma resisted the urge to roll her eyes. She hadn't heard a word Melissa had said.

"You'll come home." Melissa smiled, it was egregiously fake, even for her.

"I am home." Emma gave a shrug, trying to slough off the heavy feeling in her limbs.

"Oh, Honey." Melissa's condescension was palpable. "This isn't your home. Home is with me. It's with the Order, with your family. I've let you stay here long enough. Let you play around in this faithless filth long enough. You're coming home now."

Melissa's falsetto voice harped in Emma's ear almost as shrilly as her words. Anger was burning off whatever apathy she had been holding onto.

"We'll have to burn these clothes of course." Melissa chirped happily, so completely unaware of the fight rising in Emma's blood. She reached for the tea bringing it to her lips before catching herself and setting back down in front of Emma.

"My clothes?" Emma mumbled, her eyes on the tea, her suspicions all but confirmed.

"Well of course." Melissa gestured to the simple black dress and cardigan Emma wore. "We can't have you coming into the Temple of the Divine Mortal looking like a common whore." Melissa grabbed Emma's arm as she tried to leave the room, her patience with her mother used up. "I don't blame you, Honey, you didn't know. Iliza kept you from me, kept you from your real family, from the truth."

It shouldn't have shocked Emma that Melissa called Grams by her first name. None of the vitriol pouring out of her mouth should have shocked her, but here she was, stunned. Her limbs shaking with rage and Melissa's piss poor attempt to drug her.

"Grams didn't keep me from you." The chair behind her slammed into the ground as she snapped her arm out of her mother's grip, nearly snarling with distaste as her mother stood up to meet the challenge. "A court order kept you from dragging me out to the beach in December for a baptism. A judge kept me from having you cut off all my hair while I slept again, because I need to humble myself before the Divine Mortal. Grams didn't keep me from you, she protected me from you!"

"You don't need protection from me." The child-like voice was so strained Emma thought she might crack a tooth as she gritted out each syllable. "Drink your tea and try to calm down."

"I want you to leave." Emma took a deep breath, attempting to reel in those stray thoughts of how far her mother might actually go to drag her off to the Order.

"Nonsense." Melissa plopped back down in the chair. "Drink your tea and we'll talk this out."

"I'm done talking. I want you to leave." Emma turned to walk her mother out of the house, realizing for the first time she wasn't sure how the other woman had gotten into the house.

Her hand was on the door handle when she felt those thin pointy fingers plunge into her hair. The snap of her neck popping back was enough to make her see stars.

"This isn't over, you simpering brat!" Finally, her true colors on display, Melissa growled like the haunting beast of Emma's memories. "The Order has plans for you. I have plans for you."

Melissa pulled so hard on Emma's dark curls she fell off

balance and knocked back into Melissa with enough force that they both fell. Melissa twisted as they rushed to the ground, throwing Emma out in front of her. The table caught Emma's brow and everything went black for a moment. She thought that perhaps her mother had finally killed her. She wasn't so lucky. Melissa dragged Emma's disoriented body into her lap, those pointy fingers running over her face in a shitty approximation of affection.

"Sh... sh... sh," Melissa cooed, her rough petting jostling anger back into her daughter's limbs. "You'll be fine. You just need to calm down and you won't hurt yourself."

Still blinking blood out of her eyes and dragging herself out of the gentle pull of unconsciousness, Emma felt liquid being poured over her mouth. The bitter taste of the tea was almost a surprise to her. There was really nothing her mother wouldn't do. It was enough to force Emma into action. She flung out her arm, knocking the mug out of Melissa's hand. Vaguely, Emma registered the sound of it shattering. Melissa dug her fingers into the tender flesh of her chest. Like razors, Melissa's nails sunk into her daughter's skin, drawing little wells of blood. Emma threw her elbow back hard, catching Melissa in the stomach. The effect was instantaneous.

The table shook from the force of Melissa's shoulder shoving into one of its legs. It gave Emma enough space to wriggle out of her grasp, but not enough space to escape completely. They struggled together. Emma finally getting the upper hand for long enough to escape the cage of the chairs and table legs, keeping them trapped on the ground. The table teetered, toppling the beautiful bouquet the mysterious Vlad had gifted her. Water and petals sloshed over Emma's back, soaking her hair and clothes.

Melissa darted out from under the table. Crouched and snarling, she rushed Emma, who dodged her with barely a breath between them. A squeezing pain just above her elbow let Emma know that she had not escaped completely. Screaming with the effort, Emma pulled her arm around, whipping Melissa onto the table. It finally gave in, the spindly legs snapping on one side.

Melissa picked up the now empty vase and swung it at Emma, who ducked just under her mother's arm. The crystal connected with the glass of one of the large picture windows shattering both on impact. Its jagged broken pieces still clutched in her hand, Melissa thrust it towards her daughter, gouging into her shoulder before Emma could jerk away. On instinct Emma hauled back and threw a right hook that caught Melissa solidly in the chest with enough force to propel her through the broken window and onto the front porch.

Screaming, Melissa charged back through the window. The broken glass had to be shredding her hands as she tried to hoist herself back through the frame, but Melissa didn't stop. Nothing phased her. Emma put her fists up ready for her mother's next attack.

CHAPTER 3

V lad slid his black BMW into its space next to three others of the same make, model, and color; decoy vehicles for the occasional public event. Stepping out into the stale air of the underground garage, he felt the stiffness of the long drive to the family plot pooling in his knees and shoulders, nothing a good meal wouldn't fix. There was always something in the fridge and if not, the sun was down and with it peoples' inhibitions. After the long drive, he could use something warm in his belly and his bed. Vlad pulled a phone from the inside pocket of his coat when the parking garage's elevator door slid open. The high shine of the interior of the Wallachia Holdings private elevator cast a threatening glare of light around Vlad's Second in Command.

Sevystian was a stern man with a sharp jaw, dark brows and the stature of a gargoyle perched above everything, ready to devour its adversaries. Tonight, he looked even more perturbed than usual which meant someone was about to have a very bad night.

Vlad slipped his phone back into his pocket, dinner would have to wait a while. A long while judging by the severity of Sev's necktie.

"I take it the Caldwell meeting went well, then?" Vlad eyed him carefully.

"No." Sevystian huffed handing him a tablet. "There are many things we must discuss."

Beyond the obscenely large number that Marcus Caldwell wanted for his groaning beast of a shipping company, there was a sloppy trail of money leading right back to the Order's coffers. Sloppy at least to anyone who knew what they were looking at. Vlad flicked through the tablet to the pages earmarked by Sevystian for their bold contributions to charities and community enrichment programs, or as Vlad recognized them, the Order of Divine Mortalities outreach programs.

The acquisition of Caldwell International was on the surface a brilliant move on the part of Wallachia Holdings to move swiftly into the shipping market. Even Forbes had mentioned it in a feature, without any pictures, of course. The age of film and digital media had been a maze of new obstacles for his kind. Underneath the business grandstanding and vanity articles, the acquisition had been a chance to make a crippling blow to an old enemy. The bumbling company unaware that their president and board of directors had been funneling money to an organization like the Order that Vlad and his coven were hoping to find. It was a child's dream. Caldwell International was built on Order foundations. Money, weapons, and militants arrived on their ships and on the back of their business with just enough legitimacy to keep the law off of their trail.

"There's more." Sev flicked his hand across the screen in his grumpy dismissive fashion. "He wishes to maintain a board position."

"Tell me he is not in your trunk." Vlad's joke was only half so. Sevystian's temper was legend. "Actually, don't tell me. I don't want to know what you did with him."

"You have little faith." Sevystian kept the humor from his voice.

"Is this why you met me down here? I know it wasn't because you missed me." Vlad grimaced, hoping he could change the subject and turned on the charming salesman smile that had built his company. Sevystian simply raised an eyebrow. There was little that Vlad could hide from the man. "You don't have to check on me. It isn't the first time I have lost someone."

"Every time is the first time, my brother." Sev took the tablet and headed back to the elevator. "Kadir is entertaining in his suite. I am sure we can find something to eat. You have had a long journey."

"It felt especially long tonight." Vlad followed his comrade into the elevator, chewing over the scene at the gravesite. "She was well loved. There must have been seventy people there."

"It must have been quite a sight." Sevystian punched the button for the Kadir's floor. "She was a fine woman."

"That she was. I spoke with her granddaughter, Emma." Silence fell between them in the hard wash of anger pouring from Sevystian.

"That was not wise." Sev clinched his fingers against the tablet. "She could be one of them. Her mother was inducted when she was even younger."

"The Order of Mortal Divinity has not inducted Emma. They are the reason Iliza raised her in the first place." Vlad jammed his fist into the red emergency button stopping the elevator, squaring his shoulders against the taller Sevystian. "Emma is my family and that is sacred. She is under the protection of this Coven whether you like it or not, so I suggest you endure my actions in silence or take your leave."

"I suspect we might have to endure much in the face of your actions." Sevystian rolled his shoulders uncomfortably tapping down on the anger Vlad knew was boiling up inside him. They had been allies for centuries, it was not hard to surmise.

"I am not the one throwing a tantrum over one girl." Vlad spoke dismissively, both of them knowing the stakes of their conversation. "I gave her my card so we may very well hear from her again. If that is the case, you will afford her the same courtesy you would afford any other child of my line."

"There are no other children of your line." Sevystian straightened his tie the elevator dinging their arrival on Kadir's floor. "You have my vow. She is as you are, Sir."

A few drunk coeds stumbled out of Kadir's door giggling loudly as they traipsed toward the large pool deck, paying no attention to the two arrivals. Kadir leaned out from his apartment, his slacks low on his hips, shirt unbutton, looking thoroughly debauched. Spotting Vlad, he smiled, his whole demeanor shifting subtly as he moved to greet them.

"To what do I owe this honor?" Kadir scratched his beard with his thumb pausing to take a swig from his beer. Sevystian handed him the cracked tablet with no preamble and headed into the suite, leaving the other two to look over the abysmal offer without him. "Ah, so do I need to send Buchannan for a clean-up?"

"Apparently, Caldwell continues to live." Vlad clasp the other man around the shoulder and steered them back into the suite.

"At least he didn't kill him this time." Slinking into the black marble foyer, Kadir grabbed another beer from a passing frat boy who looked like he was ready to fight, until he got a look at the man who'd stolen his refreshment. Kadir had that effect on most people. His piercing hazel eyes and the meticulously groomed beard were pretty decorations on his large muscular frame. The smattering of scars that traced down his ribcage, up into his chest hair, and traced down from his right ear on to his neck could just barely be seen when he took a drag of his pilfered beer. The kid cowered and backed away until Kadir turned his focus back to Vlad. "Buchannan would be pissed if I dragged him away from his dinner."

Following Kadir's nod Vlad caught sight of Buchannan sprawled on one of the leather sofas the young blonde in his lap nibbling his ear with abandon. He was grinning like a fool, eyes closed and the rosy glow from a satisfying meal in his cheeks. Vlad remembered what it was like to be that young. His maudlin nature was catching up with him and his joints felt heavy again. He would have liked nothing more than to wander off to his penthouse and escape the pulsing music and well-meaning conversation of his men, but the throbbing beginning in his temple told him he needed to feed. He felt the weight of Kadir's arm settle over his shoulders steering him towards the man's private den, where he found Sevystian holding court with two gorgeous brunettes. How Sevystian knew that Vlad wasn't in the mood for a hunt tonight he did not know. He was thankful all the same.

CHAPTER 4

Simon stood over Melissa, his hand twitching over his service weapon.

"Stay down." His level drawl swept over the otherwise quiet outdoors, like a hot western wind.

To Emma's eternal surprise Melissa obeyed.

"You okay Emma?" Simon was tall and slim. He had always reminded Emma of cattle drives and the old westerns he always made them watch. Somewhere between Jimmy Stewart and Clint Eastwood, Simon's calm authoritarian demeanor had served him well as a Texas Ranger. Even the limp he had earned in a shoot-out a few years prior only added to the lean cowboy aesthetic he exuded. "Emma?"

"Yeah." She snapped out of the stupor she had hurdled into head first.

"Yeah I'm fine."

It was mostly true. Physically, Emma was alive with minimal damage. All things considered she was happy to not be in Melissa's trunk halfway to some Order compound, about to be offered up as sacrifice to the Divine Mortal.

"Shit." Emma swore loudly when Melissa tried to make a break for it.

Her worry was a needless consideration. Simon had her dead to rights. The click of his pistol cocking was deafening on the sleepy suburban street, populated almost entirely of older residences.

"The police are already on their way, Mrs. Caldwell." The timbre of Simon's voice forcing its way through his teeth gave pause, even to Emma. It was a guttural sound that felt like she was standing too close to a passing train. The way you know that as long as you stay clear of the track you won't get mowed down, still the tingle of danger persisted.

The blare of the siren broke the stare-down between Melissa and Simon. When the flashing lights finally rounded the bend, every porch light was on, and each houses' occupants were watching through their blinds. Emma didn't blame them. If it had been someone else's drama splayed over the lawn, painted in blood and flashing lights she'd have been just as curious.

As the cruiser stopped in front of the house Melissa grinned, her attention diverting for the first time from the barrel of Simon's gun, back to Emma. She made for a violent tableau, the red light pouring around her gaunt figure. That smile curling her once lovely face into something harsh and unnatural, still Emma held her ground unwilling to show her mother just how scared she really was.

A portly deputy hoisted himself out of the police cruiser, taking in the scene with depressing familiarity.

"McGreggor." The deputy lifted his hand in greeting to his fellow lawman, Simon. Tilting his head in a respectful nod to Emma he sidled up to the porch.

"They won't be able to keep me." Melissa taunted, already settling on to her knees, hands already clasped behind her head.

"Come on, Mrs. Caldwell." With the long-suffering grunt of effort the officer cuffed Melissa, taking in the bleeding bedraggled image of Emma watching them through the shattered window of a house in mourning. "Can I call you an ambulance, Ms. Emma?"

"No." Emma answered quickly, ready to quit the whole night. "Thanks, Michael."

With a gruff nod and a shuffle of his great mustache Deputy Michael grumbled his acquiescence. He was one of the dozens of so local cops who had had the pleasure, or rather displeasure of arresting her mother for the veritable smorgasbord of offences over the years. Sadly, Melissa was probably right. There was a lot of money behind the Caldwell name and no matter what outrageous stunt her mother pulled, her rich, connected husband would get her out of it.

"You couldn't just leave her alone." Deputy Michael chastised Melissa as he led her to the squad car. "Just for once, just for today, you couldn't have not shown up."

Melissa lunged at him snapping her teeth wildly. Slobber frothing at the corners of her mouth where her overly tanned skin made her look like some kind of sun-mad shipwreck survivor.

"All must humble themselves before the Order." She was stark-raving mad, and Emma felt unbearably foolish for believing anything else. Again, Melissa gnashed her teeth at them pushing herself as hard as she could manage with her arms pinned as they were, behind her. "You will be judged. The line of filth corrupts the world and you shall be judged for your collusion with this faithless whore!"

If she had been capable of blinking Emma might have missed the twitch of Simon's trigger finger. He didn't react elsewise and Emma was thankful. It was bad enough to have all of the neighborhood watch as Deputy Michael struggled with her mother to get her in his vehicle. Emma didn't know if she could stomach any further drama. Grams didn't deserve to have her final memory thus polluted.

"Don't know how long they'll hold her, Ms. Emma." Michael slammed the door to the cruiser, Melissa firmly ensconced inside. Her wordless screaming and thuds as she kicked at the metal barrier between her and the front seat mixed with the sound of the wind picking up, nearly drowning out the soft-spoken officer. "You gonna stay with her tonight? I doubt even her lawyers could get her before morning."

"Yeah, I'll be staying the night." Simon holstered his revolver, leaning on his good leg.

Relief swept over Emma with the next gust of wind. Simon was a good man. Emma was a better person for knowing him, a safer person. For each horrible stunt her mother had pulled over the years, including the time she had stormed the Chucky Cheese on Emma's tenth birthday, Simon was there. They had tried in high school to make it work as a couple, and for a while it had seemed like they would be another Texas high school sweetheart love story. There had been a piece missing though, some fundamental part of their relationship that lacked a spark. Reasonably, Simon was a smart match: safe, strong. But they would have been bored. Emma wanted more for him, and in those moments of self-reflexive honesty, Emma wanted more for herself.

"We should board that up." Simon nodded to the broken window, still propped on his good leg, his pistol thankfully holstered.

Mr. Bug zoomed across the yard, barking all the way. Miss Lily was right behind him, with Mrs. Abernathy not far beyond her. Emma wasn't surprised, they had been Grams' closest friends and it wasn't unusual to have them offer moral support after one of her mother's tirades. Tonight felt different, even from her mother's worst offenses. Tonight, she was alone with their affections. Somehow this immediate outpouring of concern swaddled her in a deeper feeling of dread. She imagined the damage that Melissa and her cult could wreak in the lives of her friends. The tingling of creeping panic began in her fingers.

Something warm and wet tickled between her toes. It was the gentlest snap back to reality she had ever experienced. Mr. Bug looked up at her with his beady black eyes, tongue lolling playfully. The little pug was the closest Emma had ever had to a pet of her own and as such she was pretty attached to the little guy. She took comfort in his warm paw weighing against her leg in his bid for her attention. Emma bent down to pick him up. Blood rushed in her ears, her vision swam. The combination of adrenaline leaving her body and whatever her mother had spiked her tea with was making her woozy. As the Earth began to wobble, a strong hand wrapped just above her elbow, keeping her on her feet. Simon.

"Steady." He was right there. Funny how Emma hadn't even noticed him come off the lawn. He righted one of the dining chairs, guiding her into it. "This might need a few stitches."

"What?" The ridiculousness of the evening, the insanity of her mother, the strange man at the grave yard, had all distorted her whole perception of the evening. Everything seemed to flit from one moment to the next with no time between them at all.

"This." Simon inspected the gash over her eye with steady warm hands.

"That looks pretty bad, Honey." Miss Lily's stout form waddled into view, Mr. Bug cuddled in her arms, his face smushed with equal concern. "Maybe you should let Simon drive you to the hospital."

"Yes dear." Mrs. Abernathy appeared behind Simon. She was tall and thin like her son, but where Simon was rugged, Mrs. Abernathy was refined. Soft blonde hair framed her kind face. "Lily and I can clean up here."

"Come on Emma." Simon made to help her up, but Emma refused.

"I'm fine." Letting out an exhausted sigh, Emma slumped into the hard chair.

Hands on his hips, Simon eyed her with his patented Texas Ranger stare. Unfortunately for him, Emma was never tired enough to succumb to his He-Man posturing.

"I'm not great, but I'll be alright. I just want to sleep. Maybe get a shower." That heavy feeling that had occupied her heart since Grams' death was leaking down into her gut, her thighs and forearms were lead. Just the idea of going to the hospital made her feel as though she was sinking through the chair. "This is just a scratch, really."

She wiped at the thick trail of gooey blood that was congealing on her cheek. It was hardly effective and Simon straightened his stance, clearly readying himself for an argument. A first aid kit smacked down on the table between them. Miss Lily looked between them eyebrows raised.

"You fix her up." Miss Lily nodded once, settling the matter. No matter that her youngest niece had taken over her bakery two years ago, Miss Lily conducted herself as a woman in charge. Emma could have wept with relief. She didn't want an argument or to spent the night twisting uncomfortably in an ER's waiting room. All Emma wanted was to be home, to be safe. She wanted Grams to hug her and send her off to bed with the promise that everything would be okay. But that couldn't happen. It wouldn't happen ever again. So Emma let Miss Lily take over, grateful for the respite even if it was only for a moment.

Emma chanced a glance at Simon and caught the desire to argue flash across his face. As the youngest division head in the Ranger's Houston office, he was just as used to being in charge as Miss Lily. He moved forward ready to make his case when his mother, Mrs. Abernathy, thrust a hammer into his out stretched hand.

"Why don't you take this, mmmh?" Mrs. Abernathy was

already setting herself into a chair in front of Emma. Popping open the first aid case she dug around for rubbing alcohol and cotton swabs. It reminded Emma of when Mrs. Abernathy had taught her how to put on make-up. Grams had never worn any and Melissa had slapped her for wearing Chapstick so hard once, Emma had seen stars. So, the burden of vanity training of all kinds had fallen to their gorgeous neighbor and mother of Emma's best friend, Mrs. Abernathy. Though she was only more recently Mrs. Abernathy, as she had seen more than her fair share of tragedy, having had to bury four husbands, including Simon's father before finding Mr. Abernathy.

Emma winced. The acrid smell of rubbing alcohol permeated the air and even though Simon's mother was being incredibly gentle, the wound on her brow was deep and the antiseptic stung. Around her Simon and Miss Lily dragged a piece of plywood out of the garage and affixed it over the gaping hole Melissa had left in her wake. Mr. Bug made himself at home on the living room sofa and eventually Mrs. Abernathy finished cleaning up Emma's face. She had insisted Emma rest while she and the others finished tidying up. Piece by piece, petal by petal the beautiful arrangement the mysterious Vlad had given her was disposed of, just another victim of the Order's destruction. Rage filled her body, stewing in her guts. She felt helpless. She felt weak. As she watched the shattered crystalline pieces of the nicest thing Grams had ever owned thrown away, Emma felt that hot liquid fury fill her throat. She didn't think grief was supposed to feel like this. Grief should be white and fuzzy. It should be a cold and lonely sort of state not something as hateful as the feeling trying to split her in two.

A clunk of ceramic hitting wood, brought her out of her thoughts once again. God, she really needed to get a hold of herself. The ceramic in question was a generic white affair with the Texas flag stamped on it: something Grams had picked up on a whim.

"Just a little tea, Hon." Miss Lily smiled sadly and bustled off, undoubtedly to finish cleaning up.

Emma sniffed the tea before taking a sip. There was nothing sharp or bitter about it confirming her worst suspicions. Emma sipped her new tea, peppermint and chamomile with the slightest hint of jasmine. It was floral and bright, gently sweet. The taste made tears threaten the corners of her vision. She swiped at them roughly in silence. Her hand hurt from where she had clocked her mother and every time she had tried to get up to assist with the clean-up Simon had pinned her with one of his, 'I know what's best', stares. Emma was too exhausted to contradict him so she stayed put, sipping tea and listening to the quiet chatter of Miss Lily and Mr. Bug. For just this moment Emma could pretend that none of the past few weeks had happened, that Grams was in the kitchen washing dishes, or upstairs writing a letter. Maybe it wasn't healthy, but Emma let herself imagine anyway.

CHAPTER 5

Hair still sopping wet and sticking to her neck, Emma adjusted her robe. She had been staring at Grams' door for a solid minute, debating on how wise it would be to go inside. Eventually she would have to, but after everything with her mother and the hours it had taken to clean up, it was past midnight. Did she really need to dig up all those memories right now? Probably not. Still she let herself inside.

Everything in the room was lacey and floral, even the walls were painted baby yellow in an antiquated feminine motif of roses and white baby's breath flowers along the crown molding. Every throw pillow carefully selected from thrift stores or bargain bins by her grandmother just to make her happy. Emma ran her hand along the bedspread, remembering the way Grams hummed "I Got Rhythm" the hem of her white house coat dancing as she made her bed every morning. Tears gathered in her eyes, different than before. Instead of the sick horrible emotion from before, Emma felt light. It was a simple perfect memory of her grandmother no one could touch. Emma let the toffee sweet nostalgia fill her up. She let the tears slide down her cheeks easily, and she built a room just like this one in her heart where the memory of the woman who raised her would live in bright morning memories. Emma would keep Grams there, in a space perfectly her own, in a place not even Melissa could ruin.

There was a little knock behind her and she jumped.

"Sorry." Simon tried to make himself look smaller, less threatening and Emma stifled a muffled laugh. Even as lean as he was, at over six feet tall, Simon was not a small man. "Just wanted to let you know I made some popcorn. There is a Buck Rodgers marathon on if you want to veg out."

His voice was so hopeful Emma would have agreed even if their feel-better ritual hadn't been so appealing. This was something they had always done. Every terrible event in her memory had been followed movie marathons, a private escape filled with too much popcorn and Simon's company. When Simon's stepfather had died they had watched the whole Lord of the Rings trilogy. When Emma's mom had called in a bomb threat to the middle school, they had watched Scooby Doo for two days straight. This was their thing.

"That sounds great." Emma hastily wiped the tears off her cheeks.

"If you don't want to I can just make up the couch. You won't even know I'm here." Simon smiled cheekily, trying to get her to laugh.

"No, I do." She sighed, pulling her wet hair out from under the collar of her robe. "I just need a minute."

"Take your time." He turned, shooting one of his sad smiles over his shoulder, before disappearing down the narrow stairs.

Alone with Grams' things once more Emma sat down at the spindly writing desk that occupied a small alcove across from the bed. A cup full of pens sat in a corner and a collection of cheery holiday-themed stamps in the other. Grams had been an avid letter writer; most of the papers she had already been through were correspondence Grams had saved.

Emma opened the desk drawer hoping to find a partially

written letter or a note, anything written in Grams' handwriting. Something to bring her back for just a moment. The drawer stuck slightly, undoubtedly warped from the high summer humidity. She tried a few times to ease it open, not wanting to break the delicate white writing desk. Finally she gave up and wrenched the drawer open with an indelicate grunt. Unsurprisingly there were more letters filling the drawer. All of them written on the same thick cream stock, all written in the same hand: Vlad. Emma felt flutters of hope and curiosity. The Vlad at the cemetery had said he knew Grams, implied that they had often been in communication and as naïve as it was, Emma wanted it to be true. She picked randomly from the pile and read.

Dearest Iliza,
I am so pleased to hear that the custody hearing has been won in your favor.

There is no doubt that you are the best hope for Emma's bright future. Your
warmth has been a balm to all those who have known you. I am honored to
be amongst them. Thank you so much for reaching out to me. Though I wish
there was more I could do to assist you. My legal team is, of course, always
at your disposal, as well as anything else you may require.
With warmest regards,
Vlad
P.S. I am terribly sorry as to the brevity of this missive. My board and I are
traveling.

· · ·

egal team? Emma wracked her brain trying to remember the name of the lawyer who had represented she and Grams at the custody hearing, but came up blank. She had been so young, most of the proceedings had just mashed together in her head, not much more than a vague sense of uncomfortable chairs and an itchy dress.

The drawer was filled with letters from Vlad. She flipped through a few of them, imagining the dark face of the man she had met earlier as she did. Her curiosity was begging her to call him, begging her to give herself some kind of context to all this new information.

She rushed into the bathroom, digging around in the pockets of her dress for the card he had given her. Hoping he meant it when he said to call any time. She dialed.

On the second ring, he answered.

he woman in the bed cooed softly in her sleep. It was an utterly feminine sound that Vlad found only mildly enchanting. She was as stunningly gorgeous in her slumber as she had been in the well-practiced mechanics of their previous activities. Somehow even after the drive, and the sex, and one good meal he'd eaten all week, Vlad felt restless. Tremors shook his legs with the need to move. There was little use in denying that flood of adrenaline, like so many nights he had lived before, Vlad slid from his lover's side to pace the barren corridors of his tower.

Perhaps it was the dip as he stood, or the absence of a warm body beside her, but the woman turned over, reaching out for him. On instinct, he reached back. Her hand was soft, and when she opened her eyes to look at him, Vlad saw Mina staring back. It wasn't her, of course, it would never be her again, but for this moment he could pretend.

"Leaving already?" She yawned, stretching her limbs akimbo, like a particularly mischievous kitten.

"I have a restless spirit tonight, I am afraid." There was a sadness in his face that even this relative stranger could hear.

"If you come back to bed, I could do my best to wear you out." She was plucky and even with sleep still coloring her mood, Vlad could hear her genuine concern.

"I am afraid I have already asked too much of you." His accent was thick tonight, the emotions of the day having already caught up with him.

"If I told you I would listen would you talk?" The dreamy lilt of her drawl almost had him protesting when she rose from the bed to slip back into her party dress. She looked over her shoulder at him, the line of her bare back tempting him to reacquaint himself with the intimate curves of her body. "Does that brooding stare mean no?"

"I am not the talking kind." For a moment longer he watched her dress before slipping back into his clothes. "Might I walk you back to the party? It is still early as yet. I am sure your friends are reveling in Kadir's hospitality."

"Please." It was the last they spoke to each other sans a kiss on the cheek as she sauntered off to a clutch of pretty girls drinking champagne and giggling beside the pool on the upper-lounge deck.

"How is it you still look so burdened?" Buchannan flopped an arm across Vlad's shoulders and stared after the woman. He smelled like sex and the lingering sweetness of cheap perfume.

"Oh, it is a hard-earned gift my friend." Vlad looked at him from the corner of his gaze. "It takes lifetimes to hone a craft like this."

"You've got a real dedication to it. I can tell." As young and tactless as he could play, Buchannan had an undeniable way about him when it came to family.

Vlad was more often than not glad that he counted the soldier among his.

"I know you ain't into all that talking shit, but if you want to spar or something you just name the time. I'll show up." For a split-second Buchannan tightened his grip on Vlad's shoulder, then let go, reaching over to grab two glasses of champagne from a passing waiter. "To Iliza King, eh?"

"To Iliza King." They saluted each other before draining their glasses.

"The low chirping of Vlad's phone was barely audible above the noise of the party. Handing Buchannan his empty flute Vlad bustled out into the hall. Party goers were still mingling between Kadir's apartment and the pool deck, but the noise inside was at least down to a dull bass pulsing down the hall. He looked at his phone; the number calling wasn't a known contact. Vlad answered hesitantly.

"Hi. It's Emma... Emma King." She sounded nervous. "Um, I don't know if you remember. You kinda gave me your number and told me to call whenever and I realize that you might not have meant at almost..." There was a pause while she presumably checked the time and hopefully drew breath. "Oh crap. It's so late. I'm sorry. I'll call back tomorrow."

"Emma." Vlad hoped to stop her before she hung up.

"Yeah." She sighed, sounding as worn out as he felt.

"The hour does not matter, my dear." Vlad was glad she had called. Her voice was a balm to the restless ache in his heart. "I find myself unable to sleep and even still should I be soundly asleep, I would welcome your call. Please, tell me what brings us to this conversation?"

"Mmmm." Emma hummed, as if she were trying to clear her throat of some condensing emotion. "I was going through Grams' writing desk."

"That sounds like quite the undertaking. If her correspondence with me was any indication of her attention to her friends." Vlad smiled as he strode down the hall to his private elevator. He spared Sevystian a nod as he exited one of the empty apartments, his dinner slipping out behind him, her eyes unfocused and dreamy, though Sevystian's read entirely opposite.

"She's got a whole drawer just for you, actually." Her voice wobbled, then steadied. "I... ugh. I didn't realize you paid for my lawyer."

"Your lawyer?" Vlad teased, it was a new feeling for him. He smiled to himself pushing the elevator call button with and enthusiasm he did not think came from his recent meal.

"Well, not mine." She fumbled for words. "The lawyer that Grams got to fight mom for custody. I found this letter that said you helped with that."

"Iliza came to me and I was happily in position to assist." For the first time since he had learned that Iliza had passed, Vlad felt hopeful as he stepped on to the elevator. "I was more than happy to help."

"Well, I just wanted to thank you." Emma sounded nervous still.

"Forgive me, but I do not believe that you called so late to thank me." The elevator doors slid shut silently and Vlad faced his reflection in the high shine of the chrome.

"No, I guess not." There was rustling noise on the phone and sniffling. "I just... My mother showed up tonight."

"Your mother?" Vlad tried to keep his voice even. "That seems eventful. Are you alright?"

"Yeah." The sniffling intensified. "I'm okay. The cops came and got her so I've got at least until morning to enjoy some peace and quiet."

"You shouldn't be alone." Vlad gritted his teeth. He stepped off the elevator into the penthouse, concern rolling off of him. It was hardly the first time Melissa had come for Emma. It was just the first time she was alone.

"Don't worry." Emma sighed sadly. "Simon, my friend, is staying with me tonight."

"And tomorrow night?" An image of Mina dashed against rocks below their bedroom window flashed in his mind. He couldn't fail his family again.

"I guess I'll figure it out tomorrow." Vlad could hear the weariness in her voice.

"Should you ever require it, my home is always open to you." Vlad contemplated going and collecting her that night, but that would make him no better than the Order. It chaffed him to be so constricted in his actions.

"These letters go back. Like way back." She paused, awkwardly as if searching for a safe topic. "You guys must have been pen pals for a while."

"Yes," Vlad agreed. "Many years. She wrote of you often. Strange though it may seem I feel as if I know you as well as I knew Iliza. She was quite the braggart when it came to you."

"Oh God, really?" Emma snorted with suppressed laughter, gasping for air as it turned into a sob.

Vlad's heart broke. Again, he contemplated leaving the tower to go to her. He doubted very much that Emma would appreciate the intrusion no matter how well intentioned.

"Emma, I would like to know you better. As dutiful as Iliza has been with our correspondence there is no substitute for face to face conversation." He was walking the line between familial duty and outright stupidity. Should Emma come to know the truth about him, the truth as to why the Order was so vehemently inclined to pursue her, he may as well paint a target on her back. By the same token, Melissa had done quite a good job of that already.

"Yeah!" Emma practically shouted into the phone and there was no disguising the trailing hiccup as she wrestled her emotions under control. "I mean, I would really like that."

"As would I." Despite himself Vlad felt a smile pull at his usually austere features. He wandered down the long hall past his office and into the main floor of the library. It was by far the largest room in the penthouse, and as imposing in its design as it was in its size.

"When?" Emma's voice still wavered between exhaustion and tears, Vlad was no stranger to either. "Never mind, I know you have to be busy. We'll figure it out."

The conversation was deteriorating along with the day. Vlad contemplated the empty fireplace that dominated one wall. For a moment it was the cold grey stone of Mina's dressing room and he could see her basking in his attention, his beautiful wife. She had been so unprepared for what the Order had wrought upon them. Emma had taken after her in stature and complexion, she had inherited his wild mane of hair though.

"Vlad?" Emma's voice broke the spell that had fallen over him.

"Rest tonight, my dear." He wished that there was anything more to ease her grief. Alas, in all his long years even time had not mended his loss and if she was his kin in any way she certainly would nurse this pain for a long time to come. "Whenever you wish to meet again I shall make the time."

"I don't wanna inconvenience you." There was a shuffling noise on the other end of the call, more papers he presumed.

"Family should be a balm to your hurt. I shall never consider you inconvenient." Vlad turned back to the room, Sevystian stood in the doorway his face a stony façade of perpetual disapproval. Ignoring him Vlad continued.

"Someone should tell my mother." A yawn on the other end of the phone told Vlad their conversation was coming to an end.

"If she is not yet aware I doubt she will learn now." With a sigh, Vlad lowered himself onto one of the long sofas.

"You're probably right." Another yawn followed by another, and another. "I think that's my cue to go to bed."

"Then I shall bid you good night." He lamented the brevity of their interactions. That lonely darkness inside him called out for another soul like his own.

"Night, then." Her voice was falsely cheerful; it was the tragic moment of silence before the call disconnected that gave her away.

Silence filled the space where the comfort of her voice had been. Still, Vlad remained unmoved, waiting for Sevystian to pass his judgment. Impatience, Vlad's ever-insistent flaw, twitched against the calm veneer he was attempting to cultivate. As true an ally as Sevystian had ever been, their opinions on Vlad's continued interference with the King family was in constant contention between the two. It would bubble up every decade or so, the ensuing fight usually leading to the kind of property damage reserved for human celebrities.

Sevystian's stony façade belied a vicious temper, and where Vlad was prone to quick, almost rash action, Sev allowed himself time to plot out his inevitably devastating revenge. Watching him now, Vlad was not entirely sure his oldest friend was not working on something for him. More than likely, some Wallachia Holdings project that would see him out of the country for months on end and safely out of direct contact with the last of the King clan. It wasn't that Sevystian was wrong, direct contact with Emma put the Coven's business in jeopardy.

So far, Vlad had been able to track the Order's trade to a local shipping magnate, Caldwell International. The initial hope had been to use the lure of a lucrative acquisition by

Wallachia Holdings to stem the flow of money into the Order's coffers, and root out the Order's Faithful who seemed to be steering Caldwell International towards nefarious endeavors. What they had discovered was much worse. Caldwell International was, at its core, just a front to funnel money, weapons, and political capital straight into the palm of the organization that had murdered his wife.

The crack of a crystal tumbler in Sevystian's hand connecting with the hard wood of the low table in front of him jerked Vlad out of his thoughts. The sweet musky smell of fifty-year-old scotch wafted up to him, the first sip just as enticing as the last. Ignoring the lurking gargoyle of a man hovering between himself and the door way, Vlad finished the glass slowly. Sevystian was positively seething by the time he was finished with the peace offering. It bought Vlad a moment's longer quiet, but ignoring the man any longer would be foolish.

"I know what you're going to say." Vlad placed the tumbler back on the table with considerable more gentleness than Sevystian. "You might as well skip to the name calling and be done with it."

"I would never, My Prince." Sevystian made a curt little half bow and Vlad winced. He only ever resorted to this kind of mockery when he was well and truly angered. "Whatever my liege believes is best, I am certain is the smartest course of action."

"Your faith in me gives me shutters." Vlad's deadpan expression was met with equal disdain from across the room. "One might almost believe you a sycophant."

"Well, let me assuage your worry, my Prince." Sevystian's voice fell from his lips and crashed onto the floor like glaciers crashing into the ocean. "You are following a fool's path. This girl is diverting your attention from where it is needed. The meeting tomorrow could cement a solution to the Order."

"I have never known you to be an optimist, Sevystian." Vlad chuckled, leaving his perch to pour another glass. "That meeting is a distant hope. Emma is known to us. She is the reality. Whatever we achieve tomorrow may very well spell disaster for her."

"And what of the Coven?" Sevystian squared his broad shoulders, straightening himself to greatest extent of his overbearing height. "What of those allegiances beyond this tenuous mortal family you cling to? What of the violence already being visited upon them?"

Vlad gritted his teeth against the insult. To question his decisions was one thing. After almost five hundred years in each other's company it was to be expected, but his loyalty was as unwavering as it had always been.

"You would leave a lone civilian to the ravages of the Order's barbarism?" Vlad hissed.

"You have done much worse to many more, without the excuse of the Order." Sev kept his tone even, making it somehow all the worse.

"That was for the betterment of my people." Vlad's words grated between his tongue and teeth, wishing they were something infinitely more destructive.

"What does that make the Coven?" Sevystian either cared very little for his own safety or very much for the dissolution of the Order and at that moment Vlad was hard pressed to see which.

"The Coven can protect itself." Vlad threw back two fingers of scotch, pinning Sev with a cold stare he usually reserved for Order Faithful. "They are not children, wandering stupidly in the dark."

"Your Emma is not a child either." Sevystian held his gaze undeterred by Vlad's cruel sneer or posturing. "She is an adult by every human standard, and far from stupid."

"Ignorant, then." Vlad spat out, disgusted with the semantics of it. "She does not have the advantages that we have to defend ourselves and still you would have me leave her alone."

"Her ignorance is an advantage." Sev clasped his wrist behind his back, standing in that authoritative way Vlad had seen him adopt a thousand times. "Iliza always had ignorance and the law on her side. It has been what has kept Melissa and the rest of the Order at bay for decades. If Emma knows nothing, if she is of no use to the Order; there is no reason to come for her."

"Melissa is beyond reason, she always has been. With the death of her mother, I fear there has been a break from the status quo." Vlad's eyes lingered on the scotch decanter contemplating another glass before deciding against it. "She came for Emma tonight."

"Was she injured?" Nothing changed about Sevystian's demeanor sans a tick in his jaw. He had always hated being wrong.

"No." Vlad set his tumbler down, stepping towards Sevystian decisively. "At least not so severely she was unable to get away. That phone call was the last of my family reaching out for comfort. Would you really have me deny her that?"

"No." Sevystian nodded curtly, his stance somewhat deflated from the bravado of before. "I would council you to practice caution, as I have always done." "I will take note, old friend." Vlad nodded in kind. "Mark my words Sevystian. She is my blood and I have neglected my responsibility to that for long enough."

"This company, this Coven is your responsibility as well." Sevystian spoke without anger his voice low and level. "The Order has not attacked our kind directly since Aleckzander took his last breath. There is no evidence to believe we are found out."

"The tide is changing my brother," Vlad sighed. "The old

doubts are dying and the with every victory I fear the Order of Divine Mortality grows in confidence. Emma would be the final jewel in their crown. They would use her as a beacon to rally the truly Faithful into violence. As terrible as they were before, the Earth would tremble for them now."

CHAPTER 6

It was already swelteringly hot when Emma left the house, self-consciously tucking some hair over the nick that her mother had left in her brow. Simon was at work and the familial comfort that his company brought with him was gone as well. None of the errands she set out to accomplish were pressing even the beta app she had yet to deliver to her client could be pushed further off. The funeral had made Grams' death real and all the more horrible. It was as if the empty places in the house that had once been filled with Grams' love were now watching her, or maybe that was some leftover paranoia from her mother's uninvited visit. Whatever reason there was behind it, Emma had fled from that hunted sensation permeating the house in favor of the summer heat of a Houston July.

She locked the front door and checked it twice before realizing that if someone really wanted in they could probably just knock down the plywood over the front window. The feeling of being watched followed to her banged up old Toyota and she wished she had parked in the garage, but that was still Grams' spot. Even though her grandmother's car was in an impound lot still being looked over by HPD, Emma couldn't bring herself to take the spot for her own. Just another reminder that she was gone.

Glancing around the block, Emma really wished that that she could chalk all her fear up to grief. She wished that Simon had laughed off her concerns the night before, thrown popcorn at her and told her to stop talking over the good parts. She knew better, her mother wasn't one for idle threats. Generally speaking with Melissa, you didn't get a threat, only the aftermath. So, Emma could forgive herself a little caution.

The car was hotter than hell and Emma's hand burned on the steering wheel. Though today she didn't give a damn about wasting gas on the AC. It took her second-hand mess of a car ten minutes to make a dent in the heat of the car's interior. Traffic closer into the city was mercifully sparse, which drew Emma's attention right to the white panel van that seemed to be on her tail. She made an extemporaneous exit, cutting off a man in a Jag, earning her the finger. The van made the same exit, keeping just far enough back that Emma might have missed it.

Through the heavy and probably illegally tinted windows Emma could just make out the figure of a man. Out of instinct Emma reached for her phone, and then dropped it when the van made a hard left. The breath that she had been holding burst out of her in a gasp of relief. The traffic thickened up and thoughts of the white van were lost in the jumble of horns and midmorning talk radio billowing out of open car windows. She hoofed it from the parking garage to a sweet little paper shop blocks away hoping that the summer heat might burn off the feeling of eyes still crawling over her skin. Emma wasn't even sure thank you notes were something you did for funerals, but it gave her a reason to get out of the house and it was the sort of thing Grams would have done.

Every shop window was an explosion of red, white, and blue trying to capitalize on the 4th of July sales. Emma waded into a crowd of people exiting one of the high-end boutiques, almost running into someone when she glanced over her shoulder for the source of the cold shiver of panic she felt skitter down her neck. There was no one, a few school aged kids, sipping iced coffees and looking more sophisticated than Emma, at twenty-six, had ever felt. Even in the light of day, in the wide-open sidewalk, she felt hunted.

Baby blue stationary with cursive gold script peaked out of the paper shop's window, Emma had never been inside the store, though Grams had bought her a journal from there when she had first left for college. It had been a frivolous thing, never intended for note taking. Lost in her memories, she walked headlong into a young man jogging down the street. Immediately she apologized, bending down to retrieve the keys that had flown out of his grip upon collision. That prickling sensation of eyes intensified, snapping the melancholy out of the air. She thrust his keys at him with another mumbled apology, flinching when a boom of thunder disturbed the otherwise sunny day. Emma was inside the shop before they could exchange the obligatory "Guess it's gonna rain."

It was a shame that grief and anxiety swamped her other senses as she walked inside. Under different circumstances she would have enjoyed the neat stacks of variously themed stationary piled in neat rows. She even jumped when the sales woman spoke to her, thinking that someone had followed her into the shop.

"Can I help you?" The sales woman was willowy thin and no more threatening than the jogger had been.

"Sorry." Emma braced her hand over her racing heart, hating that she apologized for everything like it was her fault. "You startled me."

The sales woman looked offended and Emma quelled the instinct to apologize again, while the sales woman gave her the most appraising of once-overs. The expression she wore saying clearly that she found Emma's fading yoga pants and ancient band-T wanting. She threw off the desire to snap at the woman. She was too tired and her knee still felt cramped from falling asleep on the couch.

"Let me know if you need anything." The woman's expression almost seemed fixed as she blinked at Emma, like a rubber Halloween mask. She stood there a second longer and Emma imagined that she was checking off her sales checklist before letting Emma drift any further into the store. She heard the woman's overly cheerful voice greet someone else. Emma looked up, glimpsing the man who had just entered the store but immediately turned her attention back to the stacks of powder blue card stock not wanting to speak with anyone else. Thumbing through another stack of annoyingly sincere birthday cards and novelty cards with a pastel kitten water-colored on the front, Emma felt something inside her snap.

The high-tension wires that had been holding her aloft since Grams had died pulled their ties. Her fingers ached as the tip of her nose turned to ice. Her extremities lost their respon-siveness. A black halo threatened the edges of her vision and the voice of the smug sales lady chatting up some unresponsive hipster seemed distant. The hipster and the sales lady turned to look at her their faces blurred. Everything in her line of vision was falling victim to the black shrinking halo. Emma forced herself to take a deep breath. It wasn't like she hadn't had a panic attack before. This wasn't the first time her blood felt like it was being replaced by hot lead, it was just the first time since Grams had died. Emma wanted to scream, but each breath she took was becoming more laborious than the last. With more effort than she thought she had left, Emma burst through the shop door back into the steamy afternoon heat. It wafted up from the concrete in cartoonish wavy lines leaving Emma to wonder if she were hallucinating the whole ordeal.

Trying to clear her field of vision she took short gulping

breaths until the darkened tunnel she had been staring through blurred into a soft haze. The ache in her fingers sharpened to a painful prickling sensation before fading away completely. Someone brushed against her and feeling the irritable way of self-consciousness that always followed her panic attacks, Emma turned to tell them off. It was the man-bunned hipster from the paper shop. Looking at him now she could see the dangerous marks of an Order initiate. The linen tunic he wore sported the same homespun quality of Melissa's clothing and the sweaty grip he had on her arm told Emma that their interaction wasn't some chance coincidence.

Like some passing thought drifting in the chasm of her melting brain, Emma thought this would be the right time to scream. Of all the times in the past week she had wanted to let out some unholy yell of anger and fear, now would be the time. She never did though, maybe it was the Miss Manners squatting in her mind like some belligerent toad keeping her from it, or maybe it was some deep-seeded shame she still had in regards to the Order, but she didn't make a sound. What she did do was to slam her elbow hard into Hipster's solar-plexus. His eyes bulged and he gasped for air, giving Emma just enough room to pull free of his vice like grip.

"Melissa said you were a brat." Hipster choked out, holding his stomach, still somehow sounding young and snobbish.

A bitter taste Emma recognized as adrenaline filled her mouth. Swallowing it down, Emma tried to remember every overzealous self-defense lesson Simon had ever tried to give her. She let her arms go slack, watching Hipster relax right along with her, his offensive posture reverting to the cocky stance she had seen in the paper shop.

"Your cooperation will be rewarded, Emma." The quality of his tone sent cold shivers down Emma's spine. "You belong with your family. I'll take you home."

Emma nodded meekly, feeling her guts turn over in revulsion when he nodded at her with a smile most people reserve for well-behaved dogs. It didn't matter though he had bought the act hook-line-and-sinker. A half step backwards as he leaned in to grab her arm was just enough to give her arm the momentum it needed. The punch wasn't going to win any bar fights, but Emma didn't need it to, Hipster wasn't expecting it. There was a crunch, where pain exploded in Emma's hand and she felt the man's nose smash under her fist like under-baked bread. Blood began pouring from it almost in slow motion and Emma grimaced when the warm slippery feeling of it mingled with her throbbing fingers. Even still the Hipster made another wild swing at Emma, half blind from his freshly broken nose.

"Sir, I need you to back away from the young lady." It seemed as if their little scene had attracted a few gawkers including a uniformed security guard, hand on his taser. "Ma'am, if you would please step behind me."

Emma's legs moved like taffy. The security guard said something she didn't understand into his shoulder walkie-talkie and turned his head a fraction to check on her. Hipster took the opportunity to bolt towards the far intersection where Emma could barely make-out a white van idling. Hipster dove into an open panel door and the vehicle sped away.

"Anyone get a license plate?" The security guard spoke with waning authority and the commotion now over, the crowd of on lookers was dissipating quickly. "Ma'am?"

"Huh?" Emma had missed something as she gazed after the white van. "Sorry, I was distracted."

"I can imagine." He smiled reassuringly and started over. "Are you alright? You clocked him pretty good. Your hand can't feel all to nice right about now."

"No." Shaking out the offending appendage Emma took a look at the damage. Her knuckles were already swelling, and Hipster's blood didn't make it look all that great, but Emma thought it could have been worse.

"Would you like for me to call for an ambulance?" He glanced down the street, as if some EMT might be strolling down the way at that exact moment.

"No!" Emma focused on the blood rushing from her hand. "Could you just walk me to my car?"

"You should at least stay and give a report to the police." His concern crinkled in the corners of his eyes, spreading his crow's feet well into his temples.

"No. I'm Fine. I just want to go home." She shook out her hand one last time, straightening her shoulders as if to prove she were tip-top.

"Ma'am, I really think you should sit down with an officer. At the very least it could prevent this from happening to another woman." He was laying it on thick and Emma thought about giving in just to get him to stop the guilt trip. He meant well, but as much as she wanted to tell someone what had really just happened she couldn't. Melissa was a storm that caught everyone unaware and if you didn't succumb to her rhetoric you were hurt by her wrath. Emma didn't want that for anyone.

"Can you walk me to my car please?" Even if she did file a report it wasn't like Melissa hadn't gotten away with kidnapping before. Emma could see the beady eyes of her mother's pet lawyer getting Melissa out of yet another legal pickle with a song in his heart and a retainer in his bank account. "He won't attack anyone else."

Something like realization dawned on his face and Emma knew he thought it was an ex-boyfriend or something to that effect.

"My daughter had a boy who stalked her in college." He put out his hand as if to stroke her shoulder but stopped, before awkwardly adjusting his utility belt. "I know it's hard, but when they come after you like this, that's when the police can finally do something."

She didn't have the strength to explain her mother to anyone today, let along a stranger. The part of her that wanted to spill her guts warred with the part that was ashamed to have Melissa as her mother and in the end she just wanted to be far away.

"Thanks," Emma mumbled looking over her shoulder in the direction of the parking garage, thinking wishfully of driving North into the endless Texas highway and not stopping until her engine gave out.

"Alright. Lead the way." The guard huffed in a resigned fashion. The crowd of gawkers parted as they made their way briskly to Emma's car.

The way back seemed to take twice as long as it should have the storefronts having lost their appeal. Even the car horns on the busy street next to them seemed louder, angrier.

Stepping out of the glaring sunshine and into the shadow of the parking structure felt like stepping into a cave. Emma half expected a swarm of bats to swirl and screech around her as she and the guard made it up to the concrete steps to the second floor where her Toyota was parked. The beep and click of her door unlocking for her gave Emma a ridiculous jolt of relief. The guard waited as she slid into her sedan and handed her his card with a sad smile. He waited for her to lock the doors before heading off the way they had come.

Sitting in the front seat of her locked car, the guard's card tucked into her closed palm, Emma finally let out the scream she had been holding in since Grams had died. She banged her fists in the steering wheel and cried out until she didn't have a single breath left to scream with, until her chest burned with the effort. Emma wanted to go home. She wanted to curl up on the couch and watch old MASH re-runs, listen to Grams wax poetic about Alan Alda's voice, and pretend her mother wasn't her mother, but couldn't. Melissa had gotten to her last night, hell she had gotten to her in the middle of a busy city sidewalk. Home wasn't safe anymore.

She almost started to dial Simon before remembering that he and Aaron had a Ranger's gala to attend. Aaron had taken great pains in snagging Simon a date for the event and Emma couldn't stand being a baited hook. He deserved a life outside her drama as much as she did.

The car turned over on the second try. Throwing the guard's crumpled card on the floor, it landed next to her tattered backpack. Corners of the vellum envelopes from Vlad's letters stuck out from one of the few rips in her pack that Grams hadn't sewn shut for her.

Sunlight blinded her as she pulled out of the garage, a horn blared from somewhere behind her, startling her into action. Emma pulled out into a lane of traffic, narrowly missing a collision with a black Jaguar. The driver flipped her off and Emma made to return the gesture, but her hand throbbed in protest. She had no idea where she was going, so Emma tried to focus on the mechanics of driving to settle her head. It wasn't working; an image of Melissa squatting in that white van waiting for her at her house kept popping up. Another scream was building in her throat. Emma felt a deeper fear root itself in her heart, newer than the one she had always had for her mother, but just as strong. When she was little, her mother had seemed like the Boogie Man, something you only really needed to fear when you were alone in the dark. Emma was alone now.

The light in front of her turned red. She tapped on the steering wheel with her good hand, pretending that it was as good as having a working stereo. A panhandler waved his sign at her vigorously and she wished she had a spare dollar to give him. Then someone slammed into her from behind. Her seat belt caught her tight, feeling like a steel bar wedged between her breasts. Her backpack hit the dash board with a thump, sending half of Vlad's letters crashing to the floor.

In the rearview mirror the white van idled behind her, its front grill wedged into her bumper. A semi-truck blared his horn as it raced across the intersection in front of her. Shit! Emma slammed her foot into the brakes in a vain attempt to keep her car from being pushed into the intersection by the van's continued assault. Another jolt nudged the car further into the cross walk, nearly hitting the panhandler, who shouted and waved his arms before heading back to the safety of the sidewalk. Another semi blew by, horn going, middle fingers flashing. The front end of Emma's car was nearly in the intersection with a seemingly endless parade of cars barreling through the five lanes of traffic. A buzz of traffic noise and her own blood filled her ears. She looked up into the rear-view mirror. The van was close enough now to make out the driver's face. It wasn't the Hipster, but the man had the same desperate eyes and greasy man bun. He snarled at her and her car stuttered further into the intersection, nicking the side of a blue mini-van. There was crunching sound as her headlights clashed with the mini-van's back bumper and then was a pause in the flow of cars through the intersection, a split second gap in traffic through which Emma might escape.

They were never going to stop. Maybe this is what it took for Emma to learn that, or maybe she had just been pretending that there was some invisible line that this cult wouldn't cross. Either way, it was painfully clear now, as the van pushed her inch by inch into the melee. Slamming her foot onto the gas pedal, Emma could hear something snap off her rear bumper and her car sprang free from the front grate of the van. Her head slammed against the head rest and her half bald tires thankful gripped the road with surprising agility. The gap in between perfectly sensible midsize sedans was closing by the millisecond and she shot under the red light narrowly missing the flatbed of a tow truck, only to side swipe a car turning right and losing her side mirror. It dangled limp and useless, clacking against her passenger side door as she cut across four lanes of traffic, skid under an over-pass and get lost in the traffic building up on the highway.

Emma could only hope that the white van and its occupants were stuck behind a line of predictably stagnant Houston traffic. She slammed her battered fist into the dash until the hysterical sobs that were threatening to over-take her subsided. She finally got why guys always seemed to do that in action movies. Emma needed a plan. She needed somewhere to go, somewhere safe. With a pang of regret Emma hauled her backpack onto the passage seat, digging through it without taking her eyes off the road until her fingers found her phone. One of the sharp edges of its crack screen sliced open the tip of her pointer finger, but Emma barely felt it as relief flood her system.

When Simon didn't pick up for the sixth time she thought about calling 911. She dismissed it quickly, remembering all the times mother had skated out of charges without so much as a warning. Money was power and the Order had lot of it. She checked the rearview mirror like she was developing a tick. She let it ring out waiting for Simon's familiar drawl to fill up the crushing silence of the car. A white plumbing van passed her and Emma jerked the car into the next lane before she saw the logo on the side. She left a calm message for Simon to call her as soon as he could trying to keep the fear out of her voice as best she could. It helped that there was a dozen or more exits between her and her would-be kidnappers.

The buildings thinned out as she headed out of the city heading towards the suburbs. Grams favorite barbecue place was coming up. Thinking about her white-haired grandmother flirting shamelessly with the burly tattooed bikers that frequented the dusty little joint made her lips twitch with a ghost of a smile. She was in the muddy parking lot before she had even really made the decision to stop and park. She slid her car around the far side of the building, stuffed Vlad's letters back into her bag, and threw a wave to one of the bikers she recognized from Grams' service. It felt like a sign.

Inside, she slumped into a hard-plastic chair at a back able where she could see everyone who walked in and ordered a sweet tea. The waitress jotted it down with casual apathy and sauntered away. Emma fiddled with her phone, sucking on the cut it had left on her finger. Her recent call log read like a Who's Who of people she didn't want to put in danger. Miss Lily, Mrs. Abernathy, half the neighborhood. Simon, Aaron they were both at that swanky gala. The only unfamiliar number was from last night. Emma hit send with a shaky breath listening to the dial tone ring just long enough for bile to rise in her throat.

"Hello?" Vlad's careful English was a relief.

CHAPTER 7

Vlad's phone chirped its generic factory ring tone loudly from his breast pocket, startling two of the spindly accountants perched across the conference table. The men shifted in their seats, rustling the cheap suits uncomfortably while Vlad kept his eyes glued to the figures in front of him. If he was a kinder man he might have tried to conceal the smirk of satisfaction. No one had ever accused Vlad of being a kinder man. At best, he felt an inkling of pity. Caldwell really should pay his people better if he was going to send them blindly into discussions with Wallachia Holdings. The waves of aggravation rolling off of Sevystian alone were enough to give Vlad second thoughts on their lunch plans. The room was crowded with Vlad's best and brightest, mostly mortal individuals with impressive resumes and equally impressive paychecks. The same could not be said for the Caldwell International ensemble. Vlad had grown his Wallachia Holdings with sharp acumen, accruing over time, the benefits of a stellar reputation both with its partners and its employees, Caldwell was a company built to serve the ideals of the Order. Though there were a few non-civilians working at the company as was clear by the cowering accountants seated at the table with him now. In a perfect world, Vlad would have saved them from the fate about to befall the company they worked for, but destroying the Order was more important than them. Collateral damage was a burden of war, Vlad knew that as surely as he knew the direction of the morning star. They had a new word for the Order's actions in this century; terrorism.

His phone rang out again and Vlad deigned to look up. Both accountants were blinking rapidly as if they could not imagine a world where anyone would leave their phone on in a meeting. They wisely chose not to say anything.

"Hello?" Vlad answered the phone without looking at the contact ID and Emma's voice spilled out across the connection. Frowning for dramatic effect, Vlad held up his hand, silencing the Caldwell side of the meeting. Leaving without so much as word was impulsive at best.

"Mr. Tepes, I really must insist that you stay until our business has concluded." One of the burlier associates spoke. Vlad had marked him as a Faithful the moment the man had stepped in the room. While his clothes were business-friendly, his entire appearance screamed Order of Divine Mortality, from his greasy man-bun to the barely visible marks of self-flagellation showing above his collar.

"Might you hold on a moment as I conclude some business?" Vlad kept eye contact with the burly associate while he addressed Emma.

"I can call back later." Emma's voice was clear but shaky and Vlad cared very little to have her wait on the account of the Order.

"This will only take a moment." Vlad said into the phone feeling the itch in his gums that came with the familiar tide of rage against his adversaries.

A mumble was all the he got in response, barely audible over the background noise coming from wherever she was. He took a moment to settle himself into a wider, more aggressive stance. Rolling his shoulders and neck until something popped loudly, sending a grimace over the faces of those with weaker constitutions before he addressed them.

"I do not believe that we will come to an agreement." Vlad's voice was steady and sharp and left no room for contestation. "Our offer was more generous than any other you will entertain. Seeing how you do business and those under the employ of this corporation has left me with little desire to continue further. Mr. Stevens will escort you all to the lobby."

The conference room predictably erupted in a fit of outrage, but Vlad did not linger to experience the chaos for himself. Emma was still on the line and he was far more interested in hearing from her than any more excuses the Caldwell board could come up with as to why their quarterly reports could not tie out to their ledger.

"Emma?" Vlad spoke once he was fully out of earshot from any potential Faithful. "To what do I owe this afternoon surprise?"

She was quiet still and Vlad worried for a moment that the call might have dropped.

"Uhm." Emma's short gasping breath on the other end of the call had him clenching his teeth, the bad taste from the meeting following him into the conversation. "I just... I ugh... I didn't mean to interrupt your meeting. You didn't need to shut it down for me."

"You needn't worry about my business dealings. My portfolio was healthy enough before that meeting. Money comes and goes with the seasons, it is only blood that sustains us."

Vlad let himself into an empty office. "Please Emma, tell me to what do I owe this pleasure?"

"I was wondering if you wanted to grab a bite?" Emma sounded terrified, the higher register of her voice no longer able to keep up the façade of calm. "I could really use some company."

"Of course, shall I pick you up?" Vlad leaned against the serviceable desk, mentally mapping out how long it would take him to get to Emma's home in the afternoon traffic.

"No!" Emma very nearly shouted. "Sorry. I meant, I'm not at home. There's this place Grams loved. We could go there. Do you like Barbecue?"

"Yes." Vlad could sense a creeping desperation in her voice that he didn't like. Desperate meant fear, it meant danger, real or imagined made little difference, fear made her even more vulnerable. "I am particularly fond of brisket."

That made her laugh and it eased Vlad's concern a little.

"I'll text you the address." She paused again, that tension from before still hiding in the high, tight way she finished her words. "Can you come right now?"

"Consider me already on my way." Vlad nodded to himself, assured in his decision to make contact with her at Ilza's grave.

It was by no small miracle that Sevystian had not cracked another tablet screen throughout the course of the meeting. The board of Caldwell International ran the gambit from sniveling civilians to fully indoctrinated meatheads, neither of which Sev liked. It was his job to sit across the table and make nice with them until such time as he could crush skulls or bank accounts. Until the moment that Vlad had pulled his disappearing act Sevystian had been playing through all of the scenarios in which the Coven could achieve its main priority, the total destruction of the Order's shipping channels and main source of financial support. They were bleak prospects. Caldwell International was for all the world could see, a middling shipping company that dealt primarily in the US, Western Africa, spotted with work all over Europe. It made their ties to Romania seem perfectly professional.

When Vlad's phone rang, it had almost been a relief to not have to sit with those barely contained fanatics one second longer. That relief was short lived though, as the fruit of an entire year's worth of research and hard line investigation into CI's weaknesses had marched out of the Transempirial Tower. Vlad's impulsive dismissal might have ruined the only chance the Coven would get at dismembering Caldwell International and stemming the Order's supply line. All of the hard work and demeaning concessions Sevystian had endured to tempt them this far was all for nothing. Anger simmered in his gut. Sevystian had walked the smoldering rubble of the Order's latest attack. Vlad hadn't gotten the chance to feel the desolation of their most recent trespasses. Some of those buildings had burned for days, the fires from one jumping to another and another. The Order hadn't cared that the warehouse they targeted was in a city center, didn't care that the fire had spread to one of the many apartment buildings in the area. Nothing mattered to them if it meant gaining power, if it meant hurting even a rumor of a his kind. There had been one such rumor, a story passed on by school children, and the Order had shown up with grenades.

Sevystian planted himself in the Coven's private elevator like a GQ gargoyle waiting. It was a matter of minutes before Vlad waltzed in, thoroughly engrossed in something on his phone.

"Your disapproval is noted, old friend." Vlad continued tapping away at something on his phone. "Now you will have to excuse me. I have a lunch date."

"We had a chance to starve them out." Sevystian could feel the enamel grinding off of his teeth with every word he didn't say.

"Maybe," Vlad agreed. "However..."

"No." Sevystian cut him off his voice never rising above the cool clipped tone he had affected for the meeting. "We had a chance to run the Order to ground without bloodshed. You just chose violence and you chose it for all of us."

"There will always be bloodshed when it comes to the Order, don't be naïve." The conversational cadence of Vlad's voice belied the tension between them. "Do not forget my brother, a starving beast is at its most dangerous."

The elevator door opened and Vlad beckoned Sevystian to join him.

"Am I to join you on your lunch date?" Sevystian sneered, a petty jibe to vent some waylaid frustration. "Do I need to bring flowers?"

"I daresay Emma has all the flowers she could want for a long while. You should join us though. Put a face to her name, then perhaps you will see her value a surely as you see the acquisition's." Vlad continued on to a sleek black sedan.

Sevystian held his tongue, sliding into the passenger seat silently. His mouth set in a cruel line.

CHAPTER 8

The restaurant, if it could be called that—to be clear, Sevystian thought he was being generous in doing so—was a shanty double wide that sat barely off the highway in a gravel and dirt parking lot that looked suspiciously homemade. A fat, slovenly biker waddled in front of the car and Vlad tapped the brakes. The man shot them the bird and continued on without further incident. Vlad slid easily into a parking spot beside a long row of beastly looking motorcycles. Having spent a lifetime subjected to the elements, Sevystian did not see the appeal. A pack of bikers loitered near the entrance to the "restaurant" smoking and taking turns shooting them looks of utter distain. Sevystian entertained the idea of confronting them for a moment longer than he intended and Vlad noticed. The meeting with Caldwell had left them both with pent up frustrations. An unquenched desire for violence pounded in Sev's ears as loudly as the drone of the highway.

"Shall I leave you to these bikers?" Vlad turned off the car, addressing Sevystian without ever looking at him. "I am here for Emma, but if you would prefer to indulge in a little dust-up I can leave you here. I am sure you can afford an Uber."

"You needn't frown so, My Prince." Sevystian affected the

simpering tone he knew irritated Vlad to no end. "You will crease your pretty face."

It was a petty insult, but Sevystian was feeling petty, and all together irritated. The situation was less than ideal before Vlad had decided to rush off and involve this flimsy mortal girl. Alluring as the prospect of family was to an orphan such as he, Sevystian had staked his eternity to the Coven he and Vlad had built. Yes, the Order posed a threat to this human now more than before, but they had built their religion on the eradication of his species. It seemed to him that one of those things posed a more emanate threat than the other.

The screen door creaked as Vlad opened it, waving in a leathery biker Ma before passing through himself. It was utterly ridiculous for Sevystian to see the once feared Impaler holding the door for anyone. Time eroded people in such strange ways, sharpening them so pointedly in some places and polishing them so smoothly in others. Sevystian took one last survey of the parking lot before stepping inside. Nothing out of the ordinary, sans a white van pulling next to a severely damaged Avalon Toyota. He watched them for a second longer but doubted that Caldwell's people had the balls to follow he or Vlad to the bathroom let alone across the city. Sevystian shook off the grim smile that tugged at the corners of his mouth looking for the terrified wisp of a girl he was certain lurked somewhere inside.

For as long as Vlad had spoken about her, Sevystian had imagined Emma King as a waifish, reed of a child, with soft features and brittle bones. Mostly he imagined her to have dark eyes like Vlad's and fine silky hair like Mina, and that when she blinked she would resemble a doe caught in a hunter's cross-hairs. The "restaurant" held no such woman. A few sitting in the front seemed to fit the age demographic, one with fine dark hair and large doe eyes, but Sev dismissed them immediately.

None of them suited the brittle pillar of human fragility that Emma King was bound to be.

"There we are." Vlad swaggered away towards the back of the room where a young woman sat with her back to the wall watching the room carefully.

The reality of Emma King was laughably different from the version Sevystian had created. Where he had imagined angles, she was soft and lush. Where he had conjured pictures of limbs as delicate and thin as a bird's, Emma was strong. Her hair was not fine, rather full and curled, and like Vlad's somewhat frizzled from the humidity. Faced with the fact of his own ignorance Sevystian felt the tickle of embarrassment in the back of his throat. As she stood to embrace Vlad, Sev noticed how gingerly she moved and winced slightly as they pulled away.

"This is my right hand, Sevystian." Vlad made the introduction effortlessly and Sev envied his easy charisma. "Sevystian, this is Emma King."

"Pleased to meet you." Emma reached out to shake his hand, keeping Vlad half between them. A barrier.

"Likewise." Sevystian took her hand, almost instantly dropping it when she jerked her arm in pain.

Her face was a mask of barely concealed discomfort and Sevystian worried that he had injured her unintentionally. A closer observation assuaged his guilt only slightly. Emma's cool grey eyes were overly bright, slightly too small and heavily lidded to be considered fashionable. Today they were rimmed red with unshed tears. Any unobservant man, who knew simply that she had just suffered a loss would have assumed that these were the waiting tears of grief. Sevystian knew better. She carefully folded herself back into one of the hard-plastic chairs at the two-top table, forcing him to pilfer another to sit at the side of the table not intended for another patron.

"Sorry." She fiddled with a hair tie at her wrist eventually deciding to pull her mane back from her face and off of her neck. "I didn't realize that there would be two of you." She smiled half-heartedly at Sev. "I hope you like barbecue."

"Of course." Sevystian did not. Sevystian liked fine whiskey aged for decades in burnished oak barrels and liveried wait staff. He put this all aside to observe Emma more closely.

Upon inspection, she was littered with bruises and scratches indicative of a fresh altercation. The hand that Sev had worried he might have mangled with carelessness was blotchy, red and swollen at the knuckles. Emma King was not a simpering waif jumping at every shadow. She was a fighter. Even now as she sat with them about to calmly share a meal, her eyes flitted around the space checking windows and entry points in a familiar, tactical way Sevystian employed regularly himself. He straightened in his chair, catching the delicate scent of human blood in the air. It sat under the thick smoke like an aftertaste. Emma pulled at her baggy T-shirt and Sevystian could see two crescent shaped gouges of dried blood. This was not the lunch he had expected.

"I ordered the brisket." As she spoke, a switch had flicked on and Sevystian's senses clouded over with the smell of cooking meat and his eyes watered as smoke from the pit wafted in from the cooker outside. Even Emma's voice didn't seem to match how he had imagined it. It was low and steady, lilting and dipping with the enchanting drawl of her accent. "I hope that I didn't drag y'all away from anything important."

"Nothing at all." Vlad shot Sevystian a cold look. "A meeting going nowhere, but I suspect that you did not ask me here to talk about my egregiously boring business. You look as though you have been in a fight."

"I umm...yeah mother is getting..." Emma let her voice peter off, looking down at her battered hands.

"Melissa is quite the opportunist, isn't she?" Vlad kept the venom out of his words, but not his eyes.

Emma nodded, meeting Vlad's eyes with a sad smile and

Sevystian wondered if it would not have been better to have stayed in the parking lot with the bikers like Vlad had suggested.

"Not exactly something you can say over the phone, huh?" Emma made a little sweeping gesture down her body. Other than the few visible bruises Sevystian saw very little wrong with her.

"I take it last night's visit was eventful?" Vlad took her hand gently, examining each finger with care.

"That's from today." Emma's voice was hollow, disconnecting her from her topic as well as any brick and mortar wall could ever do. "Mom had me followed. I was trying to get Thank You cards and he…"

Emma snapped her mouth shut as the blue-jean clad waitress arrived back at their table. The unfinished sentence hung in the air between all three of them as thick as the smoke coming from the pit. The waitress took that moment to slide a platter of meat and sauce between them that covered most of the tabletop. She threw down forks, a handful of wet wipes, and left without a single word. Sevystian looked down at the pile of cooked flesh, wondering if the animals that had come for Emma worked in Caldwell's company.

"I propose that we enjoy this bountiful meal and put aside our thoughts of this barbarity, for now." Vlad attempted what Sevystian assumed was meant to be a reassuring smile. It looked strained. "Then, I would like for you to come and stay with me tonight."

"We should eat." Emma smiled at Vlad, a sad half smile that accentuated her thick pink lips. "We can figure everything else from there, yeah?"

"I am happy to finally share a meal with you." Vlad slipped into the sleek veneer of charm he had always worn so easily. "Now tell me how is your business doing? Iliza mentioned you were ready to launch some sort of beta test for one of your clients."

Sevystian envied Vlad's ability to deflect more than he would ever admit. Ignoring the pitter-patter of small talk that the two picked up, Sev took the opportunity to study the room. Their waitress had several other tables, which she treated with equal apathy. The patrons ranged from the average middle class family to the hardened motorcycle clubs. Between the creaky linoleum floor and the nearly non-existent air circulation, Sevystian did not see the appeal.

A huge man with a patched-up leather vest and neck tattoo approached their table, looking every ounce the predator Sevystian was. Sev tensed; ready to counter the moment the man made his move.

"Darrel!" Emma moved first, climbing out of her seat as quickly as she could manage given her injuries.

Sevystian took note.

"Emma, Sweetie." Darrel hug her tightly, and despite the wince of discomfort Emma didn't pull away. "I'm so sorry I wasn't at the service. Me and the old lady was out in Killeen taking care of some business. Did ya get my flowers?"

"Yeah." Emma was teary eyed. "Grams would'a loved them."

"That's what I was hope'n for." Darrel looked over at Sevystian and Vlad. Showing exactly zero interest in speaking with either of them. "I saw yer car outside. It's pretty banged up. Get into an accident?"

He looked her over, for the first time he seemed to see the state of Emma.

"Yeah." Emma scrunched up her nose in a disgruntled way and Sevystian could tell that she was about to lie. "Ran a red light and didn't quite make it."

"Jesus Christ, Emmy." Darrel let out a long drawn breath and hugged her again. "This ain't the Daytona. Do me and the boys a favor and don't go getting yer'self killed. Iliza would roll over if she thought you were pulling some wild ass shit like that."

"I'll keep that in mind next time D." Emma smiled at him, too big and too toothy to be perfectly genuine.

Sevystian supposed that it was probably hard for her to lie. The man left to rejoin his crew of equally aggressive looking compatriots and all attention was back on Emma, who sat back down with the look of someone resigned to interrogation.

"Would it be far from the truth to say that the damage to your hands was the least you sustained from today's rendezvous with your mother's associates?" Vlad took a bite of the brisket, chewing it slowly while he kept his eyes glued to Emma.

"No, it would not." Emma straightened her back, and squared her shoulders, taking a breath Sevystian imagined was steeling her against whatever trauma she was about to relay to them. She was about to speak again when something caught her eye behind them and she deflated. "Shit."

Both men swiveled around to glare fully in the direction of whatever had affected Emma so completely. Two men stood in the doorway. They were hardly discernable from each other, as they both wore the same homespun linen tunics and piled their greasy hair in buns high on their heads. Their beards were unkempt and their eyes were hard as they scanned the room with intent. The shorter of the two had poorly cleaned his face from what looked like a recently broken nose, his eyes swollen and black rimmed.

A scraping noise drew Sevystian's attention back towards Emma. She had curled herself under the table using Vlad and Sevystian's bodies to block her from view. Her grey eyes pleaded with Sev from under the table.

"It is time we left." Sevystian dialed Buchannan without waiting for any further acknowledgement.

"Please don't leave just yet." Emma didn't seem to grasp

what Sevystian had intended, but Buchannan had already picked up.

"What's up boss?" Buchannan's chipper voice annoyed Sev more than usual.

"Have Fields prepare a guestroom, Emma King is staying with us."

"Oh, I love a slumber party." Buchannan poked at his nerves intentionally and not for the first time Sevystian wondered if he should have left the man-child to bleed out on that damned French beach. He hung up without further conversation.

"Emma, my dear." Vlad spoke softly, throwing a wad of bills on the table and standing. "I believe Sevystian is about to make quite the commotion. Leaving now will be our best option."

Emma nodded uncurling herself from the spot she occupied under the table and grabbed her bag tightly.

"After you, big guy." She nodded staunchly to Sevystian, tucking her fingers into the straps of her back-pack, readying herself for an attack.

In the end, it hadn't turned out to be as much of a commotion as Vlad or Sevystian had expected. The Faithful with the broken nose had lunged around Darrel's table of degenerates in an attempt to get at Emma and had promptly been felled by the violence Sevystian had sensed in the man and his company. The second Faithful had fled outdoors and attempted to snatch her in a less-than-stealthy manor. He had remained conscious just long enough to see the leather heel of Vlad's dress oxfords connect with his knee. After which he had vomited on the gravel and passed out.

Sevystian had expected Emma to squirm or perhaps vomit herself at the violence, but she did not. Emma pursed her face in distaste and walked along, allowing Vlad to lead her to his now dusty black sedan. She slipped into the back seat silently.

"Just because you were not wrong about the Order's intentions towards her, does not mean your actions earlier were not rash." Sevystian snarled at Vlad, who smirked belligerently back at him over the top of the car.

"And being rash does not mean I was not also right." Without another word, Vlad slipped into the driver's seat.

CHAPTER 9

Emma had fallen asleep within minutes of getting on the highway. The rush of adrenaline leaking out of her like a torn sieve and the hum of the engine lulled her into a difficult slumber. A mile or so from their destination, the luxury sedan hit a pothole not even its suspension could disguise and Emma jostled awake. Disoriented, she cursed, throwing her hand against the door handle. She was scared for a second that she had been taken by her mother.

"Be well, Emma. You are safe." Oddly enough, Vlad's strange accent calmed her. "We are almost home."

Home. Still groggy from the short nap, Emma struggled with the idea for a moment before watching the empty parking lots and tall grey sky-scrapers They had passed into downtown at some point. The buildings were tall and close together and when she tried to look up into the cloudy sky their height made her dizzy. Vlad probably lived in one of those slick penthouse apartments she always saw on the cover of magazines. She could picture him sitting on a one of those squared off white sofas in his neat black suit, somehow both intimidating and inviting. His associate, Sevystian, certainly seemed to fit into that category. The man had spared her few words and now that she was awake, he watched her with an intensity she wasn't completely okay with. It was as if he saw her as some sort of threat assessment in need of completion. He had the bearing of a man uncomfortable with small talk. Still, he turned to speak to her, his face straining with the effort of ill-affected charm.

"It does not seem as if we shall arrive before the storm." His voice was as gravelly as his disposition.

"You really want to talk about the weather?" Emma caught the flicker of a smirk in Vlad's eye as he split his attention between the road and his two passengers.

Fat drops of rain fell on the windshield and Emma sighed. Sometimes it felt like the only thing she could count on was the rain. A clap of thunder rattled the glass of a building as they passed. Emma smiled. The storm would be a big one she liked that. Something to wash away the day before, Houston's own cosmic Etch-A-Sketch. When they pulled into the parking garage Emma felt a little tug in her heart. Part of her wanted to stay out in the rain to watch the water puddle and wash down the storm drains until she felt like herself again.

She knew that even the comfort of the summer storm could not achieve such a feat.

They pulled into a parking garage on the far side of the Transempirial Tower, whose ornate Art Nouveau design stuck out against the sharp modernity of Houston's skyline. The entrance required a code and a palm scan, and Emma was struck by how very little she knew about Vlad and his business. Whatever he did, the man must be making bank to have a private entrance downtown. Two men waited for them next to an empty parking space, both as impeccably dressed as the two accompanying her. She felt underdressed and pulled the hem of her T-shirt further over the slight pudge of her stomach. Sweet God, she was regretting wearing yoga pants today. Why couldn't she have just worn a nice pair of jeans? She twisted around to retrieve her bag, wincing. The black and green bruise blooming like a jungle flower over her hip bone from where her mother had tackled her the night before tweaked in pain, even the yoga pants had been a little too rough against the tender flesh this morning. The sedan door popped open scaring the ever-loving shit out of Emma.

"Fuck!" Emma jerked backwards so far; she almost hit the door on the car's other side.

"I've always loved a mouthy dame." The man sticking his head inside was younger than she would have expected from anyone working for Vlad. "Com'on Doll we've got places to be."

She took his offered hand. He had a genuine look of happiness in his eyes as he helped her from the car. Not returning his smile was impossible and Emma found herself and her backpack being practically lifted from the car.

"Let me take that." He snagged her pack and slung it over his shoulder, not caring for a moment that the tattered canvas could be staining his expensive suit. "Can't have you lugging this thing around. Not when I could be showing off."

He winked at her and Emma barked out a laugh.

"Buchannan." Sevystian's growl startled Emma, but Buchannan just looked over her shoulder and rolled his eyes.

Emma peeked behind her to see Sevystian stuck on the other side of her open door waiting on the pair of them to move before he could. Emma bit the inside of her cheek hard, trying not to laugh at how ridiculous it looked. He was such a large man, built like a bear, with the bearing of a Special Forces officer. Hell, he even cut his hair like a soldier, so tight on the sides Emma could make out a scar curling over his ear, and there he was trapped by average-old-Emma.

"I vote we stand here for a while." Buchannan leaned in to mutter conspiratorially with Emma.

"Move or be moved." Sevystian growled again.

Buchannan rolled his eyes again, but tucked Emma's arm into his own, escorting her away towards a bank of elevators where Vlad and another man waited, watching the scene with mild amusement.

"Emma, I see Buchannan has already introduced himself." Vlad smiled at her in the way indulgent grandfathers do in Hallmark films and gestured to the man to his left. "Allow me to introduce Kadir, he is COO for Wallachia Holdings, and a close friend."

"Hi." Emma detangled herself from Buchannan, who pouted absurdly, and made to shake the other man's hand. Instead he raised it to his mouth kissing her battered knuckles gently. "Ummm... okay."

"It is an honor to meet you Miss King." Kadir looked up from her hand with devastating effect. His eyes were such a light green they almost appeared to glow. Even in the dim yellow tungsten of the parking garage Emma could imagine getting ensnared in their gaze.

"Right." Emma snatched her hand back, not sure she liked the overly polished charm that poured out of him. Something about him seemed fake in a way that she couldn't quite put her finger on. His thick chestnut mane was pulled high into a fat casual bun, that looked wholly different to the buns the Order Faithful had sported earlier, still it curdled her stomach. Maybe that was what had so quickly soured her opinion of him. She noticed too, a sharpness to the smile he had given her that in opposition to Buchannan seemed a poorly recreated copy.

"Let us go inside." The elevator had arrived silently and Vlad ushered her inside.

There wasn't any elevator music, which seemed odd. Without it Emma realized how disarming silence could really be. Fortunately, Buchannan was not one to let things stay quiet for long and Emma only had a moment to blink at her own distorted reflection in the chrome doors before he was talking again.

"So, I had Fields set you up in the Green Suite. Not sure if green's your color or whatever but it's nice." He shuffled around the small space to talk directly to her, sticking his body half between Vlad and Sevystian who had come to stand like centurions at her side. "I'll come back down to grab the rest a' your bags once we've got you settled."

"I don't have any more stuff." Emma shuffled around, wishing that there was some instrumental version of Free Bird playing in the background to drown out the grinding pity she could hear falling off the new guys. "I didn't exactly know I was going to need it."

"The Order?" Kadir's voice was soft and melodic, like the first note of a cello. He rolled his R's, but not like Vlad and Sevystian did.

In their reflections, Emma saw Sevystian and Vlad nod in synchronicity.

"Fucking animals." Buchannan grunted, his face screwed up in displeasure.

"Watch your language." Vlad snipped at him.

"What?" Buchannan threw his hands up dramatically, catching Sevystian in the shoulder and earning himself a very disgruntled glare from the behemoth. "She said it first. Emma's the bad influence."

When the doors opened again, Vlad was still glaring at Buchannan, who didn't seem to feel the least bit apologetic. If there were such a thing as comfortable opulence, the Transempirial's penthouse fit it to a tee. Everything from the floors to the fresh cut flowers screamed luxury. Vlad guided her through the entry into the proper living space and she worried off-handedly that the saggy old moccasins she was wearing were tracking mud onto one of the expensive rugs. The living room was appointed in dark masculine reds and browns. Each wall heavily adorned with oil paintings that seemed to come right out of her art history text book. Looking at them now she wished she had paid more attention in that class, not that anyone paid attention in that class. A massive empty fireplace beautifully carved out of white stone stood as the focal point of the room. It looked to Emma as if there should be a hidden room somewhere behind it.

"Come." Vlad steered her up the curving staircase opposite the fire. "I'll show you where you'll be staying."

"Sure," she choked out.

Vlad hummed in a small, non-committal way leading her up the grand staircase. He gave her a brief explanation of the various paintings as they passed and it became increasingly intimidating with each recognizable name he casually dropped, her shoulders tensing. Was she really going to be staying in a place like this, with a man who talked about art in the terms of lesser Degas? The amount of money on the walls made her T-shirt feel even more under whelming. She was nervous to breath too close to the walls..

"And this one was painted by Jesus himself." Buchannan turned to walk backwards, wafting his arms around yet another beautiful oil painting of Artemis hunting a stag. "It's all very impressive, isn't it?"

Emma smiled, some of the nervousness must have spilled out for Buchannan to pick up on it. He continued walking backwards until he banged into the door of their destination.

"It would seem we have arrived." Vlad lifted one eyebrow, a smirk barely curling at the corners of his mouth.

The room was dark when he opened the door. The light flicked on and she was stunned for a moment. Another fire-place graced this room as well, across from it was a massive four-poster bed draped with a green velvet duvet and more pillows than she had ever seen on one bed. She must have gaped for a moment too long.

"Or there are others." Vlad made to turn out the lights.

Emma shook her head stepping gingerly into the room to run her hand over the marble fireplace. It was cold to the touch. Her sense of awe tampered by the strangeness of her situation, by that long wait for the other shoe to hit the floor.

"The Green Suite it is then." Buchannan pushed his way into the room, depositing her backpack on an armchair and flopping onto the bed. "I say we braid each other's hair first and then the mani-pedi's. What are your thoughts?"

Emma blinked at him.

"Hey, Sev's the one who called this little sleep-over." Buchannan pulled himself up to sit against the head board, one of the trillion pillows draped across his lap. "I'm just trying to plan the activities."

"Duly, noted." Emma gave him a thumbs up taking in Buchannan's playful demeanor and relaxing a fraction, while Sevystian, Vlad, and Kadir swept into the room like over-dressed bell hops.

"Would you like for me to start a fire for you, Madame?" Buchannan wiggled his eyebrows at her, waiting for a reaction. "Perhaps, I can interest you in a bonbon or maybe high tea with crumpets."

Sev pulled the pillow out of Buchannan's hands, waving him off of the bed and replacing the cushion carefully. Buchannan made a face at Sev's back before slinking over to Emma.

"He's not a big talker, that one." He thumbed towards Sevystian before tucking Emma casually under his wing. "So, this is the Green Suite, named as such because Vlad doesn't have the sense of creativity God gave a duck. Any questions? Needs? Concerns?"

"Umm." She tried not to look as out of place as she felt. Catching the bright green gaze of Kadir Emma shivered, casting her eyes away from his unsettling focus. Spotting a set of double doors, she jumped at the distraction. "Where do they go?"

"Oh." Buchannan stood up straight and twirled her around

to face him, a serious look plastered to his face. "You must never go through those doors. It is forbidden."

"For real?" Emma said, her eyes going wide, the faint thud of the proverbial other shoe hitting the floor of her mind.

"Nah." Buchannan pulled the doors open in a flourish. "It's just the bathroom."

"Jerk." She punched him in the arm as she walked past him, and instantly wished she hadn't. Did this guy wear steel plated suits? Shaking her hand, she walked around him into the bathroom. "Jeezy Pete's."

She could feel the cold of the marble even through the leather of her shoes. Inset in the floor was a complicated spiral mosaic pattern with roses and vines that beautifully off set the deep green of the cabinets and the large green glass tiles of the shower. The affect was pure grandeur.

"Told you." Buchannan stuffed his hands in his pockets with a cocky sway forwards. "Creativity God gave a duck."

"What would you call it then?" Emma countered still wandering around touching the towels and running her fingers over the high porcelain sides of the claw foot tub.

"Don't know." He rubbed his fingers down his chin as if stroking an invisible beard. "The Vine suite? Maybe the Emerald suite?"

"Is emerald not just a synonym for green?" Vlad had snuck up behind the younger man while he pontificated, clapping Buchannan on the shoulder. He flinched and Vlad seemed satisfied that his dominance was clear. "Who's the duck now, boy?"

"I have always thought of him more as a goose." When Sevystian had managed to come up behind her, Emma had no idea.

Emma felt her whole-body jerk in surprise.

"Your fear was not my intention." Sevystian managed to

make his apology sound slightly irritated and Emma wondered what she'd done wrong.

Maybe it was just his Eastern European accent, they always sounded aggressive to her, or maybe she had seen John Wick too many times.

"It's fine." She took a step back anyway, giving herself some room. "I'm probably just going to be jumpy for a while, you know."

She was sure that Sevystian did not know.

"I can imagine." Sevystian nodded to her politely walking stiffly out of the door, where Kadir was leaning GQ style.

"Are you hungry?" Vlad asked with the whimsical look of a new father.

"I guess we didn't get to finish lunch." Emma was torn between the gnawing ache in her belly and the sticky feeling of sweat and Barbecue smoke still curling in her hair. She looked longingly at the giant shower trying to make up her mind.

"Perhaps the lady would prefer to freshen up before joining us for a meal." Kadir laid on the charm thick.

"Yeah." Emma didn't like the eerie way Kadir watched her, his eyes too focused and his mouth somehow too sharp. Vlad and Sevystian both had an air of danger about them, and even Buchannan looked as if he knew his way around a bar fight, but when Kadir spoke Emma felt as if there was some darker version of the man watching her from beneath his startling green eyes. "If I could have like a second to just decompress."

"Anything you would like." Vlad ushered everyone out of the room, and smiled stopping just short of the bedroom door. "Truly, anything at all, my home is at your disposal. Shall I close the doors?"

"Yes, please." Emma smiled wearily. "Thank you, Vlad."

He smiled back through the crack of the door, a familiar melancholy turning his lips just a little too firmly. Emma felt a corresponding pang of understanding in her gut. Now more than ever she was sure that she had made the right choice in coming here, Order or not she wanted to be with family. If her mother couldn't be that for her than maybe it was time to find a new one. Even if Vlad was only a distant cousin, probably eight times removed, she could have been dealt worse.

It took her a few minutes to figure out how to work the shower. How many nozzles did you really need for one shower? Standing the giant glass cage of the shower as the jets streamed down on her from every angle, she took it back, she understood why you needed all of the nozzles. The glass enclosure filled with steam and the scent of whatever high-end orange blossom soap Vlad had stocked for his guests. It wasn't like Emma had spent her life wining and dining herself in fancy hotel showers but she had stayed at the Omni once, and this blew it away. By the time she got out, her fingers were pruned and her skin was rosy with heat. Sliding into the plush white robe she found hanging on a hook on the back of the door, she picked up and inspected the fancy glass bottles one by one. Deciding on one with a swirl of French on its label, she hoped that the lavender-smelling goop inside was the body butter she was looking for. She felt silly for a second, then in the back of her mind she heard Gram's voice whisper, "When in Rome, Honey-Pie." Damn straight when in Rome.

CHAPTER 10

Vlad's study was exactly like the man himself. A bronze statue of a fallen angel sat on plinth in the corner; the model from which some larger statue had been carved out of marble. The paintings hung close together in overwhelming number, all featuring dark and brutal landscapes of far off lands, between which peeked a rich wood paneling. Yet another monolithic fireplace dominated one side of the room and opposite sat an equally imposing desk. The thick red Persian rug and two dark brown Freudian leather sofas finished out the space with dramatic flair. All in all, Sevystian thought it was a bit heavy-handed but at five hundred and ninety-eight years old he supposed Vlad could do what he wanted with the wealth that kind of longevity had amassed.

Some while ago, Sevystian had suggested that Coven resources diversify into real estate, prompting Vlad to build the Transempirial. The tower wasn't the only safe house style property that WH built, not that any of the tenants of those buildings would have a ghost of a clue that they worked or lived in a vampire strong hold. The tower had become the home base for much of the Coven leadership.

Kadir poured himself a whiskey before dropping next to

Buchannan on one of the sofas. Sevystian would have preferred to stand, but Vlad waved him over to the sofa and his manners won out. Sevystian's suit felt stiff and he wondered where he might get one of those T-shirts Buchannan tended to wear. God help him if he had to venture into a shopping mall. It was a well-documented fact among the Coven that Sevystian was not good with the unwashed masses. He sneered at the thought of over-crowded department stores, crossing his ankle over his knee, forcing himself out of his thoughts.

"We have a serious problem." Vlad leaned casually against his desk. His men knew better. This was his planning stance; this was the stance he took before deciding just how to pick apart his enemy, before he left them groaning on the fields of war, begging for mercy. "The Order has been a nuisance for centuries. I have tried to take measured, reasonable steps to manage their threat to our existence, to maintain our anonymity. They have killed many of our own, converted hundreds to their fanatical cause. They are systematically stamping out my bloodline. They took Mina from me and branded her a martyr, all to keep up this idiotic worship of death. Caldwell has made our alternative options void and Melissa has made peace impossible. I made a promise to Iliza that I would not let them take Emma. I am no longer willing to settle for the reasonable actions of the past."

"It's about time." Buchannan's wicked smile reached into his eyes, his feet planted flat on the floor, his body stationary for the first time since they had returned to the tower. It was funny how he got just before a fight, like a taut of muscle saving up for just the right moment to snap into action.

"Calm down, Kid." Kadir leaned his elbows on his knees, dipping his head to run his claws through his beard thoughtfully.

"Calm?" Buchannan began bouncing his leg. "You're one to

talk, your claws are out and we haven't even gotten to the good stuff."

The late afternoon rays of sunlight filtered through the gaps in the heavy brocade drapes, falling in golden stripes over their knees, casting a red glow around the room. Kadir took a fortifying breath, clenching and unclenching his fists until his nails receded to a normal length. There was a bevy of things a vampire had to have control over at all times if they wanted to survive amongst humans. Above all others was control over their fangs and a close second was their claws. They were civilized; walking around like hungry dogs wasn't an option. Self-control was a point of pride among many covens and Vlad's coven in particular was known for its relationships with human companies and individuals.

"It's been a long day." Sevystian sighed. "Measured responses protect all of us from unnecessary harm. I do not believe that these measured reasonable responses have to be merciful. It is my opinion that we need a cooling off period. Let us take our time to calculate a precision strike against The Order."

"Of course." Vlad crossed the room pouring himself a vodka, before offering it silently to Sev. "As usual Sevystian, you are correct. I am in no state to make any tactical decisions tonight. However, I will warn you brother. I want nothing less than the annihilation of these fanatics. I have grown old and tired, watching them convert or kill my family one by one. I will not let this perversion of faith bleed into yet another generation."

"And we will not." It was Kadir who spoke, draining his glass and rocking onto his feet. "But Sevystian is right. Any action we take now will be sloppy. I am not willing to risk the safety of the Coven on revenge. We have time. It is our greatest advantage."

"That and the fangs are pretty dope." Buchannan flung

himself off of the couch easily. "Bonus, I'm young and sexy forever."

"Yes." Vlad raised his glass at the retreating back of Buchanan and Kadir. "Immortality has its perks. It also requires discretion."

"It's a good thing you reminded me." Buchannan stretched.

"Ignorance does not suit you." Sevystian ground out. "She doesn't know what we are. She doesn't need to know. What she needs is to remain safe and part of that requires her to remain ignorant. The more she is involved, the more likely she will be a target."

"She's a target already." Buchannan's usual grin was replaced with the stern cold eyes that had taken him through the second world war "How does hiding keep her safe from The Order when she is staying in a Coven strong hold?"

"They do not know about the tower." Kadir was a strategist of the first degree. "She stays here until the threat to her is neutralized and then she can go back to her life, her friends, her boyfriend or whatever she has and we don't have to worry about The Order going after her for information. But if she finds out, and she tells even one of her friends what we are, it will get back to them and then they'll never leave her alone."

"What's stopping them from going after her now?" Buchannan wasn't a facts man. He was a creature of instinct and action.

"Fear." Sevystian felt the exhaustion of the day settling in his back, his neck was getting stiff and his stomach burned with unaddressed hunger. "We struck The Order a few decades ago with a well-placed attack after we received some intelligence from another coven that they were going to go after Iliza King. She was newly widowed and lived with her spinster sister in a sleepy suburb. She was an easy mark for the Order, to say the least, but the King family has the disreputable honor of being the last of Vlad's human family, the last direct line of Tepes.

The name alone would lend them substantial power, but more than anything it is the history that Tepes line shares with the Order of Divine Mortality that drives them to hunt down Vlad's family. The violence we visited upon the Order when they came for Iliza was substantial, enough to dismantle their immediate goals."

"They still took Emma's mom." The kid jiggled his leg restlessly.

"That is a different story all together." Kadir placed his empty tumbler on the mantle, slinging his other arm over Buchannan's shoulder. "The Order isn't stupid. When one tactic fails, or proves too dangerous to pursue, they switch it up. Have you ever heard of soft tactics?"

Buchannan shook his head.

"It's a technique used in long-term warfare." Kadir went on, commanding the room like a well-respected professor. Sevystian was pretty sure he had actually been one at some point. "Total annihilation is not always an option, particularly if you are trying to conquer an empire. If you are the invading force, killing everyone leaves you the ruler of no one. Changing the hearts and minds of those people gives you a kingdom. So, they tried it with Melissa and it worked. Too well for what they wanted of her. She was too manic to convert Iliza and that same behavior kept her from being able to raise Emma. They didn't take Melissa from her family, she left on her own, and we did not stop her because it would have meant revealing ourselves to the King family and taking away their chance at normal lives."

"So." Vlad drained his glass, looking into the empty tumbler, fresh waves of sorrow bombarding his chest. "I made the decision not to pursue her. I made a choice to sacrifice one life for the good of the rest. I would like Emma not to have to sacrifice more on my account. She has lost enough because of my inaction."

"Strategy is not inaction." Sevystian leaned deeply into the sofa trying to stretch out the tightness building in his lower back. "It has only ever been a matter of time before the Order attempted something like Melissa. Drawing out one's enemy with that which they cherish above all else is a tactic as old as war. There is no use in lamenting it now."

"I hate to agree, but..." Buchannan wobbled his head back and forth, in a way to let them all know he did.

"You have enough sins to atone for, let this one fall on different shoulders." Kadir walked over to the bar and poured himself another vodka.

"Ruining Caldwell's company, starving out the Order isn't going to save Emma from her mother." Vlad was choosing not to listen to Sevystian, choosing to wash down his responsibility with guilt and self-loathing. "What can we do to protect her now? She cannot stay in this tower forever."

Sevystian grunted into his tumbler, his facial expression suggesting he thought that keeping Emma in the tower indefinitely would have been his first choice.

"Why didn't they make a move on Emma while her grandmother was alive?" Buchannan's leg bounced as he spoke energy pouring out of him like the buzz of a live wire. "How scary can an old lady be?"

"Careful boy, the is my family you are speaking of." Vlad set his glass down. "The Order has a long memory and the hell we rained down on them when they came for Iliza was enough to keep her safe. But Melissa never knew that fear and when Iliza died it was enough to turn the tide in her favor. Melissa wants Emma and that barrier that Iliza represented to the rest of the Order no longer restrains them.

"So let's put the fear back in 'em." Buchannan grinned a hint of fang peeking out from between his lips.

"A consolidated strike would effectively weaken their resolve, if we were careful." Kadir studied the dregs of liquid left in his glass. "Something messy enough to make noise, but something the authorities would mistake for organized crime?"

"We need a target," Sevystian spoke calmly. "Outside the city limits preferably."

"Don't shit where you eat, got it." Buchannan stood abruptly. "I'll do some digging."

"It's decided then." Vlad looked at his men with a ghost of a smile.

CHAPTER 11

The bedroom was cut in half by a stripe of sunlight shining through a gap in the lavish emerald curtains. Man, Vlad had not been joking around when he decorated the "Green Suite." Groaning, she schlepped over to them and looked out at the Houston skyline admiring the way the light made all of the buildings shine. She pulled the heavy drapes shut, she was too exhausted and too hungry to start waxing poetic about downtown. It took her eyes a little while to adjust to the semi-darkness of the bedroom. Why couldn't her shitty mom be just a regular shitty mom, the kind that disappeared to fuck some skeevey John in Reno? No, she has got to be a nutbag cult member. What the hell was she supposed to do with that?

There was a version of her life where her mother had let Grams help, where the extraction experts they had hired had been able to do their job. That wasn't her reality though, and even when she dreamed about it, they never ended well. To be fair, they also didn't end with a car chase trying to escape her mom's kidnapping accomplices, so there was that at least.

How could she miss something that she had never had, never known? She'd seen it though, seen the way that Mrs.

Abernathy loved Simon. Seen it with families on the street. She had never been enough for her mother. When she was younger Emma had held tight to the hope that there was some act of devotion she could perform that would prove to Melissa that Emma was worthy of the love a mother should have for there child. Emma had grown out of that childish notion rather quickly.

Sometimes when people asked about Emma's mother she would tell them Melissa was dead just to see if it made the truth easier to carry. The relief was momentary if at all and Melissa wasn't the type of person that was easy to hide. More often than not a question about her mother ended with the story about Galveston and the reason Grams finally sued for full custody.

For Emma the grey rocky beach, the freezing sea wind whipping the briny stench of rotting fish was a visceral memory that still pressed sharp and cold into the soles of her feet. Melissa had held her under the water until Emma's chest burned and her hands had gone numb. The relief of that first gasp of air when her mother had finally pulled her out of the waves had been short lived as her mother had dragged her, naked, up onto the shore to kneel on the beach. Melissa had said that she needed to humble herself before the Divine Mortal, the memory of which made Emma's knees ache to this day.

Eventually someone on the beach had called the police. The pity in that officer's face was equally burned into Emma's memory. She had spent that Christmas in the hospital with pneumonia.

Ruminating on her mother's many transgressions gave her a luke-warm melancholia. Already resigned to putting on the sweat stained T-shirt and leggings from before her shower, Emma turned her attention to the bed.

Sitting on the duvet where her limp collection of laundry should have been was a sleek silver shopping bag . No note, only a clean new outfit in her size. It was simple black and soft, not entirely dissimilar to the ones she had discarded earlier. She hadn't thought to ask for them and it seemed that she hadn't needed to. Tears leaked unwanted from the corners of her eyes. She would pay him back, Vlad had already done so much.

Slipping into her fresh clothes gave Emma a moment's pause thinking about the assistant who had probably dropped them off while she had been in the shower. She shivered, uncomfortable with how unaware she had been.

She stood looking around the room for her beat up backpack, feeling slightly uneasy. Finding it by the pair of chairs next to the window, Emma dug around in it until she found her phone; her security blanket, and stared at the screen. Only two texts, one from her client asking about the beta and the other was from Simon. He was "just checking in" with her. Emma shot off a quick reply.

Can't stay at home tonight
Too much BS… call you later
Have fun XO

It would have been easier if she hated her mother, but that was another steep slope she wasn't ready to transverse at the moment.

The grand staircase was easy enough to find: it was massive and took up a large part of the main atrium. The space seemed to swallow up her footsteps and as she walked she remembered how much she disliked the quiet. Grams always had some mindless TV or radio show going in the background. She walked around the corner, following the nearly imperceivable sound of voices floating to her from a short way down the hall.

It was coming from a pair of sturdy-looking French doors as tall as the trees they had been cut from. They reminded Emma how very small she was by comparison; how weak she must seem.

She hated it. Hated that she couldn't take care of herself, take care of the issues her mother presented, it made her feel useless. Steeling herself against the hot burn in her guts that pulled her between screaming and sobbing, Emma reached up to knock.

Before her hand made contact, Sevystian opened them, stopping short upon seeing Emma standing there, hand raised. His eyes watched her with the same appraising looking he had given her at the Barbecue joint.

"Emma." His voice seemed less aggravated, thank God for small favors. "I trust you are refreshed?"

"Pretty much, yeah." She smiled oddly at him. Was he trying to make small talk? That should not be as endearing as it was. "Wish I had some other clothes to change into but..."

She shrugged, walking into the study. It seemed as though the whole crew had congregated in there, everyone drinking out of fancy tumblers and looking about as uncomfortable as she felt. Except for Buchannan who splayed himself across half a leather couch, tie untied and the first few buttons of his shirt undone.

"Emma!" Buchannan popped off the sofa like a shot, making to tuck her under his outstretched arm.

Sevystian beat him to it. Much to Emma's shock she felt a warm palm press lightly on the middle of her back ushering her into the den. Buchannan made an attempt to sit next to her, which was also quickly and silently averted by Sevystian, making Buchannan forever some over-grown collie racing around the legs of a greatly perturbed monolith.

"If you want I can go grab you some stuff from your house." Buchannan skirted the edge of the table to take a seat across from Emma, leaning over the coffee table to talk directly to her, his leg bouncing.

"I might have to take you up on that." Emma smiled at him, her stomach took that moment to rumble loudly.

"I'll have Fields put something together." Vlad put down his crystal tumbler, and reached for his phone.

"Fields is out." Buchannan slung back the last of his drink. "Said something along the lines of the cupboards being in need of replenishing. Think its code for something, boss?"

"I am quite sure it is not." Vlad smiled trying not to indulge the younger man too much. "There is a café in the lobby if you are feeling up to it."

Emma nodded quickly, her stomach already making itself known again.

"Great, I can set you up on the biometrics." Buchannan nabbed a tablet off of the table in front of him, tapping it a couple of times before turning it over to Emma. "Just put your hand in the center. It only hurts a little."

Emma put her palm on the tablet narrowing her eyes at his joke.

"Alright, you're in the system now." He took the tablet back, tapping some more. "We can do the rest whenever, but this will get you around."

He was up and out the door before he had even finished speaking, then after a few seconds he poked his head back inside to check why no one had immediately followed him.

"I would like to say that he is simply excited, but Buchannan is very much like this most of the time." Vlad pushed off of the desk he was leaning on. "Let us make our pilgrimage to the café before he comes to round us up, hum?"

The elevator and Buchannan were waiting for them in the foyer. The ride down was still without music, though considerably less awkward then before. Kadir moved to the back of the car and Emma could feel his eyes on her neck.

A man at the security desk waylaid Buchannan as they passed, asking him if they could run over some specifics. It seemed odd to her that Buchannan could be in charge of anything. Not that he didn't give off an air of competence, just that he didn't seem any older than she was. Emma felt that at best she could say she was her own boss, and most days she felt like she was barely doing that.

The group carried on to the far side of the lobby where a café style restaurant sat tucked on the west side of the building, its shades pulled down against the onslaught of afternoon sunlight. Rain peppered the windows as the clouds struggled to overtake the sky. Even at a distance Emma could see steam rising off the concrete. They sat towards the back of the space. A pleasant waitress in neat slacks and a clean, black apron took their drink order immediately, clearly recognizing Vlad as a VIP.

"I'll get y'all a cheese plate right out." The waitress called over her shoulder as she rushed back to the kitchen.

"What kind of café has a cheese plate?" Emma spoke off-handedly, looking around the crowded room. The patrons seemed to be a cross-section of rushed looking young professionals and pampered one-percenters ignoring their table-mates in favor of taking pictures of their dishes.

"West House is somewhere between Michelin Star and Starbucks." Buchannan plopped himself down on a seat across from her. "You should try the quinoa bowl, it's killer."

He nabbed a menu from the center of the table and started pointing out different things that he recommended and making jokes about different snobby-looking patrons. There was an ease in the conversation between she and Buchannan that she appreciated endlessly. Even if it was just for this moment that she was able to ignore the emanate threat of the Order, Emma was grateful.

Looking at the menu herself had her gagging over prices. Emma was so out of her league, her palms were sweating. No one else seemed to be doing the same mental math she was trying to figure out. Maybe if she delayed getting gas this month she could order an entrée. On the other side of that argument, maybe her mother would finally kidnap her and all she would have to worry about would be the Order brainwashing her into the same kind of crazy as her mom.

She ended up getting some kind of chicken pesto thing that wouldn't kill her bank account and Buchannan swore would make her weep with joy. Sevystian had the same, handing over his menu without ever having looked at it. There was a busyness about the café that made it easier for her to forget why she had come here to begin with and just immerse herself in the shallow conversation in which Buchannan was engaging them. Even Sevystian had smirked a time or two.

Their plates had been cleared and there had been some noise about getting coffee, the sun having finally given up its campaign against the storm rolling in, as sheets of rain poured over the city. Emma yawned.

"Coffee another time I think." Vlad smiled pushing away from the table. "The day has been longer than most and I for one would like a respite before taking on tomorrow."

"Agreed." Sevystian stood offering Emma a hand to help her from her seat.

"Yeah, you're probably right." Emma yawned again.

"I am always right." Vlad joked.

"That must get boring." Emma let Sevystian help her out of the chair, his hand cool and dry in her sweaty one.

"If only it were." Kadir's words seemed ominous.

Vlad nodded at the waiter as Sevystian ushered her out of the restaurant towards the Transempirial's grand lobby, the stained glass sconces and black marble flooring shining in the light of the setting sun. Once again Emma found herself situated between Vlad and Sevystain as they made their way up to the residential floors of the building in the private elevator.

"You'll have to let me know what I owe you for the clothes and dinner," Emma said disrupting the unnatural quiet of the small space, feeling sleepy and full.

"Don't worry about it Princess," Kadir purred, sliding out of the elevator as doors opened to what Emma assumed was his floor. He grinned over his shoulder as he walked away, and something like fear twisted in Emma's guts. Kadir reminded Emma of walking through her neighborhood at night and coming across a coyote. There was a dangerous way about the man, not brawny like Sevystian or clever like Vlad, but just as threatening and Emma wasn't entirely certain he was really on her side.

"I will take my leave of you as well." The ever formal, Sevystian tilted his head slightly and Emma wondered if he was fighting the urge to do a complete bow.

"So it's just us three then?" Buchannan slung his arm over Emma's shoulder, taking up the space Sevystian had just vacated as the door began to slide shut. "I say we start with facials and then..."

Whatever Buchannan was going to suggest next was interrupted by Sevystian's arm reaching through the slit of the doors and dragging him out.

"Sometimes I think it is a miracle that this tower remains standing." Vlad glanced at her sideways.

"They should have their own sitcom," Emma teased. "I really will pay you back."

Vlad raised his hand to wave her off.

"It is not required." His smile seemed sad as the doors opened onto his foyer and they stepped out. "Neither my help not my affection carries with it conditions. You are family and I will make every effort of which I am capable to protect you."

His words felt heavier than a promise, like he was making a vow that Emma couldn't understand.

CHAPTER 12

Sevystian slunk through his apartment without turning on a single light. There was no need. His eyes were already burning with exhaustion and even if he were not so run down, the extra light was really just for the benefit of the guests he so rarely entertained. It was doubtful he even knew where the switches were. Sevystian had been a vampire for a long time, his senses were honed out of necessity. Old vampires at least had had to travel at night. Getting caught on the road in the daylight was a death sentence and because of this most of the old ones still retained a sensitive night vision that made the advent of electric lights superfluous. As such, he reached his fridge without so much as scuffing the toes of his expensive shoes. Cold blood wasn't the most appetizing thing, but right now he didn't have the energy to wait for it to reach the perfect ninety-eight degrees. Blood was a lot like coffee or eggs, you couldn't just pop it in the microwave. He choked down half the bottle on his way to the bedroom.

Kicking off his shoes he tucked them under the leather arm chair that sat in the corner of his room. Normally he would have stopped to hang his ensemble back up, but tonight he would make an exception. The suit would have to be sent out for cleaning any way. Dropping the empty bottle onto his bed side table he fell into the rumpled white flannel sheets. It was the one mess he routinely allowed himself and he was particularly glad of it tonight. His body was shutting down one fine motor function at a time. Vampires could go much longer without sleep then any human, but Sevystian was pushing the limits of what even his body could do.

He wasn't always so careless with his body. Under normal circumstances he would have slept the previous nights, instead of staying up working on yet another proposal for a merger that was never going to happen. Even thinking about it now had his gums itching with the desire to tear something apart.

Marcus Caldwell had shot down every suggestion, every compromise that Wallachia Holdings was willing to concede. Sevystian understood the Coven had been taking a calculated risk in this proposed merger. Truly it was a merger in name only: Wallachia Holdings would take over all executive function and ultimately Caldwell International would be cannibalized and its most valuable parts sold off piece by piece. The flood of money, guns, and supplies running through the Caldwell channels laid to rest at the bottom of miles of red tape and iron-clad contracts. To some extent he understood how a man could not stand to see his life's work stripped down to nothing. There was a wyrm gnawing somewhere on his unconscious thoughts since the beginning of this endeavor though, some insistent rhythm of suspicion he couldn't shake, and now it seemed it was all coming to a head.

Sometimes he truly hated this century. If this was a less civilized time; if this was the time that he had been born into, he would have torn the man apart and taken the company to do with as he pleased. As it stood, now he was no longer a man of excessive and outlandish violence. Something was still not right about the whole thing, the wyrm still gnawed in his mind turning over some half-formed concern that Sevystian was too exhausted to focus on. He was drifting off into unconsciousness with an unsettled mind, which never did bode well for his dreams.

Vampires tended to dream of the past, it wasn't an absolute, as things never really are, but as far as the sleeping undead go, the past is the subject of many concerns and regrets. Old vampires have memories that fill libraries of experience and it isn't as if Sevystian could go to therapy. He shuttered to think what kind of loony bin he would end up in if he started re-hashing his regrets over the First World War or the time he spent with the Fitzgeralds in Paris, with some modern psychologist. It wasn't as if some mood stabilizer or Thorazine drip was going to do anything more than add to the cacophony of events clattering around in his mind. After the first century, the memory of his beginning had gotten muddled. Sneaking out of Wallachia in the dead of night, being hunted like an animal, those things he could recount like a well memorized verse, but dying only came back to him in his sleep. He had followed Vlad into his death, had used his final breath to ask this of his prince, to be made monster, and now only played human for the masses. Maybe he did need a therapist.

He supposed that the dreams were an adaptation that creatures like himself had developed to cope with what they had seen; perhaps more importantly to cope with what they had done. Sevystian finally let go, allowing himself to fall into the much-needed sleep he had been avoiding. It dragged him slowly under its spell, first gently and then with a hard off the cliff of his wakefulness.

A screaming pain had followed him out of mortal death. It wasn't the sharp pain of the Ottoman blade that had sliced his gut open, or even the twin punctures that had later taken what little blood he had left to offer. It was a molten hunger that had hollowed him out, his bones felt like they were splintering with the heat of it. Every sensation was secondary to the hunger, nothing existed beyond it. Vlad had poured blood into his mouth and he had choked on it. Boiling hot against his lips, it had been cool in his belly.

As long as he had lived he still could not remember the taste of that first blood, but even now in his half-waking slumber he could remember the feel of it settling cold inside his belly. It had felt as if that first swallow had knit all the pieces of him back together. Opening his new eyes into an old world, the first thing he had seen was the gaunt face of his Prince. He had seemed so surprised. Smoke had blackened the sky and the earth beneath them rendered putrid by the dead and dying. Yet, Sevystian saw without strain. Vlad poured more blood from his wine skin into Sevystian's mouth and he pulled it greedily closer, draining it of its contents. The rank odor of decay that plagued every battlefield they had ever trod together intensified tenfold, even that could not quell his hunger. He tried to drag himself up to search out another source.

Peeling back the dirty rag of a shirt he now wore, Vlad prodded the fatal gash that opened him from hip to rib. Panic set upon him, as he saw the extent of the damage. Many of the men under his command had perished from less. All his humors spilled out onto the ground. He didn't want to die, moving in a desperate scrambling attempt to escape the mood and stench of war. Determined not to die in this filth, he flung himself onto his knees, crawling over the uneven terrain.

"If you would rest, you would heal faster, my brother." Vlad leaned back on his heels, before standing. "You'll do yourself no service, moving as you are. It will only bring the hunger back faster."

"I won't die here, my Prince." Sevystian pulled himself along his arms and knees soaked in red mud. "The battle is done. Let me go further off to have my end out of this stench, where God might have mercy on me."

"There is no end my brother." Vlad followed him, stepping over the bodies in his way. "This is not your death."

"I am not your brother." Sevystian collapsed into the muck and slime, utterly without the strength to carry himself any further. He lay back to stare at the grey, sunless sky above. "You are my Prince, and I have gladly given my life in service to you, but in this you are wrong, your Highness. This is my death."

"No." Vlad squatted down beside him, smiling in a grim sort of manner that distorted his prominent features. His teeth were sharp and his lips thin. He was more animal than man, and after the enemies that he had lain waste to today it was no great wonder that he was transformed. "I gave you your death, as you asked for it, and in doing so made us brothers. This wound will mend, as will all others."

"If you have given me my death and we are now brothers, are you dead?" Sev closed his eyes fighting hard against the fear building in his chest, spreading like sickness into his limbs. "Have we died together and this gruesome place our shared hell?"

"A hell though it may be, it is not an eternal one." The screeching of carrion birds interrupted their grisly conversation. "This has been a means to an end. Our enemy will not pass through this forest of death. This empire they are spreading like a plague, it goes no further. There is no power of this world that is infinite, no army without weakness, no man without fear. I will prove this to them."

"How do we stop an enemy when we are already gone?" The wound on his stomach itched terribly and he made to scratch it, finding not his ruined belly, but thin tender flesh, newly mended.

"You are stronger than I was. It took ages for my wounds to heal." Vlad offered him an arm to pull himself up. "I told you, I had given you your death, I did not say that you kept it."

"If this hell and my death are only temporary then what damnation have I earned?" Sevystian hoisted himself up.

"I am no clergyman, Sevystian." Vlad bent over a dying Ottoman soldier, filling his wine skin with blood from a wound bisecting man's shoulder. "I do not know if this is damnation. I do not believe that it is."

Vlad offered Sevystian the wine skin. Sev wanted to turn away, needed the very idea of drinking another man's blood to disgust him, but the smell tingled in his nostrils like a fine roast and he gave in to the temptation. It was like waking after a long sickness, when the shroud of fever finally falls away and leaves your senses in peace. Standing quickly, to be quit of the muck of the ground, he could see into smoke with clear definition: the bodies of those few men he had brought with him to track their Prince to the enemy's camp. Every sound vibrated with intensity; the crackle of the still smoldering tents, the rustle of the first scavengers to make it to them, the last shallow beats of wounded hearts. The smells and sounds, even the dull light of the early evening built up like lashes one strike after another until his head was spinning, aching for relief. He pressed his hands into his eyes only to find thick claws adorning his fingers. Stumbling back, he tripped, saved only by Vlad who gripped him tight holding his entire weight with one hand.

"Come." Setting him on his feet again, Vlad picked his way across the field and into the bevy of trees that lined the base of the mountain where the rest of their army made camp. "We will find shelter away from this place. It is easier once the sun has set. You will learn to control it as I have."

Even in the forest, where the trees blocked out much of the light, Sevystian could pick out birds settling into their nests, hear the rabbits in their burrows. He could feel the eyes of lesser predators watching them as they passed between trees, drawn in by their scent. It felt like a new world, where his body was no longer his own familiar skin. All was new, as if there was a feral spirit lurking inside his bones, begging for release or relief, he wasn't sure.

Vlad lead them up a rocky path he had never taken before. In front of them Sevystian saw the thin mouth of a cave. It was really nothing more than a slit in the mountain's face and looking out from it he had no idea how they both could so easily transverse the near vertical path in the oncoming darkness. A few feet into the narrow opening, the cave widened enough to let the men walk abreast of each other comfortably. After a few minutes of walking in silence with only the gentle trickle of water somewhere deep in the mountain to disturb them, the walls opened up again. This chamber was cavernous.

"What is this place?" Sevystian tilted his head back looking into the stalactites hanging dangerously from the high ceiling.

"It is safe." Vlad made his way over to a small slab of rock that cropped out from the wall. "This is where I was made."

"Vampire?" He watched the prince for any clue that he may have been wrong, there was none. Not even shock graced his features. "The monks in the villages who tell foolish children of such creatures. They say that they are the wicked punished by the Devil on Earth. Is that what you have made me? Is this my punishment?"

"Your punishment is not mine to give." Vlad sat heavily on the stone slab beckoning his knight to join him. "There is nothing we can do now. You are made and God will judge us both for that." He offered him the wine skin again before leaning heavily on the wall. "There is still much I do not know of this new life. I think we shall have to learn together. We will protect our families, our lands from this Ottoman scourge, and perhaps then we can return."

"You think they will accept what we are now?" Sevystian drank deeply from the wine skin, barely tasting its nectar in his haste. "They would more readily invite wolves into their homes than us. Monsters do not go home."

"This monster has been home." Vlad eyed him, more annoyed at his second's inflexible understanding of the world. " My wife has welcomed me many times since my first taste of the Devil. I am still welcome in my home, and so shall you be. Even, Alekzander, the most pious of all my advisors, knows of my change and has raised no hand, nor cross to me. If that man can accept what I have become then there is nothing to fear from the rest of my people."

"And you trust that it will still be so when you return with another creature at your side?" Sevystian's query was not without merit, both men knew that their previous lives had altered irrevoca-

bly. He thought of Vlad's beautiful Mina sending them both off with a kiss upon their heads, her belly round with a second child: a girl, if the mid-wives were to be believed. "You trust Alekzander with your home, with your wife?"

"I have trusted him before." *Vlad took the wine skin from him, drinking long gulping sips until it was empty.* "He loves her well and would protect her from any enemy."

"Yes, he loves her well." *Sevystian finally sat on the slab of rock next to his prince.* "You were not dead before, and I fear that his love is a feral sort that grows wild in the absence of a stern hand. I worry that he is too attached to let her majesty return to the arms of a creature such as we. His faith will turn him against us."

"His faith has no place in the rule of my court, or the love of my wife. He knows this." *His voice was confident, overly so in Sevystian's opinion, but then again Sevystian was no prince.* "He can go to the monasteries for absolution or clarity or any other thing that his God gives to him, but in my court his deference is to me."

"My concern is that to him, you are no longer you." *Sevystian had no great love for Alekzander, nor Alekzander for him. Thought, where Sevystian reached for courtly civility, Alekzander let his distain ring out. Sevystian would have liked for his prince to throw the zealot out, for the advisor to live the rest of his days in one of his beloved monasteries. However, the many tasks of the day were pulling Sevystian into the void of unconsciousness and he lacked the energy for such a conversation.* "I worry that he may move to strike you from her bed."

"Mina would never allow any man to take my place." *Vlad growled, offended at the very notion of it.* "She loves me as deeply as she ever did. Monster, creature, or man makes no difference to her. She would never let another man into her bed."

"Sire." *Sevystian's words felt slow and cumbersome to speak.* "It is not Mina's love I question. She is a fine, strong woman, but Alekzander may not give her the choice to reject him. It is not in his nature to move past his faith no matter what is right or necessary."

"*Then may his god have mercy, for I will not.*" *Vlad's intentions were written in the cruel slash of his lips pulling back from fangs that gleamed as daggers even in the darkness of the cave.*

"*I shall follow.*" *Sevystian blinked hard, trying his best to remain awake to seek out understanding of his strange new life from his maker, but the void was calling to him. Slumping limply onto his side the last of his conscious thought left him in dark.*

CHAPTER 13

A man grabbed Emma from behind, his arm a band of iron across her tender belly. His hand large enough to cover her entire jaw as he dragged her struggling form out of the forest clearing and into the brush hushing her as he dragged her backwards into a blackened grouping of trees. His voice heavily accented and thick with urgency.

"Quiet, you mustn't let them find you." There was a familiarity to his voice she could not place. "You are the next step. Don't let them take you."

"Who?" Emma could hear people now, cackling and hooting into the night, their heavy-booted footfalls destroying the underbrush.

"Go." He pushed her forward, away from him, rushing her into the thicket of grotesque looking trees. "Go! They cannot follow you there. They'll lose their way."

"I can't." She tried to turn back to see him, afraid she would lose her way, but he disappeared in the trees already springing up behind her. She caught a glimpse of him between the sweeping tungsten beams of flashlights and flickering glow of torches that intermingled in the ever-growing forest. She could hear the traipsing of boots through the underbrush and her own bare feet padding over leaves.

She ran from the screeching and a roar of some unknown beast.

Nearly tripping over her own feet, she sprinted onward, the cold air stealing every breath from her as soon as she took them. The sounds of some battle raging behind her built higher and louder until the night was struck by silence, darkness falling like a shroud around her. She kept running, her chest stinging, her bare feet caked with mud and leaves.

Branches reached out to grab her hair and sweep across her face, but she kept moving until she narrowly avoided stepping off a cliff into a ravine. Hugging the thick trunk of the tree she looked down as the moon broke through the clouds shining onto the icy river below, a castle of sharp distorted edges sat across the divide. The silence pressed in around her and she imagined that the rushing in her ears was the sound of the rapids below crashing and swirling in her head until they met a crescendo leaving her dizzy and clutching the rough bark of the tree. The noise came to a sweeping stop and she turned to look into the darkness behind her. Her mother's gaunt form stood there lit in the horrible tungsten beam of a discarded flashlight.

"You should have come with me." Her mother looked horrible, a skeleton still chattering in the woods long after its passing. "You should have come with me. They are coming for you now!"

Screaming, her mother ran towards her forcing Emma off of the cliff and into the terrible feeling of nothingness.

Emma blinked awake, her body barely responding to direction. Groaning as she rolled on to her side, she considered just going back to sleep. It was an uncomfortable pitch black. Her room at Gram's had never gotten this dark, there was always some kind of light filtering in through the ancient drapes that covered her single window. For an instant, she was worried that she was still in the dream, but the sensation didn't stick. She could feel herself firmly in her body. Not bothering to sit up fully, she let her feet slide onto the plush rug, too plush for her to be in her own room.

The events of the past week came rushing back to her, the confused panic the dream had left her with was dampened by the shroud of sadness that had swaddled her since Grams had passed. Her head protested every movement she made shuffling herself out of the massive bed. Stretching her arms over her head she pulled to and fro, trying to work out the stiffness that came from sleeping deeply for not long enough. She moved slowly. Feeling her way to a light switch she finally saw the room in its completeness. The Green Suite was just as stunning as she had first thought. Her backpack sat on the chair where Buchannan left it the day before, the only drab looking thing in the whole room other than herself. It reminded her that she needed to work. This wasn't some vacation she had magically been able to afford. She wouldn't be here forever and her client wanted that app ready for in beta testing in a week. Grabbing her laptop and utterly dead cell phone she went in search of coffee and maybe some cereal.

Getting to the kitchen for her daily coffee was more arduous a task than she had originally thought it would be. The grand stairs were not the only ones in the apartment and it seemed as if there were an unending number of doors to open, most of which led to large lavishly furnished bedrooms and a single library that would have made any bookworm giddy. Finally, and completely by mistake she found the kitchen. It was not as large as she had thought it might be, given the almost cavernous state of the rest of the dwelling she was expecting something far larger, but what she found was a galley style kitchen with marble counter tops and black cabinets. The appliances looked like something out of Viking catalog. A copper espresso maker, the likes of which she had only ever seen in professional coffee shops, sat alone on its own counter. Checking her mouth for drool she made her way over to it.

"Might I help you with something Ms. King?" The voice was pinched with British formality and scared the ever-living crap out of her.

"Shiiiit." Emma spun around her laptop raised in both hands prepared to fend off any attacker, what she found instead was thin, finely dressed man with large expressive eyes, and slick black hair. Oddly, he seemed to match the kitchen, as if the space had decided one day that it should have a child and thus this man had been willed into existence. Lowering her weapon, she answered him. "Uhm, sorry?"

"No need for that Ms. King." He smiled and his eyes lit up with unrealized mischief. "Wouldn't be the first time I had something swung at me by a beautiful woman. Can't say it has ever happened to me in this kitchen, but I did have quite the run-in at Mr. Tepes' Paris apartment." The man leaned conspiratorially towards Emma, a twinkle of delighted camaraderie shining on his Romanesque features. "Just between the two of us there is something I still find attractive about a French woman wielding a frying pan, but enough about me. Steven James Fairchild, Mr. Tepes' personal valet, at your service. You can call me Fields if you're feeling cheeky."

"I was just going to." Emma gestured towards the copper coffee god sitting a few feet behind her.

"Please allow me." The man pulled out a stool she hadn't noticed tucked under the island. Emma hesitated, looking at the espresso maker mournfully. "I would feel ever so much better if you would allow me the pleasure of making you a coffee."

"You're worried that I am going to mess up your fancy machine, aren't you?" Emma eyed the man

"To be perfectly honest with you, yes." Fields let his smiled drop glancing around the room, making sure they were alone. "Mr. Tepes has a tendency to leave the kitchen in a state of, shall we say disarray? I would like to trust you, but experience has taught me that is nothing more than folly. So, if you would please?"

"Whatever floats your boat." Emma took the seat he offered, putting her laptop on the counter and watched him fiddle with the machine bustling around the cabinet with gusto.

"Well, Fields since this is clearly your domain, can you tell me where I could hang out and do some work? Is here a good place?" Emma asked hopefully. It seemed as good a place as any to work and given how forthcoming Fields had already been, Emma wouldn't mind learning more about her host. Wasn't there a saying about judging a man's character on the way he treats his employees, or was it pets? Anyway, Emma figured if she wanted the scoop on her white knights, Fields was the one with the spoon.

"Surely your employer would understand if you took some time." The sudden intrusion of Vlad's voice made Emma jolt out of her seat, her feet scuffling on the floor with a squeak. She hadn't even heard Vlad slip into the room until he spoke.

"Jeez." Emma put her hand over her heart. "You guys need bells, before you give me a heart attack."

Vlad laughed into the metal thermos he was drinking out of.

"You laugh now but I have been known to throw things. One time Simon snuck up on me when I was cooking and I threw a knife at him." Emma sat back down.

"I assume that he is still alive and well?" Vlad pulled a second stool out to sit next to her.

"Yeah. Oh crap." Pulling out her phone, the screen twas black. "Simon is gonna freak out."

"Why should he be worried Ms. King?" Fields put a perfectly brewed latte in front of her, complete with a delicate foam flower. "If it isn't too bold for me to ask."

"Please, just call me Emma." She taking a sip of the coffee.

"Mmmmmm, Fields if you will make me that coffee every morning I will never touch your fancy coffee machine."

"It's really for the best, Miss Emma."

"It really is." She took another sip, humming to herself with contentment. "We've been through it together, Simon and I. He lived next door all my life. We went to school together. We got chicken pox together. Whenever my mom has pulled some crazy stunt like this, he has been there."

"Why did you not call him yesterday?" Vlad interrupted.

"Like I said, he's always been there for me. I want him to have a life too." Emma took another sip. "Also, I did call him, but he was already on a date."

"Would it be horrible if I said I was glad he did not answer?" Vlad smiled, but there was a tone of sadness to his voice. "It has been too long since I have enjoyed the company of family."

"I am certain that we could scrounge up an outlet for you." The valet bustled around the kitchen talking to Emma. "I am prone to worry myself and would feel better knowing that a fellow worrier was not left in the lurch, so to speak."

"Really, you a worrier? I had no idea Fields." Vlad queried blankly.

"Your sarcasm is duly noted and enjoyed sir." Fields replied with equal enthusiasm, putting a plate of fresh fruit in front of Emma and ignoring the jealous looks from his employer. "Shall I start you an omelet or perhaps those pancakes you Americans are so fond of? I do believe I have a recipe you might enjoy."

"You have a recipes?" Emma questioned bemusedly over her coffee.

"Of course, I do." Fields puffed himself up to his full height looking forever like some indignant, overgrown crow that had wandered into a kitchen and been mistakenly put to work. "I am a modern man who cooks, cleans, and occasionally organizes his closet."

"Occasionally?" Vlad nearly spit his drink back into the thermos when he heard that, but he controlled himself. Putting the thermos safely onto the counter he turned slightly to his right to stage whisper to Emma. "The man has a larger collection of clothes than I do. Honestly, I am surprised that he hasn't turned his whole apartment into a closet."

"Don't think I haven't considered it, Sir." Field's voice remained calm, his face the epitome of distain, but his eyes glittered with dark humor. "Ms. Emma, I would be happy to perform a demonstration for you of my excellent cooking skills. If breakfast doesn't interest you, I could make something more lunch appropriate."

"No thank you, Fields." She covered her mouth with her hand, talking around a mouth of blackberries. "This fruit is delicious."

"If you are quite certain, then I will take my leave of you." He nodded his head in a tight little bow that seemed ever so proper. "If you should require any thing don't hesitate to ask."

"And what if I should need anything, Fields?" Somehow Vlad still sounded playful even through his accent. "What if I should want to avail you of one of your recipes?"

"You, Sir, should hesitate." Fields quipped.

"So that's it?" Vlad twisted in his chair to watch as Fields made his way out the kitchen. "Where could you possibly need to be?"

"Organizing my closet, Sir." The smile, Emma caught the man making as he stepped out the door, was positively ferocious.

"Don't let him fool you Emma." Vlad smiled brilliantly at her, almost obscuring the purple circles that had settled under his eyes. "I am a master of my own domain; even though it is very likely that should I touch the espresso maker again, Fields may very well risk incarceration and kill me dead."

"He told me as much when I tried to make some this morning." She squinted at her coffee concerned. "Is it morning? I haven't seen a clock yet so I've got no idea."

"I will answer you if you answer me one thing." Vlad looked around the room, checking for eavesdroppers. "Do you think his suit was nicer than mine?"

Emma did a spit take and by the grace of God it did not cover her computer in foamy latte goodness. That baby was on its last leg and probably would not survive a caffeine shower.

"How? Just how?" Then she caught the smirk on Vlad's face out of the corner of her eye. "You are a menace."

"I am well aware." He rinsed out his thermos quickly talking to her over his shoulder. "It's afternoon, almost one o'clock actually. You slept well, I hope?"

"Meh." She held her hand out shaking it to and fro in a non-committal way all too aware they were both skating around the real reason she was there, not wanting the peaceful moments of each other's company to end. "The bed was super comfy, but I had some pretty terrible dreams, which sucks. Do you have a charger for this anywhere?" She held up her dead phone. "I need to call Simon soon or he'll send out a posse, then I'll have a real mess on my hands."

"Try that drawer." Vlad pointed to a section of cabinets beside the fridge. "I think Fields hides some in there when we leave them about."

"We?" It was Emma's turn to talk over her shoulder. "I didn't know you had your family here.."

"No." Vlad's smile dimmed a little at the mention of family. While he kept up his light tone there was a sharpness to his delivery that had not been there before, something akin to sarcasm, but not quite. "No family. I meant simply myself and those few friends whom are often seen haunting the rooms of this fortress."

"Ah Ha." Holding up her query in victory, Emma brought the charger back to her stool, at last plugging in her phone to charge. "So, it's just you here? Isn't it a little big for just you? I mean not to be rude." Emma covered her face in embarrassment. Her mouth was running away with her. "Oh God, I am totally being rude. You can just ignore me. I will just sit here with my coffee, do some work and stop being intrusive."

"It is fine." Vlad lost the sharp edges in his tone. "This place is admittedly large for a single person to live here alone, but I like having some space for family should they need it. Also, my business spans several countries and three continents so it is a good idea to have room for any executives should we need a more intimate conversation than a webcam can allow. It saves on hotel fees."

"Yeah, but isn't the rent like crazy high?" Emma stuffed a strawberry into her mouth hoping that she could stop from asking horrible embarrassing questions for like a half a fucking second.

"Not really." Vlad didn't seem to notice how rude she was being and Emma was eternally grateful. "I own the building, so, technically, I do not have to pay rent, although if you think of property tax as a form of rent then yes the rent is a steep."

"Jeeze." Emma nearly choked on her fruit plate. "What do you do?"

"Not too much anymore I am afraid." Vlad was attempting to be modest. Emma had a suspicion that it would not be possible. "Sevystian runs most of the intricate business dealings and Kadir handles the heavy lifting for the US operations. Wallachia Holdings is primarily an umbrella company focused on construction and energy, though we have diversified in recent years to include some technologies' avenues." He shrugged as if he wasn't the skyscraper owning, empire building, business tycoon that he so clearly was. "For the most part we buy up smaller companies merge them with other similar companies to create a synergistic network of business." Vlad paused the litany of MBA buzzwords with a short bark of laughter. "I can see your eyes glazing over. However boring the minutia may be, it has been successful and allowed me to help my friends, and now my family, when they are in need."

"Wow, it sounds like you have been more than successful. It sounds like you are secretly running the whole freaking world." She teased him gently. "At least that explains why Sevystian is so serious."

"I am afraid not." Vlad grinned. "I have known that man since he was only a child and I don't think I have ever seen him look anything less than battle-ready, even before the war."

"So, I was right." Emma's lips quirked up in the corners, pleased to have her suspicions confirmed. "I knew he had to be in the military. I just knew it."

"Indeed, he was." Vlad tapped his ring finger on the counter. "Are we all so easily read, that you could tell his history from just a few hours of knowing him?"

"Not all of you, no. Sevystian carries himself like a lot of guys from the neighborhood who joined up right out of school. It wasn't that much of a stretch to guess he had a similar background." Emma spoke matter of fact. "What got him into all this?"

"I did." Vlad folded his hands together to rest them on the table as he spoke.

"Were you in the military also?" Emma felt like she was prying but Vlad was a particularly juicy mystery.

"In a way, yes." Damn him and his vague answers that did nothing to calm her rampant curiosity.

On the counter her phone buzzed to life, startling Emma. God she felt jumpy today. Vlad seemed to take that as his cue to end the conversation, turning away from Emma entirely and returning his attention to the sink. Damn it, she was sure she could have gotten more out of him but no way was he going to tell her all the details now.

Ugh. The phone screen told her she had eight new voice

mails all from Simon, and forty-five unread texts. Five texts were from her client asking her when the soonest they could expect the beta app to be ready and the rest from Simon; all of which threatened varying versions of sending out sniffer dogs to hunt her down if she didn't call. She sent a text back quickly telling him that her phone had died and that she was safe.

S: How do I know this isn't your mother just telling me you're alright?

S: I need voice confirmation that you are actually who you say you are.

E: As soon as I have a charge I will call. Talking with Vlad right now TTYL

S: Vlad?

E: Yeah he's family. Real family.

S: I'm not family?

E: You know you are #dramatic!

E: Call you in a bit.

S: Not good enough.

S: Where are you? I am coming to get you!

E: I am safe.

E: Need a little space. Call you in a few.

S: WHERE ARE YOU?

S: Fine. If you don't call in the next two hours I am sending out search dogs.

S: Be safe.

Putting her phone down she looked up at Vlad who had turned back and was now watching her with his black eyes unfocused. His long hooked nose cast a shadow on the right side of his face making the thin smile he wore seem crooked. It wasn't the type of smile that lit up a room, or even Vlad's own face, merely a weary one.

"Sorry." She gestured to the phone. "As I guessed, Simon was worried. Probably still is, but I'll call him later and figure everything out. Plus, my client has a bee up his butt about his app getting into beta testing."

"Iliza said something about you doing app design." Vlad took her now empty plate to the sink and began washing it. "I can't imagine that your client would expect you to work while dealing with your grief."

"Oh, I don't think he would care." Emma sighed popping open her computer.

"You haven't told him about Iliza, I take it." Vlad leaned back across the counter forcing her to look at him over the top of her computer. "You didn't tell him because you didn't want him to feel sorry for you or because you didn't want him to give the job to a different designer?"

"A little column A, little of column B." Emma hedged her answer.

"You could tell him." Vlad stared her down, giving her the best "dad brows" he could muster. "It would help to lighten your load a bit."

"Or..." She pushed back from the counter rocking the stool on to its back legs, enjoying Vlad's concerned frown a little too much before setting them back down. "...I could just bottle those feelings up until I finish this project and develop some kind of emotional trigger. Like phantom limp or maybe it'll be something cool like my eye just starts to twitch when I'm angry."

"I know you are trying to be funny." Vlad schooled his face against her eyebrow wiggles. "But you should think about taking a break after this project. In her letters, Iliza mentioned that you were doing fairly well for an independent contractor. Perhaps now would be the time to take a vacation."

"I can't, really." She sighed involuntarily. "Student loans are not to be fu... toyed with."

"Ahh." Vlad's thin lips twitched as she stumbled over the curse word.

"Plus, I'm not sure if the house is even safe anymore." Emma groaned running her hands through her hair in bewilderment. It had been on her mind since her mother had smashed through the front window. "Being there without Grams isn't great. Every time I walk around a corner I feel like she is going to be there waiting for me, or I see something out of the corner of my eye and think it's her."

"Yes." There it was again that thing he did that looked like a smile but felt like something else, some deeper sad connection that ran between the two of them. "When my wife died, I couldn't stay in Romania any longer. I left as quickly as my feet would carry me."

"I didn't know." She felt like she was seeing the echo of her own desire to escape her grief in a stranger, except he didn't feel like a stranger. "Was it recent?"

"It has been a long time. Though, not long enough." He picked a piece of melon out of the bowl Fields had left on the counter. "I knew that I loved her from the moment I saw her. She was the world in my eyes and every morning since her passing has left me feeling just the smallest bit further from her. It hurts less now. Somehow, I think that that makes it all worse."

Vlad's eyes went out of focus. Probably remembering his wife and their glamorous life together. Emma left him to his memories, watching the sadness play over his features.

Something in the way he sat changed. A hairs breath of a difference in his posture, the clinch of his jaw. Emma could hear the grinding of his teeth. The familiar sadness in his eye that called out to her own turned dark. There was an intention in his unfocused eyes that tapped at the more instinctual parts of her brain. His lips curled back just enough that Emma could make out the creamy white enamel of his teeth. Tentatively Emma reached out to put one hand on his shoulder.

He moved so fast Emma barely recognized that it had

happened. Vlad had her wrist twisted painfully in his grip, pulling her against his chest, before she heard his stool hit the floor.

"Oh God." Recognition came back to him as quickly as it had left. Shame washing the color out of his skin. "Emma."

He let her go, pushing the stool into the cabinets as he stumbled away from her. Emma's heart pounded against her rib cage. The air felt colder. Those endless pits stared at her with some regrettable fear. He didn't seem to blink, instead he watched her the way a person would if they were trying to help a lost dog about to run into a busy street.

"I am sorry." His eyes flitted to where Emma held her wrist gingerly against her chest. "I was caught in a memory. Still, that is no excuse."

Emma nodded, still unsure what to say. Her hand was throbbing, already swollen from her altercation the previous day.

"No, it's not." She stepped away from him, straightened her shoulders and looked him in his black eyes. "How did your wife die?"

"It is not a pretty story. I would not want to burden you with the details." Vlad cast his eyes to the ground, whether from discomfort or looking for a lie, Emma did not know.

"I don't need a pretty story. I need the truth. I need a reason to trust you." Emma wanted to trust him and she knew that that fact alone compromised her judgment. She had nothing else. "Start explaining or I'm gone."

"We were expecting a child." Vlad rubbed his face harshly, perhaps buying himself time, or perhaps preparing himself to relive his tragedy. "Mina and I were happy. I had come home after a long time away and in our bliss, we disregarded the signs of an impending threat. Our first night together since we had conceived, a troupe of Order Faithful broke into our home and murdered my wife and I did not save her; save them."

"Did not?" Emma felt her throat closing up.

"Could not. It makes little difference between the two now." Vlad straightened the chair, his shoulders heavy. "For all of my money, for all the power I have been blessed, I could not save the most important person to me."

"I am sorry." Emma's voice was choked with shock and anger.

"No, I am sorry." Vlad took a tentative step closer. "I have endeavored to protect you from such ugliness and now it is I who has laid it upon your table."

Emma blinked back the burning tide of angry tears that threatened to spill out of her. She didn't want to cry in front of Vlad. She didn't want to cry in front of anyone especially not in this beautiful kitchen with the sunlight streaming through window. So Emma pushed it down meeting Vlad's contrite gaze with a stiff nod.

CHAPTER 14

Simon tapped his pen frantically on the desk. He would have loved to go down to the range and squeeze off a few rounds, maybe show up those overly cautious bastards that had grounded him behind this fucking desk, but he didn't want to miss a call from Emma. That woman was literally going to kill him, forget getting his femur shattered by a bullet, forget the three surgeries it had taken to fix the damn thing. Emma King was going to give him a damn heart attack.

Tap tap tap, the pen clicked away on his desk as he stared unproductively at his cellphone sitting silently next to his keyboard. He kept replaying the scene of her mother crashing through Iliza's front window over and over. Blood and madness slicked down her face, Emma standing there drenched in tea, surrounded by broken furniture. His concern grew like a fungus until he could practically feel little mushrooms of suspicion blooming over his forearms. Dropping the pen, Simon pulled up the Ranger's criminal database and typed in Melissa King and her date of birth. Not much came up at first: a picture and an arrest record that consisted of three things: the first for a drunk in public at eighteen, a freshman at A&M, before she had Emma. The second arrest was at some kind of religious rally on her college campus, where she had assaulted a police officer and had to be dragged from the site by two officers in full riot gear. She was pregnant at the time. It was a hell of an escalation, but it had nothing on the third and final arrest: grand theft auto and reckless endangerment of a child. Looking over the record of the incident he was appalled. It was a bare bones report to be sure, stating rather plainly that the woman in question, Melissa King, had stolen a car out of a hospital parking lot in the process of taking her infant out of the care of the NICU, without the doctor's or nurses' knowledge. She then drove with the infant laying in the front seat sixteen miles away to the home of Marcus Caldwell, president of Caldwell International. A link appeared next to his name and Simon clicked it, hoping for some more insight. Melissa and Caldwell had been married when Emma was four and as far as Simon knew Emma had only met the man a handful of times, all of which had been heavily supervised by Iliza.

Marcus' page popped up with a slew of links and known associates, two requests for wire taps, both denied, and a link to a batch of surveillance photos taken last year outside his offices on the Ship Channel. Simon clicked through the photos quickly seeing several of the average-height man with a handsome face, hair graying at the temples. He shook hands with several different men all of whom looked like varying degrees of bad news and a few women who looked like they knew their way around a business end of a Berretta. One picture caught Simon's eye in particular. Marcus held the door of a black sedan open for none other than Melissa King herself. The next picture showed them kissing stiffly.

The rest of Marcus' file read like some kind of pulp fiction thriller, complete with shady connections to terror attacks in Eastern Europe. It seemed that Caldwell International had been connected to attacks on two warehouses in Turkey, both owned by a company called Wallachia Holdings. Pictures of the bombings were horrific, real scorched-earth shit. The warehouses had apparently been holding bays for some fuel tankards and the subsequent fires had over taken an apartment complex. To say that there was nothing left seemed generous to Simon.

The Rangers' files on the Caldwell connection were a mishmash of their own surveillance and what little the FBI had turned over to them. It seemed that the FBI had run its investigation to the extent it was willing to stretch its recourses. The Rangers had its own local investigation that covered a gambit of possible law breaking in Texas specifically and while the G-Men weren't about to spend money on pursuing it themselves didn't mean that they didn't want to see Caldwell International held accountable for its wrongdoing. Simon was sure that if the Rangers found anything on a national scale the FBI would sweep in and take credit for their hard work.

An organization called The Order of Divine Mortality showed up in several sections of the file, which gave him nothing he didn't already know. No suggestion as to how the group might be involved with any illegal activity or even any real connection to Caldwell other than that it was the professed religion of his wife. As he read, his frustration grew by leaps and bounds, there was precious little about the group's system of belief or how dangerous they might be. The Order did not register for tax exemptions, a bid to keep out of the any federal scrutiny. A cursory web search only provided him with a website that waxed poetic about the Divine Mortal and the blessing of life and death. Personally, he was getting major emo vibes off of the whole thing. There were other sites devoted to a historical look at The Order of Divine Mortality that suggested that the whole thing was actually an ancient sect of Christianity that had rolled out of Transylvania in the late fifteenth century that dated back to the invasion of the Ottoman Empire. The rise in the religious sect in Transylvania was due to a belief that an evil spirit was roaming the land feeding off of the people and leaving them pale; their blood drained from their bodies.

Simon swore under his breath. If the next sentence he read had anything to do with fucking vampires he was going to hunt Emma down and hand cuff her to his desk. The rest of the site did in fact mention vampires, making it a point to mention that at the time the scare tactics the Crown Prince of Wallachia had used to keep the Ottomans out of his country had been brutal, successful, and not at all on this side of crazy. Did Emma's mother really believe there were a bunch of vampires roaming around Houston?

There was a portrait of the Prince, a man with dark hair and a hooked nose, beside a paragraph listing the legends about how he drank the blood of his enemies and was most likely the progenitor of the vampire legend in the western world. Another black and white sketch depicted Prince Vlad sitting in a field of bodies having dinner next to a paragraph about how he had shaped the idea of vampires well into the present day, and that despite his brutal methods he was remembered for keeping the whole of Western Europe from Ottoman rule. The first portrait sat as a thumbnail next to a short blurb in the comments section mentioning that the website omitted the fact that his head was never recovered from the battlefields.

It all seemed very B-horror to him, but if The Order was real and so was the threat to Emma, he had better know everything that he could. He slogged through two more websites of over romanticized crap before coming across anything of substance. A local university lecturer, Professor Henry's blog chronicled classes on historical occultism. For the most part Simon found it to be the dullest of research, as it was mostly just crap about the spiritualist movement and how everyone was phony. However, he did find a single entry about The Order of Divine Mortality, where Henry called them a death cult that rose out of religious extremism and into the realms of insanity.

Prof. Henry wrote, that while there was no clear evidence that the sect had survived into modern times, it had torn its way through Eastern Europe stirring up vampire mania that had reached as far as Italy before dying down over a century later. The modern vampire myth that our movies and literature have today is heavily influenced by this cult. In fact, the notion that the undead can be killed by the sun comes directly from them, belonging to the idea that the sun is God's gift to the Earth and as such the evil scourge cannot stand its holy rays. Professor Henry's prose was a bit wordy for Simon and his wit dryer than a bag of sand, but the intel was pertinent. Simon clicked the contact button at the bottom of the page, shooting off a quick email, asking for some more information about The Order, before clicking back to Caldwell file.

Other than a parking violation outside of a psychiatric facility Marcus Caldwell had kept himself out of direct trouble. Even notes regarding his involvement with Melissa bringing a stolen car and abducted baby to his home were glowing. The arresting officer made sure to mention that he had immediately cooperated with authorities in handing over the infant and keeping the subject of the arrest, Melissa, calm. He was a first-generation college graduate and had raised his father's company out of near ruin after his father's death in a horrific house fire. Everything in the file felt like a well-plastered façade to Simon, who had only ever seen the man through the window of his childhood bedroom on the single occasion Marcus had joined Melissa for a supervised visit with Emma. Simon had had the same rotten feeling then..

He glared at his phone, willing it to ring. If Emma didn't call soon, he was going to ping her goddamned location. Who gave a shit if it was legal or not? He wanted her safe and a few text messages that could have been sent from anyone were not going to cut it. An uncomfortable fear mixed with the manic energy of his own uselessness until he could feel it vibrating in his fingertips.

He needed to hit something, running his fingers through his hair, he scratched at his neck uselessly. The sunlight always seemed harsh in this office, or maybe it was that he hated that he was in the corner office instead of in the field. The light always seemed to glint off of the other buildings downtown and right onto his desk, glaring through the remnants of yesterday's rain clouds, reflecting off every puddle that hadn't sizzled off of the sidewalk, and the sky threatened more rain. Reaching for his phone he didn't give a second thought to the abuse of power he was about to commit.

"Davis?" Simon spoke in a clipped authoritarian manner to his ex-partner. "I need you in my office ASAP."

He didn't give the other man time to reply before he hung up. He grunted as he stood up from his ergonomic nightmare of a desk chair and paced his office. Who the hell needed an office this big anyhow? The thing was bigger than his dorm room at U of H. It had a couch in it for crying out loud. His right leg protested the movement and he cursed his promotion again. His whole leg was stiff from his hip to his ankle and he knew that physical therapy was going to be a bitch the next day. One of those walking sticks that you get at touristy truckstops leaned against the wall next to the couch. It was a God-awful thing, long and twisted, made of blonde wood so heavily lacquered that it shone when the sun hit it just right, with one of those silver handles that looked like a longhorn. Simon hated the damn thing. The guys had known that when they had gotten it for him. It would have been funny if he hadn't needed it from time to time, especially when there was a shooting pain in his left thigh telling him that he should grab it before he fell on his face. In fit of displeasure he snatched the stick from the wall and continued his pacing with an angry jaunt.

There was a single knock announcing Aaron Emanuel Davis before he entered the room, a smirk on his face. Aaron wasn't a particularly tall man, just barely five ten, but what he lacked in height he more than made up for in brawn, and some would be surprised to find out, brain. His thick corded muscles pulled his button down, tight across his chest, and Simon would have laughed at how vain his friend looked with his pompadour styled hair and freshly polished boots, but he was too pissed.

"You rang, work wifey? Still thinking about Krissy from last night? She liked you man." Aaron smiled sharply at Simon, before he got a real look at Simon's disheveled state. "Oh, shit bro, what's up?"

Aaron shut the door, before stepping fully into the office.

"You still working with Sanchez on that..." Simon searched the room for the words he wanted. Nothing came to him. "Fuck, man, I don't remember. You still working on the thing, or do you have some time?"

"Nah, we finished up yesterday." Aaron eyed Simon like you might watch a wild animal approaching your picnic table. "Just doing the last of the paperwork."

"I need you to do something for me." Simon twisted the walking-stick in his hand thinking on his words before he began pacing again. On his second turn around his desk he spoke. "I need you to track a number for me, off books."

"What?" Aaron looked at him like he had grown a second head. The great and morally upstanding Simon McGregor wanted to break a federal law? "Bro, I am going to need more than that. Dude I love you, like a much older, less attractive brother, but what the fuck? That could cost me my job."

"I know." Simon paused in his pacing to look at the other man hard, wishing that he didn't need to drag him into this, but having a Ranger who was still on active field duty to run a trace would be less conspicuous. Simon trusted Aaron with his life and more importantly he trusted Aaron with Emma's life. "I would do it myself, but I want to know for sure. "

"Simon." Aaron sat on the arm of the couch waiting for his friend to stop pacing long enough to look at him. "What's going on? This ain't you."

"I need to check on Emma." Simon kept his eyes focused out the window even though he could feel his friend's eyes burning their focus into his back.

"No." Aaron stayed put on the arm of the couch.

"It's not what you think, Aaron."

"So, you aren't asking me to find out where Emma is so you can ride out and play John Wayne in the face of her mom's crazy cult shit?" Aaron waited him out, in silence. Looking entirely unimpressed by Simon's whole lonesome cowboy routine.

"No, I am asking you to find a friend of mine who hasn't checked in for a while." Simon stopped pacing behind his desk to face the other man.

"So, you aren't asking me to find Emma?" Aaron spoke sarcastically.

"Stop dicking around, Aaron." Simon gripped the walking stick tightly in his hand, the bite of the silver horns into his palm reigning in his annoyance with his friend. "Emma's mom showed up after the funeral. She broke some furniture and a window. Emma was all banged up and now her phone is dead."

"Why didn't she just stay with us?" Aaron rolled his neck trying to make the right choice. "Damn it, Simon. You haven't gotten anything?"

"A few texts earlier, but that could be anyone. Her mom might be crazy but she isn't stupid." Simon rubbed his leg the pain was turning into the aching throb he was used to. He pulled open a drawer on his desk and popped two aspirin. "I looked up her cult, the Order. None of it's good news. This thing has got roots with these crazies in Transylvania for fuck's sake."

"Like Dracula, Transylvania?" Aaron rubbed his beard contemplating just how deep he was about to sink into this.

"The very same." Simon could see his argument winning over Aaron. "You know her, you know where she hangs out. If it's some place she normally would be you don't even have to tell me. I just need to know she isn't being shipped to fucking Transylvania in one of Caldwell's boats, okay?"

"Fine." Aaron stood up and pointed at his buddy, his dark eyes deadly serious. "I'm not telling you shit unless I think she might need some help. If it turns out you're being some kinda creep I am gonna beat your ass. Then I'm gonna tell her what you did, and she's gonna beat your ass."

Aaron swung the door open and marched out of the office in dramatic fashion, an intern plastering himself against a wall to avoid colliding with him. It was a short walk to the elevator and Simon could still see him standing hands on his hips waiting for the car to reach his floor. Aaron turned around, catching Simon watching him and shot him the bird, just as the doors slid open with the elevator full of women, all of whom caught him in the act. He bowed his head in apology to the ladies and he must have said something with the hint of Spanish accent he got from his mother's side because he was grinning at Simon while he leaned over to press the button for his floor. He'd probably come out of there with at least one phone number.

Pushing out his chair with the walking stick Simon folded himself slowly into the chair. He could feel all of his bones groaning in protest. His leg wasn't going to let him stay standing for much longer. He trusted Aaron, the guy loved Emma almost as much as he did. She had been closer to the sister he had lost than anyone would ever be.

His email pinged. An auto reply from Prof. Henry saying he was out of the country on a research expedition and would be back in August.

Damn it, Simon swallowed down his frustration and tried to focus on something the Rangers actually paid him to do.

CHAPTER 15

Sevystian woke to the scorching heat of a sunbeam tracing a line across his cheek. He lay there a minute longer, luxuriating in the exquisite pain of the sun. It only ever burned this badly when he had been neglecting himself; not enough sleep, not enough blood. His body was stronger than he had ever been as a mortal, but with that strength came the inevitable need for nutrition and the general self-care that Sevystian had neglected.

It was hard to tell for a creature like himself that their bodies were atrophying. His skin was the same pale complexion it had been for centuries, the same scars he had had since his transformation, hell even the same lines decorated the corners of his eyes as they had since his last human battle. Subtlety was the way of his deterioration and it was a path he knew all too well. It started with a slow burn ache in his belly, reminding him that he needed to eat. Eventually, it trickled into his limbs, where he could feel the pressure in his fingertips. That was most often where it stopped, where he would excuse himself to go out for a "coffee" and pick up some overeager millennial for a snack. He always left them well satisfied and just dazed enough to forget that he had taken a little bite. Honestly what was one more bodily fluid between lovers? At least that is what Kadir always said when he was on the prowl.

He could feel the light forming a welt across his skin and finally he turned out of the beam. Breathing deeply into his pillow, he took in the scent of bergamot and sandalwood that clung to his sheets. They were soft against his skin and he was glad that he had spent such an ungodly amount on them. It wasn't that he liked to flaunt his wealth, or perhaps it was not only that.

Sevystian had spent so much of his life buried under carnage that in this civilized time he shrouded himself in the decadence that five hundred years of amassed wealth could afford him, and truthfully, he enjoyed every second of it. It was a shockingly shallow thing for a person who prided himself so seriously on his self-control to enjoy. Ultimately there were so few individuals amongst his pier group that he had no one to compare himself to. Vlad outdid Sevystian's indulgences ten-fold as did Kadir, and Buchannan was barely out of his first century.

His muscles pulled in a luxurious burn as he stretched. The clock on the nightstand read two-o'clock, and he lay there for a good while, ignoring every responsibility that he had amassed over the course of the previous day. He had paperwork that needed attending, the merger contract needed to be reviewed, three high ranking coven leaders had requested a conference call regarding an issue they did not want to discuss via email and there was a woman three floors above him whose blood-line demanded his fealty.

Even in the semi-dark of his empty bedroom he could smell her. Even the stale bit of dried blood he had picked up on her from the day before had enticed his baser needs. When he had been first turned, he remembered blood smelling like hers. It was indescribable, something like the smell of freshly picked oranges crossed with the feeling of contentment you have right before you fall asleep. It made no sense to him. How could anyone smell like a feeling, but he was too tired and too hungry to bother with it. As he did every day, he would soldier through the disgruntled feeling of exhaustion.

Standing with the unnatural grace that was allotted to his kind, he made his way to his slate and marble bathroom. The sleek modern style he had seen in some architecture magazine appealed to his military side, while the hidden amenities had whispered sinfully to his indulgent side, like the heated floors that would have been nonsensical for any other tenant living in Houston, but vampires ran colder than most and the warmth felt wonderful against his bare feet. The far side of the room was dedicated to a massive wet room, with a multitude of shower jets positioned on two walls and a dark slate tub sunk into the floor. He reached for the tablet that controlled the shower and pressed the master switch turning on the one side to full heat and water pressure.

He peeled off his underwear and stepped into the spray, gritting his teeth against the initial cold. It would heat up soon enough and he needed to clear his head. Sevystian had worked hard for his wealth and enjoyed the sprawling apartment that it afforded him. It was nothing compared to the nearly eleven-thousand square feet that Vlad occupied on the top two floors but he had a few thousand to himself and he wasn't planning on inviting the whole coven over for a sleepover.

Finally, the water ran scalding down his back, dropping to the dark gray floor and curling up as steam around his feet. Too soon he turned off the water, abandoning the haven of his bathroom for the kitchen and another bottled breakfast. It wasn't that he didn't appreciate the bottles of O-negative that Fields kept loaded in his refrigerator. Truly, the man did more for his brothers and himself than any other person. Still, there was something lacking when it came to bottled blood. He had heard Buchannan liken it to drinking a protein shake instead of sitting down to a meal and he had to agree. Even as Sevystian waited for the microwave to finish heating his first eight ounces he wished that he could have something warmed straight from the source. Briefly an image of Emma laying prone on his grey sheets, her fair skin almost highlighted by the moon shining through the window waiting for him, sent a shiver of desire skating down his back and settled in his thighs. Nothing good could come from him lusting after Vlad's descendant. He chastised himself for even thinking about her in such a way, but the image persisted and his vision of her grew more erotic, she whimpered, twisting his sheets and he fell completely into the fantasy of her, until a loud pop and splash brought him back into his kitchen. The microwave continued to hum away carelessly, but Sev could see most of the contents of his mug sliding down the sides.

Opening the door, he was greeted with the wretched odor of burnt blood, grabbing some paper towels from under the sink he cleaned the damned thing. It was something that all vampires learned. You can't ignore blood. It rots and stinks and invades every aspect of your dwelling and if you like where you live, never let your meals sit stagnate. Sevystian was a rigid follower of this rule. So, he cleaned up his mess and choked down the scant ounces that hadn't splashed all over his appliance. It was bitter and too thick and worst of all it was nowhere near enough to satisfy the hunger that burned through his limbs.

He picked out a sharp blue suit, a navy affair with a crisp white shirt, that he let hang open instead of wearing a tie. Usually, he would have chosen something in a black or grey, a suit and tie that made all but the most formidable opponents pale in his shadow, but he needed to square some things with Vlad and whether he would admit it or not he wanted Emma to like what she saw of him.

This was the least intimidating suit that he owned. He perused his pocket square collection picking out a white one with a simple navy "S" embroidered in the corner. Straightening his sleeves in the full length mirror he checked the gold cufflinks and smoothed his collar. It always amused him just the slightest amount every time he looked at himself in the mirror, any mirror. All those books and all of those movies that had vampire's reflections fading away. It had been the cleverest lie that any of his kind had ever told, right up there with hating garlic and not being able to go into the sunlight. His stomach burned with hunger as he looked at himself. A younger vampire might not have noticed the tingle in his gums for what it was, but Sevystian knew that he was skating the fine edge of control. He ran a thick well manicured hand through his short hair, feeling the raised edges of five hundred years worth of flaws beneath his fingertips still tingling with hunger. Grimacing at his reflection and the fine web of scars that disrupted the skin over his ear. All of his good humor wasted away. He marched out of his apartment, headed to his office on the fifth floor of the Transempirial Tower to face the barrage of emails that awaited his immediate attention, ignoring his desire to check on Vlad's new ward only a few floors above..

CHAPTER 16

Vlad had stuck around for a few moments before begging off to attend to some business. Emma still had no idea what he did for work, other than it must be very profitable if he could afford this place. Her phone beeped again signaling that it had charged fully and Emma ignored it, coding a few more lines for her client's app.

Fields popped into the kitchen with a slight bounce in his gait. He was a funny sort of man, to be sure. There was an aura a mystery about everything he did. When Fields spoke to Emma she had the feeling that she was being let in on some kind of plot. The man probably knew where all the bodies were buried in this place. She got the impression that he had probably put a few of them there himself.

"I trust your breakfast was sufficient?" Fields' accent broke through her haze.

"Oh." Emma shook off her day dreaming, only just realizing that he had asked her a question. "Right, breakfast was great. Totally hit the spot."

"Good to hear." He preened a bit as he spoke to her, working himself around the kitchen tidying the already pristine room. "Do you need another latte? I could try my hand at a macchiato?"

"No thanks." Emma laughed at his enthusiasm. She didn't know why he was so nice to her, but she enjoyed his cheerfulness. "I think I should let this caffeine simmer a bit before I go drinking any more of it."

Fields nodded good naturedly and busied himself elsewhere in the kitchen, pulling out little mixing bowls and spices before turning to her very seriously.

"Forgive the interruption Ms. Emma." He tied a very professional looking apron. "I did not ask if you had any food preferences while you were staying with us. The cov... company men usually like to eat the staples, meat, potatoes, and the like. If you were inclined I could prepare something a bit more exotic."

"Umm." Emma didn't think she really liked the idea of something exotic, but Fields looked at her with such hope in his eyes that she couldn't say no. "I will try anything you want to make, but..."

"Yes?" Fields looked at her conspiratorially.

"No bugs." He laughed a full body laugh at that.

"Certainly." The valet beamed at her. "I was thinking something Italian, ravioli maybe. I have a recipe for meatballs that is simply divine. Cake for dessert I think. Chocolate?"

"Mmmm." Emma could feel her mouth start to water. "I am going to gain weight just sitting in this kitchen aren't I?"

"I can only hope." Fields winked at her. Someone just looking in on the scene might have thought that the tall elegant man was flirting with her, but Emma had the feeling that he was simply enjoying her company. "If you want to break an old man's heart, I could make you a salad."

He said salad like the very idea of it disgusted him and they both laughed.

"Well." Emma put her hand over her heart dramatically. "I

could never break your heart. So, if I must, I shall eat your delicious fattening food."

They both dissolved into a fit of laughter, and that is how Sevystian found them, bent over the island in hysterical giggles. Annoyance bristled the back of his throat and he coughed loudly enough to dispel the noisy laughter, as they both turned to look at him.

"Sir." There was that little half bow that Fields knew he hated. "Shall I prepare something for you?"

"No." Sevystian growled out between clinched teeth. Emma flinched away from him ever so slightly. Trying to soften his initial gruffness he continued on. "Thank you, but I am not hungry right now."

That was a load of bullshit and both men knew it.

"Morning." Emma's voice was overly cheerful. "Well I guess it is not morning any more, huh?"

"No." Sev stood stiffly by the island counter avoiding eye contact. "It is well beyond morning now."

"Yeah." Emma cast around the room before falling back to Sevystian. "I like your suit."

"Thank you." Sevystian did not preen at her complement. If he ran his hand down the front of his chest that was just to check that all of the buttons were lying flat. "It is Tom Ford."

"Oh?" Emma blinked at him, her forehead furrowed in confusion. "That's dope."

Emma's eyes went wide and Sevystian made out the lovely rosy blush creep up her cheeks before she dropped her head into her hands. They seemed to have a mutual misunderstanding as she had clearly not known about his fine suit and he remained perplexed as to this human slang. Fields wasn't helping at all. He was facing the opposite counter under the pretense of chopping vegetables but she could see his shoulders shaking.

"Yes, I suppose it is... dope." Sevystian let the slang roll around in his mouth and decided he hated it. Silence bloomed around them. Finally, his eyes caught on the dented laptop that sat in front of her. "This is yours?"

"Yeah." She rubbed the edge of the screen lovingly, and it flickered ever so slightly. "This is Carl the Computer. Though he be old and just a teensy bit broken, he is mine."

"You named your computer?" Sevystian frowned at the machine amused.

Emma nodded an affirmative before deciding that it was in her best interest to distract herself from the way his suit jacket was pulling tight across his biceps. That really should not be as attractive as it was. The shoulders of his suit were stuffed full of his muscles and Emma could make out a curls of dark chest hair peaking out from his open collar. She resisted the urge to keep staring and further embarrass herself. More importantly she really didn't want to find anything attractive about anyone right now. She hoped that maybe he would move along. He said he wasn't hungry so maybe he was just looking for Vlad.

After staring at the same line for what seemed like hours she snuck a sideways look at him. Emma couldn't really see much more than his legs from this angle which was enough to make her wish that she hadn't glanced his way. He stood very still, with his legs shoulder width apart. The navy pants broke across the arch of his camel colored oxfords, score one for Emma she did a little dance in her head that she knew what those were. Since when did men's fashion become so sexy? The slender legs of his suit pants clung to his thighs in the most delicious way, Emma actually licked her lips. Closing her eyes and letting her head fall back she hated herself just a little for ogling this guy. Wasn't she supposed to be working through some emotional truama? Couldn't her mind just not go there right now?

"What is wrong?" Sevystian thought that he saw a hint of interest in her eyes, but knew he must be wrong. "Fields, bring her some water." He snapped at the other man to hurry him along, which only earned him a raised eyebrow. "Perhaps you should rest more."

"Hah." Emma rolled her head over to look up into his green eyes. She let herself want him for a moment. His cologne wafting to her; black tea and something masculine that she couldn't place. Tears choked her throat at the faint scent of bergamot, transported to Sunday mornings with Grams and her porcelain tea set. Emma wanted to hug him, this stranger. She wanted to wrap herself in that smell and his arms. She looked away from his concerned face and the unquenchable longing in her heart for connection. "Nothing to worry about."

"I did not mean to belittle your predicament." Sevystian leaned in, crowding her with his sincerity and his muscles. The move had the unpleasant effect of reminding her of Vlad's near attack earlier. "I meant only that you are safe and with people who care about your well-being. You have been through a great deal in a short amount of time. It is not weakness to desire a moment to recover."

"You make it sound so easy." Emma hummed, sitting straighter in her chair, moving as subtly as she could to put a bit of space between them. Sevystian's voice sounded like a thunder storm, rumbling low in his chest and moving outward over the landscape. She liked it. It didn't change her circumstance. "I really wish I could, but I should get this beta out the door though."

"Mmm." Sevystian moved back, giving Fields enough room to set a glass of water between them. Sevystian glared at him like he wanted him to leave. "I understand the desire to focus on work in times such as these. There is always someone here to help carry your burden, should you need it."

His cologne surrounded her, condensing in the back of her throat along with her loneliness. The shrill hollow notes of

Emma's factory-setting ringtone filled the air, snapping them all to attention.

"Crap." Emma reached over the top of her computer, grabbed her phone, and almost knocked over the water Fields had just brought. Sev caught it without spilling a drop.

"You're quick." Lightening-fast like Vlad had been. Probably just as strong. By the dower look of him Emma could guess that there was something brutal Sevystian like to keep hidden under those nice suits. Something that would be so easily overlooked when you saw his beautiful face. It was a cold reminder that she knew next to nothing of the people she was trusting with her safety. Even though she liked them, even though they had given her shelter, something was off.

"There is a beautiful balcony through the drawing room, if you would like some privacy." Thank you, Fields, you perfectly timed bastard. Emma slipped off of the stool closed her laptop and started off in the completely wrong direction. "The other door Miss."

Emma turned around avoiding looking at Sevystian, who was still holding the glass of water. She was drowning in Sunday morning memories only now realizing how alone she was without her grandmother. This place complicated those feelings. It gave her hope for families where previously there had only been Melissa. Emma didn't want to face those memories so she bolted.

CHAPTER 17

After taking two wrong turns, Emma did eventually end up on the balcony. She would not have called it that, however. The space was more like a rooftop deck or garden. Reasonably, she did not think any outdoor space that was big enough to fit topiaries and what looked like a koi pound could be called a balcony. It was stunning really. The apartment was almost too high up to hear the traffic pulsing in the city below and even though it was still threatening rain she could see a glimmer of the sun poking through the clouds. Grams would have loved it up here. She had read an article the year before about roof top gardens in New York City and Grams had wanted to go visit one.

People always talked about sadness hitting them in the chest or washing over them like a cold rain, not Emma. Her sadness tingled in the tips of her fingers, in the back of her throat, and tears started forming without her consent. With everything that had happened with Melissa and being here at Vlad's, she had forgotten somehow that Grams was gone. Taking a great gulping breath and then another she walked to the railing hoping that maybe at the very least the spectacular view might shake her out of her grief. Any reprieve really would have been a blessing.

The view over the railing was beautiful, like watching a silent film of her city rushing around a million miles away, yet it did nothing to stop her from missing her grandmother. The tingling in her hands spread up her arms until her lips and nose felt numb. Her vision tunneled and she felt like she was falling. For the life of her she couldn't stop it. Half of her butt hit the edge of one of the concrete tiles on the deck and the other half squished into the soggy grass that was woven in between them, soaking into the seat of her pants. It would be uncomfortable when she stood up, if she stood up. Right now, she didn't think that she could move, her head slumped sideways to lean against the concrete railing. It was a horribly odd angle and somewhere in the back of her mind she knew that she was sitting in water and uncomfortable, that part wasn't really in charge.

Emma let the waves of tears take her under. She sobbed until her chest burned and her head swam. How long she sat there sobbing, she didn't know. The only reality that she was aware of was the hole in her that Grams had left behind. The crying felt good, cleansing. The tears were washing some previously unreachable wound.

Gently the crushing sobs eased and the world started coming slowly into focus once again. First the startling green of Vlad's topiaries, then the sound of the wind and car horns on the street so far below. The trilling ring of her cell phone sounded far away. Turning so that she could lean her back against the rail scraped her arm harshly, and after some struggle was able to release the arm that had been trapped. Her phone suddenly sounded louder, now unstuck from where it had been wedged between her side and the railing. She looked at it dazed, her eyes filled with as yet to be shed tears. The contact and picture were too blurry to make out. She hoped it wasn't her client. She just needed a moment, taking another gulping breath her lungs burned with the effort, until she felt steadier. The chime continued on as she breathed through the sobs that hid in her chest ready for any unsuspecting moment.

"Hello." Emma's voice wobbled a little, but she held strong. "This is Emma King; how can I help you?"

"Emma?" Simon's voice bathed her in familiar comfort, like stepping into a swimming pool in the high heat of summer. "What's wrong? Tell me where you are and I'll come and get you right now."

She gasped out a hysterical sob before answering him.

"No." She took a few steadying breathes and continued. "Simon, I am so glad it's you. I couldn't see the screen and I thought that it might be my client and I cannot deal with him right now. I'm... I'm... I'm just really glad to hear your voice right now."

"Of course, Sweetie." His voice loosened, and the fight she had heard in his voice at first seemed to be sliding into the background. "Are you alright? Do you need me?"

"I'm fine." She felt her tears roll hot down her cheek and the cut above her eye stung like all hell. "I'm not fine. I am fucking awful, but I haven't been kidnapped by my mother's cult. So, I could be worse." A choked sob burst out of her chest. "When did that get to be my measuring tape for how well I am doing?"

"Don't know." Simon laughed tightly.

"How was last night?" She struggled to sit up, leaning her back against the rail, finally able to take a deep, fortifying breath.

"I don't know." He was tapping his pen so furiously she could hear him through the phone. "Krissy is... a lot. The date was fine and everything. I just wasn't feeling it."

"Not feeling it, or not feeling her?" There was a moment of silence from them both and Emma let the joke fall flat. "Sorry I didn't answer any of your texts, or calls. My phone really did die."

"Since when does Emma King let her phone hit critical mass, huh?" She could hear the tap, tap, tap of his pen hitting his desk. He sounded calm but she knew better. "Seriously, what happened? Where are you? I went by your place this morning to check on you and you were just gone and then I couldn't get a hold of you. I almost sent out a search party."

"No search party needed." Sweat started to form on Emma's upper lip and she licked it away. She didn't deserve a friend like Simon. "I had lunch with Vlad, from the funeral. I told him about Mom and he offered to let me stay with him downtown."

"The same guy Iliza was writing to?" He took her grunt as an affirmative. "Don't think I am going to let you talk around this until I forget that you ghosted on me."

"I know." Emma chewed on her lip in an effort not to throw him into the dangerous pit of her mother's design along with her. Her self-control didn't last long and Emma found herself hashing out every detail of the would-be abduction with him, knowing that she shouldn't be forcing him into this world just so she wouldn't be alone. He didn't say a single word until she was finished.

"So." He sucked in a breath, like he always did right before he planned to tell her exactly what she had done wrong. "You almost got kidnapped by your mother's minions. You went to lunch with strangers, where you were tracked down again and now you're staying indefinitely at an undisclosed location of their choosing?"

"I'm not staying indefinitely."

"Okay." He was working himself up into something. "So, when are you leaving? I'll pick you up."

"Simon." Emma let her head hit the concrete of the railing behind her. "I'm safe here, Vlad is family."

"Vlad." He choked on the name like the very utterance of it

he found distasteful. "Vlad, says you're family, but you don't know. Why didn't Grams mention him before?"

"I don't know." Emma cast around the courtyard for a plausible answer. "Maybe Grams didn't want him any more involved than he already was with the custody thing. Maybe she was too damn stubborn to accept more help. Maybe she was ashamed that her fucking daughter would make our lives so shitty."

"Or maybe he is one of Order." Even Simon could hear how conspiracy theory he sounded.

"Really?" Emma was not impressed. "Then, why did he let me charge my phone? Or insist that I call you?"

"Subterfuge." He tried half-heartedly. It was a losing battle and he knew it.

"Simon." Her tears were dry on her cheeks and the air felt heavy with rain again. She would have to go back inside any second now. "You know that sounds really stupid. Listen, I am outside and it's going to rain again so..."

They both let it hang there for a little too long before Simon finally spoke.

"I know you're tough." She could hear the scratching sound of him rubbing his scruff again. "I need you to be safe. You're my best friend, Emmy."

"Shut up Simon." Emma felt her heart ease ever so slightly. "I will text you later. I might be here for a few days, until mom forgets I exist again. It shouldn't take too long."

"Okay." He sounded at least a little bit frustrated. He wasn't the kind of person to sit around and do nothing. He was a fixer and Emma knew that not being able to help with her mother must be driving him mad. "But if you need anything, you call, okay? I don't care if it is three in the morning and you need me to pick you up in Huntsville. You pick up the damn phone and keep it fucking charged this time."

"Love you, too." Emma snickered in spite of herself.

"Yeah, yeah." He growled. "Talk to you later."

Emma hung up the phone and sat there for a moment longer letting her head rest on the railing. The wet electric smell of rain permeated the air. This high above the ground she could feel the wind picking up quickly and she wondered offhandedly if she were safe from lightning strikes. Storms had always soothed her in a strange way.

She had been born and raised in Houston, a city built on swamp land. Rainstorms had barreled through the city so regularly that when she had gone north for school she had been surprised to find that she missed the regular deluge. The thunder had been her heavenly lullaby more times than it had been a source of fear and now in her time of crisis it seemed to her that the rain was coming to comfort her once more. The drooping clouds blotted out parts of the glaring sunlight and there was an answering rumble from the distant clouds rolling in to meet the others.

She heard the library doors open with the slightest of creaks and Sevystian stood there tall and handsome, his face set in a scowl. At this distance, she was able to take him in fully, the way his suit clung cleanly to his silhouette. He cut a dashing figure, cleanly shaven, his short dark hair ever so slightly mussed by the wind. His eyes searched the balcony for her until he spotted her sitting on the ground. His face scrunched up in confusion.

She couldn't blame him. There was a set of comfortable looking loungers not three feet away. She didn't need to be sitting on the ground. Sevystian stalked his way over to her, standing for a moment to look out over the city. It seemed right for him to survey the land like that, she could imagine him reigning over some foreign castle, the lord of his domain. Then he squatted down beside her, turning all of his attention to her. It felt like electricity was tingling through her veins.

"Are you afraid of heights?" It was unfair how sexy his voice was, really. She should have someone she could complain to about this.

"No." She really didn't want to have to explain why she was sitting on the ground, because if she had to say she might start crying again and she really hated crying in front of people.

"Do you want to tell me why you are sitting on the wet ground?" He just stared at her like an infinitely patient statue.

"Not really." He nodded at her answer, not pushing any further.

"The storm is returning." He cut his eyes upwards and as if on que lightning streaked overhead followed shortly by a clap of thunder. "It would be better to be inside. Will you?"

He stood brushing out the wrinkles on his pants, waiting for her to answer. Lightning zipped through the sky behind him, making him look like vengeful creature painted by some old master against the afternoon sky. Sevystian tilted his head up and sniffed the air just as the first rain drop fell fat and wet on his cheek.

"Help me up?" Emma tucked her phone into her bra. He raised an eye brow at that, his lips turning down at the very ends of his lips. She was starting to think that he would never really smile the way other people did, though that little tilt told her that he thought she was funny. He held out his hands to her, and she reached up to take them. They were warm and calloused beneath hers. Drops began falling in quick succession, one right after the other, growing in size and intensity, distracting her from her train of thought.

She tugged on Sevystian's hand, taking off towards the door he had just come through. He hesitated for a split second, unused to the casual way Emma touched him. She seemed to oscillate between an incurable curiosity and an understandable fear. He let her lead them into the library's sitting room. His suit jacket was damp and her shirt clung to her breasts in an enticing way that he both liked and hated. That particular brand of temptation was not a vice that was visited upon him often. It was an odd feeling, and not entirely unwelcome.

"It's... uh." Emma suddenly realized how close they were standing. She could feel his warmth radiating through her wet shirt. She could feel heat creeping up her neck. "It's really starting to come down out there, huh?"

"Yes." He held her stare for too long, fighting a smile. Another odd feeling. "Did you speak with your Simon?"

"He's not my Simon." She spoke quickly.

"Mmm." He hummed in understanding and she could feel it tingle down her spine in response. "I am glad."

"Huh?" She didn't always understand him. He spoke like he wanted to use as few words as possible. His accent growled around his words, making her feel very much like she was speaking with a beast.

"I am glad that you were able to speak." His mouth turned down at the corners. "It seemed that his worry was weighing on you."

"Yeah." Emma didn't smile back, too caught between grief and intricacies of her conversation with Simon to entertain her attraction to the dangerous stranger in front of her. Emma wasn't so blinded by the nice suit and sharp jaw not to see how dangerous Sevystian was. There was not a man alive who could watch his boss kick in the face of another man without flinching that was not dangerous. She didn't dwell on the fact that she hadn't flinched either. "He was about to send out the cavalry. Simon's been stuck behind this desk at work for a couple of months now, so he is sort of looking for some action."

Her phone started ringing, muffled against between her boob. The vibration tickled and she rolled her eyes.

"See." She used the distraction as an excuse to break eye contact and dug the phone out of her bra. She could get used to that little tilt of his lips. "This is probably him just making super sure that I answer when he calls."

"Simon. I told you, I'm fine." Emma answered the call on instinct without looking at the screen.

"Hey Baby Girl." Melissa King's voice poured icy cold over Emma. All of the calmness that she was trying so hard to keep a hold of flushed away. It must have shown on her face because Sevystian's entire demeanor changed. He stiffened beside her, his face pulled tight with concentration, almost as if he could hear her mother's voice. "Where are you Baby Girl? I wanted to talk."

"When did you get out?" Emma felt the numb tingling beginning at her fingers and at the tip of her nose.

"They could never keep me for long." Melissa chuckled throatily. "There is no one alive who could keep me from you now."

"I think someone might if they knew you sent some of your goons after me yesterday." Emma nearly shouted into the phone, her breath choking high in her throat.

"Maybe." Melissa sounded calm, collected in a way that Emma hardly ever heard her. "But you never filed a police report about yesterday, did you? If you wanted to have me arrested you should have let that security guard call the police, Baby Girl." Her voice was syrupy sweet, too slow, too controlled. "I need you to come home so we can talk."

"You want me to come home?" It wasn't really a question.

"You're my daughter." Melissa crooned at her as if she hadn't threatened her, hadn't had her minions try and kill her. "I'll always want you to come home to me."

Emma hung up before her mother could say anything else. The numbness of her anger leaving her fists shaking. Sevystian stood there quiet, patient. He held his hand out. Lightning skittered across the sky, thunder chasing her anger down her arms. Her fingers tightened around her cell, until they turned white. His fingers flexed again in the universal give it here motion. Emma placed her hand in his, her fingers wrapped so tightly around the phone at the moment she doubted very much that she could let go of it. The calluses on his palms rubbed the swollen knuckles of her fingers. She hadn't noticed her hand had been so swollen until that moment. Sevystian closed it between both of his, gently pulling the cell out of her grasp.

He kept a hold of her hand while he checked for the incoming call log. There weren't that many numbers on that list. All from regular contacts she had programmed into her phone. The last call was from a private number, it wouldn't matter to Buchannan's tech. He slid her phone into his pocket and grabbed his own; his other hand still clutching Emma's. It was perhaps folly on her part that she was not more scared than she was. Sevystian put his phone on speaker, waiting in his stoic silence for someone to pick up.

"Hey Old Man." Buchannan sounded as he always did, which was to say that it seemed as if Sev might have been interrupting his fraternity's keg stand. "To what do I owe this ominous pleasure?"

"Melissa King has just made contact." Sevystian growled over the phone.

"I am on my way up." Buchannan's demeanor changed in the span of six words. "Do you have a number?"

"No." Sevystian answered with a growl. "Get Kadir."

He hung up, dragging his mind back to the present. She was standing by the window now; the sky black with rain and thunder. It was strange that she didn't look scared. He had expected that she would at the very least look frail now, but still she looked defiant. The storm had washed out all semblance of the afternoon from the sky. She seemed to be held entranced by the drops sliding down the window. The storm lit her sharply in the dim room, her hair was curling softly as it dried quickly in the air-conditioned room. He wished stupidly that she was scared, at least then he would be certain as how to react.

Sevystian had seen innumerable masses fleeing in terror.

He was a man built in war time, shaped by invasion and empire; a monster accustomed to the bitter tang of fear in his throat. Emma tilted her head and he caught a glimpse of her face in profile. She chewed on her lip, and Sevystian could smell the blood rushing the surface and her already plump lip swelled, pink and tender under her attentions. He growled low in his chest, annoyed that he was not in complete control.

"How did she get my number?" Emma spoke to the window pane, looking up only to meet his eyes in his opaque reflection. "I didn't give it to her."

"I know." Sev stared back at reflection.

"God." She spun around on her heel. "She wanted me to come home so we could talk. Was she at my house?"

There wasn't anything he could do or say, so he stood quietly. He had heard the whole of the conversation. Emma was a kaleidoscope of emotional information.

"Is that how she knew I wasn't home?" She ground her teeth, her eyes alight with anger. She was magnificent. "Are you going to answer?"

"Do you want me to answer?" Sevystian asked earnestly.

"Yes." Emma turned to face him.

"She is a member of the Order." Sevystian clenched his fist, letting the bite of his claws into his palm distract him from the hunger and anger mixing in his belly. "They have many outlets of information, and yes there is the chance that she is at your home now."

"She's at Grams'?" Anger flashed white hot across her face. "Bitch."

Sevystian grunted in agreement with her. There was a sharp knock and then Buchannan and Kadir walked in without further preamble. Sevystian handed Buchannan the cell phone from his pocket. The younger man didn't waste any time settling on to one of the low tables that were spotted around the room. He placed his WH tech division specialty laptop down on a pile of books. It was a state-of-the-art masterpiece and Sev could see Emma practically drooling over the hardware. This particular model wasn't made public, and reserved for only the most essential of Coven hierarchy.

"If your mother intends to track you down or harm you in any way I promise that you have our protection, Emma." Kadir flashed a grim toothy smile that aligned with every concern she had about the man.

"Status." Sev barked.

"We've got a full security staff on today, they have all been alerted that they are not to let anyone in the building without verbal clearance from residence or from Vlad himself. Stevens is manning the desk. He's not going to let anyone through." Buchannan didn't look up from the screen. His fingers clicked away intently as he filtered all of the data he was pulling up. Once he cracked the encryption key on Emma's phone, which he was pleased to see was surprisingly advanced for such an old model, he got everything he needed. "I like your style Emmy-doll. Kind of old school. Bet it keeps all these naked pictures of you real safe."

Sevystian nearly ripped the table in two pulling the phone off of the USB.

"Jeeze. I've had gotten what I needed from the phone, it didn't need to stay hard wired into the system any more. You could throw it in a fire for all I cared." Buchannan gave Emma a look mostly consisting of intricate eye contact and arching eyebrows. "Just joking bro. Am I the only person who kept their sense of humor? Sorry Em, but honestly one little nude wouldn't kill you."

"No." Emma's eyes twinkled slightly through the fear and anger, she leaned into his personal space. "But it might kill you."

Looking over Emma's shoulder Buchannan watched Sev

grip the phone with white knuckles. He turned the screen to face her, motioning for her to join him on the sofa.

"How does this tell us any pertinent information about Melissa?" Kadir's purring voice broke through the techno twins babbling.

"Well, strictly speaking, it doesn't." Buchannan looked back and forth between Kadir and Sevystian. "More like it tells me that at some point Emma's phone was infected with malware and it has been collecting information from her ever since. Pretty mundane stuff, contacts, locations, frequented websites that kind of stuff."

"That sounds invasive." Kadir settled his hip casually on the arm of one high-backed chairs. "Wouldn't she have noticed something like that? You are quite the tech savant yourself."

"Yeah, but that kind of information is stuff that we are all broadcasting all the time." She chewed on her lip, and Sevystian decided that it was probably a nervous tick she had. "I mean, unless it was dragging down my processing speeds I doubt I would have ever noticed it. Plus, I am always beta testing new stuff for clients and friends. One of those could have very easily piggy-backed into my system."

"You could have picked it up ages ago." Buchannan loosened his tie clearly uncomfortable with it, before leaning back into one of the throw pillows that lined the back of the sofa. "It's a super sleek set up. It wouldn't have slowed you down unless it glitched, or you know, someone used it to make an ill-advised phone call."

"How do we stop it?" Sevystian did not mince words.

"Well it's isolated to the phone so..." Before Buchannan could finish Sev smashed the phone under his heel, sneering down at the offending piece of technology. "Yeah that'll do it."

"So, my crazy mother knows where I am." Emma paused to take a deep breath, her face scrunched up in anger. "And now, I have no phone!"

"She was tracking you." Sev actually looked dismayed at her frustration.

"I've got a stash of phones I keep for just such an occasion." Buchannan bounced his knee restlessly as he thought aloud. "Their loads better encrypted than that one, so I don't think they'll be able to get in again. We will still to have to deal with the fall out." Kadir coughed loudly to get his attention, and the kid looked around the room suddenly like he was only just remembering that anyone else was in the room. "Right! Just need to check in with Stevens. Be right back."

Buchannan hopped over the back of the couch, heading for the hallway, digging the phone out of his pocket on the way.

"Do you really think that she would bring the Order here?" Emma did look a little scared now, and as much as he knew it was good that she understood the danger they posed to her, Sevystian hated that she was afraid.

"If she really wants to take you? There is a chance that she might come here, yes." He tried to speak quietly, the way he imagined would ease her fear. If anything, it ground her ill-ease into a fine point.

"I should go then." She stood up. Straightening her T-shirt and taking a steadying breath. "Y'all have been so amazing, but I can't put y'all in danger like that. Do you know where Vlad is? I would like to say goodbye before I leave."

"You're not leaving." Sevystian stepped closer. The weight that had been slowly heating in his belly since he had heard Melissa's nonsensical little voice, burned white hot. He did not intend to break the vow to Vlad; the Order would not touch her. "We will protect you."

"I can't ask you to do that." She skirted around the couch avoiding looking at Sev or Kadir's face. "You put yourself out there more than I had any right to ask you to. I don't want anyone to get hurt because of me."

"You did the right thing." Sevystian was growing frustrated.

His accent seeped out stronger as he fought to stay calm. "It is safer for you here, I cannot... We cannot protect you out there as we can within the building."

Sevystian moved as if to grab her arm, to physically stop her so that he could buy himself another moment to talk her out of this madness, but Kadir stopped him. Sevystian almost snapped his neck, barely controlling himself.

"What if you were to give us a chance to show you the kind of security we have in place for these kinds of situations?" Kadir was a smooth bastard, Sev would give him that. "A walk around the building might ease your apprehension. Let Sevystian and I show you that your mother does not pose any more of a threat knowing you are here than if she did not."

Emma moved further away from the men, folding her arms over her chest to guard against their logic.

"I know what you're doing." Panic was starting to override her rational brain and there was a part of her that didn't trust she was safe. How could she have ever be safe?. "You'll be in more danger with me here and we both know it."

"And they'll come looking for you whether you are here or not." Kadir said his accent rolling effortlessly into a melodic sort of rhythm that might have any other person rolling over to show their belly. Emma didn't trust it. "This will be the last place you were and the first place they'll look. At least with you here we can know that you are taken care of."

"I can take care of myself." Now she was just being stubborn.

"Yes." Sevystian didn't like Kadir's chances of keeping this from becoming a shouting match between the two.

Buchannan took that moment to walk back in, phone still on his ear. He put one finger up in the universal, give-me-a-second motion and Emma took that as her chance to scram. She didn't run away. She didn't really think that she had to run away from them. She could hear Sevystian following her footfall for footfall. His gait was longer than hers' and it didn't take long until he was walking right beside her, like some great hulking shadow. If she weren't so preoccupied with getting the fuck out of dodge, she might have laughed at him.

"You must stay." He sounded imploring, or at least what she thought imploring must sound like from him. The tone of his voice never really changed much from his usual growl. Emma liked to imagine there was a subtle difference.

"I can't." She opened a door that led into a bathroom that wasn't where she wanted to be. "You're not going to help me get back to my room are you?"

"Not if it means you are going to take your things and leave." At least he was honest.

She kept on moving until she came out into the main den, she almost sighed in relief. She was half way to the stairs when she heard more foot steps behind her. She picked Buchannan's out of the jumble. He walked out of rhythm from the rest, not quite falling into step with the quick thwap of their expensive shoes on the even more expensive hard wood.

"Emmy-doll." Buchannan skated in front of her and turned to walk backwards so he could face her as they walked. "What are you doing?"

"Don't even." She kept on marching up the stairs trying not to look at his distraught face. "You know that they know I'm here. I have to go."

"But." He whined solidifying forever to her that he was a human shaped puppy and should be protected at all costs. "They will come here anyway. At least if you're here we'll know that you are safe."

She didn't respond to him she just kept on walking and he kept on flitting in front of her like Mr. Bug did whenever she walked him for Ms. Lily. No way was she going to let anything happen to him, not because of her. They reached the door to the Green suite and Buchannan braced himself dramatically against the door.

"Move." She refused to meet his eyes.

"No." Buchannan shook his head like a defiant child. "I'm not budging until you hear me out."

"Ugh." Emma reached out and with a sharp prod to his ribs surprised him just enough to open the door and squeeze past. She was done listening to them try and martyr themselves for her sake. Emma was going to need a plan, first things first, she needed a place to go that her mother didn't already have on her radar. Emma could go to Simon, but if the Order had her call logs then they would see that coming. Maybe she should just get some cash and spring for some cheap motel until she had time to really think about it. She pushed between the men, ready to grab a tattered client journal that had fallen out in her haste. Buchannan got to it first.

"Emmy-doll." His voice lowering as he tightened his grip in the moleskin. She stared at it. "Please just hear me out."

"Fine." She didn't mean it. She was leaving either way. Looking down at the ground she hoped that he couldn't see the lie.

"Please, Emma." He held the journal out to her. "You could at least look at me."

Emma looked up into his eyes. It was a huge mistake.

"Sleep on it." There was a finality to his tone that was incongruous with the Buchannan that Emma knew, for some reason it didn't bother her.

Her arms and legs grew heavy and the bag that she was still holding fell to the floor. Her knees gave way and she hoped in a vague uncaring way that she didn't hit her head on the way to the ground. Someone caught her from behind before she could fully collapse. They were talking above her but she was too tired to listen, so she closed her eyes letting whoever had caught her tuck her gently into bed.

"What did you do?" Vlad's voice hissed from across the room. He moved as a silent furious beast slamming Buchannan into the ground so forcefully the hard wood cracked where his head hit.

"She wanted to leave." Kadir stood with his arms stiff in front of him, his left wrist grasped tightly in his right hand. "To protect us."

"Yes, I gathered that from your numerous texts." Vlad stared down at Buchannan, his fangs full out, claws digging into the younger vampire's throat with just enough pressure to pop through his skin. It reminded Buchannan that should he desire it, Vlad was more than capable of ripping his fucking head off. "I want to know what it was that he thought he was doing when he thralled my flesh and blood?"

"I..I" Buchannan choked around the grip Vlad hand on his throat. The older vampire eased up ever so slightly. "I wasn't thinking..."

"No, you were not." Vlad squeezed his throat again hard and Buchannan coughed wetly in pain. It was easy to forget that Vlad had been a terror that had torn through countries, who in war been made the monster who built empires in peace time. He made it easy to forget that he had sat beneath the smoke-filled sky and nourished himself on his enemies. Their blood and their fear had sustained him when the Order had tried to cut every string tying him to his humanity. It was not easy now, not as he snarled above Buchannan like the beast of legend. He seemed as if some vengeful god, come at last for his pound of flesh. Finally, Vlad let him go, slinging the blood from his claws onto Buchannan's shirt front.

"She wasn't going to stay." Buchannan stayed on the flat of his back.

"We could have convinced her, some other way." Vlad watched Emma's chest rise and fall in an acceptable rhythm. Turning away he addressed the others. "See to it that she has a new phone and that her laptop is secure. Do it quickly. I doubt that she will be out for long."

Vlad fixed Buchannan with a last withering stare before departing the room. The intention was clear, try anything like this again and you will beg for your death. Emma groaned in her sleep, rolling over onto her stomach.

"Alright we should get to it then." Buchannan was sitting up his knees bent into his chest. "We stay here much longer and we're just a bunch of guys watching a woman sleep. Bit creepy."

"Not as creepy as forcing her to sleep." Kadir studied Emma's sleeping form with the casual interest of a cat watching an interloping hamster.

CHAPTER 18

Aaron didn't bother knocking. He had access to the Ranger's database too and if Simon's reaction to Emma's mom showing up wasn't enough for him to ready the horses, then the trail of danger leading right to Emma was. The harsh light of Simon's office had only grown more bleak as the storm rolled back in leaving the room eerie flickering blue as the lights buzzed. The curse of every good detective is curiosity and damned if he didn't want to know what had pulled a twist in his buddie's leg. The file on Melissa King had seemed shallow at first glance, but once he started digging into her history, the hole just kept going. Aaron had always been aware of the Order. He couldn't have known Emma and not been at least tangentially aware that they were in part responsible for the shit Melissa put her through, but he had had no idea they trafficked in the kind of trouble those files had hinted at. Aaron was now acquainted with the danger that had Simon worried. Simon was reading through some paper-work, when Aaron marched into the office slinging the door shut behind him.

"You're going to want to see this." Aaron dropped the results of his trace on top of the paper work Simon was reading, then flopped down on one of the little-used seats in front of the desk. "Guess who owns the building Emma is staying in?"

"The Hamburgaler?" Simon looked up at Aaron without looking at the papers he had slammed down in front of him. "No? Okay, how about Chuck Norris?"

"Stop fucking around." Aaron's usually cool demeanor was shot. Wallachia Holdings had an absolute shit ton of shell companies and backdoor holdings that had left it near impossible for him to pin-point who exactly owned the Transempirial Tower, a massive land holding and work of fucking art that had been built just over a decade ago. The thing was one of Houston's most expensive pieces of real-estate and Emma was just hanging out with her long-lost cousin there? He was calling bull shit. "Listen, you wanted me to do the search so I did it, alright? Just because you are all fine and you know where she is doesn't mean I am fine with it."

"I am not fine with it." Simon tapped his pen against his desk, like he always did when he was getting anxious about something. "She told me to lay off. So, I am trying to honor her wishes."

"Yeah, well try saying that without clenching your teeth." Aaron leaned back in the chair letting his knees bounce up and down without any rhythm. "Anyways you're not the only one who can do some digging around here. She tell you that she's at the Transempirial? Did you happen to find out who owns it?" Aaron didn't actually wait for an answer. "Well I did. Wallachia Holdings."

"Wallachia Holdings?" Simon ceased all fidgeting. "The same Wallachia Holdings whose warehouses were attacked?"

"One and the same." Aaron stood up grabbing the walking stick from beside the door weighing in his hands, as Simon came up behind him. "It's not a bat but it'll do in a pinch."

CHAPTER 19

Emma woke up to the sound of thunder in the azure dark of her suite. Her body moved like she was trying to wade through mud as she fought her way to wakefulness. Emma had never liked waking up after a nap to the dark. It always made her feel as if she had wasted the day, or that she was sick, even when she wasn't. Thunder sounded again and she groaned checking the clock, 6:47. The storm must have been blotting out the sunlight. This late in summer they should have daylight until at least eight, maybe later. A storm like this could turn the sky to night in the middle of the afternoon.

Memories of sitting out on the balcony while she spoke to Simon filtered back to her. Crap, her phone had been bugged. The panicked need to flee that she had had earlier had subsided and she was glad that she had decided to give it more thought. She had to talk to Vlad before she did anything. At the very least he deserved to know that she was going to leave. She needed to get a new phone too. It wasn't really in her budget to get one, but she wasn't about to let her mother barge into Vlad's life all Cuckoo-for-Coco-Puffs.

Sitting up she felt the tell-tale scrunch of slept-in clothes.

Ugh, she hated sleeping in her clothes like that, it always made her feel like she needed a shower. She grimaced and shimmied her way to the edge of the bed. Flinging her legs out from under the covers, until she could feel the nip of the air conditioner on her toes, Emma laid there for a long while wondering if she could just pretend that nothing had happened since the funeral.

As usual, the desire to just get things over with twitched in her brain until she was sliding her toes in the plush rug under the four-poster bed. Everything was a little fuzzy from earlier and she wasn't a hundred-percent certain she remembered getting into the bed. She almost thought that she might have just passed out from exhaustion. Did that actually happen to people? Like real people, not just celebrities? She knew that she had been through a crap-ton of stuff in the past few days, but had she really just fainted? Ugh, she felt so weak. She shivered with disgust.

Standing up, she stretched her arms high over her head hoping to dust out any of the cob-webs currently making a home in her noggin. It didn't do much. She felt crooked and stiff. Straightening out her T-shirt best she could. Emma threw on her slippers someone had lain out for her and headed downstairs.

She was getting used to the size of the apartment, or at least she thought she was until she passed through what looked like a second kitchen: baffling. Fields was standing by an industrial looking cooktop, scooping the contents of a bowl into perfect little mounds on a cookie sheet.

"If that is Buchannan lurking back there, you can be assured that these biscuits are not for you." Fields seemed curt, even for him.

"Do I get one?" Emma hoped that her falsely chipper demeanor might brighten the sullen mood that seemed to swept over the man.

"Oh, Miss King!" Fields turned around with a winning smile. "Of course, you do. I was told you weren't feeling quite yourself and thought you might like some biscuits. No, that's all wrong. You don't call them that do you? Blast it! What is it you call them?"

"Cookies?" Emma supplied helpfully, as she made her way over to where he was standing.

"Quite right." Fields finished scooping the last of the batter on to the cookie sheet, putting the whole thing in the oven before turning to address her full on. "How might I help you this evening, Miss Emma?"

"You know you can just call me Emma." She leaned against the stainless-steel counter, letting her eyes flutter around the very commercial looking kitchen. This was the kind of space she had been expecting from the other kitchen she had been in this morning. Was it this morning? She wasn't even sure how long she had been asleep. She could have been out for a whole day or more. Suddenly she felt a panicked. "Fields?"

"Yes?" Fields wiped down the already immaculate counter.

"How long was I asleep?" Emma chewed her lower lip.

"Not long." Fields stopped his business to give her his full attention. "We thought you might be out for longer, passing out the way you did, but it was only a couple of hours. Nothing I wouldn't expect from someone who had been through what you have. Mr. Tepes will be glad to see you up and about. He's in his study, with the rest of his brood, if you wish to see him. I understand that you might have some things to discuss with him."

"What if I stayed here, and ate all of the cookies with you, instead?" She batted her eyelashes overdramatically at him. She wanted just a few more minutes before the world was set on fire.

"I am afraid that the cookies are as of yet, not baked." He leaned against the counter next to her, mimicking her posture.

"How about you go speak with Mr. Tepes and I promise that when they are done I will bring you a tray?"

"I would say it sounds like a bribe." Emma squinted at him sideways. "You don't like having people in your secret lair, do you?"

"Is it really a secret lair if everyone knows about it?" Fields countered with a raised eyebrow.

"That's not a... No." She teased him, buying herself another few seconds of peace.

"I would suppose it is not." He wasn't fooled by her routine in the slightest. "The far door will take you back into the dining room and Vlad's office is just off the main sitting room. I'll be along just as soon as these are done."

The door to Vlad's study was actually a pair of French doors through which the gang of them sat huddled around a low coffee table with what looked like the blueprints of the tower sitting on it. She rapped twice on the doorjamb before letting herself in. Every head swiveled in unison to look at her. Ubiquitous surprise and concern painted their faces.

"You're up!" Vlad rose from his seat, ever the graceful host and settled her carefully in the space he had just vacated. There was a bit of muttering as everyone shuffled around until Vlad was sitting right next to her and Buchannan was forced to stand.

"Sorry I conked out on you guys." She tucked one of her feet underneath her as she spoke and then immediately felt uncomfortable. The furniture was so expensive looking it was a wonder anyone ever sat on it. "I guess I was more tired than I thought."

"It is understandable." Vlad's eyes never left Emma's face, but Sevystian's were plastered to Buchannan. "I am just glad that Sevystian was there to catch you. It might have been a very different afternoon had he not."

"Oh." Emma had the uncomfortable feeling that she was

not remembering something very important. "Thank you, Sevystian."

"You are most welcome, Ms. King." His voice had a smoky purr to it that curled around the room. "I am glad to be of service."

"Sooo…" She cast around the room hoping to land on some safe topic of conversation. Her eyes landed on the smashed shell of her cellphone lying limply on Vlad's desk. "Is there anywhere to pick up a new phone around here? I am really gonna need one soon. I'm sure I could just pop out and get one."

"No." Sevystian said.

"Excuse me?" Emma gave him the evil eye. She might still need a solid eight hours of sleep, but she was not about to put up with that macho bullshit.

"There is no shop of this kind within walking distance." He paused to lick his bottom lip, before he began speaking again. "We have, however, secured a new phone for you. Buchannan says that it is top of the line. I hope you find it sufficient for your needs."

"Thanks." Now she felt kind of shitty. He was just trying to give her a new phone and she had jumped down his throat. Ugh, she really was dog-tired. "Do you think that it will be able to be tracked like my old one?"

"Hell no!" Buchannan was practically in her lap handing the thing to her. It might have been a trick of her fatigue or something, but she would swear that she had heard Vlad hiss at him. "It's, ah…" He scooted back a little until he was resting his haunches on the edge of the coffee table. "It's got all of these cool features that are built specifically for anti-malware applications and the resolution on this thing is nuts. You could probably design the rest of your app on this thing, without ever running into a problem."

"Dude, have you seen my computer?" Emma rolled her eyes

good naturedly. She liked Buchannan. He was easy going and it made the fact that she was hiding out here a little easier to swallow. "It's got one USB in the grave. I could probably do a better job on an iPhone 2"

She leaned closer to him and maybe it was her imagination but the other men seemed to tense up.

"Okay boys." It had been Gram's firm belief that issues should not be left to fester. If you had a problem it was better to let it out and in the sun. "What's got y'all up in a knot. What did I do?"

"Emmy-doll it's not you." Buchannan ran his hand down his face, mussing up his hair and looking for all the world like a distraught puppy. "They're mad at me."

"Oh yeah?" She smiled at the nickname. It was the sort of thing that seemed to spill out of his mouth before he really thought about it. It was boyishly charming and she could see how some women might find him really attractive. "Well that sounds like a personal problem."

"Yeah, it totally is." Buchanan scratched the back of his neck looking sheepish. This kid was going to break some hearts one day. Emma looked him over with his head hung low. She wondered where Vlad had picked him up. Rice, maybe? "I have a new laptop for you too if you want. The tech division has a bunch laying around that are way more secure that I would be happy to give you."

"Okay, kid." Emma squinted at him suspiciously. "Why do I get the feeling like you are trying to buy your way out of something?"

"I..." Luckily, Buchannan was saved by the doors opening and Fields sliding in with a tray of biscuits and tea, which he set on Vlad's desk and proceeded to pour a single cup and offer it only to Emma.

"Your cookies, my dear." He pronounced cookies with an air of disdain that had Emma smile into her tea cup. "It was not my intention to interrupt, but Mr. Stevens with the front desk did call to inquire about two men in the lobby looking for Ms. King."

Fear shot into her belly. She felt the tendrils of it spiraling out of her gut and lacing down her extremities.

"Emma, darling." Vlad cupped her face, turning her gently to face him. She must be radiating fear because he spoke softly, the way you might to a child who had had a bad dream. "There is no need to fear. This building and my staff will keep you safe. I am going to deal with these men and you should speak with Sevystian and the others. They have a plan to keep you safe, while we assess any threat that the Order poses to you."

Vlad kissed her lovingly on the forehead before standing to leave the room. It seemed to Emma that that gesture should have been weirder than it was. Every time she had seen someone kiss somebody on the forehead in movies it had always seemed so forced, so old fashioned, but from Vlad it was just something that he did. Like, that's Vlad for you, he's super rich, lives in a castle in the sky, oh and he kisses people on the forehead like a Dickensian grandpa.

He followed Fields out of the room, she assumed to go deal with the dudes in the lobby who may or may not be goons from the Order here to abduct her. She had just woken up and she was already exhausted again.

Buchannan slipped into the space that Vlad had just vacated, his leg rattling up and down. Even for a kid as restless as he was, this seemed excessive. They all just looked at her like she was about to send them on their respective missions, and suddenly Emma was very aware of what it must be like to be the President. The phone that Buchannan had just handed her rang with soft tinkling notes completely opposite to the shrill tone Emma had gotten used to with her old phone. It startled everyone. The guys didn't jump like she did, they only scowled at the phone.

"If somebody says the call is coming from inside the house." Emma pointed around the room making it clear that no one was safe. "I'm leaving."

"I suggest you answer it before any of us take such rash measures." Kadir spoke to her and somehow over her, his eye cutting past her to Buchannan who looked pale.

The lobby of the Transempirial was opulent to say the least. The sconces on the walls were huge Art Deco inspired leaded glass; in fact, the whole of the entry seemed to be transported straight out of the roaring twenties. It made one hell of a first impression on the two Rangers, but they were not going to be swayed by fancy décor. The security guard at the front desk stopped them before they could get to the elevators. Even a flash of their matching badges didn't allow them carte blanche run of the building. Whoever employed the staff of the Transempirial Tower kept them well trained. The guard made a short call to what Simon assumed was his supervisor before speaking to them again.

"Someone will be right down." The guard gestured to a gilded lounge area that sprawled along one side of the lobby. "There's a coffee shop through that door if you'd like to get something while you wait."

"Thanks." Simon gritted out, walking over to one of the green velvet chairs. Slumping down on the chair, his annoyance ratcheted up a few notches. The damn thing was comfortable too. He pulled out his phone and dialed Emma's number. It rang once before she picked up.

"Hey." She sounded mildly irritated the way children always sound when their parents have committed some illusory affront. "Check up on me much?"

"I'm downstairs." Simon's voice sounded exhausted.

"What?" The humor in Emma's voice evaporated, the gentle twang of her Texas accent clipped by Simon's intrusion of her privacy. "How'd you know where I was? Don't move I am coming down."

"I'm guessing she isn't happy with us?" Aaron slumped further into his chair until his head rested on the low back and his body was near parallel to the ground. "This should be good."

"She doesn't know you're with me. You should get out while you still can." Simon talked to the floor. "Just go to that coffee shop and wait it out."

"Nah man." Aaron let out a small laugh. "I'm your ride or die bitch."

Simon grinned at the floor. Well at least if he was going out, he wasn't alone.

"Besides, she won't kill me." Aaron glanced over at Simon until he looked up. "I'm too pretty."

"Shut the hell up." Simon groaned as a shot of pain spiked through his leg, at the same time a man stopped in front of him and extended his hand in greeting.

"Ranger McGregor and Ranger Davis?" The man had the accent and bearing of a 90's Bond villain and a horrible air of familiarity Simon couldn't place. "I am Vlad Tepes. Mr. Stevens, my liaison, informed me that you wished to see me about one of the tenants in the building?"

"Yes Sir." Simon stood shaking the man's hand firmly. Why did he look so familiar? "I was hoping I might speak with Emma King. She is staying here as of last night."

"Guests of the residents are not required to log in. This is not a dormitory." Mr. Tepes' demeanor changed immediately. He squared his shoulders and feet. It sent all the neurons firing wildly in Simon's brain. He gripped the walking stick hard enough to feel the bite of silver in his palm. Beside him, Aaron stood straighter, the only indication that he was ready for a fight was the slight angle of his body away from Mr. Tepes making him less of a target.

"But you are aware of guests, are you not? We need to speak to Ms. King immediately." Simon spoke around clenched teeth.

"Do you have a warrant?" Vlad asked. "I am afraid without a warrant I will not divulge any of the tower's residents whereabouts to you or any other member of the public."

"Listen." Aaron was about to go off. Simon had been in enough bar fights to know when the shorter man was about to lose his cool. They were interrupted by a shout from across the lobby.

"Aaron Emmanuel Davis, don't you dare." Emma rushed out of an elevator car towards the lounge. "I swear to God, you two."

Simon was about to speak when he got a glimpse of the squadron of behemoths standing behind her, each one just as violent looking as the last. These guys had bad news written all over their perfectly tailored suits.

"Hello to you, too." Aaron relaxed ever so slightly at the sight of her. "Babe, you can't just ditch us like that. You had us worried. Anything could have happened to you. I would have been lost without you."

He was really pouring on the Latin charm. It was getting him exactly nowhere. Aaron and Simon almost growled at the other men, sure they were outnumbered, but the Rangers were still fairly certain that they could take them. The one guy was still chuckling to himself as he sidled up to Aaron.

"That charm shit ever work on her?" He walked closer as he spoke and it became clear that he had a good four inches on Aaron, but the kid was lean where Aaron was broad. He was tall and stacked with muscle that had been pulled long by hard work, not hours at the gym. "I mean that dame is a hell of a woman. Think she could kill a man flat with nothing but a look if she really wanted 'em dead."

"We are not friends." Aaron growled at the other man.

"Not with that attitude." He slung his arm over Aaron's shoulder in a casual way that forced the shorter man to tuck himself into the crook of his arm. "I'm Buchannan, that's Kadir." He thumbed over towards the man with the carefully styled man-bun and tightly clipped beard. "You met Vlad already and Mr. Tall Dark and Serious over there is Sevystian. We're kinda like a boy band. I'm definitely the cute one."

"We are not a boy band." Vlad dragged a long-suffering breath through his impressive nose. "And you are not funny."

"I am funny." Buchannan actually looked offended.

"No, you are not." Kadir started off towards the coffee shop speaking over his shoulder to his friend. "Girls only laugh at your jokes after they see how expensive your car is."

"Emmy-doll tell him that's not true." Buchannan looked over his shoulder towards her, but was met with empty space.

Emma had dragged Simon a few paces off towards the café just out of ear shot for a modicum of privacy. His face was a ruddy splotchy mess, hair sticking out at odd angles.

"I told you I was okay." Emma flitted her eyes to the other group of men.

"You told me you were safe." Simon huffed, putting his hands on his hips in a way that told Emma he was not moved by her protection detail. "In fact, you told me that you were not fine."

"Okay, I'm not fine." Emma motioned over to where Aaron was posting up to Buchannan, his chest puffed out, his mouth bent into a cruel looking snarl. "I don't think that this is helping with things."

"Fair." Simon threw Aaron an exasperated look. "But what did you expect? You haven't called in…"

"An hour?" Emma cut him off. "Simon, I took a freaking nap. I am exhausted."

"Did you know that Vlad runs Wallachia Holdings?" Simon leaned in like he was sharing some life altering information. "Did you know that the Order might have bombed his warehouses in Romania last year? Did you know he was connected to them?"

"Yeah I knew he was connected." Emma snapped at him. "They killed his fucking wife, Simon!"

That shut him up. Blinking in the wake of that revelation, he wiped his face his argument having lost its footing.

"I need some coffee." Emma cracked her neck, looking up to make eye contact with Vlad and motion her intentions to go into West House. "You coming?"

"They got anything I can afford?" Simon looked at the stylish double doors that led into the café and sighed. This had not gone as he had expected.

"Barely." Emma smiled.

Vlad inexplicably reached the doors before they did.

"So, you're Vlad." Simon nodded at the other man, trying not to let the aura of wealth and power intimidate him.

"And you are Simon?" Vlad studied him for a moment, before reaching his hand out in greeting. "Emma has spoken highly of you. I am glad to see that she has such devoted people in her life."

They shook hands, and if Simon squeezed a little harder than was strictly necessary Vlad didn't show it on his face. Simon had really been hoping that he was going to turn out to be an asshole, but so far, Vlad Tepes was a perfect gentleman. Simon didn't like it. Where had Simon seen his face before?

The aroma of freshly ground coffee washed over them as they walked in, it was larger than he had originally thoughts taking up the whole lower half of the northwest side of the building.

"You have decided to join me. How nice of you." Emma said to Aaron as he sidled up to the booth she was sliding into, his pissing contest with Buchannan temporarily forgotten.

"Your words seem so nice, but your voice says you might kill me in my sleep." Aaron pulled a chair up to the end of the table before throwing himself into it casually. He ran his hand over his pompadour, smoothing down some non-existent frizz and leaned his elbows on the table.

Vlad and Simon slid into the opposite sides of the curved booth. Tension seemed to be growing by leaps and bounds with every passing second.

"You may be wondering why I've gathered you all here today." Buchannan stood at the end of the table as they all budged in, undisguised glee written in his eyes. Everyone groaned. "What? It was that or the one I've got about kissing a chicken's ass."

"I believe we are all thankful that you chose not to grace us with that particular joke." Vlad gritted out.

Simon was struck with how similar Vlad looked to the portrait of that prince that popped up on Prof. Henry's blog about the Order. Familiarity prickled over his skin.

A waitress came by to take their orders before he could say anything, but he was certain of it. They looked nearly identical. No wonder the Order was coming after this guy's company: they thought that he was Dracula. His head hit the back of the booth as he tried to roll his shoulders. The bang drew everyone's attention to him as he tried to play it off as no big deal. Great, now he looked like a huge idiot in front of what was probably the Dark Arts equivalent of the Back Street Boys.

"So..." Emma waited for the waitress to leave before turning her heated gaze to the two new arrivals. "You want to tell me how you found me, or are we going to speculate wildly?"

"Blame him." Aaron wasted no time throwing Simon under the bus. "He started me down the rabbit hole. I'm just here to make sure that your mother doesn't drag you off to a commune in Amarillo or something."

"So, you traced my phone?" Her eyebrow was in danger of disappearing into her mass of dark curls.

"How do you know it wasn't him?" Aaron nodded to Simon. "He has more access than I do."

"Bull crap, Aaron!" She grabbed the coffee back from him, nearly spilling half of it down his front. "We both know that you could get anything you want out of those systems."

"Fine." Aaron admitted. The waitress passed around coffees and a plate of croissants. He waited impatiently until she was gone before speaking again. "He asked me to, and don't think we aren't going to talk about why you blinked off the fucking map for no goddamn reason in the middle of the day."

"What now?" Simon hadn't heard that last part before.

"She's okay, so it doesn't really matter now does it?" Aaron tossed the accusation away like used tissue. "And the Ranger's files on Caldwell didn't help. That shit was messed up, Em. There were pictures from the warehouse explosion."

"So, you what?" She crossed her arms in front of her frustration pouring off of her in waves. "You break the law and hunt me down?"

Tension around the table pulled taught, dragging the hulking attention of Emma's newly acquired entourage fully onto the Rangers.

"Yeah." Aaron pointed at her with his mouth full pastry. "And I wish there had been a couple of idiots like the two of us to find my sister. Feel free to keep sitting there and drinking your coffee and let us protect you."

The mention of his sister visibly deflated Emma. Josie had been a few years older than them in school and her disappearance had rocked their whole world. It had certainly shaped how Aaron had seen everything from that moment on. He had become a Ranger because of Josie and now he was sitting in front of Emma telling her that he was worried about her safety. It was the guilty Ace up his sleeve he had never used before.

"Don't talk with your mouth full." Very childishly, Aaron opened his mouth to show her his half-chewed food. Emma stuck her tongue out at him. "Very adult of you, Mr. Davis. I can see now, why the girls flock to your arms."

"Hey now." Aaron swallowed smirking at her. "I haven't got any complaints yet."

"Yes, your concern is all very touching." The man in the navy suit was speaking, Sevystian. "You said that the Rangers have a file on The Order? It would be very much in the interest of Emma's safety for you to tell us more."

The man was huge, he took up a quarter of the booth all by himself and when he spoke it was with the air of carefully chosen words. Sevystian was without a doubt the most seriously intimidating man that Simon had ever met and they hoped like hell he really was on their side, because lord help the enemy of that man. Vlad lifted his hand in the air motioning the waitress back over.

"Would you have this sent up to the penthouse, please?." Vlad motioned towards the assorted pastries and coffee with a vague authoritarian casualness and Simon had to school his face against the disturbing likeness of that Romanian prince. "I think perhaps we ought to take this discussion to a more private venue."

He began walking back to the lobby entrance and the other men followed him without question. When Sevystian reached back to help Emma out of the booth, Simon had to fight back a growl in his throat. He didn't know why it pissed him off so much. It was one little gesture, one that he himself had performed a thousand times, or maybe that was why it annoyed him so much. Maybe it was the fact that she had taken his hand so easily that made him detest the man so violently. Simon was the rock Emma leaned on, he always had been and now this stranger in a nice suit was taking his place. He clench his fists with displeasure as he watched Emma snag her iced coffee from the table before falling seamlessly into the well dressed phalanx waiting for her. She caught Simon's stare over her shoulder and motioned for he and Aaron to follow.

Aaron stood up, taking a large gulp of his own iced beverage, swallowing hard before speaking. "When in Rome, huh?"

"Right." They followed after them.

CHAPTER 21

Simon tried not to get caught up in the grandeur of the penthouse that Vlad occupied. He didn't know what he had been expecting, but the medieval castle vibe the space was rocking was not it. Honestly, he wouldn't have been surprised to find an Iron Maiden leaning in a corner somewhere. It did nothing to calm his wildest concerns.

Emma sat down on the leather tufted sofa in front of the stone fireplace. Sevystian moved to sit next her. Too close for Simon's liking, some hind-brain part of him railed against the other man. Naturally, he stuffed himself in the tight space between Emma and the other arm of the couch. It could have been his imagination but he thought that he heard the man growl low in his chest, or maybe there was a dog somewhere.

"I would very much like to know what it is that you have uncovered in regards to The Order of Mortal Divinity." Vlad situated himself on a large winged back chair, commanding the room. "They have plagued my company for longer than you could imagine. If you have some information that could stem the flow of violence from these radicals I would be grateful to know it."

"Dude." Aaron grimaced at his own faux pas. He perched

on the arm of another tufted sofa sitting perpendicular to the one that Emma was currently sharing with two seriously perturbed looking men. "I mean Sir... Mr. Tepes?"

"Please, call me Vlad." The billionaire entrepreneur nodded.

"Vlad." Aaron stopped again as Fields wandered in with what looked like the pastry from downstairs and several more coffees. He watched the man as he placed the tray on the low table in front of Emma.

"Thanks Fields, you're the best." Emma scooped up the cookie he offered her.

"Got anything for me?" Buchannan chirped from his post leaning against the fireplace and was promptly met with derision.

"Terribly sorry, Mr. Buchannan, I was unaware that you had lost the ability to walk." Fields procured a napkin out of God only knows where, handing it to Emma smiling genuinely. "Any requests for dinner?"

"Enough." Sevystian snapped sitting forward. "What information do you have for us?"

Fields seemed to sink into the peripherals of the room.

"Listen buddy." Simon was on the edge of his seat as well, his hand cupping Emma's knee protectively. "I know that you're probably all mobbed up and you think that you need to protect her, but Emma is my... our friend. She is our responsibility. I can... we." He pointed between himself and Aaron. "Her friends, her Ranger friends, can help her."

"You couldn't swat a fly without paperwork." Sevystian sneered, his lips pulling viciously over his canines.

"Mr. McGregor, I believe it would be in Emma's best interest if we worked together." Vlad made a good show of trying to stem the potential violence. "The Order is well known to me and my people and while it is true that we have not had the pleasure of knowing Emma for as long as you have, I am still her family. As she is the last of mine, I am invested in seeing that she is safe and happy. Please, let us put aside our prejudices."

"Fine." Both men parroted back to Vlad their eyes not agreeing with their words. Vlad motioned for Simon to continue.

"Seriously?" Aaron interrupted before they could really start their discussion. "Are we really going to sit here like you don't have a fucking butler? Like a butler, carrying silver trays, with British accents, and shit?"

"That is my valet, Fields." Vlad picked the largest coffee off of the tray and sipped it thoughtfully. "He's been a true asset to myself and my company for decades, even if he's a little mouthy."

"Right, cause a valet is hugely different than a butler." Aaron rolled his eyes to the coffered ceiling and groaned at its craftsmanship. "Okay Vlad, you have to be straight with me here, are you Bruce Wayne? I just need to know if you have got a Batcave around here somewhere."

"Aaron!" Simon was pissed. He practically had smoke pouring out of his ears. "I don't think that..."

"Jesus, Simon." Aaron was annoyed too. "Listen brother, if you think I'm not asking Dracula over here if he and his man servant have a secret lair, you are out of your damn mind. We are here, Emma is safe." He eyed the men in the room all of whom seemed to be sitting a little straighter. "Relatively safe. Calm your tits man."

"You mentioned Dracula. Why is this?" Kadir who had said very little to either of them sat forward with his hands on his knees. Everything about him appeared severe, as if his very words could do harm if he were of a mind for violence.

"Haven't you seen the picture?" Aaron reached into his pocket for his phone, only to have every man in the room save for Simon, reach for their holsters. Any relief from the rising tension was cut down. "Just getting my phone guys." He flipped through a few web pages before settling on what he was looking for, a fourteenth century portrait of the Prince of Wallachia. "Ya see this dude is the guy Bram Stoker based Dracula off of, and he also looks just like your boss. Hence, Dracula. Hence, why these Order freaks are after your company and your family."

"Your system has this in their files?" Vlad took the phone studying it seriously. The tone of the room had gone from tense to silent, all eyes on Vlad.

"It is available to anyone with a mind to look into it." Simon took a breath. Something was off about the whole situation. These guys must be a mafia front, look at them. Maybe it wasn't the Order that they should be worried about? What if Emma was caught between her mother's crazy cult and some huge Eastern European criminal organization? Fear spiraled out from Simon's better judgment. The kind of organized crime that passed through Houston was at best bad news. Throw in the connection to those explosions in Romania and Simon felt like his head would pop off with the possibilities. "We discovered this little detail in some of our own research. We're just trying to make sure you're not just as bad as they are."

"Simon!" Emma's eyes pleaded with him to play nice. She hadn't seen the pictures of that warehouse, Simon had.

"What Emma?" Simon stood, marching around the room trying to alleviate the ache in his leg and worry in his bones. Emma was his closest friend and he couldn't stomach even the thought of losing her. "Why did he let you stay here? Vlad wants to what? Save you? Because he's your long lost uncle? He's clearly mobbed up. How can you be this stupid?"

"Fuck you Simon." She wanted to slap that self-righteous sneer off of his lips, but before she could move Sevystian was up.

Sev pulled the Ranger over the coffee table by the labels of his cheap sport coat, tipping over pastry and drinks onto the rug. Simon cocked his arm back, landing a solid punch straight into the bigger man's temple. The struggle stayed on its feet, until Simon knocked into the sofa and toppled backwards, narrowly missing Emma as she sat paralyzed by anger at the pair of them. A thickly muscled arm banded around her chest, pulling her over the back of the couch and out of the path of the fray. Somehow, Simon had ended up on top, throwing hit after hit. His knuckles came away bloodied, the sickening crunch of bone rose above the sound of heavy breathing.

Emma looked around wildly hoping that someone would stop it, no one budged. Aaron still had an arm banded around her, keeping her out of the fray. If this was some kind of mancode thing that was meant to ensure that the two could just have it out, they had better hope that this fight kills the both of them, because if she had to deal with this kind of posturing for one more second, she was going to murder them both herself. She pushed Aaron's arms off of her just as Sevystian performed some kind of ninja maneuver that had landed him on his feet with his hand wrapped in the collar of Simon's shirt, dragging him up. He flung the cowboy around him in an incredible display of power, landing him with a sickening crack in the pile of ash and burnt wood in the fireplace. He coughed, spitting up globs of blood, and smirked at Sevystian, his teeth red. Sevystian's expression didn't change as he wiped the congealed blood from his temple. It was curious to Emma that Sevystian should have bled so much yet sustained so little damage. The way that Simon had been wailing on him he should have some kind of visible injury and not some wound-less outpouring of blood.

Simon launched himself out of the fireplace. He caught Sevystian around the middle and managed to throw him off balance, sending them both crashing into the table smashing the thing to splinters. The grappling continued, until Sevystian paused, seemingly victorious on top of Simon, his arm raised high, one of the broken table legs ready to club him to death.

Emma thought this hesitation had to be Sevystian realizing the insanity of their actions when she heard the unmistakable click of Simon's service weapon being cocked. Oddly, only Aaron and Emma scrambled to stop him before the deafening bang shattered the tension. It was too late.

There could be no doubt that the bullet had hit its mark. Simon was a crack shot from insane distances. He had been among the Rangers Sniper Response Unit before his promotion. Sevystian was dead, she knew it. The moment stretched on and on like a hot rubber band until Sevystian's great shoulders heaved with effort and he stood. Listing slightly to the right he tripped over Simon on his way to the couch and slumped instead to the floor, propping himself against the leather seat. To her great shock Sevystian was still breathing. Even the blood covering his shirt seemed to drying already. Danger prickled along the fine hairs on her neck, something was wrong with the whole scene. Emma shook off the feeling to focus on Simon who she could now see in his entirety. His face was bloodied and swollen. A chunk of the coffee table protruded out of his side and his blood was pooling rapidly on the rug beneath him. The 9mm he clutched in his hand still smoking.

Where there had been stillness before there was now a riot of action. Buchannan swooped in, applying pressure to Simon's wound and Vlad knelt down next to Sevystian.

"Kadir." Vlad spoke calmly, in clipped direct phrases. "Have Fields send for Ava."

Before he could move, the valet appeared from the hallway with a large duffle bag.

"I have already summoned her, Sir." Fields knelt between the two men and began unpacking bandages and other medical equipment. "She inquired why one such as yourself would need her particular brand of help. She was most insistent so I took the liberty of informing her of our guests."

"You what?" Sevystian wheezed. "That was not your place."

He shifted back clutching at his chest, grimacing in pain. Emma knew she had to be losing it. Shit, she actually thought she saw fangs there for a second.

"What can I do?" Emma asked shaking off Aaron's grip. Being scared of her own mother was bad enough she wasn't going to let a little blood stop her from saving her best friend's life. Hopping around the sofa, and dodging Aaron's attempts to keep her out of the mess, she squatted down by Fields.

Fields had discarded his jacket and rolled up his sleeves to help Buchannan work on Simon, and she realized she had missed something crucial about the man. A thick lined dagger tattooed down his forearm was a clear indication that this man was not as he first appeared. She had mistaken him for a spindly man, but the truth was that he was indeed stacked much like Buchannan with layers of lean wiry muscle. His posh demeanor was abandoned for the quick clipped speech of a field medic. He handed her a wad of bandages, instructing her to take over for Buchannan, so the other man could help assess the full extent of the injuries. She solemnly did as she was instructed, only once glancing over her shoulder to see Sevystian staring at her, his mouth pulled tight in pain.

"Shouldn't someone be helping him?" Emma watched Simon's blood seep over her fingers as she talked. It made her a little sick. She couldn't let that stop her from doing what she could. If she needed to throw up later, then she would; right now, it was all about keeping Simon alive.

"He'll be fine." Buchannan was making quick work of bandaging one of Simon's head wounds. "We need to focus on keeping this one alive until Ava can get here."

"Fuck Ava, we need an ambulance." Aaron spoke while

dialing when suddenly Kadir snatch the cell out of his hands and smashed it on the wall behind him. "Jesus, he's dying."

"But not dead." Ava was easily the most beautiful woman that Emma had ever seen in real life. "That is a very big difference."

Ava effused calm as she swayed more fully into the room, her long dark body draped casually in one of those spaghetti-strapped dresses Emma had always wanted to look good in. She knelt by Simon's injured side, tutting her tongue at the state of him, and began digging around in the heavy cloth satchel she had with her. She pulled out a sewing kit and several glass jars filled with varying pastes and salves, handing one filled with some sticky black tar like substance to Buchannan.

"Make sure it goes over his eyes." Ava turned back to Emma who was still holding pressure on Simon's wound, arms trembling. Ava's rich Parisian accent washed over her with gentle strength. "I need you to hold tight. Can you do that for me?"

Emma nodded, straightening her shoulders, a fresh gush of blood covering her hands. He was still breathing and as long as she could hear that subtle swoosh of air in and out, she had hope.

"Listen I don't know where you found this lady but you better hope that he doesn't die." Aaron threatened Kadir..

"Or what?" Kadir's voice was low as ever, a rumble in his chest that vibrated with intention out into the room. "Your friend pulled a gun. You are not here in any official capacity. In fact, you illegally obtained the whereabouts of Ms. King. You have no threat worthy of action."

"How about this?" Aaron grabbed the lapels of Kadir's sport coat pulling them roughly down, forcing him to stoop. "If you don't call an ambulance and my friend dies, I am going to kill each and every one of you. Not even Emma will be able to stop me."

"That's quite a threat for such a small man." Kadir wrapped his hand around Aaron's throat, pressing him backwards until the Ranger was caught between the steel bar of Kadir's arm and the wall. "You wouldn't know where to start."

"Stop your bickering." Vlad was standing beside them, and Aaron for the life of him could not figure out how he had gotten there. "Get control of yourself. You are not some fledgling fresh out of the dark."

Kadir slid away from the human, chastised. He took a deep breath to regain some of his legendary control. Aaron didn't pose a great threat. He doubted the man could even fully comprehend what they were, but he did have a streak of boldness that had Kadir's well-honed instincts twitching for a fight. Kadir turned away.

Fields and Buchannan busied themselves with Ava's instructions, while Emma perched over Simon's side tremors wobbling down her arms. The hot glare of Sevystian's eyes cut a swath down his side. Kadir squatted down beside him and plucked his navy vest away from the bullet hole.

"Hurt much?" Kadir sniffed the air, it sizzled with spent gun powder. He had always hated the stuff. Maybe it had to do with all of the battlefields he had walked. It always coated his tongue and slid in great smoky gasps down the back of his throat where it would linger for hours.

"I could give you a personal demonstration if you are curious." Sevystian bit his words out from around his fangs.

"In this case ignorance is truly bliss." Kadir plucked at Sevystian's fine cotton dress shirt with a snort of derision.

"That is too bad. I thought it might be a bonding experience." Sevystian grunted with the effort to speak.

"You're funny when you're bleeding." Kadir took a closer look at the hole in his friend's chest. It had already stopped bleeding, which might have seemed like a good sign, but Kadir knew what it really meant. "You need to eat something. You don't have enough plasma to push the bullet out."

"Should I lap some off the floor then?" Sev stared at his friend cruelly. The smashed piece of lead already trying to work itself out of his pectoral. Without more sustenance, it would lodge there and the wound would heal over it forcing him to cut it out later. "Can you see it?"

"Yes." Kadir looked him in the eyes. "I'm going to need you not to scream."

Sevystian growled at him, annoyed at even the suggestion of such a weakness. Less than impressed by the show of intimidation Kadir rolled his eyes. He shook his shoulders loose and let his control drop. He could see better when he went full fang. His eyes dilated to use every spare glint of light. He dug his claws into Sev's chest, until he heard that ting that meant he had the piece of lead. True to his character, Sev didn't make a sound.

Across the room Emma was engrossed in Simon's injuries and Ava's instructions. Every time Emma would begin feeling overwhelmed by the blood or her fear, Ava seemed to know. She would turn and nod to the task at hand and for some reason all of the anxiety blasting around in Emma's head would quiet down. She was taking everything in stride until it came time to do the one thing she had been dreading since she had put her hands on Simon; the massive splinter of wood had to come out. Emma was spared any of the build-up when Ava reached back and yanked the thing out without so much as a how-do-you-do. Blood bubbled up again, slower this time, and Simon didn't react at all.

"Is he dying?" Emma kept her hands pressing in at the wound, not knowing any other way to help. "Like that should have hurt. He should be doing something, right?"

"It's good that he can't feel this." Ava was sewing him back together, not a single flutter ran down her fingers, her lightly accented voice steady. This was definitely not the first time that she had done something like this. "You can let go. The salves will stop the pain and the tonic slows the bleeding. He won't be losing anything he could not live without."

Emma drew her hands away from him, sliding off of her calves to sit fully on the floor. She watched Simon's chest relax as Ava fell into the rhythm of her stitches. Her legs burned with the effort to stay kneeling for so long. Simon's chest rose and fell in a steady motion.

Her world had narrowed down to one task and now that she was relieved of it, her eyes burned. Numbness spread from her fingertips in the familiar fashion of panic. Taking deep breaths in through her nose and out through her mouth she counted backwards from one hundred. It had always worked when Grams had told her to do it. She got to seventy-eight before the dark edges of her vision cleared. Looking around, she noticed Sevystian still leaning against the other sofa, breathing heavily, his mouth still tight. Worry shot through her again.

She crawled her way over to Sevystian and Kadir, sitting together in silence. Emma was pretty certain that her legs would buckle if she stood and even if they didn't, she would probably have slipped on the debris field that covered the floor. Kadir leaned against the couch beside him watching her in his predatory way, ignoring his friend in peril. Her hackles rose. Even though she had only known them a short while, Sevystian seemed the type of man who deserved better friends than a man willing to sit idly by and let him bleed to death. Did they both just think that the thing was just going to seal itself back up?

"Hey can you hear me?" Emma pushed herself between his knees planting her face right in front of his. "Sevystian?"

"Mm hmm." Sevystian grunted an affirmative, not elaborating any further.

"Kadir, get the first aid kit." She began plucking at his suit jacket trying to wrestle the thing off of his shoulders. He wouldn't cooperate. "Damn it Sev. Just let me help you. If we can stop the bleeding you'll have as good a chance as Simon and Ava is working magic with him."

Kadir actually laughed at that and it was the wrong fucking thing to do to her at the moment. With all of the adrenaline from the fight and her mother and a heaping dose of what she was going to call grief rage, Emma King was not to be trifled with. She leapt over Sev's outstretched leg and tackled Kadir to the ground. The attack must have surprised him, because before he could react he was staring up at Emma from the flat of his back while she wrung his throat like a bell.

"I swear to God, Kadir. If he dies I'm gonna blame you. You, insensitive prick. I don't care if it was Simon who shot 'em." Her Texas twang was strong when she was angry. She shook him a little more for good measure. "What kind of friend just sits there after his buddy has been shot? What kind of fucking asshole does that? I will kill you dead and then I'll bring you back to do it again. Do you understand me?"

Kadir didn't even have the decency to look blue in the face and that was another thing she was pissed about. Here she was covered elbows deep in viscera and these two looked like they were about to plan a night on the town. Anger gnawed in her belly, screaming for her to squeeze harder, make him as scared as she was. Kadir didn't look scared, if anything he looked bored with her attempts at violence.

"If you wanted to hurt me, you'll have to work a bit harder, darling." Kadir's voice didn't show the barest hint of strain.

"Fuck you." Emma howled, a drop of spittle landing on his upper lip. He licked it away with a leer that had Emma scrambling off of him. God, she was turning into a lunatic. The panic driven numbness was creeping up her fingers.

"Emma." Sevystian's calm voice broke through the shock of what she had just done. "I am certain that Kadir deserves all of this and more, but I will survive. It is no more than a scratch."

"Like hell it is." Emma pulled the cloth of his shirt away, intent on her own investigation of his injuries.

True to his word, all that was left of the bullet hole was a dint in his pectoral that barely oozed any blood at all. She sagged with relief against his chest and he cupped his arms around her, or more to the point he tried to. Emma pulled back to study his face, a look of hyper masculine satisfaction smothered the worry she had felt seconds before. It was the expression of a man looking at a trophy, something she had seen on the seldom occasion when her mother had introduced her to her step-father, Marcus. She hated it then and she hated it now. Emma pulled herself out of his embrace and slugged him square in the face.

"You know why." She said pointing at him, promptly climbing off of his lap, and slumped back over to check on Ava's progress with Simon. The other woman met her with a wet mushy kiss right on the lips.

"You beautiful darling, I've wanted to do that for ages." Ava was practically abuzz with pleasure. "Did it feel as good as it looked?'

"Yes and no." Emma snorted a surprised little laugh the taste of something minty lingering on her lips and shook out her hand while sending death glares at Sev who was holding his eye, perplexed.

"I can take care of that in a jiff." Ava reached into her bag of tricks as Emma was starting to think of it and produced a small jar of clear salve. It smelled wonderful and Emma instinctually rubbed it all over her hands. "That stuff's great for cramps too."

"Huh?" Emma's hands tingled with returning feeling and maybe whatever was in the salve. "I will have to try that out."

The waves of post adrenaline dizziness were crashing in her brain now.

CHAPTER 22

V lad watched the two women interact. Those two were going to be thick as thieves. He almost felt sorry for Sevystian. It was hard to see the purpose of his rash actions when it had caused such destruction and now they would have to deal with Aaron. A human knowing about their kind could be catastrophic. In the past, they might have thralled away his entire day, but with this many witnesses it could get messy. A messy thrall was the quickest path to mass discovery. A single human could be monitored, controlled, even extinguished should it become a necessity. Vlad liked Aaron well enough and he was a balm to Emma's loneliness.

Ava was wiping the tar black salve along the crooked line of stitches that was holding Simon's side together, while Emma held his other hand talking calmly to him like he could hear her. Vlad was certain that he was a million miles away by now. Even the cursory sniff at this distance told him that one of those salves was laced heavily with wormwood. The heavy smell of old-world magic made his teeth itch and he ran his gaze over Mr. Davis once more.

"Shall we." Vlad wafted his hand in the direction of his office.

"Fuck that noise, Dracula." Aaron whispered through his teeth at him glancing around to see if Emma had heard him. "I'm not about to wander into your vampire lair alone."

"You are already in mine." Vlad leveled his gaze to Aaron's, his mood towards the man quickly turning sour. "If I wanted you dead I would have killed you before you made it past the lobby."

"Fine." Aaron griped, stomping off in the direction that Vlad had gestured in, flinging open one of the French doors so hard it bounced against the wall. Vlad followed after him shooing off Kadir when he tried to follow.

"Alright." Aaron flung his arms out spinning on his heels, glaring openly at Vlad. "Let's hear it, but I'm telling you right now, man, if you say anything about making Emma one of your vampire brides there will be consequences."

"That is truly disgusting." Vlad snarled at him. "She is my blood, my kin. Do you really think I could be so craven?"

"I've seen people do a lot of fucked up shit, Dracula." Aaron flung himself onto the couch behind him and Vlad settled himself across from the Ranger. "And none of them were vampires. So, you tell me, how's this work for you?"

"She is the last known daughter of my human lineage." Vlad spoke carefully, watching the Ranger for signs of violence. "I am Royalty. We take our blood lines very seriously."

"Well Drac…" Aaron spit back.

"Do not call me that." Vlad sat forward. He was done taking heat from this fly of a man that he could so easily swat down and be done with this insipid conversation. If it weren't for Emma's fondness for him, Vlad might have done away with him, even if it would have broken a half-century streak of clean hands on his part.

"Little sensitive?" Aaron smirked at him.

"Annoyed." Vlad took a breath and collected his control.

"Mr. Davis, I believe that we can stop this cat and mouse game, seeing as we are both certain we are the cat. You know what I am, which puts me in a terribly precarious position. I do not wish to harm you, but I need to know that you do not pose a threat to my people."

"And I need to know you don't pose a threat to mine." Aaron sat forward staring hard into Vlad's gaze. "Your man, Sevystian, he didn't exactly help you out back there."

"I could argue that Simon did not help the matter either." Vlad was impressed by the calm way Aaron seemed to be handling the whole situation. Reason before reaction seemed to be the name of the game with this man, a trait Vlad valued very much. Under different circumstances Vlad might have tried to entice the man into the employ of Wallachia Holdings. "But I can appreciate that you both want Emma to be safe. Given what her mother and the Order have put her through, I believe it would be in her best interest if we put aside this contention between us so that we might better protect her."

"Does she know?" Aaron didn't fidget the way so many humans did when confronted with bigger predators than themselves.

"I had hoped that I might spare her from that bit of information." Vlad blinked slowly and leaned back into the sofa before finishing his thought. "But I very much doubt that I will be able to keep it from her now."

"And if she reacts poorly?" Aaron mirrored Vlad.

"Then she reacts poorly." Vlad sighed, a bit resigned to the idea of Emma hating the very notion of him. "If once this Order business is dealt with, she decides to be quit of my presence for the rest of her life, she will never hear from me again. But I cannot leave her to the clutches of these radicals."

"They really that bad?" Aaron scrubbed his face.

"I have memories of war and violence that spans centuries."

Vlad answered the younger man. "I have done horrible things. My journey has been dark and lined with the dead, but I take no pleasure in the injury I have caused. I have lived for more lifetimes than you can imagine trying to atone, to rise above the brutality of the past. As I live now, I am a modern man, a peaceful man, but these people worship Death, Mr. Davis. They murdered my wife and then cast her as a martyr for their cause. You would be insane not to fear their fervor."

"So that's a yes?" Aaron rubbed his palms on his knees his head tilted up, his eye barely unfocused. "I can't fucking believe I'm going to say this."

Aaron shook his head, letting his gaze skim over Vlad and fix on the floor. He was quiet for a long while, long enough that Vlad was not certain he wouldn't try and attack.

"If I trusted you," Aaron spoke to the rug, sighing deeply. "I don't have a choice, I either trust you or take my chances... Emma's chances with the Order."

"Whether you trust me or not is no concern of mine." Vlad studied the posture of the man in front of him. A study sort of resignation had fallen over the Ranger. Vlad could see it in the man's shoulders. "Emma's safety is not so easily forgotten as to be swayed by your trust."

"You seem to have forgotten Melissa," Aaron lifted his head, catching Vlad's dark eyes. "Explain how your family ends up in the Order, married to its leader. Where was your love of family then? Or is it only when it's convenient?"

"Family is never convenient," Vlad bit back his answer. He was angry and ashamed, Aaron was correct. Melissa should never been allowed to be approached by the Order, let alone inducted. "I have made mistakes Mr. Davis and my family has paid for them in blood. I do not intend to allow for such a fate to befall Emma. So I will ask you, do you mean to stand with me against the Order? Or are you content to stand in my way?"

Aaron held eye contact with Vlad, which impressed him more than he would say.

"I think we can understand each other, Mr. Tepes." Aaron raised an eyebrow at him and Vlad took it as the olive branch it was.

"Together then." Vlad smiled.

CHAPTER 23

Emma was hesitant to let Simon out of her sight, but she didn't want to crowd Ava as she instructed Kadir and Buchannan on how to get him into the elevator with the least amount of jostling. Fields stayed behind tutting his tongue at the mess they had left in the living-room, like an old hen, with no sign of the bad-ass mother-fucker who had swept in like a boss to keep Simon's insides on the inside. He was apparently the kind of man who didn't need you to know how tough he really was. He had shooed her off when she had tried to help pick up some of the debris. Sevystian had pulled himself up to stand, slightly hunched, propped against the arm of the couch, looking like warmed over liver.

"Are you okay?" Emma eyed him warily as she spoke, half convinced that a strong word might knock him down.

"No worries, sweet Emma." He smiled at her. A real honest to God smile, not one of his little lip twitches, and it was devastating. "Although I suppose you might not be as sweet as I had thought."

"I'm not going to apologize for that." Emma shoved her hands into her hips, her default battle stance. "I get that you don't like each other, but he is my best friend and I will not tolerate you hurting him again."

"Did you miss the part where your best friend shot me in the chest?" Sevystian growled his smile gone.

"No." Emma tilted her head and pursed her lips, taking a dramatic pause to really let her point sink in. "I also didn't miss the part where you started it."

"You are right." Sevystian nodded not really understanding. "But what he said to you was unacceptable. You are a princess and should be treated with respect."

"Yeah." Emma was kind of surprised that Sev was going straight for the pet names on this, but whatever, she could hang. "It was disrespectful and generally shitty of him to say, and I was handling it. Just so we're clear when I say handling it, I mean with my words, not trying to disembowel each other. That's not how grown-ups solve problems."

"It is in this house." Fields muttered under his breath as he made for one of the doors his arms loaded down with more scraps of wood than it looked like he should be able to carry for a man of his stature.

Screwing the sternest look she could muster onto her face, she rounded once again on Sevystian. She was thrown off by how pale he looked. Somehow, he was still standing, but for the life of her she didn't know how. A dark red stain had seeped through his shirt. She had seen the wound herself, he wasn't in any danger of dying. That, in and of itself, was impossible. Her stomach lurched at the thought that he and Simon could have so easily died tonight. She let her head fall forward hoping to stave off the nausea. That's when she saw it.

A glint of metal just beside the couch. Until that moment, she had been running on the idea that maybe the bullet had been faulty, that maybe Sevystian had been hit with shrapnel and not the brunt force of a 9mm at close range. The crushed bit of lead sitting on the floor tossed that theory to hell. That was a bullet. Covered in blood and breaking the laws of reality, that bit of metal was a spent bullet. Simon hadn't missed and Sevystian hadn't died. She didn't know how that was possible, but she could see the evidence of it. The panicked dizziness returned. Every breath felt like a battle, each shallower than the last. Then Sevystian was there, leaning his face down so that he could see her eyes.

"Emma." He tilted her chin up, like somehow he could see what was wrong if only he had better light. Concern colored every syllable he spoke. "What can I do? I am sorry that I have hurt you, that I let my temper lead my actions. I will not let that happen again. Let me escort you to Ava's so that you can see that your friend healed."

"And what about you?" She felt like a broken record.

"I am fine." He tucked her hand in the crook of his arm and started for the elevator, his pace slower than normal. "You saw for yourself, there is nothing for you to be worried about."

"But how?" The elevator dinged and they stepped on board.

"That is a story for later, I think." His steps faltered as they crossed the threshold into the elevator and he tucked her closer to his side. "For now, I will take you to Simon."

He looked worn, a sallow hue tinging the corners of his eyes. His mouth drawn tight in pain or contrition, Emma couldn't tell. Even so he still cut an intimidating figure against the cold steel interior of the elevator.

"Yeah." She huffed, drawing herself up to her not at all impressive five feet and four and a half inches. "Don't think I'm going to forget about this."

"I have no doubt that you will not." He grimaced.

CHAPTER 24

The elevator ride down to Ava's apartment was an endless string of intrusive thoughts all jumbling together until all of Emma's head was a blur. It was a good thing that Sevystian had guided her the whole way, a strong cool hand low on her back. The touch had sent a shiver down her spine, which she kind of hated. When Sev knocked on Ava's door. Kadir answered.

"Go ahead in. They're in the back bedroom." Kadir waved Emma inside, a peace offering of sorts. His shirt cuffs were rolled up and Emma could just make out in the thick bands of scars circling his wrists. "Sev, my brother. I would steer clear of Ava for a bit. She's..." He waggled his hand back and forth, like a tipping boat.

"Yeah." Buchannan wandered in behind him.

"He will be fine." Kadir hooked an arm around Buchannan's shoulders and Emma wondered how such a strongly built man had gotten band after band of scars like the ones he had. She stared for a second too long and he saw her. Meeting her eyes, his mouth was a thin line of disappointment, he gave his head a little shake: don't ask, his expression seemed to say.

"Let's head out huh? The witch has got this all sewn up.

Nothing we can do." Buchannan grinned toothily at his own pun. "Emmy-doll, we will leave you and your cowboy in capable hands."

Door closed, she followed the soft sound of off-key humming that was trilling through the living room. She felt like she had wandered into a bordello. Pillows and tufted cushions scattered across the floor and a large hookah pipe sat carelessly in the corner, smelling sweetly of clover and vanilla. For a moment, she stopped to wonder at the bookshelf after book-shelf stacked full of ancient-looking, leather-bound books and bottles full of mystery liquids; jars with incomprehensible labels. The humming stopped and Emma turned abruptly to spot Ava leaning casually against the wall.

"Would you like to see him?" Ava was as calm as ever, her dress covered in drying blood. "He's not exactly coherent, but it would be nice for him to hear a familiar voice."

"You are some kind of witch doctor if he is awake already." Emma felt the bands of worry around her heart snap. She followed Ava into the bedroom, admiring the woman, not for the first time.

"You can drop the doctor bit." Ava's voice was low and strong and Emma could detect the faint inflections of a French accent.

Once she stepped into the bedroom, in overdrawn moment of silence, Emma watched Simon's chest rise and fall in an easy rhythm. "So." Emma blinked slowly, trying to process Ava's confession. "Witches are a thing?"

Ava watched her with keen eyes as if she expected Emma to freak out.

Witches. Witches, the plural of witch. More than one witch. Emma rolled it around in her head, trying to picture Ava on a broom stick.

"Are you like a real witch or is this a, I-had-a-phase-in-college, kind of a thing?" Emma continued to stare blankly at

Simon's chest rising and falling. She could practically hear her heart pounding in her chest. Maybe that's why he hadn't been hurt. That didn't make sense, witches weren't bullet-proof, at least not in the stories Emma had heard.

"My mother taught me." Ava tilted her head and Simon grunted a little, squirming before falling back into an easy unconsciousness.

"So, like a real witch." Emma chewed on her lip wondering if there was some type of etiquette for talking to witches. "With cauldrons and hooked noses? Like double, double, toil, and trouble?"

"A little less Shakespearian, but you've got the gist." Ava peeked at her from the corner of her eye. "Is that going to be a problem?"

"Are you going to turn me into a newt?" Emma tried to make a joke more to make herself feel less nervous than anything.

"Probably not." Ava couldn't keep the grin out of her voice.

"Uh, well that's good." Emma nodded falling silent. She didn't know what to say and to make matters worse she still had that absurdly high-school desire to have Ava think she was cool. Maybe it was the way that nothing seemed to phase her. Ava exuded that calm confidence that every teen-movie cool-girl always seemed to have. So, Emma stayed quiet for a little while just watching Simon fall into a magic induced slumber, hoping that Ava was the nice kind of witch.

"We can leave him be." Ava's voice was low and smoky. "Come on."

Ava took Emma's blood-crusted hand in her own, and led her out of the bedroom, past the Bohemian living-room and into a kitchen that looked like something out of an architectural digest. Jesus, how much money did these people have? A huge fireplace dominated one side of the space and the other side by a massive oven range, straight off the Thermador showroom. Everything was in tones of grey and black. Even the countertop was a solid slate slab that seemed half-modern style and half ancient necessity.

"Pizza?" Ava was pulling a box of cold pizza out of the fridge like she hadn't just saved her friend's life and admitted that she was a witch.

Yep totally normal, nothing to see here, folks.

"Uh?" Emma was taken aback by the casual ease with which Ava navigated the room and the conversation.

"I'll take that as a yes." She opened the box, pulled out a slice, and flung the box down on the table between them before pulling out a chair. "So, I bet you've got questions."

Emma nodded pulling out her own chair before opening up the box of pizza and inspecting it. Pepperoni, she didn't know why but she had been expecting something more exotic, like anchovies and pineapple or something.

"There's no eye of newt, on there or anything." Ava talked around a mouth full of cheese and Emma felt a little better that maybe she wasn't completely perfect.

"Right." Emma reached for a piece but noticing the crusts of Simon's blood still coating her fingers. Ava didn't seem bothered by it. Emma on the other hand, felt her stomach roll. She scooted her chair back and it made an awful scratching noise on the floor. Ava didn't say anything, she just munched on, her eyes following Emma around the room. The sink was full of various dishes waiting to be cleaned and the soap was a thick white slab speckled with oatmeal and lavender leaves. "Is that why they called you?"

"Huh?" Mouth still full, Ava knitted her brows together in confusion. "Oh, for Simon. Because I'm a witch?"

"Yeah, 'cause you're a witch." Emma continued to scrub her hand. "How are you so calm about this?"

"It isn't like it's the first time. There is a certain amount of gore in the magic. You get used to it." Ava shrugged stuffing the last of her crust in her mouth before searching the box for her next piece.

"So, this is like a regular thing for you?" Emma wiped her hands on a clean-looking towel. "Does Vlad like call just you for this kind of thing?"

"No." Ava picked some pepperoni off of the top of a slice and popped it in her mouth, chewing and swallowing this time before she spoke again. "Vlad doesn't really need me for this kind of work. I do a bit of this and a little of that for the company. I do pretty well with some outside contracts."

"Pretty well." Emma snorted, giving Ava a smile.

"Yeah." She smiled back in her enigmatic way. "Magic has some advantages."

"So, you what?" Emma took a piece of pizza, trying to look casual. "Magicked all this into place?"

"Some of it, but it isn't like the laws of physics don't apply just 'cause I've got mad skill with a cauldron, darling." Ava leaned back taking another bite. "Everything has to be conjured from something, so is the way of the world. Mostly I trade favors."

"What did you trade Vlad for this place?" Emma's uneaten pizza hung limply in her hand, so she took a bite, more for something to do than anything else.

"I do favors for people." Her voice was thick with humor, now. "In return, sometimes they give me things. Sometimes they do me a favor and sometimes they give me lots and lots of money."

"That sounds pretty suspicious, you know that, right?" Emma took another bite of pizza, watching Ava who didn't seem offended by the accusation in the slightest. "Like you sound like a noir film, femme fatale. Like, I'm kinda expecting Humphrey Bogart to pop out of the pantry."

"Well, here's looking at you kid." Ava threw a pepperoni at Emma hitting her square in the cleavage. Both women stared at it for a few seconds before bursting out laughing. It built into a peak of tearful laughs that wheezed out of them both and left Emma gasping for breath. Ava grabbed for a pitcher of water on the table, summoning two glasses from the cupboard with a flick of her wrist, only to have Emma start laughing again and almost spilling the water everywhere.

Emma took a few fortifying breaths, sipping on her water, wanting to ask a million question but not knowing what would be offensive or not. She really didn't want to insult Ava, she had just saved Simon's life. "Do you like being a witch?"

"That's what you're going with?" Ava rolled her eyes, pulling off a bit of cheese, leaning her head back to languidly drop it into her mouth. Emma shrugged, feeling a little stupid. "Alright, I'll play." She sat forward putting her elbows on the table and used her half eat piece of pizza to gesture. "I love it. It's like being one with the universe."

"Really?" Emma was surprised that her answer was so hipster.

"Sometimes." Ava tossed the last hunk of her pizza crust back into the box. "Magic doesn't really need wands and spells and incantations. What magic needs to work is intention, force of will. Witches learned to harness our will, our intention to make magic work for us. Regular people do it sometimes, when they want something bad enough."

"So." Emma squinted into the water in front of her. "Basically, you're telling me we're all witches."

"No. Not that you wouldn't look amazing dancing naked under the solstice moon, but..." Ava's eyes twinkled with mischief again like she could sense Emma's discomfort with something so sexual.

"But?"

"Witches are born with an innate sense of power. There are thousands of legends regarding how we got our powers. I have no idea what origin story is true. The long and the short of it is that most witches are born."

"Okay wait." Emma gulped down some water. "Most? Like, if someone tried really hard and practiced a whole lot they could use magic?"

"Weirder things have happened." Ava stood up shoving the now empty pizza box into a garbage can. Looking up she met Emma's eyes. "You want to know if you could do magic, right?" Emma nodded slowly. "Theoretically, yes. But at the same time, you could also theoretically become a physicist, or a surgeon. Even cradle witches have to study and hone their craft. For regular people who didn't grow up with magic potions in their pantries, I have no idea how hard you'd have to work to get there."

Emma let herself imagine for single second what it would be like to be rid of her mother with a flick of her wrist. What would it be like to be powerful? What would be like to be free?

There was a grunt and low moaning that told them that Simon was awake. Both women turned to the large archway leading into the den.

"I should go check on your cowboy, huh?" Ava didn't say anything else, gliding out of the room with an elegance that Emma never thought she could mimic.

"He's not mine." Emma's response was second nature, a perfunctory thing she had become used to saying to other women in regards to Simon.

"Good to know." Ava winked at her and as she turned out of sight.

Emma followed her into a bedroom where Simon struggled to sit up, head still covered in the thick black salve, hand wrapped white-knuckled around Ava's upper arm. She was shushing him gently and telling him that he was going to be alright.

"Simon." Emma scooted on to the bed next to Simon and

tried not to be offended when he flinched away from her touch. "Honey, it's me. Emma."

"Emma." Simon voice was slurred and strained but he relaxed into her touch all the same. "Safe. You're safe."

"Yeah." She tried to wipe his brow, but it was covered in the salve. "You scared us."

"Home." Simon grunted, pain blooming across his features. "Ugh!"

Emma watched Simon struggle to find the words he was looking for, his features splotchy red where she could make out skin from under the mixtures of potions Ava had covered him with. By some miracle and some chanting on Ava's part Simon dipped out of consciousness. Vomit threatened at the back of Emma's throat. How had her life become this? How had she made Simon's life this? The Order had brought them all to this, chased her up into the tower, but Emma had brought the Order in to his life. The tingling numbness was back in her fingers and she had to rush out of the room.

The den was not the best place to have a panic attack, the lights were too low and the bookshelves were filled with strange objects that only served to remind her of just how far from the world she had shared with Grams this place was. Then again, Grams had spent years writing letters to Vlad. Maybe this would have been a drop in the bucket for her. That thought spiraled out of control in her mind as the countless possibilities sounded off one by one. Emma collapsed onto a low-slung sofa.

"He's sleeping now." Ava swished out of the bedroom and over to Emma. She folded the ends of her dress over her legs to sit crisscrossed on one of the thousand floor-pillows tossed carelessly over the sofa so close Emma could feel her heat. "Are you feeling alright?"

"I don't know."

"Liar." Ava had her eyes closed, stretching her finger tips to the ceiling. The scene of painted stars danced as she beckoned them. "It is normal, I would think. To worry about a wounded friend, about your place in this new world with magic and monsters."

"I don't think you're a monster, Ava." Emma watched the stars shifting on the ceiling trying to breathe through her panic attack.

"I didn't think you did." Ava stretched her arms across her chest, finally looking at Emma. "What about Vlad?"

"What do you mean?" Emma could hear how naïve she sounded.

"Are you sure you want to know?" Ava laid her head on Emma's lap.

"Not knowing wouldn't be any better." Emma looked down into Ava's large brown eyes. It seemed as if the knowledge of the world could lie somewhere in their depths.

"I suppose it does not." Ava shrugged. "But I am a witch. A real burn her at the stake, hooked nosed, if she floats hang her, witch. I will always choose to know."

"Point taken." Emma watched the milky way twirl gloriously for a moment before rolling her head onto the back of the couch. "Would you tell me if Vlad was a bad guy?"

"What do you mean?" Ava sat up crowding into Emma's personal space.

"Like." She drew out her breath taking a second to collect her thoughts. "Would you tell me if he was a murderer, and stuff like that?"

"Stuff like that?" Ava gave Emma a hard stare. "Vlad is a vampire, There are entire lifetimes of history to explain. Each of us, for however long we occupy this flesh, are bound to accumulate some wrongful deeds. I don't believe that it is my place to judge something wrong or right. And I certainly do not believe that I can make that judgment for you. Let him tell you his story and then you can make your decisions."

"A vampire?" Emma closed her eyes, trying to merge her imagination with the flesh and blood truth of the Vlad she knew. It was easier than she would have thought. "I didn't say I wanted to know."

"No, you didn't." Ava sighed, stretching out her long limbs again, sending a star streaking across the ceiling. "Does it change who he is?"

"I don't know." Emma fiddled with her hands, not looking at the witch.

"That's bullshit and you know it." She stared Emma down, until she looked up. "You're going to need to make up your mind. He's at the door."

"Sure." Emma groaned. "You're psychic too?"

"I was never a gifted clairvoyant." Ava just laughed uproariously and pointed to a large crystal ball on a book shelf, where Vlad's distorted face was passing in and out of focus. She rolled her head onto the back of the couch, closing her eyes. "If you want me to make him go away I will."

"He's your boss. You wouldn't." Emma rolled onto her knees feeling every bit the ungraceful plebian that she knew herself to be.

"A witch answers to no one." Ava just hummed, vaguely conscious. "If you want him gone, maybe I turn him into a newt."

"A vampire newt?" Emma felt the bubble of fear burst in her chest with the ridiculousness of her situation, of her life.

Ava laughed, it was a velvety sound that put Emma at ease.

"I'll let you know if I want you to turn him into a newt." Emma stood up, ready to face her demon.

"Have Fields ring me." Ava mused.

When she opened the door, Vlad was pacing. She stood there with the door half open waiting for him to speak. Twice he made like he was going to speak and then stopped, his shoulders hunched in defeat.

"So." Emma figured that if she wanted to get anything done she was going to have to do it herself; as usual. "You know a witch."

"Yes." He nodded.

"And you're a vampire." Emma kept scanning the hallway beyond the monster, she was just getting to know.

"Is it wrong that I am glad that she was the one to tell you?" Vlad seemed to sag with relief. "I know that I should prefer to have done it myself, but I cannot say that I envy her the task. Do you have questions?"

"Oh, you know only about a million." Emma tried to keep it light, sounding to herself cringingly dismissive.

"Maybe start with something small?" Vlad stopped his pacing, his body now unnaturally still as he waited for her to speak.

"Are we even related?" It came out of her mouth before she could think.

"Yes." He took a single step forward, but stopped before Emma shut the door. "I am your Grandfather eleven times removed."

"Guess I should call you Grandpa?" She closed her eyes and shook her head trying to wrap her mind around the idea.

"I think we should stick with Vlad for now." The lines at the corner of his eyes seemed deeper than they had seemed that morning. "Is Simon sleeping comfortably?" He maintained his intense stare as he cast around for anything that might be easier for them to talk about.

"Yes." Emma tried to keep eye contact, but it became too much and she looked back over her shoulder. The stars were still dancing on the ceiling. "Wow, this is harder to talk about than the time Grams tried to give me the "birds and the bees" talk."

"I can only imagine." Vlad chuckled. "Would it be too bold

to ask if you might want to join me in my office where we might sit in privacy and speak on this matter?"

"I'm not sure that I trust you." Her honesty was probably going to get her killed some day.

"Did you believe you could trust me before?" Vlad looked heartbroken, sadness in his black eyes.

"Sometimes." She kept a grip on Ava's door, ready to slam it.

"Not this morning I expect." Vlad cursed under his breath.

"Yeah, not so much." She watched him pace, trying to decide if she trusted him. "At the restaurant? Yeah, I trusted you."

"It is not an easy thing, trust." Vlad stopped. "There is little I could say to insure you of my intentions. I can only ask that you bestow that trust to me. I am the same man you called upon in your time of need. The same man whom Iliza called upon. Please give me the chance to prove this to you."

"I have a lot of questions." Emma looked over her shoulder again, Ava was gone and the stars on the ceiling were stationary once more.

"And I will answer all that I can." He tucked his head down into his chest curtly. "I need you to understand that there are some stories that are not mine to tell. All those that are, I will share with you."

"And you need to understand that I am doing my dead level best not to freak out." Emma clenched her fist, the feeling of her fingernails digging into her palms grounding her. Stepping out from the doorway felt surreal, looking forward she was starting to think that surreal would be her new way of life. "I get that this is all old hat for you but I am going to need a little adjustment time. Also, how did I not notice that you don't have a reflection? That just seems like something I should have noticed."

"I am afraid that the Vampire myths that you are used to might have it a bit wrong on that account." Vlad motioned for her to lead the way and fought a scowl of shame when she waited for him to match her speed. Keeping him in her eyeline. "I might be to blame for... well, most of them. It seemed prudent at the time to sort of build up our mystique with some misdirection."

"I swear to you, if the next words out of your mouth are pick a card, I am going to walk out." Emma laid her palm on the scanner for the private elevator and shot Vlad a sideways smirk. She wanted to trust him. Emma wanted that feeling of safety of home, of family to be true even now. He smirked back and she noticed that he didn't have any fangs. "So, do they like retreat into your skull or something?"

"Hum?" Vlad looked at her curiously, and she motioned with her hand to his mouth. "I suppose they retract into our gums. In truth, there is much about our kind that remains unknown, even to those of us who have undergone the transformation."

The elevator doors opened with their unsettling silence and Vlad boarded, his reflection twitching with a smile. Emma followed him, a tinge of humor tinting her fear.

"Why does this place make me feel like I am in a James Bond movie?" She leaned on a hand rail, looking at Vlad's refection, waiting for him to talk again. The million and one questions she had for him swirled in her head until she couldn't pick a single other one from the jumbled mess.

"I couldn't really say." He turned to her smiling in his charming fatherly way. "Maybe it's all the accents."

"Ha." Emma cupped her hand over her mouth, embarrassed she had practically barked at him. A joke cracking vampire was not how she had seen the night going.

"You know Sevystian pretends he is Bratva to win in the boardroom." Vlad grinned continuing on with the conversation, without hesitation he placed his hand on the small of her back leading her out of elevator when the doors opened into his apartment. "Well I suppose that it is not so much that he pretends to be in the mafia, more so that he does not dispel the idea that he is. I try to tell him that one day that will come back to him, but he does not listen."

As her saggy moccasins squeaked on Vlad's hardwoods, Emma realized how all those girls in the horror movies always ended up dead in the shower. It wasn't a big decision that killed you, it was the thousand little ones that paved the way for that one big stupid thing that did you in. Looking back over the events, which lead her here with this man, she couldn't see the one that had tipped the scale.

"I have no intentions of harming you, Emma." Vlad stepped into the vestibule of his apartment. "Your well-being has always been of upmost importance to me. Please let me explain."

Maybe she was being an idiot, or maybe she was about to be a late-night snack for the richest vampire in Texas. Oh God, how many vampires were in Texas? Were there like random cowboy vampires roaming the ranches of Abilene?

"I am not going to suddenly turn into a monster." The renewed panic must have shown on her face. He sat on one of the low couches and motioned for her to do the same. "I am still the same man who you trusted before. I was a vampire then, I am a vampire now."

"It isn't that simple is it though?" Emma sat.

"No, it is not." He looked weary and Emma wondered how old he really was. "I would dearly like to tell you that I am as I am because of some chance happenstance, or a curse, but I cannot. I asked to be this way."

"Why?" If Vlad had been expecting judgment instead he received only curiosity.

"The world was burning." He focused his eyes on the floor and began the story he hadn't shared since Sevystian lay cold and hungry on that cave floor all those centuries ago.

CHAPTER 25

*T*he bodies of men and women were scattered across the village streets. The children had been taken back to the enemy camps to be used for labor or converted to soldiers. This village was not the first of its kind nor would it be the last if Vlad, Crowned Prince of Wallachia, could not find a way to stem the flood of invading Ottomans. The tentative peace between the invaders and his principality had been slipping for months. Wallachian scouts had been to the edge of the Ottoman camps and reported movement on a massive scale. In this village, Vlad and the leader of his private guard, Aleckzander, surveyed a still-burning forge, its blacksmith dead on the ground.

"What is there to be done against such evil, my Prince?" Aleckzander spoke formally as he was wont to do. "Is there even a way to stop such madness, when it is so set on controlling the world?"

"If there is I will find it." Vlad stood at the mouth of the forge, watching its dying coals. Sevystian, the commander of his army, rode through the dense mist of the early evening, coming to a stop before Vlad. "What news have you?"

"More movement." He slung himself out of the saddle, throwing the reigns to a squire. "They've broken down tents, and saddled *enough horses to move half the army. Thousands of men. Your Highness, they mean war."*

"Alekzander, I need you to take Mina back to the castle." Vlad hated leaving her anywhere he could not protect her himself. "It is two day's ride to the nearest village. Sevystian, send out your fastest men to warn them. All able men must be readied for the fight ahead."

Vlad motioned for the squire to bring his own dark mount to him. The horse whinnied in displeasure, the scent of fire and rot hung heavy in the air. Before he could swing himself on to the creature, Sevystian stopped him.

"There will be no bargaining with them this time." His advisor was most certainly correct. "If you ride into their camp they will take you hostage, maybe worse. They do not wish for peace."

"You are right, Sevystian." Vlad swung up onto the horse and pointed him into the forest towards the mountains. "I am not seeking peace with these new enemies, but a truce with an old one."

What Alekzander and Sevystian spoke about as he rode away he could only guess. He doubted that it was civil. Those two were about as friendly to one another as wet cats. They would do as they were ordered should they come to blows Vlad had little doubt Sevystian could find someone else to escort his beloved Mina. The forest was dense and even the most experienced of hunters had gotten lost within its expansive wilderness. Wind rustled the leaves and vermin chattered in the branches just overhead. The trees of this forest had been there for centuries and had seen countless caravans traverse its depths in hopes of peace and of war. Never, he suspected, had they seen someone bent on the brutal alliance he now sought.

After hours of riding in the moonless dark, the canopy broke and the stars shone down on him, illuminating the steep and rocky path to his destination. He hoped in the smallest section of his heart that none of his fear was real, that this monster with whom he sought council was merely a legend. Vlad knew better. The stories the monk of Snagov told were not parables to scare peasants into the confessionals. Vlad had seen the sightless stares and trembling finger of the old men who shared such tales. Still, the fear rising in his chest hoped that he was chasing a phantasm. All around him the noise of the forest stopped, the quiet crept along the ground and swallowed horse and rider until the only noise was the heavy synchronized breathing of them both. His mount stumbled on the loose rocks covering the ground and Vlad dismounted, unable to ride any further in such terrain. Leaving the reigns to dangle, he began the climb upward to the darkest part of the cliff guided by rumor and dread in his heart.

At the highest point he could reach, the sheer rock face gave way to a thin dark cave, and Vlad took a moment to take in the expansive view of the wilderness. In the daylight, he was certain he would be able to see straight to the Ottoman camps. A strong hand gripped him by the neck of his leathers and dragged him inside the cave. Blinded by the sudden absence of light. He knew now why the old monks trembled. The rocks of the cave's narrow entrance tore at his arms as whatever had him pulled him further into the dark. Robbed of his sight, Vlad struggled to focus his other senses. Even so only the scrape of his boots against the rocky floor made a sound. His fingers grasped for purchases on the cave's walls only to find open air as the tunnels stretched out into a chamber, the dimensions of which Vlad had no concept. He was dropped without ceremony in a puddle of cold viscous liquid.

"What are you creature?" Vlad asked, sensing movement in the space around his face.

"You came to me, Prince." It was a woman's voice, light and airy. Something that he might have associated with the springtime had he been feeling poetic. "You seek something from me. It would be ill-mannered of you to cast aspersions as to what I may be."

"You are right." Vlad crawled to his knees and sat back on his heels eyes uselessly surveying the void. His head swiveling this way and that with each feather wisp of cold air as whatever she was moved around him. "I know the legends of what lurks in these woods and I am only human, and our fear makes our manners abandon us. Please, forgive me."

"You are charming, Prince." Whatever she was slid down to sit in front of him, even though his eyes had now adjusted to the shocking darkness he saw only the barest outline of her form. She reached out and brushed one sharp claw down the hook of his nose. "Though not handsome. Tell me, what is it you seek?"

"A means to the end." He swallowed hard. "Something to end the war that is coming. It is swallowing up villages. My people, our traditions will be forfeit to these invaders. I seek something that will stop them."

"And you think that I am that thing?" She continued to tap and slide her claws along his face. "Do you think that I alone could stop an army such as the Ottoman's? The Earth trembles when they march. What kind of creature do you think I am, that wields such tremendous power that a task such as yours requires? Or perhaps, the more important question is: why would a monster such as you imagine bother herself with such a human affair? Could I not sit here, watching them devour the world and then when the last one dies endure whomever comes next? I have no reason to interfere, if I am as you desire me to be, this creature of your legends."

"The priests say the villagers still bring the forest offerings of blood." Vlad fought the urge to move out of the creatures grip. How could she sit there and speak so callously of the destruction of his people? "Who will bring it to you when they are all dead? Your way of life will be gone as surely as my people will be. I am asking you to help yourself as well as your Prince."

"You are not my Prince." The claws that had tripped so delicately over his skin now sunk into his throat tearing so deeply he knew his death was a certainty. "Remember, you asked for this."

Then something pressed warm and wet over his mouth, sliding up his nose, leaving no choice other than for him to swallow. Desperately he tried to suck in air, getting only the slow drip of liquid filling him with fire. His vision dulled and the limp paralysis of unconsciousness over took him.

It was later, in shock, that he awoke. The cavern that he found *himself in was massive. He groaned and rolled onto his side to prop himself up. Any movement set his body aflame. Every inch of him was white hot with pain. Something or someone moved in the corner of his vision. As they moved closer he was still unsure if it was human or beast. Vlad blinked sluggishly, roughly wiping at his eyes unsure how they could have adjusted to such a perfect darkness.*

Plainly female, she was smaller than he had imagined. She stood over him, her heavy dark hair swept away from her face by intricate braids, her eyes wide violet gems in her pale face. Her mouth was moving, but he couldn't make out what she was saying. Sounds were filtering in as if from far away and then all at once he could hear everything, like being trampled by a herd of horses. Then she was forcing a rough-edged vessel to his lips, pouring a thick liquid down his throat.

"You will either learn to control it or you will not." She didn't bother to help him sit up, forcing him to hold the roughly-built cup she offered him. "I am sure a Prince, such as you are, will manage." She scoffed over his title with a roll of her entrancing eyes. "There is more over there, if you need it."

She nodded over to a ditch in the floor of the cave where the unmistakable color of blood, puddled. He was almost certain that it was where she had dropped him earlier. The creature shrugged on a heavy coat made of different pelts before stopping to gather some blood in a wine skin.

"You're leaving me?" Vlad was shocked. "You would make me thus, only to abandon your creation?"

"You asked for the means." She watched him with her khol blackened eyes. She seemed no more in a hurry than before she had killed him, nor more inclined to help. "I have given you the means you sought to finish this war. You are young still and your passion will lead you. They brought you here and it is they who made you as you are now. I was merely the tool. It is a rarity to see such bravery in a mortal. Your enemies know this, it is time you learned it as well."

"Yet, still you leave?" Vlad growled, the sound rippling out of his throat. "When your Prince has more to learn?"

"I told you, you are not my Prince." She eyed him speculatively, as if she might choose to end his life once more, this time with a greater sense of finality. His maker picked up a satchel heavy with goods and meandered out of the cave. "I follow no orders but my own. Your power is owed to me now. You should be grateful I did not see fit to take a pound of flesh. I am, however, taking your horse. Find your own way, Prince."

～

"So, wait, "Emma gawked at Vlad for a second. "She just freaking left you there? In a cave, in the middle of the forest?"

"Yes." Vlad rubbed his eyes, he could feel the twinge of a tension headache starting between them. "She left me to recover on my own. It took me two days to adjust to my body. The transition makes you faster, it expands your mind, your endurance. I was changed, beyond anything I had thought possible."

"Did it work?" Emma was leaning forward her face propped in her hands, elbows resting on her knees. "For your people, against the Ottoman?"

"Yes." For a moment, Vlad was lost in his own history, regret passing over his face. "There was a cost, though. Many of my people still died, some at my own hand."

"I don't understand." Emma's emotions rushed over her face plainly.

"It is better that you do not. It is a mark of the brutality of my times. A mark of the weakness in my character. You are not weak." He stood, ashamed of himself and wishing that he did not have to tell her what she had every right to know. "I used the sick and the dying people of the villages as warnings to those invaders who passed over our borders. I planted forests of the dead to ward off those who would have taken every life, not just those few who were sacrificed."

"How could you do that?" Emma felt like the churning sick in her belly threatening to make its presence known. She was sitting next to a murderer who had killed his own people. What had he accomplished? How could she have ever liked him? "I...I don't understand. How could you, just kill people?"

"I didn't just kill people." Vlad hung his head, defeat in his voice. "I built monuments of fear, in the hopes that the Ottomans would come to think of my lands as an untouchable waste ruled by a vicious monster. It only takes one story to build a kingdom of rumors. And so, I became the mad Prince, disowned by God and the church, who feasted on the blood of his enemies and his people alike."

"And you wanted that?" She felt like she was glued to the couch.

There was a lesson in his story if she could see beyond her own fear. Emma wondered what Grams would think of her friend if she had known his life was built on blood and brutality. Maybe that was the lesson Emma was looking for. Maybe Grams had known, understood that sometimes the price of things must be paid in flesh. Blinking back the gush of sadness, Emma studied Vlad, seeing now the missing piece whose absence had convinced her to try to leave the tower to protect him; power. It might be dark and unnatural, but it was what made him free. Emma was jealous and it kept her glued to her seat.

"Yes." He watched her carefully. "I wanted the Sultan's army to be so afraid that they would not march against me. The troops he sent to face us stood little chance against myself and Sevystian. We let our thirst plow through their ranks until they were driven back and we could return to our lives."

"You slaughtered people." She rubbed her hands over her

eyes. Her jealousy made her nauseous as images of the carnage that Vlad had wrought in the world played in her head. The blood on their hands was unimaginable. Sure, she had friends who had joined the army, and she was pretty sure that they had killed people in service to their country. This was beyond that. Fuck, Simon had killed the guy who had shot him in the leg at that raid and he was still messed up over it. Vlad didn't seem like he really cared one way or the other. "Do you even care?"

"I care a great deal." Vlad met her eyes with his black stare. "Every leader has had to make a choice between what is good for the few and what is good for the many. I had taken lives even before I was turned. I am not going to tell you I am a good man, if I can even claim to be one at all, but I am not some mindless creature who wants the world to burn."

"Would it really have been so bad?" Emma tried not to gag. "Would it have really been awful to just let them have your land?"

"It wasn't my pride I wanted to keep intact." Vlad dropped his head into his hands, drained and unwilling to watch Emma's disgust. "They were taking our children, our resources. My people lived in fear of the next demand they would make of us. They looked to me. They needed me to take the action they could not."

"And it worked?" She asked the question almost certain of its answer.

"Yes."

Silence strung between them as Emma searched her heart for outrage that wasn't there. She wished it were. Wished that the "forest of the dead" Vlad had created scared her more than it did. There was a worry like a termite burrowing in the back of her mind, that faced with the choice between her mother and freedom Emma would cross the same lines. Self preservation is a powerful thing.

"Earlier in the kitchen, you said the Order killed your

wife." Emma watched his shoulders tense with a sting of recollection. The subject had been a dangerous one earlier. She pressed on. "Is that why you left? Did they find you out? Did she?"

"Yes and no." The tension in Vlad's shoulders aged and the air in the room felt heavy. "I could never have kept myself from Mina. There were no lies between us. From the moment I returned to the moment she took her last breath she knew the truth of me. Blood sustains us all Emma. In Mina's blood the Order was born. I trusted someone I should not have because I was prideful and believed my position gave me invincibility. There were moments, even before my transition, that I believed I was a god among men."

"Wasn't Jesus betrayed for thirty pieces of silver?" Emma could feel his grief as keenly as she felt her own and she wanted to reach for him to comfort him as she wanted to be.

"I didn't die for anyone's sins, not when I have so many of my own to pay for." Vlad paused, taking a great shaking breath and Emma thought he might cry. "One of my advisors and the leader of my personal guard, Aleckzander, took my transformation as evidence god had forsaken me and my rule. He perverted the fear I had turned on my enemies to motivate his group of insurrectionists. They were zealots really, looking for a cause."

"He killed her out of spite? Jealousy?" A spike of worry ran through Emma veins.

"Aleckzander had always loved Mina and at first I thought it a good thing. That he would protect her all the better for that love." Vlad gave Emma a small smile. "I believe it was what planted the seeds of darkness in his heart. In his eyes, I was no longer living and so she had fulfilled her vows to me and to God. Mina refused his advances. He twisted this in his mind. To him it was only my continued existence which stood between him and ownership of her. He polluted the faith of those zealots, and eventually they stormed the castle in an attempt to kill me and save her."

Vlad broke eye contact, settling his elbows on his knees.

"Sevystian heard the whispers of dissent and took my sons to a monastery where they would be safe." His chest heaved. "But Mina and I were too wrapped up in one another and the new child she was expecting. I did not want to kill another of my people and I did not want for my wife to see blood on my hands. I believe now that I should have killed them all."

"Why?" Emma's voice sounded so small even to her.

"That was the beginning of The Order of the Divine Mortality." He held her gaze until she couldn't stand the sadness in his eyes a moment longer. "Alekzander thought I was an abomination to the life only his God could give and take. The thought that a creature such as I could exist, let alone touch what he thought of as his, poisoned his mind, his faith. That rabble of traitors chased us to the balcony of Mina's rooms and when she begged for the sake of our unborn child Alekzander forced her over the edge."

"What did you do?" Tears stung at her eyes as he spoke.

"I couldn't reach her." His voice was stiff, emotion biting at the back of his throat. "I jumped after her, hoping that I might somehow save her. There was nothing. Alekzander galvanized her death as the final act of a true and divine woman faced with birthing a monstrosity. She became the Order's Divine Mortal, an example to all and I was forced to flee my own lands. The law demanded my eldest son take the throne in my stead. I was survived and so too was The Order of Divine Mortality."

"I am sorry." Emma was sitting awkwardly on the sofa wondering if she should hug him when she felt the couch dip under his weight. He sat with his elbows on his knees mirroring her stance. Waiting perhaps, for her to run screaming out of the room. "Wow, I don't think there are any words suitable for this situation."

"No, there are not." Vlad leaned back resting his head against the back of the sofa, taking deep breathes. "I have spent five centuries and a dozen languages looking for the right words and still I am at a loss."

"Sevystian has been with you all this time?" Emma mimicked his position, with her head on the back of the couch pointedly looking only at the ceiling. "He fled with you?"

"No." Vlad rolled his eyes towards Emma, to watch her reaction. "The Order didn't know what he was; he was safe. So, he raised my sons in my place. Advised them until it was clear that he was no longer aging. By then the fevered actions of the Order had died down, but as you know, it has never truly disappeared. Sevystian faked his death and left his home in the dead of night. That is not really my story to tell."

Emma nodded and they both sat in silence for a while as she digested the new revelations of the evening. Thunder and lightning rolled past the windows, it was calming somehow to hear the relentless storm pouring down outside.

"Someday I might come to regret this." Emma spoke to the ceiling.

"I will do everything within my power to keep that from happening." Vlad took a knee beside the sofa, pulling Emma's hand over his heart and forcing her to look him in the eyes. "I will protect you. You are my family."

"I hope you mean that." Emma smiled sadly at him.

"No more." The earnest quality of his voice made her heart ache. "The Order has taken much from us."

"No more," Emma repeated like a vow and for a second her hand where it touch Vlad's chest felt hot.

CHAPTER 26

Sevystian found them sitting side by side staring at the ceiling sometime later. He knocked softly on the doorjamb, and their heads turned in unison, striking Sevystian with their resemblance; the dark hair and brow strong enough to mark them siblings.

"May I come in?" Sev waited in the door way his body half in and half out of the room. "I do not wish to disturb you."

"Come Sev." Vlad sat up straight motioning for his old friend to sit down on the opposing couch. "What is it?"

"I just wanted to check in." Sitting down, he let his eyes skate over Emma who was now sitting up, her legs crossed underneath her. "Ranger Davis has been brought up to speed with the situation. He is with Buchannan and Kadir going over tower security."

"That had better not be code for we ate him." Emma squinted at Sevystian, her eye contact was unbearable and he looked down at his hands. A family trait to be sure. "I get that you guys might want a late-night snack after your big throw down. But for real, he had better be fine."

"You know." He wasn't asking a question. "Your friend is perfectly healthy when I left he was discussing perimeter weaknesses with Kadir. He seemed particularly insistent that we assess the parking structure."

"Yeah." She seemed satisfied by that answer. "His sister was taken from her dorm's parking garage. No one ever found her, so..."

"So, you have become his surrogate sister." Vlad seemed pleased. "Perhaps I am not your only family."

"Maybe not." Emma shrugged in a limp sort of fashion, her whole body exhausted. She pushed some rogue hairs away from her face and scratched her chest where Simon's dried blood stuck her shirt to her skin, ugh. She really could sleep for like at least a week. Sweat had dried sticky on her neck and upper lip. Her skin felt tight with sleeplessness, and she had the uncomfortable feeling that the two vampires could probably smell all of her stressed out pheromones. Standing up she addressed the two men. "Alright guys, this has been great, but..."

"You cannot leave." Sevystian interrupted her, jumping to his feet, stepping deftly around the table to take hold of her hands. Holding them with firm insistence, he demanded her eye contact. "If you know about us you must know the danger that the Order poses."

"Dude." Emma looked down at herself and back at the ever-dapper Sevystian and fought the desire to laugh hysterically at the sight the pair of them must have made standing together; Her in her bloody T-shirt and yoga pants and Sevystian, slightly less bloody in his three-piece suit, a half-baked Bonnie and Clyde. "Not leaving the building. I was thinking a shower would be good. You know, maybe washing off my friend's blood." She said everything slowly, too slowly, opening her mouth too wide, as if she were explaining it to a toddler or a drunken stranger. "Do you think that would be okay with you?"

The sarcasm was not lost on Sevystian. He was a smart man who enjoyed a quick wit as much as anyone, even if he seldom showed his appreciation. He wasn't focused on the sneer in her words. As close as he was, he could now smell the slow drip of fresh human blood and his stomach growled loudly over the sound of the rain outside.

"Seriously man, eat a sandwich." Teasing him before her eyes went wide with realization. "Oh, shit. I'm the sandwich!"

"No." Vlad stood taking Emma's hands out of Sevystian's and lead her towards the door. "You are Emma. No one thinks of you as food. Why don't you go up to your room and rest? Simon and Aaron are in good hands."

"Fine." Emma sighed, already imagining the massive shower waiting for her in the Green Suit.. "But if you hear something from my mother or Simon gets worse you have to come get me."

"Is there an "or-else" coming?" Sevystian goaded her a little.

Vlad kissed her on the forehead in his fatherly sort of way and turned back to Sevystian. Emma took the chance to stick her tongue out at Sev over Vlad's shoulder before flitting out into the living-room.

He was tempted to chase after her, but Vlad wouldn't like it and the look of admonishment that he was already giving Sevystian was enough to stop him in his tracks. Vlad shut the doors with a deafening crack, or perhaps it was not quite so deafening as it was that Sevystian needed to feed. Hunger burned at his skin and in his gums. The tantalizing smell of fresh blood that permeated the main level of Vlad's home teased him with the promise of something sweet and hot. The bottles of O-negative in his refrigerator taunted him with their underwhelming nutrition. Emma smelled of oranges and smoke. Some lizard-brained part of him wanted to hunt her through the tower, imagined the chase like it had been when he had first transitioned. Another sign of his hunger taking over, of his reason giving way to the tremors of depravation wobbling out from his guts.

"You neglect yourself." Vlad had never cared much for subtly.

"My time is better spent here. I will tend to those things when there is time for them." Sevystian, who had spent his human life as the third son of a poor and lesser lord, indulged his greedier half in the finer elements of tact.

"Very well." Vlad moved around the room pulling out two crystal tumblers off of a shelf, pouring two fingers of whiskey for them both. "You are not my subordinate, no longer subject to the whims of my rule." He poured another finger for good measure and raised a brow at the clinched jaw of his companion. "Do you truly believe that you are capable of protecting my family as you are now?"

Sevystian took the glass Vlad offered him. He poured the amber liquid down his throat before settling down on the couch opposite the Prince. The sentiment hit him harder than he thought. Sevystian had known it was coming, felt it himself as Emma had drawn closer, her scent dredging up his primal, violent desires. The idea that his Prince would believe him unfit to watch over his family still struck him.

"If you wish, I can call Kadir now and you can go over with him the manner in which you wish Emma to be attended to." His voice hissed out, resentful, his fangs biting into his lip. The bottles would only sustain him for so long, and whether he found it distasteful or not, mattered little if he wanted to survive.

"There is no need for dramatics." Vlad sipped his whiskey calmly, studying his friend over the rim of his glass. "I am unsure that a man who cannot care for himself could truly take on the responsibility of another. You need to eat." Vlad held up his hand to stave off Sev's protests. "Not just those bottled dinners Fields gets for you. You need something robust, and it wouldn't kill you to put a vegetable in your mouth every now and then."

"It might." Sevystian sneered at Vlad, his fangs on full display. He clicked his claws against the crystal.

"You know, you aren't half as funny when you can't keep your fangs in your mouth." Vlad took another slow sip. Sev's growl rolled through the room like the trailing thunder of the storm outside. "When was the last time you drank something that wasn't out of a bottle?"

"Night before last." Sev lied coolly, their conversation irritating him. He sucked in an unneeded breath from between his clinched teeth, trying to center his focus on something other than the scent of blood still lingering in the room.

"If you want me to believe that you took more than a sip from that frail woman you have lost your mind." Vlad called his bluff with a wave of his hand. "Go home, go out. I don't care, but do not come back in to here until you have eaten and slept."

"I thought I was no longer subject to your law?" Sevystian slammed his tumbler down on the table, before storming out of the room and presumably out of the apartment entirely.

CHAPTER 27

Sevystian made it as far as the living-room. Emma was standing at the top of the stairs, her hair still wet from the shower, swallowed up by one of Vlad's fluffy white robes. Her mouth hung open in shock or wonder; he couldn't really tell. To say his mind was elsewhere would have been an understatement.

"Are you okay?" Her soft, rich voice swamped his senses. He noticed her bare feet, the slope of her calves as they peeked out from under the robe as she walked down the stairs. He shook his head trying to dislodge whatever fluff had lodged its way in there.

She stopped halfway down the grand staircase, her gaze following his every movement. It wasn't the look of horror that he was well accustomed to humans wearing. It was enough to remind him that he was at the limits of his self-control, enough to remind him that Vlad was correct in his assumptions.

"I have made you uncomfortable." He wanted to turn away, to walk out and leave her safely behind, but he found himself rooted to the floor. "My apologies."

"A man's gotta eat, right?" Her smile was disingenuous. Her

attempt to lighten the situation unconvincing to them both. "Do you know where Fields is?"

She swallowed hard and he followed the little clench of her neck muscles as she did. He clenched his fist, letting the sharp gouge of his claws into his palms ground him. He shook his head again, not trusting himself.

"I was hoping he might know where I could wash these." For the first time he noticed the bundle of bloodied clothes she was clutching in her hand. "I kinda need something to wear."

She folded her arms across her chest, pushing her breasts up and Sevystian groaned. Emma might actually kill him.

"No." He bit the word out. Cutting it so sharply around his teeth Emma actually flinched. He took a deep breath, closing his eyes, he tried to center himself, take back some of that control that had been slipping away the longer he went without. He could hear Vlad making his way out of his office. "I am sure that Vlad has something that will fit you."

"Okay..." Emma took a tentative step down the stairs towards him. "Are you sure you're alright?"

"I will be fine." Sevystian chanced a glance into her face, but lost himself somewhere along the slope of her neck. With her mass of wild curls pulled high on her head the tender flesh of her neck pulsed unprotected, calling out to his need for blood. Violence and hunger twisted into a hard ball in his gut.

She had stopped again, two steps from the bottom of the staircase to look over his shoulder at the man Sevystian had lost track of. Unthinkable, without distraction, without fail, Sevystian had prided himself on his vigilance. To be brought thusly by human desire, by the weakness of hunger, tore at him.

"Something I can help you with?" Vlad's cold enigmatic voice turned Sevystian's stomach.

"I will take my leave." Sevystian nodded to Emma before storming out of the apartment.

"He is very frustrating." Emma waved her hand in the direction of the elevators.

"Yes." Vlad taking his cues from Emma's now relaxed posture. "Might I be able to assist?"

"Not unless you have some clean clothes I could borrow or something not covered in blood." Emma looked mournfully down at the grimy wad of clothing in her hands. "I'd take anything at this point."

"I think we might have something." Vlad hummed.

CHAPTER 28

Emma sat half-slumped over the granite countertop of the island in what she was coming to think of as Vlad's formal kitchen, eating a surprisingly good sandwich. Vlad sat across from her, eating his own sandwich, casting a worried eye at her every time he thought she wasn't looking. Hooking one of her feet on a rung of the stool she was perched on, she watched him until, he looked at her again.

"Dude." Emma rolled her eyes playfully.

"Forgive me." Vlad put his sandwich down, dusting off invisible crumbs, tidily collecting them on his plate. "I believe I am waiting for you to run screaming from the building."

"Nah." She spoke around the bite of food in her mouth, shrugging then swallowing.

"You are a singular woman, Emma." Vlad smiled softly, the expression lighting up his dark face.

"Doubtful." Emma tapped her foot, chewing on the last of her food thoughtfully. "I don't really see how I have much of a choice one way or the other. I leave, Mom and the Order nab me off the street, and turn me into one of their minions. Or, I stay here and possibly get eaten in my sleep."

"I would never." Vlad stared at the veins in the granite.

"Maybe not you." Emma took another bite of her sandwich wondering if this was what shock felt like. Wondering if this was some post-trauma pre-panic madness setting in that she should sit unwavering, eating peanut butter and jelly sandwiches with an actual nightmare. "Life has a way of getting worse when you think you're at the bottom."

"I will not allow it." Vlad straightened his already stiff posture.

"You're not really in control of my life though." She took another bite, rolling over the feeling of confidence the knowledge gave her. "The best laid plans and all that."

"That seems rather blasé. This is your life we are talking about." Vlad watched her chew the last of her sandwich. "I should have rather hoped you would take it more seriously."

"When I was six, my mother picked me up from school early." Emma sipped her water. "She took me to this rundown old church downtown where all these guys were moving these crates and stuff. They treated her like she was the pope or something. Those guys stopped everything for her. Melissa made us kneel on the floor for so long my legs went numb. When the police finally found me I couldn't walk." Emma chewed on the corner lip. "They had to carry me out of there. The whole time Melissa was going off about the sacrifice of the Divine Mortal. She told me that no one has a choice in their lives but to serve the Divine Mortal. Hell she kept it up when the cops were putting her in cuffs."

"Where was this?" Vlad's voice was unrecognizable even to himself. The anger and dread gouging out parts of his calm veneer.

"It's gone now." Emma leaned back in her stool tilting it onto the back legs, enjoying that weightless second before it was too far to pull back. "Burned down like ten years ago. 'Snot really the point though. The point is that she took me there and told me all of these stories about monsters who forsake the divine rite of death. She was telling me about you. Don't think she knew it was you, but now... It feels weirdly right that I should stay."

"How do you mean?" Vlad hadn't been expecting this.

"Who else is there that would understand?" Emma tilted the stool back again letting go of the counter for a moment, her stomach dropped. "Simon and Aaron, they try, but are they ever going to really understand what it's like to be afraid of them?"

"I suppose not." Vlad sucked in air through his nose. "I am sorry that this is your path. I wish it were not so."

"If wishes were diamonds, honey." The legs of her stool clattered to the ground. "So, do you have to kill the people you eat or is it just like a sip here and there, and you're good? Do you only drink the blood of virgins?"

"The blood of virgins?" Vlad choked on the surprise laughter clogging his throat.

"Don't laugh at me, buddy." Emma chuckled to herself, having gotten the effect she wanted.

"I do not mean to offend." Vlad was still chuckling when a streak of lightning flashed across the darkened window. It was getting late, and even he was tired now. "I cannot speak for all vampire-kind as we all have our own habits, but no, we do not have to feed off virgin blood. I sometimes wonder if that was not a rumor started by the Order so as to bed more women." It was Emma's turn to laugh. "As for killing to feed, well that I can only speak for myself and my coven, but we do not kill those we feed from. It always seemed a rather silly notion to me, that vampires would drain their prey dry. That would be as if you ate a whole pizza every time you ate."

"Hey now." Emma grinned pointing her chip-dusted finger

at him again, mischief in her eyes. "Every pizza is a personal pizza if you try hard and believe in yourself."

Vlad smiled at her. Even if he didn't quite get the joke, he still appreciated her humor in the face of such strange circumstances.

"I took a chance. But honestly, I get it, humans don't eat a whole cow every time we want a burger." Emma joked.

"And yet ironically you have to kill the cow to get the burger." Vlad took a sip of his water.

"Hey, you aren't exactly a vegan, so don't get preachy." Emma dusted off her hands, before taking a long gulp of her own water, watching him as he watched her, until he broke and chuckled.

"I relent." He continued to chuckle wiping a tear from the corner of his eye.

"So, you are more of a take-what-you-need kind of vampire." She nodded, finding this conclusion acceptable, trying not to think what the unacceptable answer might have been. "I can see that. You probably wouldn't be able to stay in one place very long if every time you moved there the bodies started piling up."

"No." Vlad started to put away the remnants of their meal. "I have grown much attached to this city. It has a veracity to it that I enjoy."

"I wouldn't really know." Emma finished her water and stood, retying the robe over her pajamas and made to leave the kitchen.

"Off to bed?" Vlad asked.

"Not just yet." Emma yawned stretching her arms high over her head. "I thought I would grab my clothes and check on Simon one more time before I hit the hay." Vlad nodded and she made her way out of the kitchen only to turn right back around. "So, which way am I going?"

"Apartment 1904." Vlad smiled warmly at her, she could tell he was wearing out though. It had been another long day for both of them.

"Thanks." She was starting to feel the night catching up with her.

CHAPTER 29

That spy-thriller feeling didn't extend to riding Vlad's fancy private elevator alone. She still thought it was cool that she had to do a palm scan just to go down few floors. Emma found Ava's apartment easy enough now that she knew where she was going. Just before she knocked, she heard a soft crash and what sounded like Ava admonishing someone inside. Emma hoped it was Aaron; she hadn't seen him since they had moved Simon to Ava's apartment earlier. Sure enough, Aaron opened the door when she knocked. He didn't look any worse for the wear, which Emma took that to mean that Sevystian had been true to his word.

"Hola, baby-girl." Aaron stood to the side all his swarthy charm amplified by the restless energy radiating from him. "Step inside and you can watch Simon try and defend your honor."

"He's up? Like up, up?" Emma stepped inside the bohemian apartment, surprised.

"You're asking me?" Aaron chuckled closing the door. "Girly, I don't know anything anymore. This morning I was sure that vampires were relegated to camp fire stories and teen romances, but now..."

Aaron let his voice trail off with a twirl of his hand and Emma got it, she really did. They were going through pretty much the same shtick right now, grant it he hadn't just met his great great, great... wait how many great was Vlad from her? She didn't even want to think about it, she just wanted to check on Simon make sure that he was healing up okay and go to bed. She had thought that she might sleep at Ava's tonight just so he could see a familiar face when he woke up, but if Aaron was going to be here she was going back to Vlad's. For a selfish moment, she contemplated just going back up to the Green Suite and not even seeing Simon, but her guilt got the better of her.

He wasn't on the bed like he had been when she left. But some squawking and whisper-yelling lead Emma to the bathroom. Simon leaned over one of the sinks washing the black salve from his face. The battered mess it had been before was reduced to a few scrapes and a bruise under his eye.

"Ava, you're amazing." Emma smiled at the woman sitting with her legs folded under her on the counter across from the door. Simon swung around, sloshing water down his bare chest. His blood shot eyes searched for Emma.

"Emmy." He made to take a step but winced in pain and she stopped him, coming fully into the room to hug him gently. "I am so glad you're safe."

"So, you know?" She pulled back slightly from the hug, just far enough to look up into his eyes.

"Oh, he knows." Aaron sidled into the space, propping one arm on the door jam, leaning on it casually. "Yeah Six-Guns-McGregor over here tried to run back in there when I told 'em. Lucky for us Ava's the quicker draw."

"You pulled a gun on him?" Emma stared disbelieving at Ava.

"No." Aaron grinned devilishly like he had the juiciest piece of gossip. "But she does have some serious skills with that squirt bottle." Emma quirked an eyebrow at Simon who blushed all the way down his chest. "See, can't deny it, can you, bro?"

"Shut up." Simon spat at Aaron without any real malice. "But Emma, vampires? Really? I think I'm allowed to be worried."

"Yeah." Emma nodded a little stepping out of his arms and leaning against the counter. "I get it."

"I mean, if I didn't think we needed them to keep you safe I would stake them all but..." Simon didn't get to finish his thought because a spritz of water hit him dead between the eyes. He flinched, sputtering and wiping his face.

"See?" Aaron nodded to Ava who held a little purple spray bottle at the ready. "Fucking sniper that one."

"Fastest shot in the Quarter, darling." Ava twirled the bottle over her finger like a revolver, before she winked at Aaron.

"They eat people!" Simon flinched again when a jet of water hit him in the chest.

"No." Ava rolled her eyes to Emma with another shake of her head. "They drink blood, there is a difference."

"Not really." Simon threw his hands up but the action pulled on the wound on his side and he brought them back down, wincing as he held his side.

"Yes really." It was Aaron this time, instead of Ava. "It's not like there's a troupe of Hannibal Lectors running around. They take a little bit and then they let everybody go home happy. So, yeah it is different."

"Go home happy?" Simon held his hand up to Ava, ready to fend off another aquatic assault. "Are you fucking kidding me? There's no way that the people they drain are consenting to that."

"Does the cow consent to being your steak, cowboy?" Ava asked sarcasm and annoyance clear in her voice.

"People aren't cows, Ava." Simon got another spritz for that one and another for insolence.

"You didn't seemed to have the same issue when you shot Sevystian." Emma propped her hands on her hips, some part of her had known they were going to have a fight when he woke up. Emma had hoped she had until the morning.

"I was defending myself." Simon's lips pursed in disapproval. "He's fine. He's already dead for fuck's sake."

"A fact that you didn't know!" Emma threw her hands up.

"Well I know he's dead now." Simon's eyebrows rose to new heights of petulance.

"Sevystian has died, that does not mean he is dead. He is vampire." Ava cocked her head to the side and gave Simon a look that clearly said you're-fucking-wrong-dick-head. "His death was the catalyst for his transformation from human to vampire. Death is not always a permanent thing. Many human holy men do not believe death to be the end. Reincarnation, heaven, hell they all begin with death."

"Stop it." Hands still raised in a sign of compliance, Simon made his case. "Listen I'm not saying that they need to be exterminated or anything." Ava made to say something but he plowed through. "I'm just saying that we should take some distance, as soon as we can. They can have their parts of the city and we can have ours."

"Dude!" Aaron pushed off of the door jamb, tucked his thumbs into his belt loops and swaggered into the room. "You didn't just say that. That is some real bull shit."

"How?" Simon looked genuinely perplexed. "How?"

"Their side and our side?" Aaron cocked his hip out and sized Simon up. "Come on bro. You can see where I'm going with this. Should I throw down some train tracks? I mean you're stupid but you're not that stupid."

"You are seriously defending the bloodsuckers who did this to me." Simon put his arms out to highlight the damage his body had taken. All of the lightly tanned and freckled skin of his left side was covered in bruises and deep jagged gash covered in a black salve that turned his side into a ghastly flesh canyon. "And this wasn't even them making dinner, this was just a temper tantrum."

"Listen, I came down to see if you were okay." Emma felt queasy. Simon was her best friend, but Vlad was family. It had been something she had wanted since she was little, and even if it was a slim hope at the weirdest of weird situations, Emma wanted to see if it could be real. "Vlad's my grandfather, Simon. I want to know him. So, if you need me, or you miraculously decide to dig your head out of your ass, you can come find me."

"How am I the one with his head in his ass?" Simon looked around for support, completely perplexed.

"I've known he was dangerous since he talked to me at the graveyard." Emma closed her eyes with a sigh. "But hugs and kittens aren't going to protect me from the Order."

"No." Simon limped toward her and grabbed her by the shoulders, the purple-yellow bruises on his face giving him a ghoulish countenance. "I am. I can protect you."

"I can't ask you to do that Simon." Emma felt queasy.

"I think the bigger question is how you ever thought you weren't." Aaron grinned at Simon, who promptly flicked him off.

Emma walked out of the bathroom, passing a wall of windows that looked out of the sparkling lights of downtown. The traffic lights glared off the wet concrete and she imagined the swish-swish rhythm of windshield wipers of the passing cars below. The kind she used to fall asleep to as a child wishing that she would wake up in Grams old powder blue hatch back on the way home from Bingo at the senior center. She paused there long enough for Simon to catch up with her. Emma could hear Simon limping toward her. She felt her chest contract.

"Don't leave angry," he said.

She remembered sitting at his hospital bed when he had been shot, wondering if they were going to have to amputate his leg. Emma hadn't left his side for a week, and now all she wanted was to be far away from him. A dozen things had happened in the last seventy-two hours, including burying her grandmother for Christ sake, and the only people not telling her what to do or how to feel were the fucking vampires. So, he could damn well suffer if he thought she was making bad choices.

"I'll do whatever I fucking want to Simon." She turned to Ava, her voice softening ever so slightly. "Feel free to kick him out whenever you want."

"Oh, hell no." Simon posted up, puffing out his chest as he spoke. "I'm not leaving you with a bunch of monsters by yourself."

"You don't have to ask Emma," Simon sighed. "I'm your best friend, you're my best friend it's what we do. It's what I do. It's my job."

"Well, this isn't your decision." Emma's chest filled to bursting with churning feelings she didn't particularly want to examine.

"Yeah, but you're too close to it to be making the right one." Simon frowned at her, his face so disapproving Emma nearly cowed to it.

Instead she took a step back and then another, until she was out of his reach and turned away.

"What did you just call me?" It was Ava's turned to look pissed off.

"I didn't call you anything." Simon was confused again. "I was talking about Vlad and his people; that shit is unnatural, you're... you're..."

"A witch." Ava was done letting him hunt for the right words. "People like you have hunted and prosecuted my kind for millennia and still I saved your life. That unnatural shit, it isn't just vampires. There is a whole world you've never seen, you've never been a part of, and all this fear you have is just ignorance."

"I don't want to sound ungrateful, you've been amazing." Simon flapped his arms helplessly, which for such a strongly built man was pretty funny and Emma felt a hint of a smile at the corners of her lips. "But, those blood suckers are dangerous."

"You don't think I'm dangerous?" Ava snarled. "I could have let you die up there, same as them. I could run wild through the streets and bring this city to its knees, same as them. I don't, because I can choose not to, just the same as those blood-suckers upstairs. Next time you want to go running your mouth about something you know literally nothing about, think again."

"Yes ma'am." Simon, stared at the finger pressing him into the wall of windows, leaving traces of the black salve streaked across the pane.

"Ay dios mio." Aaron purred. "Girly you are some kind of pistol. I love it, take me home with you."

"You're already here, Papi." Ava blew a kiss over her shoulder at him, before looking back at Simon to give him the stink eye.

Emma had stopped her escape to watch the whole thing. Everytime she thought she couldn't adore Ava any more, the woman went and gave her another reason. She was building up a serious girlcrush on that woman.

"I'm sorry." Simon pleaded with the room, or really pleaded as much as Simon ever let himself. "Ava, you're right. Emma please don't leave like this. I'm hurt. I'm angry. I woke up in the pitch-black thinking that I was dead."

"Pussy." Aaron joked.

"Fuck you, Aaron." Simon flicked him off again. "How are you so calm about all this shit, huh?"

"Maybe I'm just tougher than you." Aaron wagged his eyebrows at him and Simon gave him, his you're a big-bag-of-dicks face. "What? Abuela, was always on about monsters and stuff. Josie and I were practically raised by the boogey man."

"So, vampires are real, and you're all calm because your grandmother used to tell you ghost stories?" Simon wasn't buying it, but Ava still had a grip on that squirt bottle. It was just humiliating, he was a grown man, not a house cat.

"That and the guys showed me around the main security bank." Aaron shrugged, flattening his hair before dropping his arm back to his sides. "There is no way the Order is getting in here without these guys knowing about it. We've got nothing on their system, Buchannan has this shit locked down."

"Really?" Simon thought about it for a moment clenching and unclenching his fists. "Alright. So, everybody stays here," Simon said stopping Emma's retort with a raised hand. "I didn't mean in this apartment. I mean in the tower, where the Order can't get to you. I don't like it, but I will try."

"I'm still mad at you." Emma crossed her arms over her chest, squinting at Simon from across the room.

"I can work with that." Simon sighed a breath of relief. At least she was still talking to him. When Emma walked out like that it usually meant he was in for a full-fledged ice out. "Let me walk you up to Vlad's, maybe we can talk some more."

"Hold your horses, cowboy." Ava put her hand on his chest to keep him from going anywhere. "I know it doesn't look like it, but you are holding together with a stitch and a prayer. You are going to lay back down. Why do you think I had them bring you here in the first place?" Ava waved him over to the bed. Emma tried to come back in the room but Ava stopped her too.

"I'm fine." Simon grumbled. "I can walk her to the elevator."

Simon's whole body jerked with his next step, his face

contorted with the effort it was obviously taking him to keep moving. His chest convulsed with the quick shallow of the deeply pained. Emma felt the familiar pull to go to him. She was about to break. She was sliding towards him when Aaron took her elbow in his warm grip. His smile was grim as he ushered her to the door.

"How's that working for you?" Ava could hardly keep the laughter out of her voice as she mocked him. "Why yes Ava, you are so wise and so beautiful."

Emma and Aaron could hear her sing-song sarcasm as they walked to the door.

"Don't worry about him." Aaron said waiting at the door as Emma stood in the hall. "I'll stay with him and make sure he doesn't make himself any worse."

"Honestly, I'm a little worried that he's going to bait one of them into another fight." Emma picked at the belt of the robe.

"Hey, baby-girl." He tucked his finger under her chin meeting her green eyes with his coffee brown ones. "He'll come around. He's scared and trying really hard not to show it, but it's all just bravado."

"Where do you hide all this smart when you're playing cops and robbers?" Emma teased him a little hoping to break the awkward intimacy of the moment, not that she didn't love Aaron, but she wasn't up for this heart to heart right now.

"I tuck it right under my balls." There it was, the totally inappropriate humor that always put a smile on her face and kept the mood light. She smacked him in the chest, before pulling him into a hug goodnight.

"Night asshole." Emma squeezed him a little tighter than necessary before letting go. He blew her a kiss and shut the door as she made her way down the hall.

Sevystian had downed an entire bottle of cold blood while pacing his apartment. It had done exactly nothing to stave off his hunger. He knew Vlad was right, he knew that he was going have to seek out something hot and fresh. Stubbornness kept him pacing his black hardwood floor, a second half drunk bottle hanging limply from his hand. It tasted awful cold, too salty, thick as glue. His stomach turned over and he stopped setting the glass bottle down on the stone counter with a crack.

This wouldn't do, Vlad wouldn't let him help if he didn't get himself under control and he wasn't going to be able to do that without getting something real. Sev looked at his watch. If he left right now he would still have enough time to pick someone up at one of the bars close to the tower. He grabbed his jacket, balling the collar up in his fist. No one would see the wrinkled lapel in a dive bar, but huffed in frustration anyway, compulsively straightening it out as he slipped out the door.

A scent of smoke and citrus wafted around her. He didn't need to see her face to know it was Emma. Sevystian took a deep breath full of the fresh-washed scent of her hair before he even realized he had done it. He opened his mouth to apologize but the scent of fresh blood hit him and then suddenly it didn't matter what he said because the savory sweet scent of her was coating his mouth. Gone was the stench of the Ranger's dried blood. This was something altogether more luscious. He looked her up and down and she pulled her robe tighter around her freshly washed clothes, a barrier between them.

"You surprised me." He took a step back, feeling the door against his shoulders.

"I thought you vampire types were supposed to be able to sense us mere mortals from a mile off." She gave him a half smile. She seemed calmer now. "Sorry, bad joke."

The moment slowed nearly to stopping she scratched at her temple where the cut from Melissa's first attack began to ooze and Sevystian's control snapped. He darted forward, grasping Emma by the back of her neck. His claws digging into her hair and holding her just so. The flavor of her exploded on his tongue. She tasted of oranges and hearth herbs. He licked the blood off her temple his eyes closing of their own volition. Her skin was soft and lush under his tongue. A soft hiccupping sort of gasp drew his attention back to her face. The cupid's bow of her mouth barely open, pulling in shallow breaths.

A rush of cold shame ran over him and he pulled away from her. Emma was Vlad's flesh and blood not some one-night stand. There was a hazy, almost disappointed look in her eyes that Sevystian didn't understand. This should never have happened. In this state, he could have killed her, might have.

"I guess you never got that sandwich huh?" Her tone was light, but there was a rawness to it that had Sev taking a dangerous step closer.

He shook his head, his jaw too tight to push words around. He took a step closer, his eyes not focused on hers. More blood rushed up to her skin's surface and the struggle he had already lost once, became unbearable.

"Sevystian?" Her voice was so soft, unsure, maybe even scared; he couldn't tell for sure.

His jacket dropped in a swoosh to the floor as he gently cupped her face in one hand, turned her around, and backed her into the closed door. He cushioned her between the slick steel door and his chest bringing his mouth back to her flesh. Her skin felt hot on his cold lips.

He lapped up the smudge of blood that had pooled on her temple. Their breathing was getting heavier. She put one small, warm hand on his chest, sighing into his touch. A growl started low in his guts and he pulled at her hair wracked with a desire that he couldn't remember feeling since he transitioned. It was an entirely human desire to take her somewhere only he could see her, hold her, taste her. She gasped, high and breathy, and Sevystian felt like a bastard. Satisfied that he had cleaned every morsel of blood from her skin, he licked the gash softly. Already he could feel the wound closing, she needed to keep still. With a final swipe of his tongue he tugged her face back so he could inspect his work, his mind a haze of primitive needs. She whimpered, her teeth biting into her bottom lip as her eyes searched his face, the reality of his actions began to sizzle through the fog.

He let go of her hair and stepped back, not meeting her eyes, staring at his hands in horror. His shell colored claws still curving out like little daggers of betrayal from his fingers. He tried to swallow, just to clear his throat so he could explain himself, but his tongue felt thick. His mind spiraled with the thousand horrible things she was probably thinking about him at that instant.

She searched his face for an answer to his actions. He took another step back hoping that the space would be enough. The smoky bright scent of her followed him into the hall. The image of her braced, soft and breathless chased him until his back hit the wall. There was nowhere else for Sevystian to run and worse he didn't want to.

"Sevystian?" Emma's warm honey accent dripped over his name and he lost the fight for control. He stepped towards her.

CHAPTER 31

Simon laid back on the bed, breathing shallowly, hoping that he didn't look as weak as he felt. He didn't want Ava to think he was weak. She was the kind of woman that he would have had a hard time talking to at a bar. She looked like she might have wandered off some Riviera beach, that long dark mane of hair kept away from her face with a lattice work of thick braids. She walked back into the bedroom, arms full of jars and something that looked like a bundle of sticks. It was probably something witchy.

As if he wasn't in enough pain with all the new injuries he had sustained, his leg was aching. He rubbed it unconsciously. The pain must have shown in his face. Ava frowned at him, dumping her load on the sheets next to him. Someone had stripped the bed down to just the bottom sheet, which was probably for the best considering he was lying in a smudge of something black and slimy. Simon hoped that it wasn't coming out of him, because he was pretty certain that that wasn't a good thing.

Ava rounded the end of the bed, pulling the hem of her dress up to kneel at his hip and Simon absolutely did not look at the expanse of thigh laying against his. She pressed the edges of the tar like substance covering his side, grimacing when he flinched away from her touch. She didn't draw her hand back, walking her fingers firmly across his abdomen, she watched his face looking for how far out the pain radiated from his injury. Shrugging to herself she sat back, closed her eyes, and mumbled something to herself that sounded to Simon like mumbo jumbo; probably more magic.

"You're not going to like this." Ava exhaled, folding her hands in her lap and watching his face carefully.

"Not going to like it 'cause it's gonna hurt?" Simon's already thick Texas twang doubly so as he tried to fight the gnawing pain in his thigh. "'Cause I gotta tell you, honey, I think I've just about topped out on that one."

"I need to take this off." She nodded at his side. "I need to see what's going on under there. I don't like how much pain you're in. This should be helping more than it is."

"Honestly, honey." Simon gritted his teeth against the pain shooting up into his hip. "It's my thigh more than anything. It's been a... stressful day, to say the least."

"Old football injury?" Ava's hazel eyes sparkled with mischief.

"Nah." He struggled to sit up against the pillows to no avail. Ava leaned over to help rearrange him and he caught a whiff of hops and sunshine. "Caught a bullet in there awhile back, nicked the bone, it was a whole mess. It's all healed up now, got a rod in there now. Still hurts like a son of a bitch if I put too much stress on it, though."

"Well, I would say a death match with Dracula's right-hand man probably counts as stressful." She was half-laughing and Simon was too distracted by the smoky tenor of her voice to realize why she was patting his bandage. Without any warning, she ripped the bandage off.

"Oh, fuck you." He shouted, his voice raw. Bolting up in surprise, before his exhaustion got the better of him, he fell back into the pillows, his breath rushing out of him in gush of hot air.

"You look like you are in perfect shape to do that, cowboy." She wasn't looking at his face, she was already gently prodding at the hole in his side.

"What?" He was confused, breathing hard, only half aware of the room anymore.

"Looks like it is coming together nicely." She reached for one of her jars, leaning her whole body over his legs, the soft jersey of her dress feathering over his bare stomach. "You really need to rest. It's mostly done, but you could still tear it open, if you move too much."

"Can't you wave your magic stick bundle over it and make it all better?" Simon grunted. "I thought you were supposed to be a witch."

"Sleeping is old school magic." She popped open a lid of one of the jars. Digging her fingers into it she pulled out something slimy green that smelled faintly bitter, like burnt sugar.

"Sleep's sleep." Simon winced as she plopped a large dollop of the slime right where the torn pieces of his flesh were knitting back together. "No need to pretend it's something it's not."

Once the cold shock of the goo wore off Simon realized the discomfort that had him rolling onto his hip was gone. He felt each intercostal muscle relax individually.

"Think what you want." Ava muttered, used to non-believers. "Doctors can't decide why we need it, or how much we need, or why when we don't have it our bodies shut down, but you're probably right. Nothing as simple as sleep could ever be magic."

"See, your words say I'm right, but your voice says, I'm a bag of dicks." Simon felt like he was high. Whatever she had just rubbed on him was good shit.

"Oh, does it?" The sarcasm dripped out of her mouth.

She was fiddling with another jar, black stuff this time,

rubbing it between her hands and muttering her nonsense words again. Simon knew he was running to the far field of intoxication when it started to glow red. He felt like he was being told some incredible secret of the universe, so he knew he had to be totally shit-faced. What the hell was in the green slime? When did he ever contemplate the secrets of the universe? The closest he ever came to that was drinking Shiner on his crappy old couch watching Ancient Aliens on the History channel. Then she put her hands on him and it was like a crest broke in his chest, spilling all the exhaustion out into his limbs.

"What is happening?" His voice felt like it was coming from so far away. She was standing up and he tried to reach out for her but his arms were too heavy. He should have felt panicked, he was injured in a stranger's apartment, a witch's apartment, and yet he wasn't in the least bit concerned.

"Just a little magic to help you get to the good part." She winked at him grabbing her bundle of special sticks and walking into the bathroom. She peeked back around the doorway to add, "Now I'm going to take my magic sticks and smudge all of your shitty prejudice out of my bathroom. Thanks for that by the way."

Simon didn't know what smudging was but he smelled smoke and heard Ava singing Hotel California softly as he drifted off, so he was going to assume it meant something witchy. The better question was why he had always associated that song with witches. Man, he was fucked up. The world was drifting out, blurring into darkness at the edges, it felt like ecstasy. Maybe Ava was right and sleep was magic.

CHAPTER 32

"Hey Sev!" Buchannan ran down the hall in front of a small harem of beautiful women he and Kadir were heralding to his apartment.

"What?" Sevystian stopped dead in his tracks the space between them just barely respectable.

"Thought you might want to join us." Buchannan clapped Sev on the back and Emma screwed on her most casual "I was definitely not just lusting after your bestie" smile ." Emmy-doll, I thought you went to bed."

"I was just about to." She blinked slowly, trying to collect her thoughts. "I wanted to check on Simon before I went to bed."

"Yeah?" Buchannan was an artist at the craft of casual conversation. "Ava's a genius, right? Easy on the eyes too. Don't tell her I told you that though, she's a viper when she wants to be."

"Your secret's safe with me." Emma felt her smile turn genuine. Sevystian was crowding her again.

"Hey Sev." Buchannan spoke to him softly, his grip on the taller man's shoulder digging in. "Think you might want to come with Kadir and I."

It was a not -so-subtle hint and Sevystian took it. Stepping back, he shook off whatever spell had captured him. He waved them off and Emma didn't try and analyze why she was so pleased he did. Buchannan nodded with a little salute to Emma and jogged back to door Kadir had disappeared through.

"You should go with them." Emma whispered, a hiccup in her voice. "Just point me towards the elevator."

"Please." Sevystian sounded woefully confused and disheartened. "I have frightened you. I will not leave you until I know that you are well. My actions were brutish. I have let myself go too long without proper feeding and I lost control of myself. For that I am deeply ashamed. Can you find it within your power to forgive me of this transgression?"

"Consider yourself forgiven." Emma pulled the belt of her robe tight enough that she could feel it nip in at her ribs. "I'll leave you to your victim."

"Don't use that word." Sevystian growled slamming his fist into the wall. His lips pulling tight over his fangs. "It makes it sound like I'm attacking them in alleyways. Leaving them for dead, or worse."

Sev crowded into her space, leveraging his weight on the fist still planted on the wall beside her.

"I know you're not." Emma looked up into his eyes, still glazed over from something Emma hoped irrationally was lust. "Vlad and I talked it out. You're hungry. You should go with Buchannan."

She was interrupted by Sevystian passing her to unlock the door to his apartment. It brought him nose to nose with her, or more accurately nose to chest. He pushed the door open, waving her in before bending to pick up his rumpled sport coat. She watched as he desperately tried to shake out some of the wrinkles. It was a lost cause and he stopped when he realized that she was watching him.

"Please." He held his hand over the threshold of his home. "Let us speak somewhere we can converse freely."

"Oh, right." Emma stepped lightly into the apartment. It was mostly dark except for the ambient city light streaming in from a wall of windows that cast a moody grey wash over the space.

Inside was a stunning work of minimalist design, the kitchen stretched across the entire wall to the right that opened completely into the living-room. On the other side of a huge black leather sectional was a wall of bone-colored stone with a pass-through fireplace, around it she could see a massive wooden dining room table that was long enough to stick out on either side of the wall. The place barely looked like anyone lived there. It was more of a show room than anyone's actual apartment. Sevystian put his hand on the small of her back guiding her to the sofa.

"Your apartment is amazing!" Keeping the false cheeriness in her voice.

"Thank you." Sevystian's voice was clipped more sharply than usual, or what Emma had come to think of as usual for him. "You have questions."

"Some." Emma ran her fingers through the soft throw, folded carefully along the back of the couch. "Can't you just steal blood from a hospital or something?"

She paused in her perusal of the room.

"Interesting that you are okay with stealing from a hospital." Sevystian lips tilt down at the corners. "Couldn't that kill someone just as easily?"

"I see your point, but the people who gave the blood are doing it... doing it... I don't know, willingly?" She was waving her hands around looking for the right collection of words to make her point.

"No one is going to willingly feed a vampire." Sevystian smiled sadly at her naive argument. "Even those who have donated blood wouldn't do so if they knew there was a chance that we would take it. Vampires are predatory by nature; it frightens everyone in the end."

"I would." Emma said standing straight and defiant.

"You would, what?" Sevystian studied her. "Feed me?"

"Yeah." She nodded slowly. "You said you don't kill your vic… dinners."

"No." Sevystian took a step back. "You are Vlad's…"

"I am my own person." Emma followed Sevystian into his personal space, pulling the robe away from her neck. The smoky orange scent of her invaded Sevystian's apartment.

Emma sounded strong but her hands were shaking. He bent down resting his forehead on her shoulder, his breath tickling the pale strip of her neck she had offered up to him.

"You should never bite someone here, not unless your intention is to kill them." Sevystian's lips ghosted over her skin.

He was trying to scare her off. Emma didn't intend to let him. The feel of him pressed into that bare strip of skin was a weighty temptation she wasn't expecting.

"You said vampires don't kill their victims." There was that word again.

"I did not say that." He pushed her away, his tone painfully serious. "Young vampires or careless ones, they have killed countless people, as well as the ones who take lives for fun or for revenge."

"Careless?" She asked, her bravado wavering in the face of his reality, seeing his fangs glint in the low light for the first time.

"It is easier than you think, to take a life." Menace laced through his voice, in an attempt to send her back to the safety of Vlad's penthouse.

"How?" Emma' set her shoulders unwilling to be sent off like a frightened child.

"Easy enough." He looked into her eyes and reached out to

slide his grip around her throat. "Most people think that we bite here." He was rubbing a circle with his thumb around her pulse. "It is a stupid mistake, you cannot hope to control the blood flow this close to the heart."

His hand slid down cutting between the lapels of the robe, so his hand was resting on her chest. His skin was slightly cooler than hers. Those cool fingers ran over the still raw claw marks Melissa had left her with. His finger traced over the half-moon scratches light as a breeze and Emma closed her eyes to avoid facing him. When she opened them he was watching the gentle glide of his fingers over her chest. She could feel a blush crinkle up her breasts puckering her nipples and chase up her cheeks. His hand returned to her throat putting a hint of pressure right at the hollow dent where her clavicles met her sternum. It was a test, his eyes kept flicking to her face, watching her for signs of distress or fear. Emma was not so easily deterred. The seed of rebellion that lived in her heart would never have allowed her to be cowed by such an obvious tactic.

"So where do you bite?" She cut right to the quick.

"I suppose it depends on how hungry you are." Sevystian pulled his hand back slowly.

Emma could feel the intentional scratch of his claws tickling across the tender welts left by her mother.

"Maybe we should do a little less talking and you should do a little more eating?" Emma peeled off the offending robe. There was a "if you dare" glint in the way that he looked at her that spiked Emma's sense of competition and had absolutely nothing to do with the flutter of attraction she felt whenever he opened that sinful mouth of his. Nothing at all.

"You don't have to." Sev motioned vaguely to the discarded bit of terry cloth.

She cocked an eyebrow as she sat on the shiny low coffee table, her posture perfect.

"I am not getting blood on that." She offered the sleeve to

him to feel, he declined. "Suit yourself. Okay so where's the damage gonna be?"

Silence settled around them, filling up the near empty room, pressing tightly into her ears, making them pop. The standoff lasted just long enough for Emma to start to doubt her decision. Just when she felt the tight embarrassing grip of rejection at the back of her throat he relented. Sevystian stalked around the couch to stand in front of her.

"A bite needs to be somewhere that I can control the amount of blood you lose." He sat down opposite of her on the sofa. Where he had been unyielding before, Sevystian was now limber. His legs spread wide as he rolled up his sleeves up his thick forearms, inviting her to watch. "Your forearm, your inner thigh."

She made a noise in the back of her throat completely unintentionally. He seemed larger now than when they had both been standing, now that they were on level ground. Now that they both understood where their collective intentions would take them, Emma looked at him. There was an animosity about him that before this moment Emma would have assumed accounted for in his muscular stature or the perpetually grim demeanor.

He took her hand in his grip, turning it over to expose the pale underside of her forearm. His calloused fingertips brushed along the delicate blue line of her vein. She wished he would get on with the biting. The longer his touch lingered on her skin the more vulnerable she felt. Despite the rather tame pajamas she wore, somehow, she was naked to him and even in the high heat of summer Emma shivered. It was a reminder that he had not always been a well-appointed businessman, that air of intimidation she felt rolling off of him was just a byproduct of centuries of war, blood, survival.

"Here." He tapped the pulse of her wrist, jerking her out of her own thoughts. "You run the risk of them noticing before it is fully healed." He brought her forearm up to his nose to breath in the scent of her pulse. "The Order's propaganda has made it impossible to seek out our needs in the open."

"How do you hide it?" She felt too warm, her breathing was shallow. His nose was still tucked into her skin, each of his breaths matched her own, shallow unmeasured, erratic.

"I bite somewhere else." The tip of his tongue lapped a stripe from her wrist to the palm of her hand. Sevystian's eyes zeroed in on hers. Emma met his gaze, there was something of a challenge in it that excited her. His lips tilted down at the corners, his approximation of a smile. Twisting her hand over again, he laid it palm flat on her thigh, cupping his own much larger hand over it. Sliding them both up the inner seam of her thin pants until his thumb brushed the crease of her hip. "Here."

"That seems intimate." Emma was overwhelmed by the intensity of his eyes, and the feel of her own pulse throbbing in her ears. Her cheeks felt hot and her hand tingled where his tongue traced the blue lines of her veins.

"You're nourishing another being." He took his hand away, leaning out of her immediate personal space. Not so far that she lost the pressure of his thighs crowding hers or the scent of his soap in the air between them. "Intimacy should be preferred over anonymous violence, should it not?"

"You're intimate with all of your..." She paused, there wasn't a word for what it felt like to be here, preparing to do what she was. "Partners?"

"They come to me for sex." His voice trembled through her body, everything about him, about this moment, felt explicit. "I give them pleasure and they give me sustenance."

"They don't notice that you're biting them?" Emma stared at his fangs as he took her hand into his grip, turning it over so the pale skin and blue veins where once again visible to his impenetrable scrutiny. He ran his thumb along her vein and she let each firm stroke carry away scraps of her reason as she imagined she might have let him if he had been any other man she had met in any other manner.

"My partners are usually distracted with other more enjoyable matters." His eyes flashed, and she could almost see him imagining her laid out for him, naked and wanton.

"Oh." She questioned. Her brain was going fuzzy, it might have been for the best. "It doesn't hurt?"

"At first, yes." Sevystian was holding onto his control by the most delicate of threads.

"Then how do they not try and stop you?" Not that Emma imagined that anyone could stop him if he set his mind to it, which set her heart pounding for an entirely different reason.

"There is a point." He skimmed the razors edge of his claws across the center of her palm, sending tendrils of lust spiraling down her arm. "In the course of desire when all things are just sensation. If your partner is skilled enough and the intention right."

"Oh." Her voice was high and breathy. "You should probably, you know... do the biting now."

"Here." He rubbed a little circle in the middle of her forearm.

He pulled her onto his lap as if she weighed nothing, looping one arm around his shoulder and laying her head in the crook of his neck. She let her chest mold against him. His dress shirt rumpled and soft against her cheek. His nose was swept lightly over her arm tracking a nervous tremor scuttling through her. That was all the warning she was allotted before he struck. His fangs sank into her vein with the accuracy of a well-seasoned phlebotomist. Emma giggled half-heartedly at the thought.

Sevystian had been correct, the pain sizzling through her arm turned into a dull throbbing molten feeling she couldn't name. Emma couldn't think, she felt dizzy and euphoric. With each beat of her heart she could feel her desire for rationality leave her just a little more. The fear and grief that weighed cold and dense in her heart didn't matter, they were another person's problem. Tears puddled hot and waiting in the corners of her eyes. Closing her eyes, she felt them leak down her cheeks in rapidly drying streaks.

Emma didn't want to think anymore, didn't want the burden of her mother or her beliefs dragging behind her, dead weight. She didn't want to think about waking up tomorrow only to remember that Grams would never again wait impatiently for her to get home from a client consultation, just to ask how it had gone. Emma wanted what Sevystian offered, relief, distraction and so she let the warm gentle waves of pleasure float her away.

"Hush," Sevystian murmured brushing her hair back from her face settling back in the chair.

Despite the steamy weather, Emma shivered. How much time had passed as she sat curled on his lap, or how much blood had passed between them, were far off concerns. She didn't even know why she was crying anymore. Passing his thumb gently under her eyes, Sevystian swept away her tears, watching her face for signs of distress.

"Was that enough?" Emma could feel new tears welling in her eyes, completely contrary to the relief she felt in the diversion of his arms.

"I am satisfied." Sevystian spoke in a tone much softer than the one she had come to think of as his.

New tears rolled down her cheeks and he let those fall, watching them as they passed her chin where finally Emma reached one lethargic arm to catch them.

"Would you kiss me?" Her voice was light, unhindered by the tears that seemed to be ebbing now as the euphoric high of Sevystian's bite eased.

"What?" Sevystian was taken back by her request.

"You don't have to mean it." She sighed leaning back so she could look him in the face. "I just want to kiss you. I think I would like that."

He didn't wait for her to change her mind. The dark scruff on his jaw rasped along hers. His hand moved to cup her cheek dominating the kiss. His calloused hand slid up her thigh sending heat spiraling up her hips, making her curl into his embrace. She whined, struggling to get closer to him. He chuckled and so she bit him. Sev growled back, his lip still caught between her teeth. She scraped his lip between her teeth until she had tortured him enough and let him go with a pop. Turning herself with a great shuffle of arms and legs so her back was against his chest she made to push herself out of his lap. He caught her tight against him.

"That wasn't very nice of you." Sevystian's low voice was back to its demanding timbre. He brought her back settling her ass into the crease of his hips, keeping her legs from reaching the ground.

His mouth by her ear, one hand in her hair, the other an iron bar across her waist. Emma was trapped against him, his breath on her neck. She felt dizzy again, before reality was sinking in on her. Emma knew she wasn't ready fall into bed with him. There were a million reasons to keep her head on straight, even as she looked back at what she had just done, she felt the crippling doubt sneaking in. Whether her actions were an act of insanity or not, she might never know.

Placing her hand over his, she tugged herself free, he let her go easily enough. Her legs wobbled and she would have fallen down, but Sevystian caught her helping over to the large sofa where she could get some space from him. They sat there watching each other for a long while in the blue silence of the room. She let her head fall back onto the soft faux fur of the throw and contemplated just pulling it over herself and going to sleep.

"I dreamed about you." Her voice sounded throaty.

"A nightmare?" He teased.

"Yes." She let her eyes wander the room. "My mother pushed me off a cliff. You tried to warn me."

"I didn't scare you?" He sat with his elbows on his knees, the entirety of his focus on her. It could be either terrifying or wonderful to have all of his attention.

"No." She looked back at him, half smiling.

"Fear can be informative." His attention didn't waver.

"I suppose." A yawn over took her.

"You are cold?" He tensed on the edge of the coffee table.

"I should go back to Vlad's." She wanted to get up, really, she did. She wanted to be smooth and say good-night, maybe wink at him over her shoulder as she left. That was cool, right? She couldn't seem to make herself move, her arms suddenly felt like they were filled with warm sand. "Or you could just toss that blanket over me and I'll be real quiet."

Sevystian chuckled again, that was twice in one night.

"You'll stay with me." He didn't wait for her to decide. "I want to keep you close."

"Hmm." Her thoughts were drifting again, this time from the inevitable exhaustion from the previous days grueling events.

She was drifting in and out of focus as he slid onto the sofa behind her, lifting her up so she could lay with her head on his chest, rising and falling in time with his breaths. Emma wondered why vampires had to breath.

"Stay here tonight." He pleaded brushing his fingers through her hair. His fangs had retreated, claws too. Pity, she thought winsomely, she was starting to like them. Nodding, she yawned, content to stay exactly where she was as she gave into her exhaustion in the safety of his arms.

· · ·

Sevystian counted her breaths as she lay in his arms, watching for any sign she was in distress. The holes in her arm were pin pricks now, closing rapidly. He licked them anyways, enjoying the soft murmur of pleasure she made each time he did. Finally, they closed completely and he felt strange tending to them further. He sat in the quiet room with her now asleep on his lap trying to decide what to do. After the days on end of grief and violence, they both needed sleep and in the lazy spell woven around them, Sevystian wanted to stay as they were. It wouldn't do for the night, already Emma was wriggling in efforts to more comfortably situate herself. A cramp as new blood tried to force itself into his legs pushed him into action. He pulled her tight into his chest hefting himself onto his feet and made his way into the bedroom.

The sheets were in their usual heap in the middle of the bed and he settled her down on one side, pulling them neatly around her. It didn't make much sense to him but there was something nice about tucking her into his bed. It was a real tangible way to care for her, and he drew out the process by smoothing out both sides before stripping down to his boxer briefs. He took the time to fold the mussed clothing before putting it in the hamper. The suit jacket and robe were still in the living-room somewhere and the thought gnawed at him. With a look at Emma sleeping peacefully he darted out of the room, he didn't want to leave her to wake up alone. She was in the middle of the bed when he returned, and finally with everything in it proper place he curled up beside her.

CHAPTER 33

The smell of coffee woke Emma up. Not in the blurry way she had woken up every day since Grams had passed. Finding instead the warm flannel sheets of an unfamiliar bed. She stretched wide, half-expecting to fall out of her tiny twin bed onto the floor of her room at home. A streak of mid-morning sun fell across her face and she opened her eyes a slit, looking around the room. Neat as a pin, even her robe was hanging over what looked like a fancy coat rack, not like a hook on the back of a door, like some kind of outfit display thing. She was thoroughly impressed. The coffee called to her, but so did nature, and after opening a couple of wrong doors she found the bathroom, another crazy lavish room with double vanities and a shower that had its own tub. Well, if she had a few hundred years to save up her pennies, she guessed she could have nice things too.

In the kitchen, Sevystian whipped some cream with vanilla for the waffles he was making. He had slept for a few hours and then unable to lay still any longer gotten up to start breakfast. Normally he wouldn't have bothered for himself, but Emma needed to build her blood sugars back up and it was another excuse to keep her close. To his disappointment, she had wrapped herself in the fuzzy white robe, by the time she came into the kitchen.

"Smells amazing in here." If she thought that dry humping like teenagers in his living room was going to keep her from blushing like crazy at that sight of him making breakfast in nothing but his underwear, she was wrong; very very wrong. The fabric of his boxer briefs bunched high around the thickest part of his thigh and slouched low at his abdomen, giving Emma plenty of him to drool over. Emma liked this casual Sevystian, relaxed in his domain, seemingly unburdened from whatever responsibilities kept a scowl on his face.

"You need to eat something sugary this morning." He smiled at her, the one that broke whatever idea she had of him being a grumpy tycoon. "I should have made you eat something last night."

They both knew why he hadn't made her eat something the night before.

"I... ugh." He looked so completely human in that moment; whisk in hand trying to think of something clever to say that wasn't along the lines of: *you taste good, or wanna try that naked sometime*? "I made waffles."

As if to make his point for him, the waffle maker beeped insistently, and he pulled out a perfectly golden waffle and added it to the already tall stack next to a little pot of syrup.

"How many waffles do you think I can eat?" She laughed nabbing the fresh one and piling it high with his now finished whipped cream.

"The first one was..." He chewed his word options for a moment as she took her first huge bite. "Imperfect."

She busied herself building another bite and he put one of the bowls in the sink and started to wash it.

"Nope." She stood up, talking with her mouth full of

whipped cream. "No dishes, I've seen you eat, I know you can do it. Sit your ass down and have a waffle. They're perfect."

"Perfect?" He sat carefully on the stool beside hers and meticulously loaded his plate with the bare bones of waffle toppings, before taking a small, neat bite and chewing thoughtfully.

Emma watched him, eyeing the oddly precise mannerisms she had not noticed until they had a quiet moment together. He swallowed and moved on to another bite and Emma nudged him with her elbow, curious what he thought of his own culinary work.

"Acceptable." He slid the second bite into his mouth watching her.

Returning the favor, Emma studied Sevystian in the calm daylight of his apartment. Large scars bisected his shoulder on the right side and one near his hip on the left made her bite her tongue against the barrage of questions she wanted to ask him, but the morning so far was perfect and she didn't want to darken it with old memories.

CHAPTER 34

Buchannan stood at the monitoring bank of cameras stuffing a doughnut into his mouth with little finesse. A box of them sat on the desk between Stevens and himself. The dayshift guard, Mark, had brought several boxes from his wife's bakery, and despite Stevens having spent the entire evening at his post, he was happy to stay a while and eat a few while giving his boss the run down on the night's events. Buchannan had been particularly interested in the couple that had stayed so late, asking question after question about their clothes and demeanors. Stevens couldn't really say more than he already had on the strange couple. They were a burr in his paw. He couldn't shake the feeling that they were not just some hipster duo looking for Wi-Fi and air-conditioning.

"Who's that?" Buchannan pointed to the Toyota pulling into staff parking, mouth full of plain glazed.

"Heather." Stevens squinted at the car. Something was off but with such bad picture he couldn't quite tell. "Funny I didn't know she was pulling the turn around."

"What?" Buchannan licked a bit of sugar off his finger, already looking in the box for another.

"She worked last night." Stevens put his cuff mic to his

mouth, directing his inquiry to Mark at the front desk who was just finishing up with the morning security brief. "Hey Mark, you got Heather on schedule for today?"

"No sir." Mark's tinny voice buzzed through the comms. "Why, we got an issue?"

Buchannan's eyes scanned over each of the screens with mechanical precision, searching for irregularities.

"Might be." Stevens mirrored the younger looking Buchannan, arms crossed over his chest. Then the Toyota passed directly in front of the far camera and they got a look at the driver. Greasy Man-bun from the night before pulled Heather's car into the space closest to the service door. "We have a breach in the staff entrance. I need a lock down now."

Buchannan held his phone to his ear, waiting for Kadir to answer and watching the screen with a low, simmering rage.

"I need you to run point from here." Buchannan had a stillness about him in situations like this that Stevens was certain underlined an extensive military career.

"Yes sir." Stevens nodded. "Should I call the authorities?"

"We are the authorities." Buchannan snapped, before scrubbing his face with his hand. "Don't call anyone until I, or Mr. Tepes gives the go-ahead. We don't want to make this any messier than it is."

"Yes, Sir." Stevens nodded again, watching the screens for further development. He had been with Wallachia Holdings and specifically at the Transempirial long enough to know not to question the happenings of the company's upper echelon.

"Kadir, we have a breach." Buchannan didn't react to the loud curse from Kadir on the other end of the phone. As they spoke five figures crawled out of the car pulling up tattered grey rags over their faces.

The new barista from West slipped out of the middle of the backseat and Stevens felt vindicated for every bad thing he had ever thought about the kid. Skeevy little punk was coming in to his building like a bad heist job. Two of the perpetrators were clearly female, but none of them were blonde or tall like Heather, which didn't bode well. Stevens felt the bottom drop out of his stomach. Something had been off last night and he should have done something, and now for all he knew Heather was at the bottom of the bayou. He clinched his jaw until his teeth squeaked against one another in protest. Beside him, Buchannan rattled off details of the situation to the COO, clicking out of the call without acknowledgement.

"Is Heather among them?" Buchannan's voice was deeper than Stevens had ever heard it.

"No." Stevens pointed to the shitty barista crouching by the service door, clutching... was that a wooden fucking stake? Lunatics! "That one is the new barista downstairs, though."

"Have West House evacuated. I want all commercial spaces emptied." Buchannan dialed another number putting his phone to his ear. "Sev we've got a problem."

CHAPTER 35

Noon in the heat of a Texas summer always seemed to Vlad like the scene from an old spaghetti western. Even in the city, heat would sizzle off of the sidewalks or rise from the concrete pavers of his penthouse patio in almost cartoonish waves. If he blocked out the buzz of traffic from the street below, he could imagine a penny whistle interlude just before the big showdown. Standing here today he certainly felt as if he was waiting for one. Since Iliza King's death, almost five days ago, his family had had no rest. If it wasn't the Order beating down their business, or trying to corrupt the last of his blood kin, then it was tensions riding high between the new arrivals and his Coven brothers.

Vlad drank deeply from his thermos, the blood was warm and fresh. Lord only knew how Fields managed to keep it that way. He heard the door to the balcony open and shut behind him and knew without looking that it was Emma. Her presence carried with it a wash of contentment. He had not been able to enjoy the lives of his own children, but Emma for whatever reason seemed to be content to let him indulge in hers. He smiled into his meal, the steam of it hardly noticeable from the air outside.

"Ugh." Emma came to stand next him at the railing, looking over at the bustling city with a long sigh. "I love the storms, but boy howdy, do I hate the humidity."

"Do you really wish to speak about the weather?" Vlad glanced sideways at her. She looked happily rumpled.

"It's called an ice-breaker." She turned around to lean her back on the rail, so she could watch his face as they spoke. She was really hoping that he wasn't super mad that she had a thing for Sev. She had only known the guy a few days, it wasn't like she was planning a spring wedding, she didn't want to break up the band. "Or didn't they have those back in the stone ages?"

"Hum?" He tried to hide his amusement behind his thermos. She could see it peeking out from behind the stainless steel.

A slight breeze wafted around the corner of the building, and Emma's delightful mix of lavender and citrus scents mixed with a dark familiar sandalwood.

"You look brighter this afternoon. Might I inquire as to whom might have boosted your spirits?" Vlad took another sip giving himself time to study her. Emma looked more relaxed this morning, glowing around the edges.

"How do you know it's a who?" Emma blushed furiously. Vlad tapped his nose with his index finger, before taking another long gulp of his breakfast. "Oh, gross. Tell me that's a joke and Sev just called you to gloat."

"I am afraid not, my dear." He turned to face her, still smiling. "The transition changes many things. It isn't all hissing at strangers and turning into bats you know."

"Hold up." She looked at him wide eye. "You can turn into a bat?"

Vlad tried to keep a straight face to no avail. He cracked and was half-bent over laughing when the door opened again and Kadir and Aaron rushed out.

"There's been a breach of the exterior." Kadir stopped in front of Vlad, arms folded behind him.

"Where's Sevystian?" Vlad spoke with his full authority. The calm that had enveloped the early afternoon was extinguished.

"Buchannan is alerting him now." When Kadir spoke, it was with the simmering predatory glee Emma suspected was his more natural demeanor. "Stevens confirmed that all commercial spaces are empty of personnel."

"Residential areas?" Vlad clenched his jaw, fighting the itch in his gums.

"They are being told to stay in their apartments while we deal with an uninvited guest in the lobby. As far as they know, they are not in danger." Again terse, Kadir seemed to lack any of the frills he had tried to dazzle her with before. "It seems they have taken advantage of a small break in surveillance in the parking structure. Five members have breached the exterior service entrance and are making their way up the North-West emergency stairs."

"Stay here." Vlad thrust the warm thermos into Emma's hand and stalked off in the direction of the library.

"Fuck that noise." Emma tossed the thermos down, cringing slightly at the thick red liquid pouring out onto the concrete pavers. "I'm not a hightower kind of princess. I know how to fight. I'm not staying put."

"And if they have guns?" Vlad stopped to looked at her full on, both annoyed and impressed with her gumption. "How do you intend to defend yourself against a bullet? I won't have you hurt by another one of the Order's minions."

Aaron tapped her arm gently with something warm and metal. She palmed Aaron's off-duty 38-snubbed nose six shot revolver. Effortlessly flipping out the cylinder, she checked for ammo and flipped it back into place.

"They might wanna be worried about her." Aaron looked so proud he might have burst right then and there. "It'd be easier to quit arguing with her and go get these guys. She's gonna win anyways."

Kadir's phone rang in his pocket, startling the small group of them, he answered it quickly talking angrily in some Eastern European language that she couldn't place. He ended the call just as quickly.

"They are on ten." He spoke to Vlad directly. It was time to make a decision, if Emma was going with them or not, it didn't matter, but if they got much higher it would be more than a little hard to explain what a bunch of mad men were doing in the building to their civilian tenants.

Whether Vlad intended to argue anymore was moot, as Emma stalked off to the elevators, Aaron jogging behind her.

"The question is answered then." Kadir's voice traveled across the patio. Emma didn't stopped to see if they were following.

CHAPTER 36

They exited the elevators on the last residential floor and walked down the stairwell to the Wallachia Holdings offices in a single file line with Emma at the rear. It was the last floor the public had access to and the one that Vlad and his team could most effectively contain an altercation. Before stepping out of the stairwell Vlad had tried once more to convince Emma to leave the violence to the men folk. She responded by cocking the revolver and assuming the tactical ready position Simon had taught her.

Taking point Vlad lead them through the halls in near silence. Vlad stopped them at a bend in the hall to peer around the corner. It was dark and Vlad pushed them back into the lip of an office doorway, signing for them to be quiet. Her heart pounded in her ears, which she supposed should have been alarming. Aaron adjusted his stance next to her and the brush of his body against hers jolted her out of her thoughts.

Finally, Emma heard the footsteps of the intruders picking their way down the hall, until they passed the little nook unaware they were being watched. They weren't wearing sneaking around clothes, not the skin-tight cat burglary ensemble she had imagined. Instead they donned shabby linen tunics, poorly dyed black. They were a motley crew of individuals, in their hand-sewn garments and utility belts full of random weapons around their middles. One of them had a hammer and a wooden stake like some terribly dressed Van Helsing. Each of them walked pressed tightly to the walls and Emma thought that they must have trained for this. They were out of earshot when Kadir's phone vibrated; a text from Sevystian.

On their flank.

Kadir motioned for them to head out, taking off down the same hall their enemy had just moved through. He made some technical bullshit with finger gestures and aggressive eye contact, to which Aaron flipped him off as he moved past him. The hall opened up into a large reception area, with one of those tall stately desks with Wallachia Holdings' logo on the front of it. It would have been impressive if it weren't for the five Order Faithful lying in wait for them. Aaron huffed out a chuckle, pointing his weapon at the ground, watching the Order unwittingly display their incompetence.

Emma didn't have the other's training and as such didn't notice the sloppy novice mistakes that had the others snickering. Emma didn't see barely trained baby soldiers, she saw the hunger seething in the grit of their teeth. Crimson veins webbed the whites of their eyes, pupils blown wide with some unknown stimulant. They looked desperate and if nothing else Emma knew not to underestimate the acts of desperate people. She took long breaths, counting to ten on every inhale until she could no longer hear her blood rushing in her ears.

A tremor vibrated down her arm and into her hand, ignoring it she adjusted her grip on Aaron's gun and studied the invaders. Even with her mouth and nose covered with a strip of greying linen, Emma could pick out her mother amongst them. The Order circled them slowly, in the manner that always seemed to be menacing on TV. Here, it made them seem like amateurs. As if having caught them they had absolutely no idea what to do with them. Fucking Wile E. Coyote shit. Emma wasn't fooled, though. She had seen what her waif of a mother could do on her own. With a squadron of eager disciples, Melissa King could rain down havoc.

"You're on private property." Vlad seemed content to let them be in charge for the moment. "You have not been invited by this company or any other inhabitants of the building, and as such I must ask you to leave."

One of the Order faithful chuckled, setting off a series of nervous tittering through the group, sounding like hyenas. Melissa made a jerky motion with her hand, throwing the pack of fanatics into silence.

"You know why we're here?" Even muffled by the strip of fabric coiled around her face, Melissa's strange, childlike voice was unmistakable.

"I could venture a guess." Vlad raised an eyebrow in distain.

It was clear that Melissa was expecting more from him. She stopped her wobbled circling to stand in front of Vlad and pulled down her makeshift mask, baring her teeth at him. The others stopped in their tracks spread out in a crooked half-circle their backs to the reception desk. All their nervous energy pouring out of them as they bounced and jittered in place. The invaders faced them with misplaced confidence. Vlad surveyed then with his calm authoritarian stare, seemingly undisturbed by the rising tension or the rattle of their garden tool weaponry.

"This company is an abomination, supporting the filth that runs this world." Finally, a tall bony cultist broke the silence with her snarling gibberish. Fidgeting with pent-up aggression. She threw herself at Aaron.

Chaos broke like an egg, slashing at him with a hammer.

. . .

Emma watched a second longer than she should have, nearly getting caught by one of the Faithful, a boy by anyone's definition. She dodged his weak attempt at tackling her and tripped him as he fumbled past. Melissa launched herself teeth-first into Vlad's throat, earning a grunt from the vampire and distracting Emma for a second from her would be assailant. When he lunged again his chokehold caught her unaware. The initial panic was a white-hot blur of elbows, her's, and cursing, his. It would be a cold day in hell before Iliza King's granddaughter let a cheap shot like that take her down.

Emma let herself go limp, all of her weight dropping into her attacker's surprised arms. Unsurprisingly he dropped her, just like she had expected. Emma hit the floor, rolled over, and kicked him squarely in the balls the second she had the chance. He fell onto his knees groaning, tears in his eyes. Scrambling away from him Emma got to her feet quickly. He lunged, one hand still clutching his testicles and was met with the butt of the revolver connecting with the bridge of his nose. Blood sprayed everywhere.

Emma grimaced when some splattered across her face. She had always sort of thought that that was just something directors put in movie for dramatic effect. Yet here this guy was proving her wrong. He clutched at his nose, blood drenching his linen mask, and tried to stand up. Before he could reestablish his footing, Emma kicked out, cracking him hard in the kneecap with a nasty click, hyper-extending his knee. All but screaming, he sank to the floor, pulling off the slip of fabric from his face, gasping in painful gulps of air. Even through the blood, Emma could tell he was far too young to be risking his life for someone as crazy as her mother.

• • •

I f Aaron had ever questioned the brutality of the Order, he never would again, even with a broken collar bone, his opponent lunged switching the knife to her other hand. Aaron dodged, narrowly missing the business-end of the blade. He reached out with his empty hand and grabbed her wrist and twisted it until it snapped into an unnatural angle finally dropping the knife. He had hoped that that would end the erratic attack. She surged forward.

He wasn't dealing with a sane person, he wasn't even dealing with a sober one. All of these Order elite had to be hopped up on some good shit. If his adrenaline was keeping his pain to a minimum, they couldn't even feel theirs. She ran at him again, teeth bared, pushing her forearm hard into his throat, knocking the breath from his lungs, forcing him backwards through the other clashing bodies and into the wall. She watched him gasp for breath, hate scribbled over her angry face as she tried to choke him to death. Aaron's eyes watered and his face turning from red to purple until he brought his arm down swiftly on his attacker's broken clavicle.

She shrieked, stumbling back and then she was gone. Not slumped to the floor, or preparing for the next attack, simply gone. Blinking away his confusion he saw Sevystian and the woman he had been fighting now slung lifeless on the floor twenty feet away, her neck cocked at a sickly angle against the large desk. Sevystian didn't even acknowledge Aaron, his eyes glued to the sight of Emma standing victorious over one of the Order, the gun he had given her cocked and pointed at the man's forehead.

S evystian felt his anger rise like a cold tide as he came into the reception area from the back stairwell. His oxfords didn't make a sound as he slid into the fray, twisting out of the way of Kadir as he brawled with a taller Order member. Before Sevystian could get to her, Emma had dropped out of her attacker's grip and nailed him right in the crotch. It was almost enough to make him smile. He paused, gauging whether or not Emma would need him to step in and help when one of the Order barreled up to him. If these guys were supposed to be the elite of the Order's hit squad, they were not half as good as the Coven thought them to be.

The Faithful was brandishing a stake and hammer, his eyes wide and wild. Restlessly bouncing from foot to foot, lunging forward only to skitter back, scared, but too radicalized to give up. He could write a textbook on this guy's behavior alone. Sevystian had had enough of this dance.

Stepping into the man's next attack, Sev grabbed his wrist and snapped his arm at the elbow, just as the sharp tip of the minion's stake pierced into Sev's stomach. The scream the man let out was muffled, his already dilated eyes watching in abject horror as his arm flopped the wrong way. Turning back to Sevystian with a terrible spark of hatred the Faithful leaned into the stake. Sev felt it pop through the thick web of muscle over his abdomen, squishing into his intestine where it could do real harm. It didn't matter that it wouldn't kill Sevystian, a belly wound could still do enough damage for his opposition to get the upper hand. That was not an option.

Ripping off that ridiculous little mask the Faithful wore, Sevystian grabbed the back of the man's head, twisting it so as to expose his neck. It had been a long time since he had killed anyone this way. He would have to feed, if he wanted to keep fighting. His fangs bit into the flesh just under the man's chin and forcing their way through the tough rubber walls of the carotid. It only looks easy in Dracula movies; real life took more effort. The taste of the stuff was rancid, like the man had died weeks ago. It would do the trick all the same. Sevystian could only stomach a few swallows. He let the man fall to the ground to finish bleeding out and rubbed his mouth on his sleeve.

Sev took two loping steps, grabbing the neck of the nearest Faithful and tossed her grey-clad body into the reception desk. There was a sick crack as her head hit the ply-wood fixture. He surveyed the battlefield, checking on his men. Emma stood victorious over her attacker, gun raised keeping him cowed beneath her.

"Fucking rat's blood." Kadir spat out a mouthful of red, hot liquid onto the industrial ply carpet, drawing Sev's and Aaron's attention away from Emma. "Don't know what they're on, but it tastes terrible."

Sev nodded, letting his eyes slide back to Emma.

"It's been a long time since you killed a man like that." Kadir said, nodding to the body on the ground by his feet. "Like riding a bike."

"What kind of fucking bikes did you guys have?" Aaron picked his way towards them holding his bleeding arm tight to his chest. "I have had better nightmares than this shit." Kadir jerked Aaron's arm up, licking a slobbery path all along the wound the crazy bag lady had gouged out of it. "Did you just lick me? I am not okay with that!"

"It stops the bleeding." Kadir rolled his eyes. "Fucking cowboys."

Kadir was grinning from ear to ear, mischief glinting in his eyes. It was irritating especially with the sour taste of bad blood still hanging in Sevystian's mouth.

"That's hot, Emmy doll," Aaron whistled, still twisting his arm back and forth to inspect the cut that had already stopped bleeding.

"Eat a bag of dicks, lover boy." Emma said, her eyes never wavering from her hostage.

. . .

Vlad could hear the rest of them talking, embracing their post-battle high. He didn't indulge in any snarky banter. His concentration was focused on Melissa. She had been stronger than he had anticipated, her small frame gave no indication of its power. Vlad supposed that her hate made her strong. There was a sizable chunk missing from his neck that was just the size of her mouth. Pain lanced down his shoulder as he put a bit more pressure on the wound. He was bleeding like a spigot, staining his hands and suit jacket, just another reason he detested Melissa King. Contrary to the popular history of his kind and certainly contrary to the Order's opinion of him, Vlad didn't enjoy killing.

It was the only reason Melissa still drew breath. Pulling the madwoman off of him had been a task in and of itself. Even without fangs she had been able to latch hard onto his throat and detangling her had involved prying her off and with her a chunk of one of the tendons in his neck. He was going to be weak on that side until he fed. It sent all of those primeval instincts firing away inside his brain.

Melissa came at him again and Vlad caught her arm. Twisting her off balance and trapped her by the throat to the back of one of the reception's sofas. Melissa scratched and gurgled her displeasure as she turned a ghastly pink color and he turned away, sick of the very sight of her.

Melissa's gurgling went quiet and Vlad turned back to her, the movement pinching his wound uncomfortably. She was finally unconscious. Vlad loosened his hold on her, letting her limp body sag to the floor. He stood, straightened his sleeves, and hoped that Fields had restocked the blood stores. It was going to be a thirsty evening.

One glance around the waiting area told him that he had been right to leave her alive. The rest seemed to have laid waste to their enemy, leaving no one alive for questioning. With the exception of Emma, who had her prisoner dead to rights. The young man was shaking as he took in the sight of his fallen comrades. Yes, his darling little Emma was a glorious creature, pride swelled in his heart. Maybe he was getting a little soft in his old age.

"Still think I should stay locked up in your ivory tower, Grandpa?" Emma sassed, tipping her head towards Vlad while keeping one eye on her wayward little cultist.

"I think I would live a less stressful life, if you would." Vlad snorted, another gush of blood pumping down his shirt front as he moved beside her. He aborted his efforts, slouching instead onto the stiff sofa Melissa was laying against. "Alas, today is not the day of granted wishes."

"Shit, Boss." Aaron squatted down next to Melissa and poked her hard in the ribs like she might pop back up. "She got you good. Didn't even need fangs."

"The human jaw is strong enough to crush its own teeth." Fields strode into the reception area with the annoyance of a long-suffering nanny.

Emma and Aaron exchanged looks, yep, definitely need to get that guy a bell. Fields handed Sevystian and Kadir a bundle of zip-ties each, eyeing the dead bodies like they were each personally responsible for pissing in his cereal.

"So, are we concerned by this or is this more of a 'rub some dirt in it' sort of situation?" Emma touched Vlad's coat sleeve gingerly, her hand coming away with a generous smear of thick gooey gore.

"I wouldn't recommend rubbing dirt on any open wound, Miss Emma." Fields handed Vlad a metal thermos and turned his attention to Emma.

"You know what I mean, Fields." She squinted at him.

"I wouldn't presume." He flicked one of his eyebrows heavenward and grinned at her. Vlad handed Fields the empty thermos, wiping his mouth on his ruined sleeve.

"I believe now would be a prudent time to take our guests somewhere a bit more secure." Vlad's voice had an unmistakable mark of authority to it.

"The Brothers Grimm over here, have got those two trussed-up like rodeo calves." Aaron let out a long-satisfied groan as the last of the adrenaline left him. "You need help with these guys or are we going to pretend like I didn't see some holding cells in your security dungeon?"

"I would settle for not being in the middle of the reception lounge with easy access to at least three main exits. They have already availed themselves of at least one." Vlad snipped, the cold black pits of his eyes digging into Aaron. Aaron held his ground. "Good. Kadir, if you would please take our new friend to one of Buchannan's holding rooms. Sevystian and I are going to question Mrs. King."

"No." Emma grunted. "I'm going to."

"Out of the question." Sevystian stood up from where he was finishing tying Melissa's ankles together.

"First of all, I have the upper hand when it comes to getting information out of her, she's my mother. And second." Emma had never liked being told what to do, not even when Grams had done it. "I would like to remind you that I still have a loaded gun and now that I know bullets won't kill you, I might just shoot you for being stupid."

"You do you, Sweetheart." Kadir smirked at her and she had to admit he was growing on her. "Sevystian help me with the boy. I think they have that one."

Sevystian growled something in what Emma assumed was Romanian and Vlad barked back. For a moment, Emma was sure Sevystian was going to sling her over his shoulder and take her away. Shooting her a withering look Sev begrudgingly hoisted the boy up by his arms and followed Kadir to the elevators.

"Alright." Aaron clapped his hands together causing Emma to jump. "What's next Dracula?"

"Do not call me that." Vlad scrubbed his brow.

"You know you like it." Aaron stood, walking around to stand at Melissa's feet. "Alright, Fields you get the head."

CHAPTER 37

On the other side of a pane of two-way glass, Melissa King looked to Emma as she always did: messy. Her hair was tied back in a low frizzled bun, her clothes screamed bag woman. Her appearance was not helped by the random snarls she made at no one in particular, or the ring of blood around her mouth from where she had taken a chunk out of Vlad's throat. After several attempts to pull herself free of the zip ties binding her hands and feet, she flung herself childishly into one of the wheelie chairs pushing herself to the far wall of the private conference room. They were waiting to move her into one of the Tower's holding cells until Fields could finish patching Vlad together. The wound in his throat had been rather extensive. Fields had suggested to a snappish Vlad that he required tending more than Melissa required questioning.

Vlad stood stoically a few feet from Emma on the other side of wall of a two-way glass that cut the room in half. Fields carefully stitched up the gaping wound in Vlad's neck. He jerked sharply earning him one of Fields' stern scolding looks.

"Didn't think vampires needed stuff like that." Aaron shrugged.

"Can't say I ever thought too hard about it." Emma looked over at Vlad and Fields before shrugging and turning her back to her mother.

Aaron tapped on the glass curiously and Melissa immediately swiveled around, trying to find out where the noise had come from. Noticing the mirror, she scooted closer until she pressed her face against it. Steam puffed out in little plumes of distress around her nose and mouth.

"I don't believe that this was an organized strike." Vlad made his way closer to the glass, waving Fields off. The other man departed, presumably to clean up the gaggle of dead bodies just down the hall. "This is too messy for anything sanctioned by Caldwell. He would not have given us this opportunity. The information she has, the leverage she has walked into our building could mean an end to this cycle of destruction."

Vlad let his voice trail off. Emma struggled to feel remorse or guilt, something for the useless loss of life that had occurred. She wanted to feel badly, she wanted to get choked up and cry over all the violence, they were people. Human life was supposed to be sacred, but the disturbingly rational voice in the back of her head just kept telling her that they had made their own choices.

"I want to talk with her." Emma squared her shoulders, prepared to fight them both on the matter.

"I suppose there is no point is there in arguing the matter?" Vlad didn't look at her when he spoke knowing the answer to be a resounding no. He merely watched Melissa slump back into her chair and wheel around the room some more. "She is as much your enemy as mine. You have as much right to her answers."

"You don't want to...I don't know." Emma sighed feeling strangely defeated. She was expecting more push back. "Don't vampires like... hypnotize people to do their bidding?"

"Not you." Vlad's jaw ticked with frustration and Emma

regretted asking. "The term is thrall, and anyone who uses such a tactic against you will face consequences."

In the conference room Melissa was now on the floor back against the mirror, trying to gnaw through her restraints. Aaron banged on the window again and she stopped like a dog who had been caught licking its stitches.

"So, why not thrall her, or whatever." Emma put air quotes around the word thrall like it was some offensive slang word she didn't trust.

"An effective thrall requires a calm mind." Vlad cast his eyes around the tableaux of the conference room, settling on the feral-looking woman in the middle munching on the hard-plastic restraints. "I am not sure that I could manage that kind of emotional distance at the moment."

Vlad itched his neck, his mouth set in a scowl. She got what he meant, if anyone could understand the states of uncontrollable anger her mother could rouse in a person, it was Emma.

"She might lie to me." She shrugged, crossing her arms, a little shiver of nervousness skittering down her spine.

"There really isn't anything we can do about that." Vlad pinched the bridge of his nose and rolling his shoulders uncomfortably. "It's the human prerogative."

"I'll get her talking." Emma nodded, wiping her sweaty palms against her thighs.

"Do you want me to go in with you?" Aaron nodded towards the room.

"Nah." She sounded more casual than she felt, and more relaxed than she had ever been around her mother. "I think she'll talk more if it's just me. Maybe she will just forget and just tell the truth you know?"

"It's not the worst plan." Simon limped up behind her, looking if it was possible more banged up than the last time she had seen him. She was pretty sure those yellow rings around his bruises meant he was healing.

"Hey look who made it all the way to the elevators." Emma smirked at him as he sidled up to her.

"Yeah, yeah." Simon hung his head, leaning heavily on his walking stick. "You can save your next rant about prejudice or whatever. Ava beat you to it."

"I think I love that woman." Emma sighed off-handedly, before turning back to the conference room and her mother. "I guess now's as good a time as any."

Opening the door, she found herself standing ten feet from her mother. Melissa didn't seem to notice that anyone had entered the room, too busy chewing at the plastic zip-ties around her wrists. Emma slammed the door shut, and her mother jumped at the sound, growled and scooted along the wall in absurd little half-hops, working her way on her haunches towards her daughter.

"Mom." Her mother's eyes went soft. That milky, blissed out, look that junkies get after their first hit in a long while. "I wanted to see you, to talk to you."

"I knew you would come to your senses." Melissa hobbled closer, holding her hands up to Emma in an expectant manner. "Untie me, baby, and we can take them all out. We can be a family again."

"Again?" Emma couldn't stop the disgust from bleeding into her voice. "You left me as a baby."

"Because I had to." She was getting too close for Emma's liking, her hands still raised. "Honey, the Order needed me. Marcus needed me."

"Marcus?" Emma took a deep breath. She had watched all those cop shows with Grams. She could do this. Start with the little things and build up to the real stuff, once she got her mother talking Melissa King would probably spill her guts before she even realized it. "Why did he need you?" Emma let her voice go soft, affecting that childlike cadence her mother always used. "Mom, please."

That did it. Like magic, she saw the heavens open in her mother's eyes and she started to speak.

"Oh, Baby." Melissa's voice warbled with unshed tears. "I had to come here, even when he said no. I knew it was the right thing. The Divine Mortal told me so. She speaks to me, Baby. She's so beautiful, baby. So, beautiful."

"Marcus told you not to come?" Emma needed to get her mother back on track, she could see her slipping off the rails already. "Why didn't he want you to come?"

"He doesn't understand." Melissa blinked at Emma, her arms tucking into her sides, slack. The restraints bit into her wrists but she didn't seem to notice now, too distracted by her daughter to worry about them. "He said that it would interrupt his plans for the company."

"What company?" Emma squatted down next to her mother making sure her mother couldn't hide away from her eye contact. "Mom?"

"Caldwell of course." Melissa tilted her head to and fro, and Emma could tell that her charm was wearing off. She was going to need a new tactic. Her mother was a fanatic, but she wasn't stupid. Eventually she would catch on.

"What's the Order like?" Emma made her face relax in what she hoped was a fair facsimile to her mother's dreamy expression.

"Oh, honey." Melissa's voice lit up. "It's perfect. They're gonna teach you all about the world. Baby girl, it's okay, 'cause the Order is gonna fix it. We'll take them down together. I'll teach you how to shoot and Marcus will take you to the ship-yard and show you the business." Melissa reached out for her daughter again, and Emma took her hands, trying to keep her talking for as long as she could. "You aren't his but that's okay. And you'll marry one of our Faithful and we'll be a real family. We'll have to burn these clothes of yours, but I'll make you something before you are confirmed with the Divine Mortal."

Melissa squeezed her hands tightly, looking down at her daughter's fingers. "Baby?" Her voice was hard, her grip on Emma's hands so tight she could feel the circulation cutting off. "Why don't you cut me free and I can take you home. Your real home."

When Melissa met Emma's eyes she was not the same person who had waxed poetic about the Order and the beauty of the Divine Mortal. Her eyes were cold, despite her best attempts to flutter her lashes sympathetically. Emma tried to pull her hands out of her mother's grasp, teetering awkwardly in her crouched position. Melissa pounced, the momentum pushing Emma fully onto the ground trapping her left arm underneath her. Knees digging purposefully into Emma's throat, throwing all her weight into the attack. The edges of Emma's vision turned fuzzy even as she clawed and bucked trying to dislodge Melissa, but her arm was still trapped beneath her.

"How dare you!" Melissa wheezed with the effort to strangle her only daughter. "I made you. I gave you life." She was screaming now, leaning her body weight onto her arms. Snarling at Emma's grunts of pain. "I should have never had you. Marcus was wrong about keeping you, just like he was wrong about coming here. I'll show him. Your precious filth will see when my son is finished with you all, you won't be able to keep me here forever."

With a violent jerk Emma was finally able to free her arm. Grabbing a chunk of her mother's hair Emma pulled. The hair came free at the root and Melissa screamed, letting go of Emma's throat. It was just enough for Emma to twist her hips dumping her mother on the ground.

With her arms tied together, Melissa was unable to stop her body from crashing into the ground. She smashed into the carpet and Emma scrambled away. Taking painful gulps of air, Emma put another foot of distance between her and her mother. Melissa crawled after her, undaunted by her daughter's hard elbows or sharp kicks, the woman clawed and screeched. Where the hell was Vlad, Aaron? Where the hell was her backup? The fight continued on and they rolled together until Emma was on top, her hand smashing Melissa's face into the rough industrial carpeting.

"I'm so tired of being scared of you." Emma whispered. "I am tired of worrying if you'll show up and ruin another graduation, or if you're going to break into my dorm room in the middle of the night. I am sick of it. You are not my family."

That enraged Melissa and she thrashed uselessly, her arms stuck flat against the floor, trapped. Emma wasn't surprised as her mother tried uselessly to dislodge her. The woman had no leverage. She pushed herself up and stood over the woman who had abandoned her, who had turned every major life event into to a game of will-she-won't-she, and she felt nothing. That sliver of pity and love she had kept reserved for her mother was gone. Melissa had used up the last of Emma's mercy.

Melissa rolled to her shoulder just enough to lash out. Emma stomped her wrist before she could do any more damage. The crunch made Emma's stomach protest, but she wasn't going to play victim for the sake of her civility, not anymore.

The door opened and Emma looked away from the woman groaning on the floor, to see Simon standing there, his face a hard plane of stone. He nodded at her once in that curt way she was starting to associate with a job well done. She stepped over the woman's upper body and narrowly avoided Melissa's last-ditch effort to trip her. Simon made a move to help, but Emma stopped him with a look. She hadn't needed his help when she had almost been strangled and she could manage fine now that she was on her own feet. She slid past him and out into the hallway where Aaron and Vlad stood, in all their stoic machismo.

"What, no help?" Her voice was raspy, and a ring of bruises was already turning dark around her throat, her sarcasm just this side of mean. A smile broke across Vlad's face and the worry in his eyes faded slightly. It was a good feeling knowing that Vlad thought she could handle herself.

"Nah." Aaron slung his arm over Vlad's shoulder, winking at her in his own cocky way. He lifted his chin ever so slightly to show off his own set of bruises. "I thought we'd watch."

"Fuck you too, Aaron." She rolled her eyes at him, rubbing her neck. She felt the small half-moon cuts Melissa's nails had dug into her skin, and she wondered idly if she was ever going to get used to the feeling of being covered in blood. She really hoped not. Letting out a breath, she let her body relax against the door frame. The worst of the day's action was over, her mother was tied up, locked up, and not getting out any time soon. Stress poured out of her, folding her body in half as hysterical laughter bubbled out of her in great shaking guffaws.

"I know I'm funny, babe, but you're freaking us out." Aaron moved to stand next to her rubbing her back until finally the laughter stopped, her limbs still shaking. "Maybe we should get you a drink, or like ten."

"I could dig a burger." Emma wrapped her arms around his waist hugging him tightly. She let her arms fall away, taking a few steps towards the elevators, before a thud stopped her.

The noise was soft, unobtrusive. There was another thud and then another, Emma didn't want to turn around. Without looking, she knew what she would find. Her mother was throwing herself into the glass of the observation window. Blood was seeping down her forehead from where she was hitting it against the glass. Each of them stood transfixed by this act of madness. The glass was thick, but persistence is a heavy hammer. Her body slammed the center of the glass and a web of broken glass stretched out from her mark. Melissa stood back watching as the cracks spread out to the edges of the window frame. Tilting her head to and fro, Melissa poked the center of the broken web, her eyes alight with violence.

The sound of the mirror shattering was like listening to another storm roll through the city. Glass fell in large jagged pieces breaking anew when they hit the floor laying there like field of grisly knives. Some sticking out of the sill at odd angles, framing the insanity that was Melissa Caldwell-King in the jaws of some grotesque fresco. There was a kind of standoff where they watched one another, gauging who would move first, and then she was climbing through.

Emma's ears buzzed, her nose went numb and the tips of her fingers tingled. Her mother made it through the window frame, her arms and shins cut open, her boots crunching on the glass. Melissa grabbed one of the shards holding it with both hands. The ties held her hands together forcing her to hold the glass between her palms where it dug into her flesh.

Melissa was bleeding badly. With her hands still tied together, the blood ran down her forearms and into her shirt. Melissa didn't even look phased, she looked invigorated. Bleeding like a stuck pig with a mad grin, she rushed Emma.

It was the easiest decision that Aaron ever made, easier even than joining the Rangers. He hit Melissa straight on, knocking her off course and sending them both into the sea of glass. He heard the squish of Melissa's improvised dagger slide just under his ribs. There was a moment where it didn't hurt at all and then the glass popped through something, probably his diaphragm. Really, he had no idea what it could actually hit in there, it seemed like it had hit something important. Pain bloomed out from the puncture like television static, somehow both innocuous and terrifying. He knew it should be hurting worse than it was. Pain told you something was wrong, pain told you, you were alive. Aaron's pain had turned on like a TV turned on full volume and then muted out, while the ghostly static fizzled in his gut. Funny, he had always imagined killing him would have been harder to do. But hell, he had been wrong about shit before.

Beneath him Melissa let out a wet cough, blood sputtering up every time she tried to breath too deeply. He could hear people moving around him, Simon was saying his name over and over, all warbled. Someone strong was rolling him off of Melissa, he could feel their hands gripping his shoulders. Then the panic set in, he tried to sit up, to pull out the glass, but his body wouldn't cooperate. His arms felt cold, every breath he took he could feel that static sensation of pain. The fluorescent lights glared in his eyes, shuttering in their eerie flickering light, until Emma leaned over him. The tightness in his chest eased ever so slightly. She was okay. Everything from that thought didn't matter, he had saved Emma. He blinked, Emma's face smearing into someone else. At least this way he would see Josie again.

"Get Ava!" Emma cradled Aaron's head in her lap and tried not to look as afraid as she felt.

CHAPTER 38

Ava finished tying the last stitch closed on Aaron's stomach and rubbed yet another salve gently over the neat row of black x's with a resolved frown. There was a lot that her magic could accomplish, but the kind of malice that was laced into Aaron's wounds was more powerful than her potions. The spells she knew to draw it out would almost certainly do more damage than good. Worry twisted a knot in her belly. There was nothing to do about it now. The time for her to act would have been before, when she could have sapped the strength right out of that vile woman. Healing Melissa would be all too easy. Ava shuttered against the thought of doing anything to help the person who could spew such powerful hate. It permeated the air around Aaron's wound, like a noxious plume of gas. Every magic left its own kind of signature and Melissa Caldwell-King, left trails of slimy hate-fueled power behind her, even if she didn't know she was using it.

"You don't look happy." Emma stood next to Ava as she scrubbed her hands as best she could on her skirt hem. "How bad is it?"

"He's going to live." Ava forced herself to smile, it was tight and did not reach her eyes.

"But?" Simon spoke from across the conference table Aaron was laid out on. He stood over his friend, watching for every breath he took.

"But…" Ava checked his pulse and replaced the damp cloth on his forehead. The sleeping draft would keep him unconscious for the worst of it. "…there is such a thing as the power of intention." They stared back at her, their eyes blinking slowly, children on the cusp of understanding. "Sometimes, the act violence is so powerful, or the intention to cause harm so great, that it coats the wound in opposing magic. I'm sorry. Aaron will never walk again. I'm not even sure he will even be able to speak."

"That's crazy." Emma voice was still raw from before, breaking at the ends of her words in a hiss. "My mother isn't a witch. She's a lunatic."

"You don't have to be a witch to do magic, Emma. You know that." Ava looked at her sternly but softened when she saw the tears threading silently down her cheeks. "Magic exists whether I do or not. Everyone interacts with it. Takes from it; adds to it. Your mother wanted it to hurt, wanted to cause this suffering. I've stopped it from spreading, but that's all I can do, without killing him."

"There has to be something you can do." Simon didn't cry, he wasn't the type, but his lips pulled tight over his teeth as he bit out his words. "Some way to fix this."

"I am afraid that this is beyond me." Ava had never in her life felt as useless. Here she was, wishing for some hope that she did not have. "We can wait and see if he gets stronger, and if he does, we can try again."

"If?" Emma was shouting, breaking Ava's heart. "I'm sorry. I have to…"

Emma rushed out of the makeshift medical ward Ava had

turned the conference room into. Here was another soul swallowed up by the Order that Ava couldn't save.

Simon watched Emma run past the broken window, a struggle playing on his face. Ava could see he wanted to follow. Still, he stayed put.

"You're not going after her?" Ava slumped into one of the forgotten rolling chairs and began mindlessly tracing healing sigils on the table.

"She doesn't want me to." Simon settled himself painfully on a chair next to Ava's. Their conversation consumed by the terrible rhythm of the shallow rise and fall of Aaron's chest.

CHAPTER 39

Melissa struggled against the restraints that bound her to the chair, in spite of the pain that it caused her. With every twist, a fresh jolt of agony would fissure through her back, feeding her rage. She was nourished by it. Laying on the floor with that oaf of a man dying on top of her she was certain that she too would greet the True Mortal End. She could not think of a more beautiful gift to be given than to be martyred for the Order, just as Mina had cast herself from the parapet to escape the corruption of her husband. That traitor bitch had ruined everything, slathering some putrid black paste all over her back.

Now, her tunic stuck to her, and she sat here, her wrists tied to the arms of a metal chair. It didn't even have wheels to move herself away from the table that she was pressed up against. All of her struggles were in vain. The filth were clever, she would give them that, but they wouldn't keep her here forever, nothing could.

The door on the far side of the room swung open and the man from before strode in; calm. He looked very much like the bastard Prince Vlad from the sacred texts, save for the modern garb and finely groomed hair. She watched him unblinkingly, as only the truly fanatic can do. He pulled a chair over to sit, not across from her as she thought he might, but perpendicular, so that when he sat his knee bumped into hers. The more she watched, the more she was convinced of her faith. This man, whomever he may claim to be now, was the father of filth and she alone had found him. Vindication boiled in her belly.

"You know who I am." His voice had no intonation, no fear of what she could bring down on his head. She was furious.

"You sit here before me as proof of the corruption of humanity." There was no slow build. Her rant began volcanic, destructive and aimless. "You are the proof of my beliefs. The vile evidence that every Faithful Mortal has been right to pledge their lives to the Order, to the name of the Divine Mortal herself. You are filth and all those who follow you are tainted by your putrid curse..."

She continued on speaking in circles until Vlad pushed his chair out and made to leave.

"Coward." She hurled at him with the last of her breath, before leaning back and letting the pain surge down her back and breathe fire into her.

"Tell me, Mrs. Caldwell." Vlad forced her to make eye contact with him. The second he had her gaze she went slack. He had scarcely had an easier target. It was for the best, for he was by no means as calm as he let on. The Ranger had been a good man, and Vlad could read the writing on the wall. The chance that he pulled through his injuries was slim at best. An easy mark was truly a blessing, anything more and he would have been fighting through his own fury, for a few seconds of usable thrall. "Where is the Order's base of operation?"

"Caldwell Incorporated offices in the ship yard." Her voice was hollow, like it was coming down a tunnel.

"Is that where they prepare for the missions against us?" Vlad kept his voice monotone, listening for the second her heart rate fell out of sync, for any indication that the thrall was failing.

"No."

"Where, then?" Already, Mrs. Caldwell was hugely infuriating with her answers. Short and to the point, covering exactly the scope of the question. He wondered if she was trying to be evasive. All of her vitals indicated that she was well and truly under his thrall. It was unlikely.

"The Order meets at the Caldwell Estate." She took a wispy breath, her voice fluttering, like she was remembering something happy. "But we train at a ranch outside of El Paso."

"Anywhere else?"

"Yes." Her eyes squinted, still she didn't blink, held entirely captive by Vlad's gaze.

"Tell me where?" Vlad gritted out, his neck itched where she had bit him. The wound was long since closed, Fields' careful line of stitches needed to come out. He twisted his neck letting the stretch of the skin ease that nagging tickle trying to distract him from his mission.

"When we were first married, Marcus took me to a camp along a river in Transylvania. I don't remember the name." Melissa was sinking further into his thrall, the beat of her heart slowed. The tension in her arms released and Vlad felt secured in his control for a single moment before an image of Emma kneeling over a wounded Aaron filled his mind. Melissa made a little humming sound that drew him back to the task at hand. "There was an old castle high on the cliff and he showed me where the Divine Mortal sacrificed herself for the good of the Faithful, so the line of filth would not grow any larger, so that we might have the chance to wipe them from this Earth."

Melissa's body was near slack as she continued.

"How do you plan to do that?" Vlad felt the familiar pinch of his fang growing out of his gums. He clung to his control with the tips of his claws, wishing that he had sent Kadir or even Buchannan in to interrogate this woman in his stead.

"By the will of God and the faith of man." She took a shuttering breath. He was losing grip on the thrall. "God gave us the water to bless and the trees to grow by the light of the sun. As long as we remain pure of heart every Mortal is a weapon."

"Do you have guns, grenades, real weapons?" Vlad's voice faltered and he heard her heart skip, before falling right back into rhythm.

"Of course, we do." Her unblinking stare and relentless cheerfulness while speaking about the destruction of his entire species was disarming. He slammed his fists on to the table, thrall be damned. She blinked.

Vlad snarled at her, his fangs on full display. He probably looked to her like every nightmare story she had ever been told. The Order had long since set her fragile mind against all of his kind. The look of abject horror as she fell out of the thrall and shrank away from him was only mildly satisfying.

"I knew you were real." She whispered to him. "Marcus wrestles with his doubts, but I knew. The Filth are not some make-believe devil painted on our walls. You are real, and I know."

"Good." Vlad growled.

He lunged towards her, his desire for the scent of her fear a petty revenge he was willing to indulge. She didn't flinch. The horror that crossed her face moments before replaced by a satisfied smile. It was the look of victorious politicians and snake oil salesmen the world over. She tilted her head to the side exposing the vein leather of her throat.

"Do it." She said, not a trace of fear in her voice, her heart throbbing steadily. "Deliver me unto the Mortal's embrace."

Vlad felt sick, felt the rage double its weight in his heart. The perversion of his wife's memory bitter in its sincerity. For all his desire to see Melissa dead he could not give her that gift.

"No." Vlad pulled away. Standing straight, he collected his composure, straightening his tie and cuffs. "You will live."

CHAPTER 40

Emma wasn't entirely sure how she had gotten lost again. The plain cream walls of the corporate floors of the Transempirial tower, made every hallway look just that same as the one before. Which is possibly why Emma found herself in a ball sobbing on the landing of the stairwell. She wanted to be strong and push herself up from the ground; declare war on the Order, but grief washed over her at every turn. Just when she thought there might be a moment to breathe, a streak of hope, it was snatched away from her. To think that made her feel selfish. It wasn't her lying on the table in some antiseptic office, waiting to see if she was going to be a vegetable. Grams would want her to fight, Aaron would want her to fight, she wanted to fight, but every move felt like a snake squeezing around her belly. Every breath she took the snake would squeeze a little tighter.

Sobs shook her body, as the cold of the bare floor soaked through her clothes. She lost track of time, giving in to the emotions flooding over her. Building in great waves of tears that swept her up and threw her into the shore only to pull her back out to sea again. She was gasping for breath, all of her thoughts tossing around rapid fire, every good memory of Aaron mixing together with all the ones she had of Grams, until everything was confused. Someone wrapped their arms around. Her first instinct was to fight them. Sevystian's low voice whispered calmly to her as he pulled her into his lap.

"Shhh." How he found her, she didn't know. "You will weather this too, my sweet Emma. Shhh."

He rocked her back and forth, petting her hair softly and kissing her temple. Eventually the sobbing slowed to sporadic hiccups that would crest and burst with tears and little snot bubbles. Emma King did not cry pretty. Still, Sevystian said nothing. Only taking out his pocket square and dabbing at her eyes, letting her use it to wipe her nose. The quiet and the odd blue light of the stairwell lulled them both into the weightless trance, half between sleep and wakefulness. Emma was slipping fully into sleep, when Sevystian's phone beeped in his coat pocket startling them both out of the reverie.

"I got your shirt all wet." Emma made no move to extricate herself from the cocoon of his arms.

"You don't seem very sorry about it." Sev kept his voice soft, his hands still stroking up and down her back.

"I'm not." She blinked up at him.

Sevystian's phone beeped insistently from his pocket until he relented and they moved apart so he could answer it.

"What?" There was nothing but ice for whoever was on the other end of the phone. "Call off the dogs, Buchannan, I have her. We will head there now."

He hung up without preamble and stood, offering her his hand. She took it, not meeting his eyes and wiping her nose on his silk pocket square. She crumbled it up in her hand, not wanting to hand the snotty thing back to him.

"I have many more." He waited patiently for her to look up at him.

She tried to flatten out some of the wrinkles quickly before peeking up at him through her wet lashes. His shirt was wrinkled and his sleeves were rolled up his forearms. He was thoroughly rumbled and still devastatingly handsome. "I bet you cry pretty too, don't you?"

"I wouldn't know." Sev took her hand in his and led her back into another bland hallway. "I only ever cry alone." He squeezed her hand tightly. "In the dark, like a man."

A broken smile cracked across Emma's face at his jest and she followed him down the hall, knowing all the while she was going back to that horrible room where Aaron would be. The snake twisted a little tighter around her belly, and she felt her breakfast make a bid for freedom. She squared her shoulders and fought down the urge to vomit. Sooner or later she was going to have to see him. It wasn't right to stay away just to make herself feel better.

CHAPTER 41

Vlad glared at the beast of a woman who slumped unconscious over the table in the bland little interrogation room. There were no cameras in this part of the tower. This was by design, unlike the accidental flaw that had led to death of the young Miss Heather. He let himself imagine what it would be like to open Melissa's throat and be done with it. Rationally he knew that it would not be done, the Order did not fold from the loss of one inconsequential fanatic. Their ranks were legion, their faith was strong, and growing stronger if Melissa was to be believed.

It would be a momentary relief from the situation; however, he did not believe he could look Emma in the eye if he did it. Emma had a kind heart but she could not forgive him killing her mother, so Vlad settled for fantasy and the bitter metallic tang of drying blood that coated his hands. He could lie of course. Tell Emma that her mother had succumbed to the wounds she sustained in both attacks and there was a part of him that very seriously considered the idea. It would all come out eventually, though. If he had learned nothing else in his life, he had learned never to underestimate the will of the truth.

Some things cannot be hidden for long, no matter how deep they are buried, the truth is always one of them.

He let his breathing slow until it stilled into nothing and listened, Melissa's heartbeat wasn't the slow monotonous thrum he had learned to expect from a thralled human, skipping a few beats faster or slower every few seconds. It was nothing too unusual. He had seen humans with heart murmurs sleep for hours under even the lightest of thralls, and Vlad spared her no mercy. The soft thuds of the prisoner in the other room were nothing like Melissa's, they shuttered out of sync with the young man's breaths. He could imagine what it must feel like to be under the scrutiny of someone like Kadir and for a moment he almost felt sorry for the boy.

In the right hands, a thrall was as much a weapon as fangs or claws could ever be. Human minds were strange complex mechanisms that responded tenfold to any stimulation. Push too far and you run the risk of shattering their grip on reality, not enough and you risk exposure. A thrall was a precision tool that needed a deft confidence to strike properly. Fledglings spent most of their first decades attempting and failing to master the art of it. To synchronize the body and mind of the intended prey until they were entirely under your command was not an easy thing and even at his most controlled, Vlad was not the deftest practitioner. One look at Melissa's slack face told him that he had lost himself. At least she had passed out before he could wreak any permanent damage. Shaking off the gloomy ambiance of the room, Vlad slid out, letting the door click softly shut behind him.

A glance through the little viewing window of the other holding room didn't shed much light on the boy's interrogation. Kadir leaned back in one of the plain metal chairs, feet propped up on the table, cutting open a pomegranate, while the boy struggled in his own plain metal chair. He jerked at the restraints, holding his arms and legs to the chair and if Vlad concentrated he could smell the fresh blood rushing to the boy's raw skin. It wouldn't do to have him fearful. It would make him irrational, savage even. What was Kadir thinking, not putting him under?

Stepping into the room, a bitter, almost chemical scent hit him like a physical blow and he understood. Adrenaline was a serious combatant to the effects of a thrall. Even the oldest, most skilled vampires had trouble putting someone fully under in the heat of an adrenaline spike. Kadir was conserving energy. They had their enemy in their control, there was no need to waste time trying to crack that shell, if he could just wait him out. The boy's eyes flashed between the two vampires and the bitterness permeating the air increased exponentially.

"You're killers." The boy growled, doubling his effort to extricate himself from the zip ties. He slammed the chair up and down in futile little hops, until he wore himself out and stopped with a huff of impotent rage.

"Are you having better luck with the other one?" Kadir didn't bother looking at the boy. He tossed him a sideways glance when the boy hopped the chair again, the metal legs screeching.

"Yes." Vlad nodded, pausing as the boy interrupted them with a scream of some unintelligible vulgarity continuing on after a moment like he wasn't even in the room. "She was a wealth of information."

"Was?" The boy screeched. There was more chair-hopping and Vlad worried briefly that he might disturb the floor below them. "Was?"

"She is no longer talking?" Kadir sunk his teeth into the fruit, waiting patiently for Vlad to answer his question. It was the most frustrating gift Kadir had been blessed with, his ability to endure the silence of a place, a person, until there was only madness or submission. It had proved very useful in a variety of situations.

"It is hard to speak when you are unconscious." Vlad sighed drolly his calm perusal belying his fervent desire to be quit of the room and see to the well-being of Emma and the injured Ranger downstairs.

"What did you do to her?" The boy was shouting again, his voice cracking in high octaves. They ignored him as he continued pulling at his restraints, cutting deep gouges into his wrists. "What have you done? Where is she?" His voice was wearing thin, the raw edges of it crumbling into exhausted sobs as the adrenaline seeped out of his muscles. "Please, please don't hurt her. Don't hurt her."

"We are not the invaders here." Kadir's voice purred through the room, filling up the corners with his warm accent. "She hurt herself."

"You're a liar." The boy spat at them. His saliva landing pathetically on his shirt, miles from his target. "My father told me the truth. You're all liars and filth."

"Coming here was his idea?" Kadir spoke softly.

"No." The boy said. "He's given up on saving her."

"Saving who?" Vlad tried to keep his voice flat.

"My sister!" He screeched. "Emma. You're keeping her captive here. You're going to turn her into one of you."

Despite the venom in his voice, speaking to the boy didn't feel like talking to Melissa. Where Melissa spoke coldly with rigid conviction, the boy spat out the Order's rhetoric like a toddler reciting Bible verses.

"Emma?" Kadir turned an interested eye to Vlad.

The rush from fighting was slipping away from the boy faster and faster now. It might be time to slip him under, but the kid was churning out plenty of information on his own.

"Melissa is your mother?" Vlad kept his focus entirely on the young man tied to the chair, ignoring Kadir's question.

"She is the mother to all of the Order's True Faithful." He squeaked.

"Yes, but you are her son, made of her flesh and born to her name?" Irritation was creeping into Vlad's voice.

Kadir coughed pointedly into his fist, jolting Vlad back to the present. Claws curled into Vlad's fist, cutting into his palms and dripping blood down his sleeve. The boy swallowed hard, starring at the drops of blood with terror in his eyes.

"Mother told me you were real." The kid whispered. "She said our faith wasn't about fables or shadows. She said our devil was real and here you are."

The kid couldn't have been any more than nineteen. It was a hell of thing to live your whole life under the control of a maniac like Melissa King. Even so, they were all sick of hearing about his kind being the Devil. When was the last time you heard about vampires trying to blow something up, or rob a bank? Never. Kadir cracked his neck and took a deep breath drawing their captive gazes into his own. It looked too easy, and the kids heart slowed so quickly Vlad worried he might pass out.

"What is your full name?" The purr of Kadir's voice filled up the room.

"James Marcus Caldwell." The kid responded. He looked and sounded like he was sleep walking.

"Alright, James." Kadir lowered his feet from the table and leaned into his subject's personal space. "Is Melissa King your birth mother?"

"Yes." James blinked slowly back at them waiting for their next question.

"The True Faithful, who are they?" Kadir ran the interrogation with the hand of a master, while Vlad stood silent watching the proceedings

"They are those who Mother has chosen." James licked his lips.

"James?"

"Yes." He answered.

"Does your father know you are here?" Kadir let his voice drop and octave, and the boy shivered, a sign of complete control over the thrall.

Vlad's phone vibrated in his pocket. Fields' contact blinked across the screen. He stole out of the room careful not to disturb either of its occupants.

"What?" Vlad growled into the phone.

"The Ranger has taken a turn for the worse." There was a pinch to Fields' British formality that let on more than the other man was saying out-right.

"Is there anything to be done?" Vlad took a long useless breath

"Just the one thing, sir." The butler's voice was dark.

"You're sure Ava cannot save him?" He was grasping at straws and he knew it.

"Ava is sure." There was no room for question in Field's voice. "If there was something to be done, some way to save him, Ava would not hesitate."

"This is not the outcome I would have hoped for." Vlad looked in at Melissa, still face down in the table. Again, he thought about snapping her neck.

"Nor I, sir." Fields, for all of his quirks, was a good man and a good friend.

"Bring Ranger Davis to the library." Vlad turned away from Melissa, ignoring the skip in her heartbeat. The woman had a heartbeat like a drugged rabbit and he had much more pressing matters that needed his attention.

"Yes, sir." Fields hung up and Vlad prepared himself for what came next. The door to the second holding room opened and Kadir stepped out, James was slumped over the table.

"The kid doesn't know much." Kadir peered into Melissa's room watching her for a minute. "She has a lot to answer for."

"Yes." Vlad replied.

"You could kill her now." Kadir tilted his head back and forth, like he was contemplating the best way to do it. "Down here, where no one would see it was you."

"You would see." Vlad stared into the room, not looking at his accomplice.

"But I would not tell." Kadir didn't look at Vlad either, his focus still on Melissa.

"She is still Emma's mother." Vlad crossed his arms over his chest as if that finalized it. It was clear Kadir did not think it was so cut and dry.

"She's James' mother too." He nodded towards the boy's room. "That didn't stop her from bringing him here, knowing he might die. It didn't stop her from abandoning Emma. There are people who do not deserve the chances they have been given."

"It is not that I believe you are wrong, my friend." Vlad relaxed his shoulders, scrubbing his brows in frustration. "Emma would never forgive me."

"You have not known her for long, Vlad." Kadir turned to face Vlad, his expression cold. "Do not presume to know what her reactions will be. Melissa King has mistreated everything she has touched. Just because she is Emma's mother does not mean that Emma wouldn't forgive you."

"I find it hard to believe that she could forgive me for taking away the last of her family." Vlad felt guilt and spite roil in his gut.

"She would still have James." Kadir paused, sizing the older vamp up with his stare. "She would still have you."

"A brother she doesn't know and the man who killed her mother?" Vlad snorted. "Not much of a consolation."

"It might be the kindest thing you could do for her." Kadir looked away.

"How so?" Vlad studied his friend's silhouette in the harsh florescent light.

"So, she doesn't have to kill Melissa herself." Kadir's voice had gone flat, and distant, his thoughts far away. "That is not something you want her to carry."

"Do you really think she could?" Vlad would like to have said he was shocked, but there was a lawman dying upstairs and three more dead Faithful littering the halls of the building below them. There was only so much destruction a person could wreak before they had to be taken out of the equation.

"I have no doubt." His voice still seemed far away. "She puts up with what Melissa does to her because it doesn't hurt anyone else."

"But?" Vlad knew there was more.

"But." Kadir shook his head his thoughts coming back to the present. "She won't allow others to endure this just for her. The cowboy, the Coven, they are all going to be more important than the life of this foul creature. Even her brother may come to mean more to her. Anyone could see the damage that Melissa has done to him." Kadir let his voice trail off.

"You think I should stop it here." Vlad wasn't asking a question.

Kadir nodded in agreement anyway.

"What about the boy?" Vlad turned his gaze away from Melissa to consider the door to James' cell.

"I think he is young." Kadir walked over to look into the room where the boy was tied unconscious to the chair, his head resting on the table. "I think he was raised by cruel people who beat their beliefs into him like a stray dog."

"You would give him a chance, but not his mother?" Vlad frowned.

"I think it is foolish to punish dogs for following the orders of their masters." Kadir crossed his arms over his chest and Vlad knew that the conversation was going nowhere.

"Leave it be for now." Vlad cast a final glance at the two rooms, their occupants well leashed. "They are not going anywhere, but Ranger Davis might. Go back to James. See if there is anything else we need to know."

CHAPTER 42

The scene Sevystian and Emma walked into wasn't quite what Emma had been expecting. Fields and Buchannan were tucking Aaron tightly on to some haphazard looking stretcher while Ava packed up the remnants of her work.

"They're taking him up to Vlad's apartment." Simon pushed off the wall where he had been leaning and limped over to them. "Ava thinks there might be a way to save him, but it didn't really seem like a good idea to stay here. It's not as defendable as Vlad's. Buchannan says the place is some kind of fortress."

"It is." Sevystian nodded in agreement. "It was built with the Order in mind."

Fields and Buchannan hefted their cargo gently, walking swiftly out of the room. Emma frowned, never having realized before how in step they were. Without a single word, they had coordinated Aaron's extraction. It must have taken a long time to build that kind of synchronicity, yet she had hardly seen them in the same room together. Ava handed her one of her satchels and she let the thought of the two vampires float away on the clouds of worry gathering up again.

"You can save him?" Emma clutched the bag tightly. "Like really save him, not just keep him alive?"

"I can't do it, but...." Ava chewed on her lip clearly unsure if she was making the right choice or not. "...I think I have a way to make him whole again. We need to speak with Vlad."

Emma didn't like the ominous way Ava kept chewing on her lip. From the short time she had spent with the woman, Emma was convinced that there was probably next to nothing that would knock Ava sideways. Whatever this solution was had her on edge, it didn't bode well. Regardless, Emma decided not to question Ava, letting her thoughts land on Aaron. He was so pale, stretched between Fields and Buchannan, his shallow breathing the only noise in the space. Emma pulled her gaze away from Aaron only to be confronted with her own distorted reflection in the metal doors. When they finally opened to the penthouse Emma felt the breathless squeeze of panic and hope waring inside her. Stumbling out behind Ava, she was glad only Sevystian was there to see her hesitation.

They passed through a set of large double doors into the library. Buchannan rushed around, closing the heavy brocade drapes over the massive windows that looked out onto the patio garden, while Fields carefully situated Aaron on to a low sofa. The light of the late afternoon sun was shocking, cutting red lines across the rug. Emma didn't know how it was still light outside, it felt like she had been awake for years now. The easy morning she had spent with Sevystian was decades behind them.

Certainly, something so horrible hadn't happened by the light of day. Everything bad happened in the dark, all the horror movies said so, yet here they all were in the harsh light of a burning Houston day waiting for her vampire grandfather to see if he could save her friends life. Yeah, her life was firmly on track, nothing to worry about here folks, move along. Aaron groaned as Buchannan and Fields moved the stretcher out from under him. It was more than any of them had heard out of him since Ava had started her work. Whether or not it was a good sign, Emma had no idea. Ava seemed encouraged so she would take that as a win.

"Is this his only option?" Sevystian was watching Aaron, his focus laser-fine. The shallow pump of his heartbeat was thready, even with all of the impossible things he had seen Ava do, he was doubtful that Aaron could be saved.

"No." The meaningful look that she gave him said it all. "But some might argue that this is the lesser of the two evils."

"Sir might argue that it is not." Fields still hadn't bothered to put his uniform back on, and Emma was now aware of how very intimidating he really was.

"It isn't Sir's life. The things I can do to save him, they have risks, known risks. With the transition, there is a wealth of unknown." Ava sat down gently at the end of the couch, pulling out one of her salves and rubbing it at Aaron's temples gently until his whimpering died down. "Vlad is going to have to get over his hang ups."

"What are they talking about?" Emma's head was still spinning and she really hated that they were talking like everyone in the room had their Master's in occult studies.

"She thinks Vlad should change him." Sevystian looked down into her eyes. "Whatever damage that has been done to him; the transition will be quit of it."

"It would work?" Emma turned to Ava who was mumbling something over Aaron. She finished her incantation and turned to Emma.

"Transition magic is second to nothing." Ava nodded as she spoke, her mouth pinched down at the corners. "All of this." She gestured to the shuttering rise and fall of Aaron's chest. "This is rudimentary intention magic, she probably didn't even know what she was doing. It's strong, but I've seen people get turned on their last breath and still make it through. There are no certainties with any kind of magic. If I was going to put my hopes in anything, it would be on the transition."

Somewhere between the interrogation room and the elevator, Vlad had lost his cool. Something about the way the space around him looked so completely unaffected by the chaos pissed him off. Or possibly it was that he had been looking at his own damned face for ten floors and had nothing to distract him other than the truth. All of this destruction was his fault. He had asked for this, he made the choice and now Mr. Davis could not. He should have taken the stairs. Standing there, his own distorted image reflecting back at him in the polished steel, he lost it smashing the reflection until the doors dented and his knuckles bled. When the doors opened, he rushed into the library not sparing a thought to his disheveled appearance.

Emma had never seen him like this. Sure, she had known that he was a vampire and in the dark places of her imagination she could picture what a pissed off vampire might look like. Somehow, she had never imagined him quite so terrifying. Vlad's eyes that had been so gentle before were now filled with rage, his fangs curled uncomfortably long in his mouth.

"Out." Vlad snarled around his teeth.

"No." Simon protested. "I'm not leaving you alone with him."

"Do you really think that Aaron wants to be a vegetable? Do you think he wants to die? Simon?" Emma felt like she was sinking into the floor. "If Ava says it will work, I believe her. Can't you just put your stupid prejudice aside for one fucking minute and let him save Aaron?"

"Jesus, Emma." Simon ran his hand through the short hairs

at that base of his neck, tugging at them hard enough to hurt. "Do you really think that I give a shit if he's going to be a fucking vampire or not? Look at him, he's not in control. He'll tear Aaron's head off like this."

"Do not mistake my anger for lack of control, Mr. McGregor." Vlad's voice was barely a hiss of air between his fangs.

Even though she knew it wasn't really directed at Simon, Emma felt the need to stand between them anyway. Vlad's knuckles were still pale and bleeding.

"Aaron should have had the chance to choose, but that is a luxury no longer afforded to him." Vlad drew in a breath his nostrils flaring wide giving the look of a charging wolf. "Let me bring him back to you."

Simon stared him down, his sharp eyes cutting into him from across the room. No understanding passed between them, no one backed down, they simply stopped their bickering.

"What happens?" Emma's voice was louder than she thought she was capable of at the moment. "How do you turn someone?"

"It's very simple." Vlad blinked, turning his gaze from Simon to his granddaughter and she let out the breath she had been holding. His hands were no longer clinched, even his fangs seemed to be smaller, or maybe it was an optical illusions. "Mr. Davis needs only to have been bitten and to share blood with one of our kind. A sufficient amount of our blood will see to the rest."

"Am I missing something?" Simon was leaning heavily on his cane, the entire length of his side burned with the effort to stay standing. Ava had warned him that he needed more time to mend, obviously, he ignored her. Looking around now everyone seemed confused by his sudden outburst. "Why haven't we had Buchannan turn him already or the fucking butler?" Fields straightened immediately his hand to his chest, somewhere between shock and affront. "Don't give me that, dude. We all fucking know you've got to be one of them."

Fields made to speak, but Vlad put his hand up, stopping any further argument in the room. He looked as if he were about to lay down some kind of ancient truth for the room at large until Ava beat him too it.

"Buchannan is too young." Ava's tone was matter of fact, like it was the easiest thing to see, like they all should have known that that was somehow important. "The older the vampire, the older the transition magic. Vampires grow stronger with every year they survive. We need to give Aaron every opportunity we can afford."

"Your mother had a lot of hate in her when she stabbed him." Ava explained. "I've been keeping it isolated, but I can't do anything to heal the affected area with it infecting him like it is. Aaron needs serious magic, anything I can do to help could destabilize him and he would die before Vlad could turn him. I don't want to risk his only shot on Buchannan."

Aaron moaned. It was a pitiful sort of noise that children make when they have been sick for too long and their fevers have gotten too high. All eyes turned to him.

"This needs to happen now." Emma sucked up all the confidence she could muster. "Vlad, or not, I am not just going to let Aaron die. Whatever it is you have to do, do it."

"We should leave." Sevystian's voice was as soft as he could make it. "It is not gentle thing. "

"You think I'm going to leave because it's not gentle?" Emma pursed her lips, her voice sharp and hollow. "This is my mother's fault, everything that he is feeling right now is because she had to come for me. This is happening to him, to all of you because I am here. Do you really think I care if it isn't pretty? He's my friend, if you want me to leave you're going to have to drag me out of this room."

"Then we are decided." Vlad looked from Simon to Emma,

both their faces painted with identical scowls. "Whatever is to come from here, I believe that this is the correct decision."

The sun streamed in through the barest gap in the drapes, scattering its now hazy red glow around the room. The light of day made it all worse. Emma would have preferred to have had the dim twilight that glowed golden orange this time of year, the kind that could hide things from her eyes. As it was, nothing stayed hidden. There wasn't some easy lead up to the bite like there had been between her and Sevystian. Vlad had crossed the distance to the sofa in three steps, shooing Ava out of his way and sunk his teeth into the crook of Aaron's arm. Closing her eyes didn't help either, the wet sounds of the whole process made her stomach roll. She wanted to be there, she needed to be. Simon tucked his arm around her shoulder, it was something familiar that did as much for him as it did for her.

When Vlad pulled away, she could only see him in profile, barely catching sight of the corner of his mouth, rimmed crimson in blood. Taking a bite out of his own flesh, Vlad held his arm over Aaron's listless body. She watched as the initial rush of his blood trickled into a slow drip falling into Aaron's slack maw.

Vlad's blood stopped flowing. He pulled his arm back, rolling his sleeve back over his wrist, it wasn't healing. Emma couldn't let herself think about it, Vlad knew how far he could push his body.

"That's it?" Simon took a wobbly step towards Vlad, leaning harder on the silver-headed cane than Emma had ever seen him. "What happens now?"

"We wait." Vlad took the handkerchief that Fields offered him and scrubbed the blood from his lips. "It could be moments or it could be days."

"So, we're just going to sit here waiting?" Buchannan asked and earned him only the glares of the other occupants of the room. "It's just... We have other matters to deal with, very important ones. Kadir can't be the only one keeping our... guests in check."

"She isn't dead?" Emma's voice sounded far off to her, like she was listening to a recording of herself.

"No." Vlad spoke in a soft voice. "There are still things that we must learn from her. And there is the fact that she is still your mother."

"You're wrong." Emma snapped back to herself, the fog of grief and uncertainty she had been wading through for days finally clearing. "Melissa King is not my mother. She isn't capable of being a mother. Get what you need from her and then get rid of her."

"Emma." Shock drenched Simon's voice. "You don't mean that."

"Why shouldn't I mean it?" Emma was frustrated, how could Simon possibly know what she meant? "She's done nothing but hurt me. She killed Aaron, you get that right? The only way we could save him was by turning him into a fucking vampire. Who knows if it's gonna work, or if he even wanted that.

How many of Grams's windows did she break when I was growing up? How many times do you think I caught Grams sobbing in her room over her? And that's just what she's done to us. What about the things she did for the Order; the stuff we don't know about?" Emma paused for a long while, letting her resolve sink in. "She doesn't get to do this and live her life like it isn't her fault. We're standing around waiting for Aaron's corpse to rise from the dead."

The room went silent waiting for Simon or Emma to back down, to cower away from the other's resolve. Neither of them gave an inch and Aaron remained unmoving on the sofa. There was a burning pit of worry in Emma's belly that kept telling her that this wasn't going to work. Aaron was not coming back to them. Finally, Emma turned away from Simon, understanding that this was perhaps one of those situations where they were both equally correct, or both equally wrong.

Sevystian stood for a few extended minutes weighing his strategic options. In the end, he made eye contact with Vlad, before signaling to Buchannan, to make his way out of the room. Emma felt his warm hand on her back and looked up into his eyes, knowing that he was needed elsewhere. There were bigger issues to attend to, if any of this was going to be stopped, they were all going to have to suck it up. Plans needed to be made. Waiting them out was no longer an option and with Melissa in their custody, escalation was absolute. Buchannan stood at parade rest by the door, waiting patiently for Sevystian to join him.

"Stevens will want to do an overhaul of the tower's security system and he will have to be debriefed, at least partially, on the situation." Gone was the casual charm Buchannan spread so easily, and in its place, was a still militant precision that set off alarm bells in Emma's head. "Melissa should be further interrogated and I would like to hear what Kadir has gotten from the boy. From there we can better formulate our plan of attack."

"Attack?" Emma didn't mean for it to sound like a question, of course they were going to retaliate. She would have been more surprised to find out that they didn't want to. It was more of a realization than anything. Suddenly she had a purpose, a mission she could focus her so far aimless energy towards. Yeah, attack sounded really nice right about now.

Emma could feel Sevystian's eyes tracing her, studying the shape of her profile. She turned to meet his stare with hard eyes, ready for another fight. Instead, she found approval. The corners of his mouth pitched downward in his tight facsimile of a smile and Emma was glad. She didn't have it in her to back away from a fight, it wasn't in her blood. He nodded to Buchannan and followed him out of the library.

"Emma." Vlad moved his attention fully to his granddaughter. "You are fully correct about Melissa's misdeeds. However, I do not want you to feel that it is your duty to bring an end to them. Just because she gave birth to you doesn't make her any more your responsibility."

"No, it doesn't." Emma looked curiously at him for a second. "Just the same as me being your relative doesn't make me yours."

"That's different." Vlad seemed taken aback.

"How?" Emma raised her one battered eyebrow, her bruises and scrapes making her appear ferocious in the red light of the afternoon.

"I suppose we will just have to respect our choices." Vlad grinned at her. It felt good to have her know him. Know who he was, what he was, and still side with him.

CHAPTER 43

When Sevystian and Buchannan arrived at the security hub, Kadir was stepping out of one of the holding room's doorways. James sat handcuffed to the chair inside, passed out face-first on the table. Sev thought for a moment that some kind of violence had been perpetrated on the young man until he saw the steady rise and fall of his chest that suggested a masterful thrall was keeping him unconscious. Still, the heavy stench of old blood filled the air, Buchannan quirked his head in question and Kadir thumbed towards the next room.

"The King woman." Kadir shook his head as he spoke. "She's in rough shape, nothing that would end her life. Though it is enough to fill up the whole place with that putrid smell."

Sevystian studied the door, thinking about what his next move should be, what the best outcome he could hope for in this situation. A thick smear of blood lingering on the back side of the knob caught his attention. Curious, Vlad was almost obsessive about keeping interrogations as peaceful as possible. Unexplainable injuries were holes in the delicate web of a thrall. The bigger the thrall the easier it is to break and ultimately compromise the safety of the entire Coven, but perhaps the rules could be bent for the Order. It was not unreasonable that Vlad would have lost his temper with the woman.

Something was off. The convergence of noise was a sonata played in minor. No note out of place but somehow wrong. Standing just outside the room, he closed his eyes, focusing on the sounds all around him. Sevystian could pick out Kadir's subject clearly under the buzz of fluorescent lighting, his steady heart beat slow and even. The feel of Buchannan's eyes skated over him, leaving a bristling sensation in their wake.

The sound of abrading fabrics and softly clinking metal let him know Kadir was adjusting his cufflinks, but nothing else. They were missing a heartbeat: Melissa King's. It wouldn't be the first time a member of the Order had died to prevent their secrets from being known. They weren't usually the cyanide capsule in the back-molar-kind of lot, it wouldn't surprise him.

Clenching his fist around the cold sticky handle of Melissa's cell, the feeling of wrongness overwhelmed him. Even through the door the smell of fresh blood overpowered that left over from her still healing injuries. Slamming open the door, Sevystian was met with an empty room, the sight of which filled him with a terrible fury. Pieces of the zip-ties lay scattered around the floor next to her chair. They looked the way attic wires do after the rats have gotten to them. On the table the word filth had been written in congealing blood. Melissa had chewed her way out like a rodent.

"Call Stevens, make sure no one leaves the building." Sevystian snarled, stalking across the short hallway to the security headquarters. "Kadir, notify Vlad."

"Stevens isn't answering." Buchannan was already redialing, but they all knew what that meant. If Stevens wasn't answering a call from the Chief of Security it was because he couldn't. A cursory evaluation of the CCTV turned up nothing. Still no answer from Stevens.

"Kadir." Sev didn't look to see if he was following him, he

didn't have to. "Stay with the boy, there is no trusting them to stay under. Kill her if she returns for him."

Buchannan's phone buzzed in his hand, he answered, putting the call on speaker.

"Mr. Buchannan." The guard sounded nervous. "Sir, we've had a possible breach in the staff garage. Neither unit has checked in and Stevens is not responding. How would like us to proceed?"

"I will investigate myself, maintain perimeter security. Do not let anyone in or out of the building until you hear from me directly." Buchannan hung up the phone cursing.

"She's already gone." Sevystian spoke through clenched teeth.

Buchannan broke into a trot to keep up with him as he made his way to the private stairwell that lead to the staff garage and the lobby. Fat drops of blood trailed down the steps confirming their worst-case scenario. The door for the garage sat slightly ajar, the hand-print scanner had Stevens' ID still flashing on the screen. Sevystian turned to Buchannan with a grimace, reaching for the door. The door slid open with a grinding noise and the unconscious body of a tower security guard slumped into the stairwell. Buchannan bent to check his pulse, giving Sevystian a wave to move ahead of him into the parking structure.

Two gunshots rang out from one of the levels below and Sevystian sprinted towards the sound. He skidded around the corner of a concrete pillar in time to see Melissa crash Stevens' car through the gate. The second guard raised his gun to take another shot at the retreating sedan. Sevystian laid his hand on the barrel shaking his head. The young man was bleeding heavily from a head wound and there was a slim chance of the kid hitting her anyways, better not to take the risk with an unknown number of civilians on the street.

"Stevens?" Sev asked, his voice hard and flat.

"She has him, Sir." The kid responded, blinking sweat and blood out of his eyes. "I...I tried to..."

He pointed his gun in the direction the sedan had taken off in, uselessly. The mangled metal remains of the parking gate swung back and forth before crashing into a heap, startling a gaggle of passers-by. Sevystian herded the guard back up into the shadows of the garage and out of the curious stares of the mortals on the street. There was a shuffle behind them and the kid swung around in a panic, gun raised. Buchannan put his hands up, taking a few steps out of the dark.

"I'm not the enemy." The Guard fell into Buchannan's thrall as easy as breathing. "There was a break in and you did your job admirably. Collect your partner and report to the security desk for first aid."

The guard nodded once and then took off at a lazy trot to the entrance to the stairwell.

"We won't be able to do that to all of them." Buchannan tucked his gun back into its holster, flipping his jacket over the tell-tale bulge it left in the small of his back, and making his way back into the building.

Sevystian scowled out at the mouth of the gate, watching a smartly dressed couple walk into the restaurant across the street, completely unaware. "If we can't settle this quickly, it won't matter."

CHAPTER 44

Emma didn't really need anyone to tell her that Melissa had flown the coop. It was in the air, in the way Vlad shifted his eyes to her when he thought she wasn't paying attention. Her mother's absence damped the air around them with unrealized violence. Kadir opened a door to her left, his shirt sleeves rolled up to his elbows, showing off an untidy set of scars that webbed across his forearm. Wariness sliced hot down Emma's spine.

It was unnerving to watch Vlad pace the line of the security hub's narrow isle, his dark eyes cold and unfocused. The blue light from the wall of monitors cast one side of his face in an eerie blue shadow leading Emma's imagination to supply an unkind comparison to the predatory prowl of a long-worn alley cat as he navigated the empty swivel chairs and sharp desk corners without a glance. Vlad had received a call on the way down; Emma didn't know who it had been. He had managed an even keeled response and hung up, his body language turning almost languid. In the minutes since, they all waited in front of the bank of computer monitors for Sevystian and Buchannan to return.

A soft grunt came from somewhere next to her and Emma

blinked. She had zoned out thinking about Vlad and all the times he had likely prowled rooms. Would this be where they finally came up with the plan that would see her mother and the Order brought down?

Another grunt and Emma shook her head, freeing it of the cobweb of thoughts. Turning to face Kadir. He stood in the doorway to a holding cell of some kind, the young man Emma had overpowered in the attack slumped over the table inside, his chest rising and falling in a gentle rhythm.

"The boy has nothing more to give us on Melissa." Kadir's soft accent purred melodiously, and Emma wondered if the accent was real. She could imagine it as some dedicated affectation. Paired with his darkly handsome features and those green eyes she could see how the accent would open certain doors for him.

"Try again." Vlad's voice was sharp, his own thick accent cutting his words strangely.

"It will not matter." Kadir leaned against the same desk Emma had propped herself against. "None of this is premeditated. He won't have any answers and you risk breaking him while there is still vital information to be learned."

"How do you know?" Emma's voice was unintentionally hard. Kadir more than anyone in the Coven put her on edge. She didn't know why, but there was a gut feeling, the kind of feeling that raises the hairs on the back of your neck that Kadir was dangerous. It was the same feeling that told her that Kadir never shared everything he knew.

"He has been raised in the Order. It is no stretch of the imagination that he should have knowledge that we do not." Kadir crossed his arms and leaned back, stretching out his neck with a wicked crack that sent shivers down Emma's arms.

"How do you know that Melissa's escape wasn't premeditated? How do you know that he doesn't know where she is heading?" Emma's voice sounded shrill.

Kadir studied her for a moment, as if he were taking account of her flaws and setting up some plan of attack. Anything he had to say was cut off by the metal doors of the security hub slamming open, narrowly missing Vlad in his continued circuit around the room.

"We fucking missed her." Buchannan snarled, pushing past Vlad unceremoniously to reach the monitors. "I don't know how she did it, but two of my best are on their way to the hospital. Now Stevens' is riding shotgun to this freak show."

Emma slid out of his way, happy to have an excuse to put some distance between herself and Kadir. Buchannan eyed her sideways.

"Sorry Doll," he mumbled. "Your mom's a real piece of work."

"You're telling me." Emma felt a warm cup-of-coffee sort of affection towards Buchannan fill her chest. "You've got nothing to be sorry for. She only came here because of me."

"No." Sevystian filled up the doorway. "Melissa would have come, with or without your presence. You are only the catalyst for a rushed, unorganized attack."

"He's right." Vlad nodded, ceasing his pacing.

"And yet somehow, that doesn't make me feel any better." Emma smirked at her grandfather.

"Nor I." Vlad replied with equal solemnity. "Her actions are not your responsibility. Neither I, nor my men, hold you accountable for what has happened."

"Tell that to Aaron." Emma ground her teeth. God, she wanted to punch something, desperate to tear her mother apart. Years of abuse and neglect fanned the newly kindled revulsion for Melissa. "Tell that to Stevens."

"We'll have to find him first." Buchannan wasn't paying attention to the conversation anymore. His fingers were flying over one of the many keyboards in front of him, sending up window after window of CCTV footage up onto the dozens of monitors that spanned the largest wall behind them.

"These can't all be your cameras." Emma watched stunned as what looked like an ATM camera flashed across the screen.

"No." Buchannan was distracted. She suspected she wouldn't get much more information than that.

"There." Sevystian pointed to a monitor that featured a parking garage. "That is Stevens' car."

"Where is that?" Kadir leaned over the desk, staring intently as the door of the sedan opened and a bedraggled looking Melissa stumbled out, a gun held tightly in her hand.

"Hold on." The keyboard chattered noisily as Buchannan ran through whatever system he was using to hack into the cameras. "Down by the stadium."

"There's a home game tonight." Emma stared dumbstruck by the image of her mother dragging the grown man out of the passenger side of his own car. He said something to her and a grainy Melissa slapped him across the face with the side of the gun. Emma felt her stomach roll with disgust. "That garage is going to be packed. We need to call the police."

"And tell them what exactly?" Kadir's distain was clear. "That your insane mother has taken one of our security guards hostage in the name of her vampire hunting cult?"

"How about something like a woman with a history of violent and erratic behavior is in a crowded public parking garage with a gun and a hostage?" Emma snapped back. "Or were you planning on running down there and taking care of it? Think you can take her out and get Stevens to safety without being seen by someone?"

"You have no authority here." Kadir set his shoulders straight pulling himself to his full height.

"I don't need any to see that a bunch of vampires running into a situation that is currently sans vampires would be a bad idea. What if it's a trap?" Against Kadir's large frame, Emma felt diminutive, weaker. She stood her ground. "Melissa is insane. You said it yourself. It doesn't matter what she says to the cops but if you go in there fangs out and the Order is ready for you... hell even if the Order isn't there. It's better to let HPD take care of it."

"It exposes all of us to the human authorities." Kadir took a step closer to Emma.

"And running out there to kill her in broad daylight doesn't?" Emma held the glint of his sharp green eyes.

"Doesn't matter now." Everyone's head swiveled to Buchannan, who was watching Melissa's feed with uncharacteristic somberness.

The grey image showed Stevens standing on shaky legs between Melissa and a terrified parking security attendant. Stevens had his hands up in a placating gesture. Emma could see his lips moving, but the scene played out in silence. Even the noise of the office had stopped. Every breath stilled, only the clicking of Buchannan's fingers against the keys disturbed the tension. Melissa was shouting something, her lips pulled wildly as her image snarled silently at the two men she had at her mercy. The attendant hit the ground. Even the low-quality image picked up the pool of blood flooding out from the attendant's body.

"Shit." Buchannan's efforts doubled and soon images of panicked civilians rushing out of the garage filled the screen. "That's all the angles we've got."

An outside camera picked up two uniformed patrol officers rushing into the garage drawing their weapons. Kadir snarled something in a language Emma didn't recognize and leaned once again on the desk.

"It would seem you shall have your wish." The fight drained out of him like the attendant's blood on the greasy concrete.

"It would seem we are no longer in control of the situation." Vlad's voice was now unnervingly calm.

"Were we ever?" Emma tucked her chin into her chest, trying to ignore bile climbing up her throat. It was a futile effort and a plastic trash can was thrust under her nose as she chucked the acid of her empty stomach into the bin. She reached out for support and a darkly tanned arm reached back, holding her upright while her body continued to convulse. It took several minutes until the last of her empty retching ended, her face red and eyes watering.

"Here." Kadir handed her his handkerchief, his face unreadable.

"Thank you." Emma dabbed at her eyes, ignoring the unsettling attention of the rest of the men. "Is there... anything we can do to... uh, mitigate the damage?"

Kadir looked over his shoulder at the scene. Every monitor now filled with a different angle of the parking structure.

"Not much." Buchannan went back to his keyboard. "There are already several 911 calls for that location and ETA for on site is 3 minutes. They'll have SWAT in 10. They might just take care of the problem for us."

"Buchannan!" Sevystian's voice swung through the room like a hammer.

"Sorry." Buchannan looked sheepishly at Emma. "I kinda forgot she's your mom."

"I wish I could." Emma gritted her teeth against the unwelcome onslaught of tears threatening her. "What's next?"

... TO BE CONTINUED

Emma's story continues in Fall of Kings coming in the winter of 2021.

Not done with the world of the Transempirial?

Join the Coven today and immerse yourself in Emma's adventure. Click now and receive three exclusive deleted scenes.

https://eawilliamslit.com/contact/

If you enjoyed this book please remember to leave a review. When you post a review you are helping to support the authors you love and helping readers like you find books like these.

ACKNOWLEDGMENTS

This book would not have been possible without the support of my family. My father who didn't let me give up, my sister who encouraged me, and my mother who has read every piece of paper I have put in front of her since day one.

www.ingramcontent.com/pod-product-compliance
Lightning Source LLC
Chambersburg PA
CBHW051209190726
48288CB00006B/1884